THE GATE THIEF

BY ORSON SCOTT CARD
FROM TOM DOHERTY ASSOCIATES

Empire
The Folk of the Fringe
Future on Fire (editor)
Future on Ice (editor)
Hidden Empire
Invasive Procedures (with Aaron Johnston)
Keeper of Dreams
Lovelock (with Kathryn Kidd)
Maps in a Mirror: The Short Fiction of Orson Scott Card
Pastwatch: The Redemption of Christopher Columbus
Saints
Songmaster
Treason
The Worthing Saga
Wyrms

THE TALES OF ALVIN MAKER
Seventh Son
Red Prophet
Prentice Alvin
Alvin Journeyman
Heartfire
The Crystal City

ENDER
The First Formic War
Earth Unaware
Earth Afire

Ender's Game
Ender's Shadow
Shadow of the Hegemon
Shadow Puppets
Shadow of the Giant
Speaker for the Dead
Xenocide
Children of the Mind
First Meetings
Ender in Exile
Shadows in Flight

HOMECOMING
The Memory of Earth
The Call of Earth
The Ships of Earth
Earthfall
Earthborn

WOMEN OF GENESIS
Sarah
Rebekah
Rachel & Leah

THE MITHERMAGES
The Lost Gate
The Gate Thief

FROM OTHER PUBLISHERS

Enchantment
Homebody
Lost Boys
Magic Street
Stonefather
Stone Tables
Treasure Box
How to Write Science Fiction and Fantasy
Characters and Viewpoint
Pathfinder
Ruins

THE GATE THIEF

A Novel of the Mither Mages

ORSON SCOTT CARD

A Tom Doherty Associates Book
NEW YORK

This is a work of fiction. All of the characters, organizations, and events portrayed in this novel are either products of the author's imagination or are used fictitiously.

THE GATE THIEF

Portions of *The Gate Thief* appeared in *Orson Scott Card's InterGalactic Medicine Show,* Issues 30 and 31, as the short story "Flying Children."

A Tor Book
Published by Tom Doherty Associates, LLC
175 Fifth Avenue
New York, NY 10010

www.tor-forge.com

ISBN 978-0-7653-2658-4 (hardcover)
ISBN 978-1-4299-4703-9 (e-book)

First Edition: March 2013

Printed in the United States of America

0 9 8 7 6 5 4 3 2 1

To

Rick Fenton

and

Gordon Lundrigan,

my companions in

spiritual, moral, and philosophical searches

and my exemplars in shepherdry

CONTENTS

1. Flying Children 11
2. The Morning After 18
3. Intervention 42
4. Captive 59
5. Assassins 65
6. Angry Gate 79
7. Amulets 90
8. Search 113
9. Visitors 127
10. Confession 154
11. Reunions 164
12. Mittlegard 179
13. Trust 192
14. Loyalty 214
15. Running on Automatic 229
16. Frostinch 248
17. Ka and Ba 259
18. Clear Memory 281
19. Treachery 297
20. Worries 318
21. Intimacy 328
22. The Queen 348
23. Resolution 359

THE GATE THIEF

1

Flying Children

On a certain day in November, in the early afternoon, if you had just parked your car at Kenney's burger place in Buena Vista, Virginia, or maybe you were walking into Nick's Italian Kitchen or Todd's Barbecue, you might have cast your gaze up the hill toward Parry McCluer High School. It could happen. You have to look somewhere, right?

You might have noticed something shooting straight up out of the school. Something the size and shape of, say, a high school student. Arms waving, maybe. Legs kicking—count on that. Definitely a human being.

Like a rocket, upward until he's a mile above Buena Vista. He hangs in the air for just a moment. Long enough to see and be seen.

And then down he goes. Straight down, and not falling, no, shooting downward just as fast as he went up. Bound to kill himself at that speed.

You can't believe you saw it. So you keep watching for a moment longer, a few seconds, and look! There it is again! Too far away to be sure whether it's the same kid or a different one. But if you've got someone with you, you grab them, you say, "Look! Is that a person? Is that a kid?"

"Where?"

"In the sky! Above the high school, look *up*, I'm saying straight *up*, you seeing what I'm seeing?"

Down comes the kid, plummeting toward the school.

"He's got to be dead," you say. "Nobody could live through that."

And there it is again! Straight up!

"That's one hell of a trampoline," somebody says.

If you noticed it early enough, you'd see it repeated about thirty times. And then it stops.

Do you think they're dead? I don't know, how could anybody live through that? Should we go up and see? I'm not even sure it was people, it could have been, like, dummies or something. We'd sound so stupid—hey, you got a bunch of kids getting catapulted straight up and then smashing down again? It can't be what it looked like. Maybe we'll see it on the news tonight.

Three different people got it on their smartphones. Not the whole thing, but the last five or six, and one guy got fifteen of them. High quality video it wasn't, but that actually made it more credible. All three videos got emailed to people. All three ended up on YouTube.

Lots of comments: "Fake." "Why do people bother making crap like this?" "You can see that the lighting's different on the flying dummies." "Cool. Something new and fun to do with your old G.I. Joe's." The usual.

The local news stations aren't all that local. Lynchburg. Roanoke. Staunton. They don't give a rat's ass about Buena Vista—the town never amounted to anything even before it died, that's what people think in the big city. If those are big cities.

And the footage is so implausible, the flying figures so tiny that it wouldn't look like anything on TV screens. Besides, the fliers were so high that at the top, all you can see is a dot in the sky, not even the mountains. So it's sky, clouds, and a dot—makes no sense. Has to be a bird. Has to be a trick of the light. So it doesn't get on the news.

But scattered through the world, there are a few thousand people who know exactly what could cause those kids to fly. Straight up, straight down, incredibly fast and yet no news stories about dead kids at a Virginia high school. Oh, yeah, it makes sense to *them*, all right.

It's an act of a god. No, not an "act of God," to use the weasel-out-of-it words in insurance policies. Not God. *A* god.

Or at least people used to call them gods, in the old days, when Zeus and Mercury and Thor and Vishnu and Borvo and Mithra and Pekelnik were worshiped wherever Indo-European languages were spoken.

Nobody called them gods anymore, but they were still around. Weaker now, because they could no longer pass through the Great Gates that used to carry them from Earth to Westil and back again, greatly magnifying their powers.

Only a gatemage could send someone from one place to another instantaneously, but there hadn't been a gatemage since 632 A.D., when the last Loki of the Norse destroyed all the gates on Earth, disappearing through the last Great Gate and closing it behind him.

In the North Family compound, only a few miles away from Buena Vista, one of the kids spotted the longest YouTube video only a few hours after it went up on the web, and within twenty minutes the most powerful mages in the family piled into a pickup truck and headed for the high school. They knew it was Danny North who had done it, Danny the son of Odin and Gerd, a boy who had seemed to be drekka until one day he up and disappeared.

Now they knew that he hadn't gone as far as they thought. Now they knew he wasn't drekka at all, but a gatemage. And a strong one. Because the video didn't show somebody suddenly appearing in the air, which is how gates usually worked. No, the flying figures could be seen as they moved upward. They were moving fast, yes, but it wasn't instantaneous. They rose into the air, visible the whole way.

That meant it wasn't just any gate. It was an attempt at a Great Gate. A spiral intertwining of many gates at once, rising straight up from the surface of the Earth. And even if it only reached a mile into the air, it was one more mile of Great Gate than had existed in nearly fourteen centuries.

Here's the thing. Some of the gods on that pickup truck were heading for Parry McCluer High School in order to find Danny North and kill him. Because that's what you *did* with gatemages—they brought nothing but trouble down on the Family, and if the Norths had a gatemage and allowed him to live, all the other Families would unite against them and this time they wouldn't be allowed to survive the war that was bound to start.

The Norths had to be able to show Danny's dead body to the other Families—it was their only hope of survival. If history had taught them nothing else, it taught them that.

But other gods on that truck had a different plan entirely. Danny's father and mother had known perfectly well that Danny was a gatemage—it was in hopes of creating a gatemage that Gerd and Alf had married each other back before Alf became head of the Family and took the name Odin. The two most powerful mages in generations: lightmage Gerd with her power over electricity and light; stonemage Alf, with his strange new talent for getting inside the workings of metal machines. Everyone expected a child of theirs to be extraordinarily talented.

But Gerd and Alf had studied the genealogical tables and they knew that gatemages, rare as they were, came most often to couples with very different affinities. Like stone and lightning, or water and fire. And never to beastmages. So they hoped. And when Danny showed no sign of being able to do magery, or even raise a clant—even the most minimal abilities—they hoped even more. Because yes, he might have been drekka, worthless, devoid of power; but he might also be a gatemage, unable to raise a clant because his outself was fragmented into all the potential gates that he could make in his life.

And a year ago, when Danny ran away, Thor had used his clant to converse with Danny before he got too far away, and had confirmed that yes, Danny was making gates and yes, Danny finally knew what he was.

So the gods on that truck were evenly divided between those intending to murder Danny before he could make a gate and get away, and those determined to enlist his power in the service of the Family.

They got there too late. Danny had already made a Great Gate, and the Gate Thief hadn't eaten his gates. Danny had friends—Orphans who didn't belong to any Family—and some of them had passed through the Great Gate and returned. It made their power irresistible. The Norths were sent home in utter and ignominious defeat.

But none of them had been killed. It was a good sign that Danny and his friends had refrained from doing any serious damage. They still might be able to work something out—especially if they eliminated the faction of the North family that still wanted Danny dead. Times have changed, Uncle Zog! We can't kill our gatemage, Grandpa Gyish!

We have to get Danny to let us pass through a Great Gate! You saw how powerful his friends became—a Cowsister took your eagle right out of the sky, Zog! A mere Cobblefriend was able to open up a rift in the ground and swallow our truck! Imagine what Odin will do with his power over metal and machinery, what Gerd will do with electricity, when they pass through a Great Gate.

And imagine what the other Families will do to *us* if Danny lets any of them through a Great Gate before us. No, that's not a reason to kill him—how will we even get near him now? He's warned, he's ready, he'll just gate away from us. You know the stories. The winged feet of Mercury, seven-league boots—gatemages can be gone before your attack comes close to them. Or they can suddenly appear behind you and kill you before you turn around.

Gatemages are slippery! Once they come into their power, you *can't* kill them. Even if you sneak up on them somehow, passing through a gate heals any wound. We're no threat to a gatemage. We need him—alive and on our side. So we have to talk to Danny. Appeal to his family loyalty.

And if you can't stop trying to kill him, then we'll have no choice but to put *you* in Hammernip Hill. For the good of the family.

You understand, yes, you do—you'd do it yourself. There's a gatemage in the world, one who created a Great Gate and wasn't destroyed by the Gate Thief. And that gatemage is our own Danny. He knows us, he grew up among us. He has roots in our garden. We need to play that up. We need to bring him back to us. Not irritate him with foolish attempts to murder him. Get it? Are you going to leave him alone? Keep him safe? Make *friends* with him?

Yes, you say so now, but can we trust you? Stay away from him. Let Odin and Gerd do the negotiating. Or Thor. Or Mook and Lummy. People he likes and trusts. Don't let him see you. We want him to forget all the nasty things you did to him growing up.

THE NORTHS WEREN'T the only Family that spotted those YouTube videos—they were just the closest. The Illyrians, for instance, were already aware that there was a gatemage in the North Family. That's why they were spying on the Norths constantly.

And when their own gatefinder, Hermia, went missing, their suspicions were confirmed. For a while, they thought the Norths' gatemage had killed her—gated her to the bottom of the ocean, for instance, or out into space. But then one of their clants had spotted her, still very much alive, and she was using the gates.

Now the YouTube videos confirmed that the Norths' gatemage was powerful—a Gatefather, able to raise a Great Gate all by himself, or perhaps drawing partly on Hermia's abilities—and it was time to get Hermia back under Family control. Chances were good that the Norths' gatemage could be turned, recruited into the Argyros Family. Hermia was their tool to accomplish that. To get Illyrian mages to Westil and back again.

Once mages were restored to their full power, who could stand against them?

Left to themselves for fourteen centuries, the drekka had made a mess of things, and they were only getting worse. It was time for Earth to be ruled by gods again.

2

The Morning After

It was early morning, and Coach Lieder was still at home, Danny had run here from the tiny cottage where he lived alone. He could have created a gate, but that would have made a mockery of his decision the night before, after confronting his family, not to make any more gates at the high school. Technically, Coach Lieder's house wasn't the school, but since his promise had been made only to himself, who would he be fooling?

Besides, he had hardly slept last night. He needed the run in the brisk—no, *cold*—morning air. It was better than coffee, when your goal was to become alert rather than jittery.

He knocked lightly on the door, avoiding the doorbell in case someone in the house was still asleep. He also waited patiently before giving another couple of raps. Then the door opened.

Coach Bleeder—sorry, Coach *Lieder*—stood there in all his half-dressed glory. Apparently he slept in boxers and an old teeshirt—no one would change *into* such an outfit first thing in the morning. And he looked bleary-eyed, tense, worried. This surprised Danny, since at school Bleeder usually showed only two emotions: contempt and anger. Now Lieder seemed vulnerable somehow, as if something had hurt him or might hurt him; as if he were grieved, or expected to grieve.

"You," said Coach Lieder. And now the contempt reappeared.

Danny expected Lieder to say something about the rope ladder incident yesterday in the gym. But he just stood there.

"Sir, I know it's early," said Danny.

"What do you want?"

Well, if he was going to act like nothing happened, that was fine with Danny. Only now he had to have a reason for being there. Instead of doing damage control from showing off his godlike powers in the gym, what else could plausibly have brought Danny here? "I wondered if you could time me."

Lieder looked puzzled, suspicious. After all the months in which Danny had taunted him by never letting Lieder time his fastest runs, it was natural that Lieder would suspect a trick.

"I'm tired of the game," said Danny. "I'm in high school. I should care about high school things." And even as Danny said the words, they became true. It might be fun to be a high school athlete, even if Lieder was a complete jerk.

"Like waking up your teachers?" asked Lieder coldly.

Had Lieder really still been asleep? It was early, but not so early that someone coaching the first team of the day at seven shouldn't already be up and dressed.

"I stepped off a hundred yards," said Danny. Actually, part of his gift was a very good sense of distance, with reliability down to a foot in a hundred yards, or a twentieth of an inch in a foot. "Do you have a watch?"

Lieder held up his left wrist. "I'm a coach, I wear a stopwatch."

Danny jogged easily down to his starting place. "Ready?" he called.

Lieder, looking annoyed, put his finger to his lips. Then he put his right hand to his watch, looked at Danny, then nodded.

Danny took off at a sprint. A hundred yards wasn't that much—it's not as if he had to pace himself. He gave it everything—or at least, everything he had at six-thirty in the morning after a night of no sleep.

When he came parallel to the walkway leading up to Lieder's door, Danny burst through imaginary tape and then jogged to a stop and faced Lieder expectantly.

"Can you do it again?" asked Lieder.

"Do you want a couple of miles?" asked Danny.

"Just those hundred yards again."

So Danny jogged back to the starting point, waited for the nod, ran again. This time he let his after-race jog take him up to Lieder's porch.

"Do I make the track team?" asked Danny.

"On probation," said Lieder.

"Because I'm only marginally fast?" asked Danny. "Or because you want me to suffer a little for being such an asshole so far this year?"

"Everybody starts out on probation, till I see whether you'll listen to a coach."

"So I'm not fast after all?"

"Even the fastest can get better," said Lieder. "The fast ones are worth the time you spend working with them."

"Just tell me. Am I any good?"

"You'll be starting for us," said Lieder. "Now can I finish my breakfast?"

Danny grinned. "Knock yourself out," he said.

Lieder closed the door behind him.

As Danny headed back down to the street, Lieder's door reopened. "Have *you* had breakfast?"

"I don't eat breakfast," said Danny.

"From now on you do," said Lieder. "My athletes eat."

"I'm not an athlete," said Danny. "I'm a runner."

Lieder stood there, looking angry, but hesitating.

"I have to stay light if I'm going to be fast," said Danny.

"You're either on the team or you're not." Lieder glanced into the house, then faced Danny again, looking like he wanted a fight after all.

Danny could see that Lieder wanted to yell at him. Something was keeping him quiet. There was someone in the house he didn't want to wake. Or someone he didn't want hearing him yell at a kid.

"Listen, Mr. Lieder," said Danny. "I want to do my bit for the team. But I won't belong to you. You just timed me. If the speed you clocked for me is good enough for me to compete, then I'll compete for you. I'll listen to your advice and I'll try to get better. I'll try to get stronger and build up stamina. Stuff that makes sense. But you don't control what I eat, and you don't control my time. I come to practice when I can, but when I can't, I don't, no questions asked."

"Then forget it," said Lieder. "I don't need a defiant little asshole like you."

"Your call," said Danny. "I offered, and you turned me down. Now I don't have to hear any more complaints from Mr. Massey."

"You didn't offer shit," said Lieder, getting even quieter as he took a step down from the door. "If you're on the team, then you have to play by the same rules as the other kids."

So Lieder still wanted him. Danny must have been pretty fast.

"I can see how you wouldn't want to have one student getting special treatment," said Danny. "But I don't have any choice. My time isn't my own. I sometimes have to pick up and be somewhere. It's not my call, and I don't want to have to put up with crap about it if I miss practice."

"So go, then. Thanks for waking me up, you little prick."

"Cool," said Danny. He turned away, headed back to the street.

"You haven't heard the last of this," said Lieder.

Danny turned around and came right back up to the porch. "Yes I have," said Danny.

"You're a student. Unless your parents provide you with a note for each and every absence, you aren't going to get away with disappearing whenever you want."

"I stay throughout the school day," said Danny. "I don't miss classes. But before and after school, there's stuff I have to do. I offered to share that time with the track team, as much as I can. That wasn't enough for you. I get it—I even agree with you. I shouldn't be on the team. But that's it. No more crap about it. I let you time me and you didn't want me enough to take me on the only terms on which I'm available."

"Who the hell do you think you are?" asked Lieder, the bully in him at last coming out, his voice rising. "You sound like you think you're some world-class star, negotiating with a pro team. You're a minor, and a student, and the law says you belong in school, and the school says I'm a teacher with authority over you."

"What is it?" asked a weak voice from behind Lieder. A woman's voice—barely. It was such a husky whisper that it would have been hard to tell, if Lieder hadn't whirled around, revealing a little old woman in the doorway.

A small woman—just the right size for bullying, thought Danny.

But no, Lieder had been trying not to disturb her. And now that Danny looked closely, he saw that the woman wasn't old, just faded and sagging. Not his mother, as he had first supposed. Nor was she small—or at least, she wasn't short. Average height, and since Lieder was no giant, they looked about right together as man and wife. Except that she was wasting away. Something was seriously wrong with her, her robe hung on her as if she were a child wearing a woman's dress.

Cancer, thought Danny. At home Lieder deals with a wife dying of cancer or something just as bad. Then he comes to school and takes it out on the kids.

On Danny's tall and skinny friend Hal. It was because Lieder was humiliating Hal that Danny had made a series of gates to help Hal get up the hanging rope to the ceiling of the gym yesterday. A series of gates that intertwined and turned out to be the start of a Great Gate.

It was too easy, to think that a dying wife was the reason Lieder was a bully. It came too naturally to Lieder, a habit, an aspect of his personality. He was probably always a bully. Only now he's a bully with something else to worry about.

"It's all right, Nicki," said Lieder.

"Why don't you invite this boy inside?" asked Nicki. "He looks cold."

"I'm fine," said Danny.

"He's fine," said Lieder.

"Come in and have some cocoa," said Nicki.

"He has to get to school," said Lieder, "and so do I."

Danny had been willing to shrug off the invitation before, but the woman was insisting, and the trickster in Danny couldn't help but enjoy the fun. Plus, he was tired and cold and pissed off at Lieder. "Actually," said Danny, "I don't have to be there till eight-thirty. I'm not on one of those teams that practices before school."

"But cocoa's not good for my athletes," said Lieder.

"I think of it as an energy drink," said Danny. "And I could sure use some warming up."

"Come on in, then," said Nicki.

As Danny came past him, heading for the door, Lieder gripped him harshly by the shoulder and whispered fiercely in his ear, "You're not coming into my house."

"What?" said Danny loudly. "I couldn't hear you."

Lieder didn't let go. "You heard me," he whispered.

Danny gated himself just an inch away. Yesterday morning he couldn't have done that—created a gate and passed it over himself so tightly that it took only his own body and clothing, and *not*

Lieder's hand. But the gates he had stolen from the Gate Thief last night consisted of the outselves of hundreds of gatemages, and every one of them had been a trickster during his life, and every one of them had had more skill than Danny. He had managed to contain them in his hearthoard—his stash—but wherever that was kept inside him, he was able to access some of their knowledge, or at least some of their experience and reflexes and habits and talents.

He must have absorbed these things unconsciously, because he hadn't thought of doing it, he had simply done it.

If I had known how to do this last year, in Washington, I wouldn't have had to drag that murderous thug with Eric when I gated him out of the back room of that convenience store.

But there was something else that happened, something Danny hadn't expected. When he gated himself an inch without moving Lieder's tight-gripping hand, it moved his own body into space that Lieder's fingers occupied. Lieder's fingers were ejected from that space at such speed that the bones didn't just break, they were pulverized.

Danny heard the gasp of pain, then saw the limp and empty-looking fingers and realized at once what had happened. Before Lieder had time to turn the inhaled gasp into an exhaled scream of agony, Danny passed a gate over Lieder's body, which healed him instantly.

That meant Lieder no longer felt the pain, but he still remembered it, very clearly.

"Don't ever touch me like that again," said Danny.

"Come in and join us, daddy," said Nicki from the other room. Apparently they were one of those married couples who still called each other mommy and daddy long after their children were grown. "You have time. The kids will just run laps till you get there."

Danny knew that the kids would sit around chatting or napping, but he had no reason to disabuse Nicki of her fantasy. He had to deal with Lieder, whose face was still showing the shock and horror of that pain.

"Don't you learn anything?" asked Danny softly. "When I tell you that there are some things I'm going to do, whether you like them or not, it's a good idea to believe me and step aside."

"This is my home," whispered Lieder.

"And that was my shoulder you were gripping," said Danny. "Boundaries, Coach Lieder."

Danny walked into Lieder's house.

Lieder stayed outside for a while. No doubt trying to figure out what it was, exactly, that Danny had done. What had it felt like to him? Agony, yes—but had he understood that for a moment, his fingerbones had become tiny shards inside limp sacks of skin? Had he felt Danny move by an inch, instantaneously, or had he registered it only as Danny pulling away with incredible strength?

Danny walked into the house and quickly found the kitchen, where apparently the cocoa was already made, for Nicki was pouring it into three cups. She moved slowly. She held the pitcher with two hands. It trembled in her grip—if it could be called a grip. Danny half-expected it to slip out of her fingers at any moment. No wonder Lieder didn't want his wife trying to show him hospitality.

It was not deliberate, not planned. More of a reflex, as if Danny had seen the pitcher slipping from her grasp and lunged out to catch it. Only the pitcher was not slipping, and he didn't lunge with his hands. Instead, he sent out a gate, passed it over her, around her, and brought her out of it without having moved her more than a hairsbreadth from where she stood.

She seemed to register it as a shudder. "Oh, someone stepped on my grave," she said, with a tiny laugh, and then flinched as if she expected to cough, only she didn't cough.

Because passing a gate over her had healed her. It always did. Whatever was wrong with a person, passing through a gate always healed it, as long as their body parts were still attached and they weren't fully dead.

Not that she immediately became strong and hale—she looked completely unchanged. Except that her hand didn't tremble holding the pitcher, and there was color in her cheeks and she didn't seem so fragile as she continued pouring. "Isn't that odd," she said. "I felt a chill, and yet now I'm suddenly warm. I'm never warm anymore, but I am right now."

"Furnaces are like that," said Danny. "One minute you're cold, the next you're hot. But remember, you're holding a pot of hot cocoa."

"Of course," she said. "No wonder I'm warm! I should feel downright *hot*."

"It's nice of you to give this to me," said Danny. "I don't usually eat breakfast, but it's cold enough today that even a good run didn't warm me up the way it usually does."

She laughed as she set down the pitcher. The cups were full. Then covered her mouth. "I don't know why I laughed," she said. "Nothing you said was funny."

"But I said it in a funny way," said Danny.

"You say everything in a funny way," she said.

"I lived in Ohio for a while, but I didn't think I picked up an accent."

"No, not an accent," she said. "You talk as if you got the joke, but didn't really expect me to get it. Only just now I think I *did* get it. Isn't that funny?"

Danny smiled. And as he looked at her, he realized that the hand to the mouth, the way she was looking at the cups instead of at him—this woman was shy.

Not really shy. Just sort of generally embarrassed. He saw this all the time, but not with adults. No, he saw it at high school. He saw it with girls when some guy talked to them. A guy she kind of liked, or maybe liked a lot, and she couldn't believe he was paying attention to her.

This isn't Coach Lieder's wife, thought Danny. This is his daughter.

She called him daddy, not by the habit of a husband and wife, but because he really was her father.

"Do you mind if I ask how old you are?" asked Danny.

"How old do you think?" she asked. But her face showed that she hated the question.

"I'm deciding between sixteen and eighteen," said Danny.

"What's wrong with seventeen?" she asked. But there was relief in her voice. Nobody had guessed so young an age in a long time. How could they?

"Seventeen is a nothing age," said Danny. "Sixteen is driving and eighteen is voting."

"You can get into R-rated movies by yourself at seventeen," said Nicki. "Not that I go anywhere."

"Not that there's a theater worth going to," said Danny.

"Not in BV," said Nicki. "But there's a theater in Lexington. I just . . . don't go out much. I don't even watch movies on TV anymore. I lose interest, somehow. I fall asleep. No point in renting a movie just to sleep through it."

"You've been sick."

"Oh, I'm dying," she said. "There are ups and downs. Right now I think today might be a good day. A very good day. But probably that's just because of the company."

"This is very good cocoa," said Danny.

"Daddy buys me only the best. There's not much he can do for me, but he can get me first-rate cocoa. He's so gruff with other people, but he's really very kind to me. I like to think that only I get to see who he really is." She looked at him over the cocoa cup as she took a sip. "I know he was angry with you. That's why I came to the door."

"Thanks for saving me," said Danny. "I think your father has a low opinion of my team spirit."

"He cares so much about his teams," said Nicki. "He wants

everyone to do their best, but Parry McCluer High School isn't noted for the ambition of its students." Then she touched her mouth again. "I can't believe I said that. I haven't . . . I haven't been sarcastic in years."

"Then you're probably overdue," said Danny. "I think everybody needs to say something sarcastic at least once a week. Of course, I'm years ahead."

"And I'm years behind," said Nicki. "But it's getting late. I don't want you to be called in to the vice-principal's office on account of me and my cocoa."

"I'm far more afraid of Coach Lieder than of any vice-principal. Besides, when I get in trouble I end up talking to Principal Massey."

"Only the best for you," she said.

"Or else it's only the worst for him," said Danny.

She laughed. So did he; but he also got up and carried both their cups to the sink. Coach Lieder's cup remained untouched on the table.

"I'm sorry you only know my father in his grumpy moods."

"I'm glad to know that he has any other. I'm assuming you've seen nongrumpy moods yourself, and aren't just repeating a rumor."

"That would be gossip," said Nicki. A moment's hesitation. "Will I see you again?"

"I doubt it," Danny answered truthfully. "I think your father is very unhappy that I accepted your invitation this time."

"But if I invited you again?"

"Does your father own a gun?"

"Yes, but he doesn't know how to use it. I think he bought it to make a political statement."

Or because he was afraid of some student coming to assassinate him some dark night, thought Danny. "Thanks for the cocoa. I'm very warm now."

"Me too," she said.

He made it to the door unescorted, but Coach Lieder was waiting outside by his car. Danny expected to be yelled at, but instead Lieder only said, "Get in. I'll drive you to school."

Danny tried to assess what Lieder was planning—was he only speaking softly because he was afraid Nicki could hear him? But then he thought: If I don't like what he says, I can always gate away.

Then he rebuked himself. I've already made three gates today, and it hasn't been a full day since I vowed never to make another here in BV.

Except the one that would take him to Marion and Leslie in Yellow Springs, and the one that Veevee used to get back and forth between his house and Naples, Florida. He'd reconstructed those last night, when he got his gates back from the Gate Thief.

Inside the car, Coach Lieder was strangely silent. But when he spoke, he sounded as menacing as ever. "What do you plan to do with my daughter?"

Danny wanted to say, You mean besides healing her of whatever was killing her? Instead, he answered, "I don't plan to do anything. She invited me in for cocoa. I drank cocoa. We talked. That was it."

"She likes you," said Lieder.

"I liked her," said Danny. "But no, in case you're worried, I don't like her *that* way, she's just nice and we had a nice conversation and that's it. Nice. So you don't have anything to worry about."

Lieder was silent for a long time. Not till they were going up the last steep hill to the school did he speak again. "I've never seen her talk so freely with anyone."

"I guess she was having a good day," said Danny.

Silence again until the car came to a stop in Lieder's parking place. Apparently even coaches who didn't have a lot of winning seasons still got their own named parking space.

"You haven't asked me what's wrong with her," said Lieder as Danny opened the car door.

"Nothing's wrong with her," said Danny, letting himself sound puzzled.

"She's obviously sick," said Lieder, sounding annoyed.

"It wasn't obvious to me," said Danny, lying deliberately, since by the time he got home tonight she would be markedly improved, and in a week she would probably look fantastic, compared to before, and Danny wanted Lieder to think it had already been happening before Danny even got there.

"Then you're an idiot," said Lieder.

"Oh, I'm pretty sure of that," said Danny. "Thanks for the ride." Then he was gone.

It occurred to him as he walked into school that Lieder was thinking that Danny might be useful to brighten his daughter's spirits during her last weeks of life. While it might be amusing to watch Lieder try to be nice to him—it was clearly against the man's nature—it wouldn't be fair to Nicki. Especially because Nicki was not going to die. At least not of her disease, whatever it had been. When Lieder realized this, when the doctors told him she was in complete remission, he'd very quickly want to be rid of Danny. So Danny would spare them both the trouble and never go back there again.

The real problem today was going to be dealing with the kids in gym class, who had no doubt spent the whole evening last night telling everybody they knew about the experience of going up the magical rope climb and ending up viewing the whole Maury River Valley from a mile high. Whatever Lieder had seen yesterday, he hadn't mentioned it today. Yesterday, he had seemed to blame Danny for the whole thing. "They're riding it like a carnival," he had said. "You did this," he had said. But today he hadn't mentioned it at all.

And as Danny walked through the halls and went into his first class, he didn't see any unusual excitement and didn't hear any mention of the magical rope. It bothered him—how could high school kids *not* talk about such a weird experience? But he wasn't going to bring it up himself.

It wasn't till he saw Hal in his next class that Danny was able to ask about it.

"Are you kidding?" asked Hal. "Nobody's telling anybody about it because they'll all think we're crazy. Hallucinating. *On* something."

"But you know it really happened."

"I do *now*," said Hal, "cause *you* apparently remember it. What *was* that, man? What happened?"

This was so weird. People claimed miraculous things happened all the time, even though nothing happened at all. But this time, when it was something real, they weren't talking about it. It's as if when something really scares people, the blabbermouth switch gets turned off.

"I don't know any more than you do," said Danny. One of the gifts of gatemages was that they were good tricksters, which meant they were good liars, since it's hard to bring off any kind of trick if you can't deceive people.

Hal looked hard at him. "You look like you're telling me the absolute truth, but you're the one who told me to hang on to the bottom of the rope and spin, and then I shot up to the top. You're the one Coach Bleeder told to get me up the rope, and so what am I supposed to think except that *you* did whatever it was."

"And if I did," said Danny, "what then? Who would you tell? How far would the story go?"

"Nowhere, man," said Hal. "You saved my ass all over the place, you think I'm going to do anything to hurt you? But you took off yesterday, you went outside when the rope trick stopped working, and when I went out after you, you were gone. Vanished. What are you, man? Are you, like, an alien?"

"A Norse god," said Danny.

"What, like Thor?" Hal laughed.

"More like Loki," said Danny.

"Is this your final answer?" asked Hal. "Am I really supposed to believe this one?"

"Believe what you want," said Danny. "Class is about to start." He went to the door and Hal followed him into the classroom.

HERMIA WAS SITTING in the Applebee's on Lee Highway, looking out the window at cars pulling in and out of the BP next door, when her mother slid into the booth across from her.

"Have you already ordered?" Mother asked.

Hermia felt a thrill of fear. She was too far from the nearest gate to make any kind of clean escape. Mother was a sandmage, which should have meant she was powerless in a place as damp as western Virginia, but as Mother often pointed out to her, her real affinity was for anything powdered or granulated, from snowflakes to dust, from shotgun pellets to salt and pepper and sugar. The table was full of things that Mother could use.

Besides, wherever she was, Father would not be far away, and he was a watermage—a Damward, able to choke her on her own saliva, if he chose. If they wanted Hermia dead, to punish her for running off and not reporting to them about the gatemage she had found, she could do nothing to stop them or avoid them.

So apparently they didn't want her dead. Yet.

"They're getting me a hamburger," said Hermia. "There's not much you can do wrong with a hamburger."

"They could leave it on the counter for twenty minutes, letting it get cold while the bacteria multiply," said Mother. "And then they bring it to you, without apology, assuming that you're the mousy little thing you seem to be and won't utter a word of complaint."

"I'm not mousy," said Hermia.

"They don't know that," said Mother. "And you look so Mediterranean—they know you don't belong here in this hotbed of Scotch-Irish immigration."

"So you've made a study of American demographics and genealogy?"

"I study everything," said Mother. "People are like grains of sand—from a distance, they all look alike, but when you really study them, each is a separate creation."

The waiter came over and Mother ordered a salad. But before the waiter could get away, she said to him, "What do you think of a daughter who suddenly disappears and doesn't tell her mother and father where she's going and whom she's with? What would you call such a girl?"

The waiter, who had flirted with Hermia a little when he took her order, answered instantly: "Normal."

Mother laughed, one of her seal-like barks. "Hope springs eternal, doesn't it, dear boy. But I assure you, you're not her type."

The waiter, looking a little baffled, muttered something about putting her order in and left.

"You do enjoy toying with them," said Hermia.

"Observing them," corrected Mother. "Seeing how they respond to unusual stimuli. I'm a scientist at heart."

She was Clytemnestra and Medea rolled into one, that's what was in her heart, thought Hermia, but she knew better than to say it. "So you found me," she said.

"Oh, we've known where you were the whole time," said Mother.

Hermia didn't bother to answer.

"I know you think we couldn't possibly have traced you, with all your jumping through gates, but you see, when we first realized you might have gatemaking talent, we implanted a little chip just under your jaw. We track it by satellite. We Illyrians are truly godlike in our prescience, don't you think?"

It had never crossed Hermia's mind that they might have installed a tracking device in her body. She had given Danny away every time she used one of his gates.

Or maybe not. When she made a jump through one of Danny's gates, it would take time for them to get to where she was. Knowing where she was wasn't the same thing as being there to observe her.

But last night they'd had plenty of time to get to Parry McCluer High School.

"You spent the night here?" asked Hermia.

"In the Holiday Inn Express," said Mother. "It has a nice European feel to it."

"Meaning that the rooms are tiny and have no space to put your luggage?"

"We didn't make ourselves known during the festivities. But we saw some of the Norths challenge you, and watched as a couple of mere Orphans brought old Zog's eagle down and then cracked open the earth and swallowed up their truck."

"They gave it back afterward," said Hermia. "Or did you fall asleep before the end?"

"From these actions, we cleverly deduced, in our Aristotelian way, that somebody had passed through a Great Gate. I think it wasn't you who made the gate, because if you were able to make gates, you would have disappeared the moment I sat down."

"No, I can't make gates. You know I can't."

"I know you have always said you can't. But now I believe you. Maybe."

"I'm not telling you who—"

"It's Danny North who's the gatemage," said Mother.

"Don't you dare lay a hand on him."

"No habanero powder in his eyes or up his nose?" asked Mother. "Why must you always spoil my fun?"

"He's not just a gatemage, he's a Gatefather," said Hermia. "In all the history of the world there's never been a gatemage like him."

"The world has a lot of history. And there are two worlds, for that matter."

"He beat the Gate Thief," said Hermia.

"Isn't that nice."

"What do you want, Mother?"

"My darling daughter to tell me she loves me, even if it's a lie, and to pretend she's glad to see me."

"I'm not reporting to you anymore."

"You don't have to report, as I just explained," said Mother.

"Danny and I and the other gatemage—"

"So you *are* a gatemage, and not just a Finder."

"I'm a Lockfriend," said Hermia.

"And the other gatemage? Victoria Von Roth?"

"A Keyfriend."

"How lovely. It's like you're twins, born thirty years apart."

"The next time Danny makes a Great Gate, we're going to make sure *all* the Families and the Orphans have equal access to it."

"Even the drowthers?"

"We aren't going to let a Great Gate give one Family an advantage."

"But you already have, silly girl," said Mother. "That cow Leslie now has the power to snatch other people's heartbeasts away from them, and Marion can crack open the earth without causing so much as a three point oh on the Richter scale. They could take down every Family right now."

"And yet they haven't done it," said Hermia. "Doesn't that tell you something?"

"Doesn't the fact that we didn't kill you tell *you* something, too?"

"It tells me that your hope of getting through a Great Gate is greater than your desire to keep anybody else from getting through it."

"It *should* have told you that we mean to play nice," said Mother. "We're going to let you and your boyfriend Danny and his aging mistress Veevee set out the rules, and we'll play along."

"Till you see a way to get an advantage," said Hermia.

"Wasn't it nice of me to come and inform you? Some of us wanted to kill you and then deal with Danny North separately. We would pretend we didn't know where you were. They're very angry with you for betraying us."

"I didn't tell him anything," said Hermia.

"You didn't tell *us* anything," said Mother. "But . . . water over the dam, isn't that what they say?"

"You got your physics degree at Stanford, Mother. Don't pretend to be uncertain of your English."

"We're going to station an observer at the high school," said Mother. "And we're going to expect you to stay there, too."

"I'm too old for high school," said Hermia.

"But you're such a little slip of a thing, they won't doubt that this is your senior year."

"I don't have to be at the high school. I can gate in and out whenever I want to talk to Danny."

"As long as he keeps gates available to you," said Mother. "No, we want you there where *we* can watch you both."

"And where you can threaten to do violence to me in order to get him to do what you want."

"Would that work?" asked Mother.

"I don't think so," said Hermia, "but with Danny you never know. He's not in love with me. I don't think he particularly likes me. But he's a compassionate kid. You could probably just point a gun at a puppy, take a picture, and then send it to him along with the threat, 'Do what we say or we'll shoot this dog.' "

"Well, we aren't going to threaten to shoot you *or* a puppy. We think—some of us think—that now that you know that we've known where you are all along, and didn't interfere with you, you'll return to us with renewed trust and loyalty."

"Are you among those who think so?" asked Hermia.

"I'm only one vote among many," said Mother. "But it's pleasantly needy of you to ask for my reassurance."

"You know that whoever you send, Danny can just gate away."

"Oh, I hope he doesn't do that," said Mother. "We'd have to shoot the dog."

CEDRIC BIRD STOOD in a circle of tall standing stones on the brow of a grassy hill. Sheep grazed on the gentle slope below him, but Ced saw no sign of a shepherd.

He had meant to do what the others did. Step into the Great Gate, and then, the moment he was in Westil, take the next step and go back to Earth with his power greatly enhanced.

Only in the moment they arrived—in daylight on Westil instead of night the way it was in Buena Vista—he felt a touch of breeze on his cheek. And as a windmage he couldn't go, not without first feeling the movement of the air, getting a sense of the way the sunlight warmed the air and the grass moved in the breeze.

It was only a moment, a second or two. Out of the corner of his eye he saw the others step forward and disappear. And then he stepped forward—and felt the grass brush against the cuffs of his pants. The Great Gate was already gone, and just like that, Ced realized that he had decided to stay on Westil.

He felt a momentary thrill of fear. All the bedtime stories his mother had told him about the faraway world their ancestors came from. The place where the gods of legend lived. It was a terrifying place where huge storms could be conjured by the anger of a sandmage, where Stonefathers could fashion copies of themselves in stone, where a lake could be swallowed up in stone, or an island be overswept by a Tidefather's wave.

Yet he could also feel the wind.

He had always felt the wind, even in his sleep, it would wake him by whistling through the eaves and trembling the windows, and he would get up and open the door and go out into the wind. Mother would hear him and rush out after him and gather him up and say, The wind is a terrible thing, Cedric, it carries birds far from shore and sweeps nests out of the trees. But Cedric would say, It never hurts me, Mother. I love the wind.

Yet he had never really felt the wind until now, today, as he stood in this gentle wind on a grassy hill in Westil. He felt it shape itself around the standing stones and sensed all the eddies within the circle. He was aware of the play of the breeze in the wool of the nearest sheep, and the sweep of it through the grass exhilarated him.

It's not the breeze of Westil that's different, Ced realized. It's me. I've been through the Great Gate, and now I have all the awareness of the wind that I ever wanted. Now I'm the mage I always was in my dreams.

He couldn't resist the temptation now; it wasn't enough to feel the wind. He had to shape it. He had been studying with Norm Galliatti, an Orphan Galebreath in Medford, Oregon, and he had raised his abilities from making tiny whirlwinds and raising a slight breeze on a still day to the point where he could direct a breeze, narrow it like a dart, blow out a candle from a hundred yards, change the flight of a ball in midair.

But here . . . just by thinking of doing it, it happened. A whirlwind rose all around him, spinning inside the circle of stones, whipping his hair and clothing, and it was so much larger and stronger than anything he'd ever been able to do before that he laughed aloud, then cried in joy. Oh, Mother, can you see me? O Bird of my Youth, O my Hummingbird, Calliope, are you watching now? See what I can do!

The whirlwind created so much suction inside it that he rose up into the air, but he was in no danger. This was no tornado, snatching up creatures and flinging them here and there, randomly. No, the air that spun around him *knew* him, cared for him, carried him. The wind rejoiced in him as much as he rejoiced in it. Here you are, it was saying. We are sheep too long without a shepherd, cows with udders full and no dairyman to ease us, till you came.

Carry me, he thought. Carry me away from here. Show me this world.

The whirlwind raised him higher and he could see now over the nearby groves of trees. There was a shepherd's hut just beyond the river, and out of it stepped the shepherd, looking upward at Ced as the whirlwind bore him along the river's course, downstream because that's what Ced felt like, but the wind might have carried him anywhere.

Now I know why people called us gods, if we Mithermages of Westil could pass through Great Gates and to *this*. When they painted Hermes with wings on his feet, was it a windmage like me that they remembered?

Ced had only to think of going to the crest of a rocky outcropping, and the whirlwind bore him there and gently set him down. What had once been such a labor to him, just to make a whirlwind go where he wanted it to go, was now effortless, and he could ride within it. Here is how a magic carpet flies. This is the wheel Ezekiel saw in the middle of the air.

But now that he was on solid ground, Ced stretched out his arms and gathered more and more wind into the vortex. He moved it away from himself and made it spin and spin and spin. The top of it rose up, and at the base it began to gather dirt and dust and bits of grass and old leaves and insects from the ground and now the whirlwind became darker, more visible as a column, more like the television image of a tornado, only it wasn't in the distance, it was here, and he was in control of it.

This is the real god, thought Ced.

No: In his mind he was speaking to the wind itself. Thou art the god, O whirlwind of my making. I have wakened thee.

With the realization that the wind was alive and could hear him, Ced crossed a threshold. His outself went into the wind. It became his clant. It became his heartsblood, and he was riding in the wind the way his mother flew in hummingbirds, riding it and guiding it, both as companion and controller, passenger and pilot.

He never left his body; he still stood watching the tornado from the tor. Yet he also *was* the tornado, not seeing through it, for tornados have no eyes, but rather feeling it with the kinesthesia of his body, the way a person can sense with eyes closed just where the hands are, and what the fingers are doing. He could feel the location and dimension and speed and strength of the tornado just as he could tie his shoelaces in the dark, the fingers moving smoothly through well-remembered patterns.

He rode the tornado for a hundred miles before he was sated with the joy of it. Enough, enough, enough. He let go of the wind and immediately felt it slacken and fade, the air also rejoicing with the memory of such rapid, powerful flight. His outself returned to him. He stood, whole again, and yet bereft because the wind was just a gentle breeze again. He had been a giant; now he was only a man.

He climbed down from the outcropping of rock. It wasn't easy—a windmage can fly to a place where a goat can't climb. But there was a grassy way, a step here, a jump there, that let him get down from peak to riverside.

Then he began to walk downstream, looking for people. But he found none.

Instead, he met the wreckage of a village, the houses torn up by their roots.

He had to raise a little whirlwind to lift him over the tumble of a broken forest, with trees uprooted and cast upon each other like a game of pickup sticks.

And then he came to a city where the trapped cried out from inside collapsed walls, where men and women keened aloud over the bodies of the dead, and children wandered looking terrified and lost.

He could not understand their language, though he recognized that it sounded somewhat like the language his mother sometimes spoke to him in snatches, the language she spoke to the birds that gathered around her when she fed them or sang to them in the yard.

None of them seemed to think anything of this stranger among them. They were too caught up in their own misery and fear, in the struggle to release the victims trapped in the fallen buildings. Ced joined in, helping to pull away the wreckage, to lift the broken bodies, to carry the living to safety.

I need you to heal these people, Danny North. I should not be here alone. I can't be trusted. It's too much power. Look what I did without even realizing it. I felt the devastation of this town as a kind of crunching underfoot, like tramping over fallen acorns on the pavement near a city oak. But it was these buildings I was kicking aside, and in the wind of my passing I never heard my victims' pleas and cries, for the wind sings and screams, but it has no ears and never listens.

I have ears. I have eyes. Yet I was far away on a rocky hill, standing there in the ecstasy of power. It was a drug.

I have been a god for only an hour or two, and look what I have done.

Yet as Ced struggled to save people in the aftermath of his tornado, he also felt a dark and terrible pride. On the one hand, he wanted to weep and beg forgiveness, to take responsibility and bear the consequence: I did this. I will help undo the damage, as much as I can.

But the most powerful feeling deep inside him was much simpler, and filled with the fire of pride:

I did this. Look what I can do!

3

Intervention

Danny thought he was going to Laurette's house that night for a birthday party. Not the teen-movie cliche of a party so huge that it overflows the house and infests the neighbors' yards and results in the police being called. It was just a get-together at Laurette's house in honor of Xena, Laurette's friend and, since he arrived at Parry McCluer, Danny's.

But when Danny showed up at the house, and the door opened at his knock, he knew he'd been had. His friends were all there—the girls, Laurette, Sin, Pat, Xena, and the boys, Hal and Wheeler. But a big banner high on the wall, plainly visible from the front door, said nothing about birthdays or Xena.

It said "Intervention," and Danny knew at once that he was the target, the patsy, the subject.

"What am I supposedly addicted to?" he asked.

"He doesn't even get the *How I Met Your Mother* reference," said Sin.

"He doesn't watch television," said Hal.

"Wow, we should have intervened about *that,*" said Xena.

"When are you going to intervene with Laurette about always showing off her cleavage?" said Danny. "It scares the teachers. They think they're going to fall in and get lost."

"Let's stick to the plan," said Laurette.

"It's not *my* plan," said Danny.

"You're not going to dodge this one," said Sin.

"You still haven't told me what you're intervening about," said Danny. "Maybe I'll agree with you and we can move on to the party portion of the evening."

"We want you to stop hiding who you are," said Hal.

Danny turned to him. "I'm President Obama's love child with a Chicago waitress. I'm actually black, but I act super-white and it fools everybody."

"We know you have powers," said Sin.

"You're a fairy," said Xena. "The Tolkien kind."

" 'Elf' is a better word," said Pat.

"No, it's definitely 'fairy,' " said Xena, "because it's more fun to say."

"I'm not an elf and I'm not a fairy," said Danny. "These days I'm on the track team. I'm going to get a letter and be an athlete and then I'll be too cool to hang out with you."

"We know you healed us," said Pat. "My complexion has cleared up totally, and Sin's infected piercings got uninfected."

"You didn't do anything for my weight problem," said Xena, "which wasn't very nice."

"Maybe he likes you the way you are," said Wheeler.

"I'm trying to think how I did this magical stuff," said Danny.

"It all started happening after you got here, that's point A," said Xena.

"Post hoc ergo propter hoc," said Danny.

"He's talking Logic," said Hal. "I wish Ms. Schrader hadn't done that unit on fallacies."

"Point B," said Xena, "is the tripping place."

"So I heal people *and* I make them clumsy," said Danny. "Sounds like a contradiction."

"And there's that flying thing with the rope climb," said Hal. "You're the one who set it up. You told me to move my hands as *if* I was climbing. That means you thought I'd somehow get up there without actually climbing."

"Is that how you remember it?" asked Danny.

"Notice how he's not actually denying it," said Hal.

"I *would* deny it if I knew what you were accusing me of." Danny realized once again that it's always a mistake to equivocate. If you're going to lie then just lie. Don't try to make it technically true or almost true or truish.

"I didn't think we should call it an intervention," said Hal. "I thought we should call it an ultimatum." He seemed really angry.

"Admit to this crazy stuff you're accusing me of, or else," said Danny.

"That's what an ultimatum is, all right," said Hal.

"What's the 'else'?" asked Danny.

"Or else you're not really our friend."

Danny knew they were right, but also they were wrong. They couldn't possibly understand what telling them would mean. It's one thing to think your friend has some connection with mysterious stuff. But if they found out what he was, they either wouldn't believe him or they'd pressure him to demonstrate it, and he wasn't going to make any more damn gates at Parry McCluer.

"If you were really *my* friends," said Danny, "you wouldn't decide what the answer is and then threaten to ostracize me if I don't tell you that you're right."

"Then what's the answer?" asked Sin. "We're not going to tell anybody."

"Let's say I admit I'm some kind of fairy. You promise not to tell. But since you already think you know it, and you also promise not to tell, then how would my telling you change anything?"

"You don't trust us," said Wheeler.

"What if I'm some kind of magical guy. Have I done anything evil with it? Hurt anybody?"

"I think Coach Bleeder landed on his ass a couple of times because of you," said Hal.

"Did it ever occur to you that *if* I had these powers, maybe I was keeping secrets from you for your own good?"

"There are some things that humankind is not meant to know," intoned Laurette.

" 'If I tell you, I have to kill you,' " quoted Xena.

"Let's put the shoe on the other foot, where it belongs," said Danny. "If we're such good friends, why would you threaten to *stop* being my friends if I don't tell you something that, *if* it's true, I clearly want to keep to myself?"

Sin stuck out her feet. "How does that put my shoes on the other feet? These are the only feet I have."

Nothing he did was going to help. Because Danny knew from the family history where this led. You tell drowthers what you are, then you have to show them. And once they see it, they get scared of you, and either they avoid you or they try to become your servant because it's human nature to want to be close to power.

Danny didn't want to find out which way his friends would go. He'd never had friends before, and now he was going to lose them no matter what he did.

Better to lose them *without* their knowing for sure what he was and what he could do.

"I accept your terms," said Danny.

They leaned forward expectantly.

"I'm not going to admit to any of this stuff, so I guess that means we're not friends." Danny walked back to the door.

"Wait!" said Laurette.

"We didn't mean it!" said Xena.

"*I* did," said Hal. "He sent us a mile into the sky, and if he says he didn't it's bullshit."

Danny opened the door and stepped outside.

He could hear someone—several people—rushing toward the door. He didn't want to play out this scene on the front lawn.

So he gated back to his house and pulled the gate in after him.

Had he even closed the door behind him? For all he knew, they had seen him disappear.

But he was pissed off at them. Why would friends try to force him to tell what he clearly didn't want to tell? They weren't his friends. He barely knew them. So why did he have this gnawing feeling in his gut?

"Where did you gate from?" asked a voice.

Hermia was sitting in his living room.

"How did you get in?" asked Danny.

"I used Veevee's gate," said Hermia. "I was visiting her, and I wanted to visit you, but you weren't here so I waited."

Danny looked at her steadily. "What are you doing here?"

"My family came to me," said Hermia. "My actual parents. I was so honored."

"Was it a happy reunion?" asked Danny, sitting down across from her in the only other chair in what passed for a living room.

"It was all about you," said Hermia. "They want you to trust them. They say they won't try to control you, they don't want a war, but they think you need training."

"Like I'd ever let any of the Westilians anywhere near me."

"I'll tell them that," said Hermia.

"Are you in their pocket? Do they have some kind of control over you?"

"Meaning, can you trust me? Yes and no. You can trust me to keep my word. But they have some kind of tracking device imbedded in me, so wherever I go, they know where I am."

Danny thought about that a moment. "So they've seen you jump."

"Yes."

"By jumping from Veevee's place to here, they know where that gate is."

"Yes."

"Everywhere you go, you show them the gates."

"Yes," said Hermia. "But I told you as soon as I knew, didn't I? What was I supposed to do, seal myself in a coffin like a vampire and never go anywhere again?"

"So they know where I am right now."

"They know *I* came to these exact map coordinates," said Hermia. "They don't know that you happen to be in this place, but yes, they probably will, very soon."

"Shit," said Danny. She really didn't have much choice, if her own family had decided to track her.

"We have to make contact with all the Families eventually," said Hermia. "Including my Family. If you intend to make a Great Gate and share it."

Three cars pulled up out front, one of them actually screeching on the pavement.

"How long have you been waiting here? Does your Family just hover over you in choppers or balloons or something?"

Hermia peeked out the threadbare front curtain. "No, and it isn't your Family, either."

Danny joined her at the window. His friends were getting out of three cars.

"Damn," he said.

"Make a clean getaway," said Hermia. "Or gate *them* somewhere."

"I never told them I live here," said Danny.

Hermia flung open the door. Danny said "No!" the moment he realized she was doing it, but by then it was already done.

"He's here, isn't he!" It was Laurette's voice.

"We drove three different routes and he wasn't running on any of them," said Sin triumphantly.

"And there's no way he's fast enough to already be here," said Pat, "not on foot, not even running."

Now they were at the door, piling in. But Danny wasn't there.

Instead, he was behind the house, out of sight, watching the living room through a peephole—a tiny gate right in front of one of his eyes, so when he closed the other, he could see what was happening in his living room—and he could hear pretty clearly, too.

"Whom are you looking for?" asked Hermia.

"So he's got a girlfriend," said Xena, sounding pretty put out about it.

"Danny North," said Wheeler. "He lives here."

"How interesting," said Hermia. "Who are you?"

"His friends," said Laurette.

"Sounds more like you're stalking him," said Hermia.

"You still haven't told us who you are," said Xena.

"I actually *am* his friend," said Hermia.

"You sound British," said Xena.

"Cute British accent," said Pat disgustedly. "Boys are so predictable."

"But she has little boobs," said Laurette.

"You're still the fairest in the land, Laurette," said Sin.

"How did he get here so fast?" Hal insisted.

Listening outside, Danny thought: Hal is able to stay focused. Hal is something. Which is probably why Coach Bleeder zeroed in on him, tormented him. Because he has the potential to accomplish far more with his life than Bleeder ever has. No wonder the coach had to take Hal down a peg every chance he got.

"He's a gatemage," said Hermia.

With a thrill of fear, Danny thought: Hermia was telling me to gate them away. Now she's spilling it to them.

Nobody was asking what a gatemage is.

"He opens up holes in spacetime," said Hermia. "He links one place with another, regardless of distance. He makes them adjacent."

"Do you think you've actually explained something?" asked Pat.

"I've explained it like gravity," said Hermia. "I described the results. I have no idea of the process. That's all that Newton ever did."

"And Danny can do this," said Hal. "Connect things with each other."

"He may be the greatest Gatefather that ever lived," said Hermia. "But so far, he's mostly used his power to create little gates at your high school."

"What do gates have to do with his healing people?" said Pat.

"Danny doesn't heal anybody, but the gates do," said Hermia. "If you pass through a gate alive, your body arrives in optimal condition."

"No zits," said Pat.

"No piercings," said Sin.

"So why did he lie about it and pretend he wasn't doing it?" asked Xena. "It's way cool."

"Because it's *too* way cool," said Hermia. "There are a lot of people who want him dead. By making gates at your school, he ran the risk of being discovered. That business with the rope climb? The worst thing happened. His family showed up and tried to kill him."

Silence.

Then, in a smaller voice, Laurette said, "His own family?"

"I thought his parents were dead," said Hal.

"A lie," said Hermia. "His parents are actually very powerful mages. To their credit, *they* didn't try to kill him. It was his grandfather and uncle who attempted his assassination."

"Sick," said Wheeler.

"There's a lot of history that you don't know," said Hermia. "And most of it is unbelievable to people like you."

"What do you mean, 'people like us'?" asked Pat.

"Normal people," said Hermia.

Wheeler laughed. "Did you hear that? She called us normal."

"Let me help you understand this," said Hermia. "Danny's father is named Odin. He was born with the name Alf, but when he became head of the North family, he took the name Odin."

"Wow," said Wheeler. "You're talking, like, a god."

"I'm telling you that the gods of mythology are real people. Only each name has been recycled again and again. We're not immortal. But the names are."

"So who is Danny?" asked Hal. "Is he a god?"

"If his family stops trying to kill him and accepts him for who he is, then the name he would be given is Loki."

"Thor's nasty brother in *The Avengers*," said Wheeler.

"There's no magic hammer," said Hermia. "But yes. There's a Thor in the family, but he doesn't amount to much. None of them do." And then she explained how the Great Gates work. Danny sat outside, listening. Hermia was good at explanations. Why shouldn't she be? Gatemages had the gift of language.

It terrified him to hear her telling his friends. But he also knew that this is what he had wanted to do. This is why he didn't gate away from them. This is why he hadn't left Parry McCluer High School. This is why he had carelessly let them realize his power, as he returned home far faster than his feet could have carried him. He wanted them to know; he wanted to be honest with them. But he couldn't bring himself to answer their questions. Hermia was doing it for him.

When she finished her explanation, she said, "Now I've told you the answers to your questions. Do you believe me?"

"Yes," said Pat and Wheeler and Sin and Hal.

"Why?" asked Hermia.

"Because I rode the rope," said Hal.

"Because he cured my piercings," said Sin.

"My face," said Pat.

"Because it's so cool," said Wheeler.

"And the rest of you?"

"It's pretty hard to swallow," said Laurette. "How do *you* know all this stuff? I never heard of you."

"I'm a gatemage too," said Hermia. "A lesser one. I can't make gates, but I can see them and I can lock them. And I can help Danny. But now you all have a choice to make."

They waited.

"Are you with him or not?" asked Hermia. "That's why he was afraid to tell you, because once he did, you'd have to make the choice."

"What do you mean, 'with him'?" asked Hal. "He's got this incredible power. What does he need from us?"

"What the gods have always needed," said Hermia. "Servants."

Consternation. Outrage. "I thought we were his friends!" said Laurette.

"Are you his equals?" asked Hermia. "Are you? When the others come to kill him, what do you think you can do? When Danny's mother electrocutes you or his father makes your car stop working, and any gun you point at them fails to work and a hawk comes to peck out your eyes, can you stand up to them?"

"Duh," said Laurette.

"We're useless," said Hal. "So why would he need us?"

"That's why I didn't say that he needs soldiers. Or allies. He needs servants. He needs people he can send with messages. People to watch and notice things, and tell him about them."

"Spies," said Pat.

"And messengers," said Hermia. "The Families will know you're powerless. With any luck, they won't kill you. But they could. If you piss them off. Do you understand? You're powerless. But you can help Danny to put together some kind of peace treaty. Some way to unite the Families and share some of his power with them."

"And why would we want to do that?" asked Xena. "*If* these *gods* actually, like, *exist*, why would we want Danny to give them more power?"

"Because if he doesn't, they'll kill him," said Hermia. "It's a matter of time, that's all. Are you his friends or not? You're the ones who demanded the truth, so here it is. Now you have a choice. With him, or not with him."

"With him," said Hal.

"Slow down," said Pat. "This is major."

Hermia had done all she could—all that Danny needed her to do. Now it was time for Danny to face his friends again. He had been a coward to leave it up to her.

So he gated into the house.

He appeared in the middle of the room. They stared at him in fear.

"It's true," whispered Laurette.

"Cool," said Wheeler.

Danny turned to Wheeler. "This isn't a comic book, Wheeler. It doesn't go from panel to panel until the good guys win. In the real world, good guys lose all the time. What wins is power. I have a lot of it, but I don't have enough to protect you all the time. I advise you to get the hell away from me and pretend you never met me. With any luck, none of the Families will notice you and you'll be as safe as anyone."

"How safe is that?" asked Pat.

"If I create a Great Gate and the Families send people through, so they become gods again instead of elves and wizards, the way they are now, then you won't have a choice anymore. You'll stay out of their way, and if they notice you, you'll do what you're told or you'll die. Our Families aren't nice people. They call you drowthers. They think of you the way you think of cars. Useful when you need them, but fun to crash into each other and watch them blow up and burn."

They were looking sick and scared. So Danny was communicating.

"Do you see why I tried not to tell you?" said Danny.

"I think you're just trying to scare us," said Xena defiantly.

"Is it working?" asked Danny.

"Yes," said Laurette.

"Good," said Danny. "I came here in hopes of having a normal life. Two years of high school. But then I got stupid and did that thing with the rope climb and Hermia saw it and told me that it was a Great Gate. I finally got the knowledge to do some really powerful stuff."

"But it sounds terrible," said Sin. "Why would you let them through?"

"Here's how it'll work," said Danny. "Either I'll work out a way to give all the Families equal access to a Great Gate, or one of the Families will kidnap somebody I care about and kill them if I don't give them *exclusive* use of a Great Gate."

"Who would they kidnap?" asked Hal.

"Hermia. The woman who pretends to be my aunt. Or maybe you, Hal. It depends on how much they've observed already."

"And if they kidnapped Hal," said Laurette, "what would you do?"

"He'd let them kill Hal," said Hermia. "He'd let them kill me. Because if he lets one Family have a Great Gate, and not the others, then that means that the most violent and evil Family will rule the world. But if they all have a share of the Gate, then maybe, just maybe, they'll balance each other out. Maybe they'll avoid a war. Maybe you drowthers won't all end up as collateral damage."

"Is she right?" Hal asked Danny.

"I hope so," said Danny. "But if it came down to it, I don't know if I could do it. Let them kill you or her or anybody. Up to now, the only life I was risking was my own. But once I made a Great Gate, everything changed. Now the whole world is at risk."

"But you can do things," said Hal. "Like, if you'd been around for 9/11, you could have made those planes—"

"No, I couldn't have done a thing," said Danny. "Because I would have found out about it when everybody else did, by watching television. I've got a couple of talents, but I'm not really a god. Not like you're thinking—a god that knows everything and can do anything he wants. I can do a few specific things, and I don't know very much at all."

"Then what good is it?" asked Pat.

"Not much," said Danny. "All I can do is try to keep the damage to a minimum."

"So what's your choice?" said Hermia. "My Family's on the way here right now, you can count on that. If you're going to choose *not* to stand with Danny, then he's got to get you away from here before they come. Go get in your cars and drive away and forget you ever knew Danny. Don't do anything to tip off the Families that you're his friends, or you'll end up as hostages. Get it?"

"Shit," said Sin. "That's just—that's terrible."

"Exactly," said Hermia.

"Why did you make a Great Gate, man?" asked Hal.

"Because I'm a servant of spacetime," said Danny. "Because it's what I was born for. Because I faced a powerful enemy and beat him. Because I'm stupid."

"There's a feeble chance," said Hermia, "that it will be better. For instance, Danny's father and mother, if they went through a Great Gate, maybe they'd come back and use their power to destroy all the nuclear weapons in the world."

"Could they do that?" asked Hal.

"The question is, *would* they," said Hermia. "The Families don't have a history of trying to make life better for the drowthers."

"Drowthers—that's us?" asked Xena.

"It sounds like the N word," said Pat.

"It's exactly like the N word, the way most people in the Families use it," said Danny. "But some of us want to use our power to protect you."

"Don't let them through the Gate, man," said Hal.

"I told you how they'll make him do it," said Hermia.

"Then kill yourself first," said Hal. "That's what I'd do."

The words hung in the air.

"Maybe you would," said Danny. "But I'm not that kind of hero. I'm not any kind of hero."

"'With great power comes great responsibility,'" intoned Wheeler.

"If only," said Danny. "In the real world, with great power comes great suffering—by the people who don't have the power."

"I wasn't kidding," said Hal. "You shouldn't exist. If you didn't exist, things would keep on going the way they have been since 632 or whenever."

"Spacetime would only create another like me," said Danny. "And maybe the next guy would be even worse than me."

"He did use his power to help us," said Laurette.

"You were knocking Coach Bleeder on his ass," said Hal.

"Yes," said Danny. "And making him drop his watch."

"To protect me?" asked Hal.

"And because it was funny," said Danny.

"It *was* funny," said Hal.

"Are you going to destroy the world, Danny?" asked Sin.

"I hope not," said Danny. "Here's what I hope. I hope that the Families will unite to use their power to stop all wars, to stop all the terrorists, to put an end to all the shit."

"Did they ever do that before, back before the gates were closed?" asked Hal.

"No," said Danny.

"Why would it be any different now?" said Hal.

"Because Danny's here," said Hermia. "If one of the Family starts acting like Stalin or Pol Pot or Idi Amin, Danny has the power to gate him to the bottom of the Atlantic, and they know it. They've got no way to stop him. As long as Danny's alive, he has a chance to keep it all under control."

"So you're going to be, like, the god of all gods," said Hal.

Danny sat down. "Yeah," he said.

"Plus graduate from high school on schedule," said Hal.

"Maybe I'm not going to be able to pull that off," said Danny.

"Why did you ever think you could?" asked Pat.

"Because I didn't know I could make a Great Gate when I came here," said Danny. "I didn't know anything. I just wanted to be normal."

Hal made a weighing motion with his hands. "Normal, or supreme god. Supreme god, or normal. So hard to decide." Then Hal reached out his hand to Danny. Offering a handshake.

"I'm in," said Hal.

"In what?"

"In the same shit soup as you," said Hal. "I'm your messenger. Or servant. Or whatever you need. I think you're a good guy. I think if anybody's going to have this kind of power, I'd rather it be you than anybody else I can think of, except maybe Winston Churchill, and he's dead."

Danny solemnly took his hand.

"So Hal gets to be your right-hand man," said Wheeler. "Just because he was willing to talk to you when you came to Parry McCluer High."

"Because he's my friend," said Danny, "and he volunteered."

"Well I volunteer too," said Wheeler.

And in a few moments, they had all agreed.

"So get in your cars," said Danny, "and get away from here."

"I thought that was what we'd do if we said no," said Laurette.

"I don't want Hermia's people to know about you. Not yet. Go. You're my friends. Your intervention worked. We've told you everything that we know. We didn't pretty it up. And you chose to stand with me. So the first thing is, if I say get out of here, you get out. So they can't use you as hostages to control me."

They nodded.

"Don't act like drowthers," said Hermia impatiently. "He doesn't want *nodding*. He wants *going*!"

And with that, Danny gated them all, one at a time, out to the cars.

After a moment of disorientation and confusion, they scrambled into the cars and drove away.

"That was what you wanted, wasn't it?" asked Hermia. "You wanted me to tell them, right?"

"I didn't know that's what I wanted until you did it," said Danny. "But yes. They asked for the truth. They're not children, they're people. They deserve to have the knowledge to choose for themselves."

"They made a stupid decision," said Hermia.

"True," said Danny. "But all the decisions are stupid. I've made nothing but stupid decisions. You too."

Hermia grinned. "When there aren't any smart decisions, I suppose you just have to pick the stupid decision you like best."

"Your Family is coming, right?" asked Danny.

"I can't imagine they're not."

"Then it's time to move to a different location," said Danny.

"It's time for me to move to one place, and you to another," said Hermia. "Until we're ready to set up the meeting we want. Because they'll always know where I am, and we don't want them to know where you are."

So Danny gated Hermia to a place she knew in Paris. Then he wrote a note to the Greeks and left it on the table in his own little house in Buena Vista.

"I will let you send two people through a Great Gate," said the note. "Go home and wait for my messenger. After today, anybody from any Family who comes to this town will be sent to the Moon. Leave now."

Danny opened the front door, so they wouldn't have to break it down. No reason for the landlord to lose money.

Then Danny gated to Washington, DC, then on to Staunton, to Lexington, and then to Naples, Florida, gathering in his gates behind him so they couldn't trace him if they happened to have a Gatesniffer that Hermia didn't know about.

Veevee knew at once that he had come through a gate into her condo. She came up from the beach through the gate he had left there for her. "Just in time for the season finale of *The Good Wife*," she said.

"Is that a TV show?" asked Danny.

"It's pure fantasy," she said. "There are no good wives."

"What about good husbands?" asked Danny.

"We'll see—when you grow up. Want a sandwich?"

"I'll make my own," he said. "We told all my friends about what I can do."

"Well, that was selfish and stupid of you."

"They insisted," said Danny.

"That was stupid of *them*, but they didn't know what they were asking. You have no excuse."

"I know," said Danny. "But other people are going to be involved whether we like it or not. Might as well have some of them on our team, on purpose, by their own choice."

Veevee shrugged, then laughed. "It's going to be so entertaining, to see how this all comes out. Right up to the moment when everything goes up in smoke."

"We're gods," said Danny. "What could go wrong?"

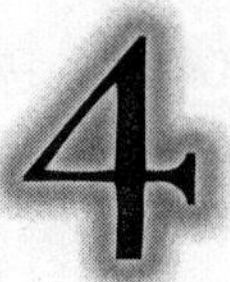

Captive

Wad was so very old that even his own grief and rage could not hold him deeply, not for long. The being who had dwelt inside a tree for fourteen centuries, watching for only one thing, a gate between worlds, was not fully engaged in being a human being, not yet, perhaps not ever.

Wad was a watcher above all. Yes, he had been taken as the lover of a queen. Yes, he had loved his son, had tried to protect him, and then had been outwitted by his lover, his enemy, Queen Bexoi, and his son was dead. Yes, he had imprisoned an innocent woman and her sons, then set them free. Surely this qualified as having been truly alive.

But Wad was still watching. Not only seeing what lay outside himself, as he had done creeping through the castle at Kamesham, but also what was happening inside himself, where his gatesense lay.

In his early life as Loki, and then for centuries as the Gate

Thief, Wad had captured and held the gates of other mages, but never had a gate of his own been taken from him. So he had not understood what it was like to have his outself captive in another mage's hearthoard.

Of course it was well known what happened to other mages when their outself was taken captive. How they lay inert, comatose, waiting for their wandering self to return.

But they were not gatemages. Their outselves were usually indivisible. Only the greatest of mages could control multiple clants or ride several heartbeasts at once—and even they suffered from the self-division.

Gatemages, though, were divisible by nature. They could leave bits of themselves here and there forever, as gates that others could use, always aware of where they were, but never putting their whole attention into any one gate.

Which is why, when Wad stole all the gates from mage after mage, he did not leave their bodies empty and helpless. They were able to continue their lives almost normally. Wad had therefore believed that he had done them no real harm. They were still themselves, still alive and aware, still able to control their own bodies.

He had not understood.

When the new Gatefather from Mittlegard stole most of Wad's gates from his hearthoard, including all the gates that Wad had stolen from others over the years, at first Wad could only think about the handful of gates that he still had under his own control. He had used those gates to save Anonoei, King Prayard's concubine, and her two sons, Eluik and Enopp. He still had some power. He was still a mage.

But now, without an urgent task, he realized what he had not understood before. More of the gatemage is in his gates than Wad had ever supposed. For he was still aware of his stolen gates. He still knew exactly where they were. He felt them all the time. He just couldn't *do* anything with them.

Yet, like the outself of a beastmage, riding with the heartbeast, or like a clant raised from plants or stones or sand or water or fire, his stolen gates were aware, alert, sensing what the possessor of the gates was doing, seeing, hearing.

And the longer Wad concentrated on his stolen gates, the more he was able to get glimpses of what the other gatemage wanted, what he planned, what he needed, what he hungered for. It was not quite words; always the words remained just out of reach. Unless this thief, this Gatefather, this Danny North spoke his thoughts aloud, Wad could not gather them up and study them. But as surely as if he were a beastmage, Wad could feel the inner longings of this man—no, this *boy*.

He could not change anything, could not take control of him—Danny North was master, and there was not enough of Wad within his captured gates for him to hope to take control. The deepest self of a gatemage was not in his outselves, the way it was with other kinds of mages. This was why gatemages could raise no clants. But the gates were still a part of him, and so now he was a part of Danny North.

And all the gates that Wad had stolen over the centuries, they had felt the same. The mages were not as strong as Wad, and so perhaps they had not felt themselves inside him as clearly as Wad now felt himself inside Danny North. But they must have been aware.

And because Wad had lived on and on inside the tree, the captured gates had not faded and died after their mages died. They were all still alive.

Wad had suppressed them, kept them silent. But they had been watching. They *knew* him as no one could ever know another human being, from the heart out—unless manmages also had such deep understanding.

In only a few days inside Danny North, Wad knew him intimately, the *feel* of him, the kind of man he was, the loves and fears and hopes and hates of him. So in these fourteen centuries, how well did the other gatemages still shadowed in Wad's hearthoard come to know him?

And now their knowledge was inside Danny North.

Wad could feel them, too, the gates that were fellow captives of this boyish Gatefather. He realized now that he knew them all, that even as he suppressed their cries, the tumult of their rage and despair, their surges of will, he had come to know them. They had been a part of him, and now that they were gone, he missed that intimate connection. At such great distance, in another man's hearthoard on another world, he longed to listen to them now.

The trouble was, they hated him. Even inside Danny North's hearthoard, they stayed as far from Wad's gates as they could. For even there, Wad's power was great, his hoard of gates vast indeed compared to theirs—though all of them were puny before the billion gates that belonged to Danny North himself. The other gates—the remnants of so many dead mages—still feared and hated Wad.

And loved Danny North.

That was what astonished Wad, when he understood it. These gates were no less captive than they had been before. Danny North had not set them free. Yet they responded to their new master as if he had liberated them. As much as they had hated—still hated—Wad, they loved this boy.

That was what Wad now struggled to understand. I was a good man, thought Wad. When I walked two worlds under the name of Loki, I saw the great danger that both worlds faced from the dark manmages from the world of Bel, the possessors of men's bodies and souls. And I sacrificed everything to save the worlds from the dragons of Bel. Did that not make me the best of men?

Yet they never came to understand the nobility and greatness of my cause. Centuries inside me, and their hatred never relented.

Inside Danny North, though, they seemed to blossom, to come

to new life. A pathetic, shadowy life, but life it was. They were still alert, still aware, but calm, not seething as they had done inside Wad.

They liked Danny North. They liked living inside him. They liked seeing the world through his eyes. They were at peace with him.

And they were not fading even now.

Nor are my gates fading, though they are apart from me, thought Wad. In fact, my gates thrive there. I, too, am more at peace inside Danny North than I am inside myself.

That was Wad's great discovery: The reason he could bear the death of his son, the betrayal of Queen Bexoi, the agony of his own guilt for what he had done to Anonoei and her sons, and the terror of having lost almost all his power, was that Danny North held a huge part of Wad inside a heart that was astonishingly pure and at peace.

Danny North was good.

Undisciplined, untrained, raw, confused, afraid—young.

Yet even so, his character was fully formed, as it is in all people by the time they reach the age of understanding—as it is, perhaps, from the moment they are conceived. And the person that Danny North revealed himself to be, by those who were held against their will inside his heart, was decent to the core.

Am I not decent, too? Why was dwelling in my hearthoard such a torment, and dwelling in his is an experience of healing, rest, calm, comfort?

Maybe the difference is this: The first thing I tried to do, when I realized I was still alert and aware inside of Danny North, was to exert some kind of control over him.

My first instinct was to rule.

But Danny North does not want to rule over anybody.

The poor child. So much power, and no idea of what it's for.

He did not eat my gates because he saw me as a rival. He was merely trying to survive, to hold on to himself. He does not want to rule the worlds. He does not even want to be the hero who *saves* the worlds. What does he want? Who is this boy?

And why, when he is so utterly different from me, do I find myself so glad of his company?

Danny North was such a compelling presence in Wad's mind that it took Wad days to realize that he knew something very important about events here on Westil.

There was a new mage in the world. A mage who had passed through a Great Gate. The powers of the Great Gate still clung to him; it was as if his footfalls reverberated like temblors through the deepest rock of the world, and made the slightest of vibrations in Wad's gatesense. Even though the Great Gate had not been of his making, the disturbance in spacetime could not be hidden from an old Gatefather like Wad.

What was he? What magic was this interloper doing? Whatever it was, the world was waking up before this surge of magic. No one had exercised such bright power since the closing of the Great Gates fourteen centuries before. Whatever Danny North was doing in Mittlegard, Wad was here on Westil, and this new greatmage was Wad's business.

And because Wad was *not* as decent, as unambitious as Danny North, his first thought was this: How can I harness the great power of this new greatmage and use it to wreak vengeance on my enemy, Queen Bexoi, and make her suffer as I have suffered?

5

Assassins

By the time Danny got to the farm in Yellow Springs, Marion had already suspended a rope over the central beam of the cowbarn. "Ladder work?" asked Danny.

"I'm a Cobblefriend," said Marion. "I can't fly, nor can my clants, such as they are."

"Then why didn't you wait for me to make a gate and carry the rope up there?" asked Danny.

"Hard for you to believe, I know, Danny, but before you ever came to this farm, I was able to wipe my butt all by myself."

Danny grinned. "Are you suggesting that you want me to install a rectal gate? Outbound only, I promise."

Marion made as if to smack Danny, though he never had and never would. But then he stopped. "Could you?" he asked. "Not rectal, but a gate that's attached to a person instead of to a place?"

"When Hermia gets here," said Danny.

"Hermia. Veevee. They'll only know what's in books."

"And I only know what I've tried," said Danny. "All those years I tried to figure out how to lock gates and how to take them back inside myself, and I couldn't figure any of it out until I saw it done."

"Somebody had to be the first gatemage," said Marion. "And from what Hermia says—if you can trust a Greek—"

"It's only a problem if they're bearing gifts," said Danny. "And she's Pelasgian."

"From what she says you may be the most extravagantly gifted gatemage ever. So you're going to have to break new ground to reach your potential."

"Parents always think their children have more potential than they actually have," said Danny.

"What about gatemage surgery?" asked Marion. "Those tracking devices inside Hermia—can't you gate them out of her?"

"I have a map in my head of all the gates I've made," said Danny. "But I can't map the inside of a person's body. Going through a gate heals people of any injuries or dysfunctions, but if I start making gates to remove bits of Hermia, it would only be by chance if I found the tracking devices her family installed in her."

"At least now I understand why you want to gate up to the roofbeam to hang a rope—it's something you know you can do."

"Don't you mostly do things you know you can do?" asked Danny, a little resentful now.

"Yes," said Marion. "Tell me. If you took one end of the rope down here, then gated to the roofbeam, would the rope just follow you and string out from here to there, or would it get cut off where the gate began?"

"It would look cut off," said Danny. "But it would still be connected. It would go up to the mouth of the gate down here, and the very next inch of rope would then emerge from the gate up there."

Marion shook his head. "Stonemages like me believe in solid connections. Not sudden leaps through spacetime."

"Where's Mom?" asked Danny.

"Out scouting for anybody's clant or heartbeast. You're making a Great Gate again, which is exactly what all the Families want, not to mention rogue Orphans we might not even know about."

"I can't believe that passing through a Great Gate allowed her to sense anybody's outself within a couple of miles," said Danny.

"And I can feel all the disturbances in the rock, not to mention the flow patterns, for a hundred miles in every direction. There's a reason why people had to go through Great Gates before the drowthers deigned to call them gods."

"So that's what you and Mom are now?" asked Danny. "Gods?"

"If I had already been a Stonefather, and then went through a Great Gate, then yes, I think I could put on a show that would make drowthers feel a strong desire to let me have my way. But as a Cobblefriend? Let's just say that my affinity is much more useful. I have more to give the stone, and so the stone replies with greater strength. That's all."

Danny stood there, looking at the ground, thinking of how Marion had opened up the earth near Parry McCluer High School and swallowed a pickup truck. Thinking: What will I be able to do, after I go through a Great Gate? And Veevee and Hermia? What does it do to a gatemage?

Wasn't that what they were making this Great Gate to find out? With no Gate Thief left to threaten him, and with Marion and Leslie primed to keep all danger at bay, Danny could experiment a little. He could stay a minute or two on Westil. Not very long—not long enough to be in danger. But long enough to see the place where Marion and Leslie had lingered for only a fraction of a second. "We blinked and then came back," Marion explained at the time. "It was daylight and there were rocks and grass, that's all I know."

"And he only knows about the grass because I told him," Leslie had said. "Stonemages don't care about grass, but Cowsisters have a real eye for it."

Danny put a little weight on the rope that Marion had suspended. He was so hungry to make a Great Gate that he almost couldn't wait until the others arrived.

No, that wasn't true. *Danny* wasn't hungry for it. What he was feeling as a powerful yearning was coming from many of the outselves trapped inside him. The Gate Thief's old prisoners, not the Gate Thief himself—*his* gates were all about blocking Great Gates, stealing them, not using them, and certainly not building them.

Could Danny use some of the captive outselves in making a Great Gate, as if they were his own? Hermia had told him that in the old days, mere Pathbrothers would sometimes contribute to a Gatefather their three or four or dozen gates to help reach the critical mass to make a Great Gate. Could he use these captive gates the same way?

Danny tried to use one on an ordinary gate. That is, he did the inward thing that felt like gatemaking, only tried to access one of the captives to do it. The result was almost a physical pain, the rebuff was so sharp and strong.

No!

It felt like a shout from somewhere deep inside him. Not the *word* no, but the meaning of it, the idea of utter rejection.

It made sense. Danny could not force another mage's gate. In Hermia's account, the Pathbrothers would donate their gates willingly. These gates had all been stolen, from gatemages who most assuredly would not want their captor using their long-lost outselves to make his gates.

It would have been interesting to see the result of a Great Gate made out of so many different mages' gates at once. But if they wouldn't let him, the question was moot.

It made sense. If Gatefathers could make use of stolen gates, then they'd have done it all the time. The Gate Thief wasn't taking gates in order to use them, he was taking them in order to prevent their being used.

And again he wondered why. Something about the Semitic gods. Something about Bel, the ancient Carthaginian deity.

I won a battle when I beat the Gate Thief, but I didn't even know what war I was fighting in. For all I know I just intervened in the American Revolution on the side of the British. I have no idea who the good guys are. There are so many enemies; but what if my enemies are right to want to destroy me? What if my defeating the Gate Thief was the worst thing that ever happened in history?

"Stop brooding, Danny, it makes your mouth turn sour," said Veevee.

So she had taken the gate from Naples, Florida. She was almost quivering with excitement. This Great Gate was more for her than anyone. After all her years of not knowing whether she was a gatemage or not, her complete vindication upon finding Danny's gates and realizing she could unlock them had been the greatest joy of her life. But then came the frustration of not being able to do anything *but* unlock gates—that and teach Danny all the gatelore she had learned in a lifetime of study.

Now she had hope, however meager, that by passing through a Great Gate she might have her power augmented in some interesting way. It was all she had talked about, whenever there was nothing else to talk about, so that Danny knew that it was where her thoughts always turned in moments of idleness. She hadn't nagged him, but he felt the pressure of her yearning all the same.

He felt some of the same curiosity himself, and Hermia was, if anything, even more in need of some kind of boost to her abilities, since as a Lockfriend she could only close gates that Danny wasn't leaving open anyway. But Hermia's presence here would be dangerous, since she would bring her Family soon after. So she and Danny, left to themselves, might have waited.

Danny, for his part, was afraid. Yes, he had beaten the Gate Thief before, but that might have been a fluke. What if the

Gate Thief was waiting for him again, this time prepared for him, this time armed in some terrible way. It could be something as simple as a sword. Danny appears, the Gate Thief swings a mighty sword, plop goes Danny's head, and even if somebody dragged him through a gate, even a Great Gate, and even if they set his head on his neck and held it there through the passage, Danny didn't think the healing properties of gate travel would do the trick.

It wouldn't happen. There was no way the Gate Thief could know where Danny's new Great Gate would appear on Westil. *Danny* didn't even know.

"It does look so unfortunately like a gallows," said Veevee, looking up at the rope and then down to the dangling end. "Did Marion have to put a noose in it?"

"It's not a noose, it's a loop," said Danny. "It's so I don't have to hold on so tightly while I spin. I want to have my mind clear."

"You could just spin around on the ground, like a dervish," said Veevee.

"I made the gate on the end of a rope last time," said Danny, "so until I know more I'm doing it the same way this time. For all we know, the strength or endurance or power of the gate depends on the speed of my spin."

"Or it has no effect at all."

"Time to experiment with that is after we gatemages have passed through the gate ourselves."

"And back again," said Veevee.

Danny knew what she was thinking of. "We don't know for sure if Ced decided to stay there or not. All it would have taken was a moment's hesitation. The Gate Thief was on me almost instantly. It could easily have been Marion and Leslie trapped there as well."

Stone appeared at the tail of the gate to his house in Washington, DC. "Hello, Veevee," he said.

"'Veevee'?" she said indignantly. "Not 'My darling' or 'My love' or—"

"O glorious Gatemage," said Stone. "O most admirable of women. O thou wife."

"There we go," said Veevee, preening playfully. "It may take a little prompting, but you know how to make a girl feel all princessy."

"It'll be interesting to see what a Meadowfriend becomes after passing through the Great Gate. I have visions of being able to make every lawn in America grow so rapidly, with grass so tall, that people can't find their houses."

"And the buffalo herds return to roam all over North America, consuming lawn grass at a prodigious rate, and yet the grass leaps ever higher," said Veevee.

"Grass growing from cracks in the sidewalks and asphalt tears it all into little chunks," said Stone. "In this profuse jungle of life, no vehicle can move; even helicopters can't land for longer than a minute or two before grass grows up so thick that the blades can't turn again."

"And three hundred million people die of starvation," said Danny dryly.

"But the vast lawns make such a lovely cemetery," said Veevee.

"Don't worry, Danny. Even if I could do it, I wouldn't," said Stone. "Lawns are the least interesting plants in the world. Everything interesting has been bred out of them. A true meadow has at least a hundred different species of grass, clumping here and there, with a thousand wildflowers and bulbs and tubers and mosses and ferns and—"

"Day lilies," said Veevee. "I do love day lilies."

"The poodles of the plant world," said Stone scornfully.

"So pretty," said Veevee. "Alone or in great fields of them. Don't leave them out of our meadow, darling."

Stone looked at Danny and rolled his eyes.

"I saw that, Peter," said Veevee. "Eyerolling is rude."

"Rude but necessary," said Stone. "For your own good. Make your gate, Danny. The longer I stay here talking with Veevee, the more extravagant the trouble I'll get myself into."

"I'll tell Hermia we're ready," said Danny.

Because his gatesense already told him exactly where the gate he had made for her in Rio was—her latest hiding place, the theory being that if she had to keep moving around, at least she could go to warm and interesting places—he was able to make a new gate straight there.

She wasn't in her hotel room. That was a surprise. She knew that it was nearly time for the making of the Great Gate. She was supposed to be waiting.

Danny immediately made a return gate and stepped toward it just as the shotgun blast went off. He felt the pellets tear through his body and then . . . no pain at all, because he had passed through the gate back to the barn. He still gasped from the pain he no longer felt, and the others turned toward him.

"They found Hermia," said Danny. "She wasn't there, and they weren't waiting around to talk about it."

"Are you hurt?" asked Veevee, fingering his tattered shirt.

"I was, for a moment," said Danny. "I may still have all the pellets in me. I can work on that later. The gate healed the wounds, and I have to find Hermia."

"It can't be her own people," said Stone. "The Greeks may do many terrible things, but they wouldn't kill the world's only living gatemage."

"But they're the only ones who could track her," said Danny.

"They might be tracking the trackers," said Marion.

"Or they might have a sniffer of their own, whoever they are," said Stone. "The Greeks track Hermia, but a sniffer could simply have found your gate and then waited for you."

"Some fanatic group that really thinks we shouldn't go back to Westil?" asked Veevee.

"Or some minions of the Gate Thief," said Marion.

"I'm going to look," said Danny. He made a tiny gate, really just a viewport, that showed him the room where someone had shot him.

Two men were standing there, one carrying a shotgun. "I know I hit him before he disappeared," said one.

Danny made a gate and pulled it over them.

They arrived twenty feet above some spot out in the Atlantic Ocean, far from the nearest land. Danny's new viewport was in place before they hit the water. The shotgun sank at once; the men cried out for help as they tried to swim.

They weren't good at it. In fact, one of them was panicking and clearly had no idea how to swim.

Not Greeks, then. Hermia's Family were proud of their heritage among the thalassocracy, and they were all taught to swim as babies.

Danny needed a way to hold them in place, where they'd be helpless, unable to escape, but in no danger.

Gravity would have to do the police work for him. Danny made a gate that scooped them out of the water, then dumped them twenty yards over it; he moved the mouth just under them to catch them. They fell a half inch into the gate's mouth, which tossed them back up that half-inch and dropped them again. It gave them a continuous sensation of falling, but they could breathe and they could hear.

Through the viewport, Danny spoke to them.

"I could have put you a thousand feet down and the ocean would already have crushed you."

The man who had held the shotgun was weeping. But the other seemed capable of listening.

"Where is the woman who lived in that hotel room?" asked Danny.

"Woman?" asked the man.

Danny moved the mouth of the gate so now they fell twenty yards before rising again. He let that go on for a minute and then returned them to a half-inch fall.

"Try again," said Danny.

"She go to the beach," said the man. "Then we go in her room. She not come back yet."

Now that Danny had a chance to study the men, he could start making guesses. "Persians?" he asked. "Hindi?"

The assassin managed to look scornful in the midst of his ongoing terror.

"Tell me what Family you're from," said Danny.

"Never," said the man.

So it *was* a Family—an Orphan would have declared his non-Family status proudly. And it was a Family that regarded hiding its identity as more important than life itself. Any of the known Families might have wanted to do this assassination stealthily, but the secrecy wouldn't be important enough to die for it. After all, killing gatemages was something they were all sworn to do.

A Family, then, that everyone thought was extinct?

Danny ran through a mental list. Middle Eastern, from the look of them. But all the Families were Indo-European, and in the Middle East that list wasn't very long. "Hittites?" he asked.

"No!" shouted the man.

Hittites they were, then. Interesting. Exciting, even. How had the Hittite Family remained hidden all this time? They were supposed to have been wiped out before Pompey came to Syria, though some Family historians speculated that they might have adopted the Armenians and helped them surreptitiously.

But historical interest would have to wait. "If Hermia is dead," said Danny, "so are you."

"Alive!" the man cried. "We not touch her."

"No Great Gates!" shouted the other man, the weeping one. "Bel comes! Bel goes to Yllywee!"

So they *were* allies of the Gate Thief. Or shared his fear; Yllywee was an ancient name of Westil. Danny remembered the runic inscription in the Library of Congress. "We have faced Bel and he has ruled the hearts of many." Manmages from another world—a world not Earth and not Westil. "Loki found the dark gate of Bel through which their god poured fear into the world." Why would it matter whether Danny made a Great Gate if Bel already knew how to make gates of his own?

The Hittites knew something, and he had to find out what it was.

Danny moved the tail of the gate that suspended them to the barn. They plopped in a sodden mass amid the straw near a milking stall. At once Danny brought back the mouth of the gate, scooped them up, and hung them in the air ten feet above the barn floor.

"What's going on, Danny?" demanded Marion. "How can you bring strangers to—"

"Hittites," said Danny. "They shot me, and they know something about Bel."

There had been enough discussion of the runic passage that everyone immediately understood the significance.

"I need you to question them while I'm gone," said Danny to Marion.

"I'm not an interrogator," said Marion.

"I didn't say *torture* them," said Danny. "Ask them questions."

"*You're* torturing them," said Marion. "Look how afraid they are! They're falling and falling!"

"People pay money to go up in airplanes and freefall like this before they open their parachutes," said Danny. "It's not torture, it's just a way of keeping them where we want them."

"Not here," said Marion.

"Fine," said Danny. "I'll put them back out over the Atlantic till I find Hermia."

"No!" shouted Leslie from the door. "Let them go at once!"

"They killed me!" shouted Danny. "They're assassins."

"And Hittites," added Veevee. "So they're evil *and* interesting."

"This is not what a good man does," said Leslie coldly.

Danny knew at once that she was right. His fear and anger had made him act by reflex. Yet he had also shown restraint, and he wanted credit for it.

"I could have killed them," said Danny. "I didn't kill them."

"They're sopping wet," said Leslie.

"I didn't know they couldn't swim," said Danny. "But I pulled them out of the water, didn't I?"

"Get them out of my barn," said Leslie. "Now."

Back to the ocean, then. Again, Danny had to move the tail of the gate first, which put them back in the water, flailing and sputtering, and screaming whenever they could catch their breath. Then he got them back up in the air. By now they thought of that continuous freefall as a good thing, no doubt, compared to drowning.

Danny followed them this time, suspending himself in the air. No falling in the water—when he was moving *himself* through space, he was much quicker, more deft about it.

"I'm going to go see where my friend is," said Danny. "If she's hurt or dead, I'll do the same thing to one of you while the other watches."

"We not to touch her, we not talk to her!" the less-panicked man insisted.

Danny gated himself back to Hermia's hotel room in Rio. It was empty this time, no shotguns waiting. The door was undamaged—they must have bribed their way in. Danny went to the balcony and looked out over the broad beach. So many people lying there or milling around. But after a few minutes he spotted someone who might be Hermia. He made a gate near her. If it was Hermia, she'd see it and step into it; if it wasn't, she wouldn't.

It was. She did.

"Is it already time?" she asked as soon as she was in the hotel room.

"I came here for you," said Danny, "and I was met by a shotgun blast."

Hermia saw the pellet pattern on the wall, Danny's punctured clothes, and exclaimed softly. "My Family wouldn't—"

"Not your Family," said Danny.

"They just shot to kill? Without a warning?"

"No negotiations. Just . . . bang."

"Who was it?"

"Hittites, I'm pretty sure." He grinned.

"Extinct gods with shotguns," said Hermia.

"Extinct for two thousand years, no less. They didn't actually admit to being Hittite, but it's the one they denied instead of being evasive. I have them hanging over the Atlantic."

"I want to talk to them."

"You want to lock the gate they're using so they drop into the water and drown," said Danny.

"Eventually, yes," said Hermia. "You're too soft, Danny. People who shoot first can't be left alive."

"People who talk about Bel have some explaining to do," said Danny. "And they didn't actually kill me."

"They killed your clothing," said Hermia. "Walk around like this and you'll start a new fashion. Perforated clothing. Shotgun Style by Calvin Klein."

"I want to make the Great Gate before anything else happens," said Danny. "Those clowns aren't going anywhere. We'll have plenty of time to question them after."

"If we make it back," said Hermia.

"If we don't, then someday somebody will find a heap of bones and some empty clothing hanging in the air over some spot in the Atlantic. It'll make the cover of the *Enquirer.*"

"You sound like you don't care," said Hermia, "but I know you do."

Danny sighed. Leslie thought the worst of him, Hermia thought the best of him, and they were both right. Danny gated the two men into a single cell in the county jail in Lexington, Virginia. "They're on dry ground now, all right?" he told her. "Now let's get this gate made before somebody notices them and lets them out."

"Where are they?" she demanded.

"In jail," said Danny. He made a viewport into the cell and showed her.

Hermia spoke to them. "Don't make a sound," she said. "If you try to get out or if you talk to anybody at all, it's back to the ocean for you." Then she added a few words in a language Danny had never heard.

"Yes, they understood me," she said to Danny. "The Hittite-Armenian theory seems to have some merit."

"You speak Armenian?" asked Danny.

"It came up," said Hermia. "I'm a gatemage, it's a language."

Danny reached out his hand, and the two of them gated to the barn.

6

Angry Gate

What did you do with them?" demanded Leslie.

"They're alive," said Hermia. "And safe."

Leslie looked at Danny suspiciously. "I want to hear it from him."

"Because you think you can tell if I'm lying?" asked Danny.

"We assume you're lying," said Stone. "Because we're all hoping you killed them and had done with it."

"I'm hoping no such thing!" said Leslie.

"We can't control a gatemage anyway," said Marion to Leslie. "He did what he did, he'll do what he does."

"I can make him feel guilty about it," said Leslie.

"That's not very sporting," said Veevee. "Danny feels guilty for being alive."

"Make the Great Gate," said Hermia. "If the Hittites are onto us, then everybody knows that there are gatemages in the world again, and they'll be looking for a Great Gate."

"That's an argument *against* making one," said Stone.

"It's an argument for making one *now*," said Hermia, "and all of us going through it except Marion and Leslie, because they've already gone and somebody has to keep watch."

"You're coming right back, aren't you?" Leslie asked Danny.

"Unless the Gate Thief gets me this time," said Danny.

"Do you think there's any chance of that?" asked Veevee.

"He's weaker than he was," said Danny, "but he knows a lot more than I do." Danny walked to the rope, took hold of it, pulled the noose wide open.

"I hate that noose," said Veevee. "It looks so grim."

Danny made no answer, just pulled the noose down over his head and shoulders, then tightened it under his armpits. Now he could put his weight on the rope while keeping his hands free.

His feet were still on the floor of the barn. He turned around and around until the rope was so twisted that it lifted him off the floor. Only the tips of his toes touched.

"Want us to wind you tighter?" asked Hermia.

"I'm pretty tightly wound already," said Danny.

"Very funny," said Veevee.

"I'm still not sure whether I should go through it," said Stone.

"Do it," said Veevee, "and keep me company."

"It will give you the power to make plants grow and cover everything," said Marion.

"That's kudzu," said Stone. "It doesn't need any help from me."

Veevee took hold of his hand. " 'Come and go with me to that land where I'm bound,' " she sang.

"Is that a real song?" asked Stone.

"A very old one," said Veevee. She sang again: " 'I'm gonna walk the streets of glory on that great day in the mornin'.' "

"I need to concentrate," said Danny. "And I need the two of you to be watching, so you know when to go through the gate."

Veevee smiled. " 'They'll be singin' in that land, voices ringin' in that land. There'll be freedom in that land where I'm bound.' "

"Nobody's ever heard of an obedient gatemage," said Stone.

"Serves you right, Danny," said Leslie.

Danny silently raised his feet, leaned back, closed his eyes. He began to spin. Twenty gates at once this time.

Only this time he wasn't alone—there were all the other mages' gates inside him, and many of them, *most* of them, were clamoring, demanding that he use them to make the gate.

One by one he drew them in, until now he was spinning a score of other mages' gates along with his own. He couldn't tell if they were making the Great Gate stronger, by adding more threads to the connection, or weaker, by adding new textures that didn't fit well with his own. Danny knew nothing about what he was doing. Yet it seemed fair to him to include the outselves of these long-dead mages, which had been stolen from them because of their attempts to make Great Gates.

You lost your magery by doing this. Did I capture you to keep you imprisoned, or to set you free and let your power live again in the world?

Free free free, answered the gates inside him.

Me me me, demanded so many gates that he had not yet used.

Enough, thought Danny. Twenty of mine and twenty of you.

He was spinning rapidly now. Not as fast as he had been spinning in the gym, but it was enough. This time he could feel the power in it, this time he understood that what mattered was not the speed of the spinning, but the intertwining of the gates. It truly felt like a rope—four great strands, each consisting of ten gates. Because he had made a Great Gate before, and learned so much in the making of it, he could understand it better this time.

Two of the strands were made entirely of Danny's gates, and the other two were made of the other mages' gates. He wove all of his into the return gate, whose tail would be here in the barn to bring them home, and all of theirs into the gate of sending, whose mouth would be here. They spun themselves together like forty slender tornadoes, all of them spinning on their own, weaving their own patterns.

And then he cast them upward and outward, with all the strength of his inself, and felt rather than heard the song of rejoicing as the strangers' gates leapt out into space, into time, carrying his own gates with them.

They connected in another world. The Great Gate was made.

"Now," said Veevee.

"Untie me," said Danny, still spinning.

Strong hands stopped his spin; other hands loosened the noose and pulled it over his arms. He still hadn't opened his eyes. He didn't need them. It was with another sense that he saw the Great Gate. It was very different this time, as if the earlier gate had been woven of one color of thread, while this one was of many bright colors that combined and recombined. Gate of many colors, thought Danny. What does it mean to have a gate of many colors?

He felt Veevee and Hermia take him by the hands. The mouth of the gate was wide. Danny stepped into it. Joined to him, they did not need to step; they were with him as the gate gathered him in and there they were, in bright sunlight on the other world.

Danny opened his eyes. The light was dazzling after the relative darkness of the barn. But he could see that they were surrounded by tall stones, rough-hewn, set on end into the grassy ground at the brow of a gently sloping hill.

"Stonehenge," said Danny.

"A gatecatcher," said Stone.

"Fool," said another voice. A stranger's voice. A man.

Danny turned to where the voice had come from. But it wasn't the voice that told him who the man was. It was the inself. It was the few gates the man had inside him.

"Gate Thief," said Danny. "Why are you here?"

"Fool," said the Gate Thief. "To use those angry Wild Gates."

"They wanted—"

"Centuries in prison have made them uncontrollable. Insane." The Gate Thief spoke Westilian with a strange accent, but Danny understood him perfectly.

"They wanted to be part of the Great Gate," said Danny. "Are you here to do battle with me again?"

"He wants to come through the gate," said Veevee.

"He's here to kill you," said Hermia.

"You know nothing," said the Gate Thief. "Someone has to teach you."

"Lock the gate behind us, Hermia," said Danny.

"Do we have to go so quickly?" asked Veevee. "This is Westil, and the sun is so bright I can hardly claim to have seen it."

"I don't want him to follow us," said Danny.

"You'll be back here soon enough," said the Gate Thief. "Begging me to teach you how to undo this terrible thing you've done."

"Why did you eat all the gates?" demanded Danny, his curiosity overpowering his good sense, making him stay long enough to ask.

"You know why," said the Gate Thief. "My captive gates have told you."

"They say the name of Bel."

"Bel, the gatemage from the other world," said the Gate Thief. "The world of soul stealers. The world of manmages. Fool."

"Let's go," said Hermia. "Who knows what he's plotting to do while he keeps us talking?"

Meanwhile, Stone knelt in the grass, his hands splayed out, digging into the soil. "It's so alive," he whispered.

"It's you that's alive," said the Gate Thief. "Coming through the Great Gate has made you strong. All of you *too* strong. You have nothing to fear from me."

"That's what he wants us to believe," said Hermia.

"Gatemages are such liars," said Veevee—rather proudly, Danny thought.

"What do I call you?" asked Danny. "Loki?"

"Wad," said the Gate Thief. "It's my name since I came out of the tree."

Danny had no idea what that meant. "I'm not giving you back your gates," said Danny.

"I don't need them," said Wad.

"Do you know what happened to Ced?" asked Stone. "He came through the earlier gate and he stayed."

"A windmage," said Wad. "I know where he is."

"Is he safe?" asked Stone.

Wad laughed. "Is Westil safe, with him here? The most powerful mage in the world now—the winds that he blows!"

"Is he causing harm?" asked Veevee.

"He doesn't know how *not* to cause harm," said Wad. "Any more than you do. And there's no one to balance him, no one to teach him. That's what you're doing here. Setting monsters loose in the world."

"Becoming monsters ourselves, by that reckoning," said Danny.

"We're all monsters," said Wad.

"Let's go back," said Hermia.

Danny could see him clearly now, standing between two stones, leaning on neither. A slight man—like Danny, he was neither tall nor short, neither strong-looking nor weak. And his face was neither young nor old, but ageless, with eyes like deep water, gray as the belly of a thundercloud, looking into Danny with such sadness, such anger, such understanding.

"Don't look at him," said Hermia. "He's too strong for us."

"I'm weak," said Wad. "You have most of my outself inside you now. What do I call you?"

"You don't," said Danny. He gathered the mouth of the Great Gate around himself and they were in the barn again.

The sunlight was gone. The stones. The grass.

Stone knelt, his fingers pressed against the floor. He was weeping. "It's a desert here, compared to there," he said.

"We met the Gate Thief," Veevee told Marion. "He was almost as pretty as Danny, and as old as the stars."

"I can't lock the other gate," said Hermia. "The outbound gate, the one you made from the hearts of strangers."

Danny could see that she had locked the return gate, and was trying to close the other. "You can't control it because there are twenty mages in it," said Danny. "You have to close them one at a time." He began pinching off the gates.

But by the time he got to the third gate, the first was open again. "It won't stay closed," he said.

"I see now," said Hermia, and instead of trying to close the whole Great Gate, she began to join him in closing the individual gates. "I can see everything more clearly. I'm so much stronger. You'd think I could close them."

Danny could see that she was getting no better results than he was.

The inbound Great Gate, the one made entirely from Danny's own gates, was closed and locked, but the gates of other mages were not so obedient. They willed themselves to be open, and though Danny and Hermia could close them, they would not stay closed.

"We have a wide-open public gate here," said Veevee. "I can see what you're doing, and they won't stay closed. They don't *want* to be closed."

"Wild Gates," said Danny. "'Angry Wild Gates,' he called them."

"Angry at him, not us," said Veevee.

"I held them prisoner, too," said Danny. "And it doesn't matter who they're angry at. They aren't *people,* just the wraiths of people, the lingering memory of them. But strong."

"Going through a Great Gate strengthened us," said Veevee. "But they *are* a Great Gate. How strong is that?"

"Let them stay open," said Danny. "It isn't going to work, no matter what we do."

"Are you saying that you can't close the Great Gate?" asked Marion.

"I closed the one coming back to Earth," said Hermia. "But not the one leading to Westil from here."

"So my barn is now a Great Gate, and you can't close it?" demanded Leslie.

"Why did you use those gates?" said Hermia.

"They wanted it," said Danny. "It seemed only fair, after so long in prison."

"But you didn't know them—what kind of men they were," said Hermia. "A wraith preserves the character of its maker, and these might have been very bad mages."

"Yes, that seems obvious now," said Danny. "I chose the most insistent. The most selfish. But it never occurred to me that I couldn't control these gates."

"You've never faced a gate that wasn't under your control," said Marion. "You've never *seen* a gate that wasn't of your making."

"But he did make it," said Veevee.

"I wound them together, I threw them into spacetime," said Danny. "But Marion's right—they aren't my gates."

"Then move them," said Leslie. "Get it out of my barn."

Danny tried. The gate wouldn't budge. Only when he stopped trying to move it did it move—in the opposite direction. And it widened.

"It's trying to eat us," said Hermia, alarmed.

It was true. The mouth of the Great Gate was seeking them out.

"Take them!" cried Veevee. "They were captive before, capture them again!"

Danny tried to unmake the gate as he had done with his previous Great Gate, but these were not his own gates, and they dodged him. He could work on one at a time, but they all resisted him. They refused to be captive again.

"I thought passing through the gate was supposed to make me irresistibly strong," said Danny.

"They're stronger, too," said Veevee. "Dead as they are, it made them more powerful, to be part of a Great Gate."

"Wad took them, though. Loki, I mean," said Danny.

"They weren't all woven together like this," said Hermia. "And he knows more than you."

Now Danny understood what Wad had meant: "You'll be back here soon enough, begging me to teach you how to undo this terrible thing you've done." Danny wanted to go back right now, to demand answers from Wad.

"No!" shouted Hermia.

"No what?" asked Danny.

"Don't step into that gate!" she cried. "Don't you see? It's *not yours*. What's to stop it from moving itself into the depths of the sea?"

"What have we done?" asked Veevee miserably.

"You don't control it at all," said Leslie. She wasn't just angry now. She was afraid.

"It could go out and look for the Families that are hunting for it?" asked Marion.

"I don't know what it can do," said Danny. "Wad was right, I *am* a fool."

"At least the return gate is closed," said Hermia. "If the Families go to Westil, they can't get back."

"But that's terrible," said Danny. "What right do we have to set them loose in that world? I have to reopen the other gate. I have to make it so there's no space between them, so that if you go through the gate you come back here immediately. No pause, no chance to see the sights."

Danny acted even as he spoke. But no sooner did he move the mouth of the return gate directly in front of the outbound gate than the Wild Gate moved its tail away. Not far—the two Great Gates were so woven together, so inseparable, that it was only a few yards between the tail of the Wild Gate and the mouth of Danny's return gate.

"It can't get away from my gate either," said Danny in relief. "As long as I keep mine anchored, it can't go far." Danny tethered the mouth of his own part of the Great Gate to the walls of the barn. It was like hobbling a horse. The Wild Gates could move the mouth of the combined gate, but only a few yards.

"This is our worst nightmare," said Leslie. "A gate you can't control, here in our barn. Do you understand what the Families will do now?"

"Whatever it takes to get to this gate," said Hermia.

"They don't *know* it's gone wild," said Veevee. "I don't plan to tell them. Do you?"

"The gate is hungry," said Danny. "It wants to be used. It'll find a way."

"Then let's feed it," said Hermia. "Negotiate with the Families, let them each send a couple of mages through, exactly as we planned all along. They don't have to know that we can't close the gate or move it or . . . anything. You gate them here, two at a time, and send them through—how will they know that you aren't as much in control of the Great Gate as you are of the gates you make here on Mittlegard?"

"Or make another Great Gate, one you control completely," said Veevee, "and starve this one to death."

"I don't know what to do," said Danny. "Wad was right. I have to go talk to him. I have to ask him."

"Terrible idea," said Stone.

"If you *do* go back, make another Great Gate," said Hermia. "Don't ever step into this one again."

"She's right," said Veevee. "This is an angry gate, isn't that what Wad said?"

"Who's Wad?" asked Marion.

"Loki," said Danny.

"The Gate Thief," said Hermia.

"He's dangerous," said Stone. "He makes me believe in the devil."

"I'm screwing everything up," said Danny.

Stone was sitting on the floor now. "What else did you expect?" he asked. "Nobody's done this in fourteen centuries. And it's not *your* fault that the Gate Thief had all these captives. It's *his* fault, not yours. The only thing you did was *not* let him capture you."

"That was my first mistake," said Danny.

"No," said Leslie. "Not a mistake."

"We'll figure this out," said Marion. "We'll find a way to get it all under control."

"But first," said Leslie, "we're getting all my cows out of this barn."

Amulets

Danny had first come to Parry McCluer High School as a long-dreamed-of adventure. And the dream had come true. He had made friends. He had learned how to use his power and he had done good things with it. A few pranks, too, but he hadn't used it to win races and he hadn't hurt anybody, unless you counted humiliating Coach Bleeder.

Now, though, he came as if he had graduated, then found out he had flunked a test after all and had to come back. Only nobody knew he had been gone. Nobody knew he had failed. His friends didn't believe him when he told them.

They were gathered in the old smoking area—the one that the teachers regularly checked. But since they were only talking, not smoking anything, it was a good place for Danny and his friends to gather.

"So can we use the gate?" asked Pat.

"I told you, nobody can."

"I thought you said it was wild," said Wheeler. "Anybody could use it."

"We're not letting anybody get near enough to use it," said Danny.

"Then what's the big deal?" asked Hal. "Is it, like, the last gate you can ever make?"

"No, I can make as many as I want."

"So can you take us to that other world?" asked Laurette.

"Why would I do that?" asked Danny. "You're not mages, it wouldn't do you any good, and what if you got stranded there? It isn't a safe place."

"You're right," said Pat. "Here, you can only get run over by cars or catch some hideous disease or get blown up in chemistry class."

"I didn't blow anybody up," said Hal.

"But you *tried*," said Wheeler.

"I tried to get them to cancel school for the day," said Hal.

"Can we stop talking about your failures, Hal?" said Xena.

"Yeah, let's go back to talking about mine," said Danny.

Xena gripped his arm and spoke so earnestly and pressed so close that he could feel her breath on his cheek. "You haven't failed at anything, Danny North," she said. "You're, like, a god."

"The god of screw-ups," said Danny.

Xena kissed his cheek. "Your screw-ups are better than other people's successes."

"So you went to the other world. Westil," said Laurette. "That was supposed to make you more powerful."

"I don't feel any different," said Danny.

"Well, can you do stuff you couldn't do before?"

"I don't know."

"*Why* don't you know?" asked Laurette.

"There isn't a manual," said Danny. "They *kill* mages like me. They don't exactly provide me with instructions."

"Who reads the instructions?" asked Laurette. "Haven't you *tried* anything?"

"I wouldn't even know what to try," said Danny. "I made gates before. I can still make gates." He shrugged.

"So you can take us to Disney World?" asked Sin.

Danny hadn't expected that—not from the goth with constantly infected piercings. "You want to go to Disney World?"

"I'd say Paris, but I don't speak French," said Sin. "Come on, I've never been."

"Me neither," said Xena.

"I don't want to go," said Pat.

"I don't like using gates to steal," said Danny.

"Who said anything about stealing?" asked Sin. "Just get us in."

"And then get us through all the lines and into the rides without tickets," said Laurette. "Is that so much to ask?"

"They'll catch me," said Wheeler. "I always look guilty."

"How about Cape Canaveral?" asked Hal.

"You provide the security badges, and I'll get us in," said Danny.

"This isn't even fun," said Pat.

"What about all those people trying to kill you?" asked Xena. "Are you safe now?"

"I don't know," said Danny.

"And what about teaching us how to help you?" asked Hal. "Or is that off, just because you screwed up and made some gate angry?"

"I can't have you help me," said Danny. "I'd just screw that up, too, and then you'd get killed."

"Wow, he's really down on himself," said Laurette.

"He needs cheering up," said Xena. She kissed his cheek. Not a sisterly peck. Her lips brushed his cheek and lingered. It made him feel a tingle in his legs and in his butt. He didn't know that tingling could be so weirdly dislocated.

"Don't go there, Xena," said Hal.

"Even if you *are* a warrior princess," said Wheeler.

"Jealous?" asked Xena.

"Yes," said Wheeler.

Everyone looked at him in surprise.

"It's just Danny, and all of a sudden you're getting all kissy with him," said Wheeler.

"Yeah," said Laurette. "Just because he's a *god*, why would you want to *kiss* him?"

"You're right," said Xena, clinging to Danny all the more tightly. "I want to have his baby."

At that, Danny pulled away. Joking around was one thing. This was something else. "I just have to think," he said.

"He can't think if all his blood has rushed out of his head," said Laurette.

"I'm just trying to figure out if there's a way I can keep you guys safe," said Danny.

"We'd be safe in Disney World," said Sin. "It's the safest place on earth."

Danny thought of what he needed his friends to do. Gate them as emissaries to the Families, to explain the terms they'd have to agree to in order to pass someone through a Great Gate. Danny couldn't go himself, and he couldn't send Veevee or Hermia, either. The Families would set traps for them. But what would be the point of trapping drowthers?

That was the problem. Since the Families didn't regard drowthers as having any value, they wouldn't hold them as hostages. If they got annoyed, they'd just kill his emissaries.

In fact, as soon as anyone realized that Danny *had* friends, they might try to use them against him. Threaten them. Follow them. Kidnap them. Kill them. Without waiting for Danny to send them anywhere.

He couldn't concentrate on all of them at once. He couldn't keep them safe. "What have I done to you guys?" asked Danny.

"What are you talking about?" asked Laurette.

Danny explained his worry.

"Cool," said Wheeler. "It's like being inside a comic book."

"Except we're collateral damage," said Hal.

"We're the red shirt guys," said Pat.

Danny made a gate, a very small one, and put it directly above a small stone lying in the clearing. "Hal," said Danny. "Would you pick up that stone?"

Hal didn't bother looking to see exactly which stone. He just lunged for the general area, reaching for any stone, and when his hand brushed the gate, he fell into it and he was sitting ten feet away. "*That* is disorienting," he complained.

"That wasn't what I wanted," said Danny. "I'm trying to see if I can tie a gate to a thing instead of a place. Just move the stone, somebody. Laurette, keep your hand low and move it slowly and I'll tell you which stone."

She moved carefully—though Danny also noticed that she bent over at such an angle that her considerable cleavage was aimed right at him. Was that because it was her habit, or because she was thinking the same way Xena was, that because Danny could do magery he was suddenly cool enough to be worth flirting with?

"That one," said Danny.

Laurette picked up the stone.

The gate stayed in the air above where the stone had been.

"Damn," said Danny.

"Didn't work?" asked Laurette.

"I was hoping I could do it because I went to Westil. The enhancement of my powers."

"Bummer," said Hal. He was back in the circle now.

"Who cares?" asked Sin. "It's just a rock."

"He wants us to be able to carry gates around with us," said Pat. "So we can stick a finger in a gate and be somewhere else."

Sometimes she surprised him. Sour as she was, she was always thinking. Maybe when you don't care whether other people like you, you have more brainspace for analysis.

"Well, there's no reason it shouldn't work," said Hal. "Whether you went through a Great Gate or not."

"What do you know about magic?" said Xena contemptuously.

"What I know about is physics," said Hal. "Basic, elementary, pathetic, every-semi-educated-moron-should-know-it-level physics."

"Xena slept through the physics unit in eighth-grade science," said Laurette.

"Danny always attaches his gates to small moving objects," said Hal. "He's never done anything else."

Danny looked at the gate he had just made, the mouth and tail of it, and couldn't figure out what Hal meant.

"The surface of the Earth is spinning one complete revolution per day," said Hal. "At the equator, that means it's moving at a thousand miles an hour. Here, it's about eight hundred miles an hour. The Earth is also moving around the sun at sixty-seven thousand miles an hour. So when Danny's gates seem to stay in the same place, they're really moving incredibly fast—so they're attached to *something*."

"You said 'small moving objects,'" said Laurette.

"Compared to the Sun, Earth is a small moving object," said Hal. "Compared to the galaxy, Earth is a blip. The only reason we think it's big is because we're even smaller."

"Thanks for the info, Science Boy," said Xena.

"Like he said, everybody knows that," said Wheeler.

"Oh, *you* had sixty-seven thousand and eight hundred miles an hour sitting there in *your* brain?" said Pat.

"No, but I knew that the Earth spins completely around once a day," said Wheeler. "And I knew it went all the way around the Sun once a year. That means it's a seriously fast-moving object. Duh."

"If you're so smart, how fast is the solar system moving around the center of the galaxy?" Pat asked Hal.

"Four hundred eighty-three thousand miles an hour," said Hal.

"And how fast is the Milky Way moving toward Andromeda?"

"That's impossible to say," said Hal, "because they're moving toward each other and there's no stationary point of reference."

"The whole galaxy is moving one point three million miles an hour, compared to the CBR," said Pat triumphantly.

"What's the CBR?" asked Sin.

"Cosmic Background Radiation," said Hal, "and that's not what you asked, Pat, you asked about how fast the Milky Way was moving toward Andromeda."

"This is all so sad," said Sin. "While other boys were memorizing football players' stats, Hal was memorizing the stats of astronomical objects."

"I wonder if Earth will make the playoffs this year," said Laurette.

"And you girls memorize what George Clooney eats for breakfast," said Wheeler.

"That walking fossil?" said Xena.

"The cast of *Twilight*, then," said Wheeler.

Apparently the girls couldn't argue with that one.

It was no secret that Hal was smart. And Pat was the smartest of the girls. And Danny knew all this stuff too—he knew everything he had ever read. The difference was that Hal had realized it applied to this situation.

"I get the point," said Danny. "I'm attaching the gates to a point on the surface of a spinning, moving object, so there's no reason I can't attach it to a pebble except that the pebble is smaller." Danny gazed steadily at the stone, trying to figure out how to attach a gate to it the way he had attached the gate to a spot in the air above the stone.

Meanwhile, Sin had a question. "How do you wizards or whatever you are, how do you know *we* don't have magic?"

"Don't talk to him, he's making gates," said Laurette.

"We *don't* know you don't have magic," said Danny. "Our blood has been mixing with the rest of the human race for thousands of years, so you probably have some Mithermage ancestry." He tried to hold the image of the stone in his mind and create a gate solely in relation to the stone, not distracted by any other surrounding feature.

"So send us to Westil," said Sin. "Maybe we'll come back with superpowers."

"Yeah," said Hal.

"Cool," said Wheeler.

Danny's concentration broke. He was impatient with himself, but they only saw that he was annoyed.

"Sorry," said Laurette.

"Stop distracting him!" said Xena protectively.

"Why don't you hold it in your hand and really focus on it?" asked Pat. "Disconnect it from the ground."

Laurette handed him a stone. Danny took it, bent over it, stared at it, made a gate.

He moved the stone a little to the left.

The mouth of the gate moved with it.

It was that simple. Remove the pebble from its context, concentrate a little, and he had an enchanted stone.

"You look happy," said Xena. "Does that mean you're thinking of me naked?"

"It means he attached a gate to the stone," said Pat. "We all try *not* to think of you naked."

"So . . . what now?" asked Hal. "You give us each a stone to use if we need to make a quick getaway?"

"A stone's a lousy idea," said Laurette.

"Why?" asked Danny. He had thought it was a pretty good idea.

"First," said Laurette, "what if we drop our stone? How could we tell which one was ours, except by brushing our hand against it and taking off like Hal just did? And then we *still* don't have the stone—but maybe whoever was chasing us finds it and follows us."

"Don't drop the stone," said Wheeler.

"Right, like none of us ever drops anything," said Pat.

"Second," said Laurette, "suppose somebody handcuffs us and searches us and finds a stone in our pockets or purses or whatever? How many people our age carry rocks around?"

"Okay," said Danny, "Not a stone. I was just learning how to do it, and there are plenty of stones."

"A ring," said Sin.

"A nose ring," said Xena. "Then every time you blow your nose, you'll transport somewhere."

"Or you sniff and you get sent to the moon," said Wheeler.

" 'One ring to rule them all, one ring to find them,' " intoned Hal. " 'One ring to bring them all and in the darkness bind them.' "

"Are you saying we're on Sauron's side?" asked Wheeler, a little angry.

"Sauron doesn't have a side," said Danny. "You forget, the Families are all the gods, all the fairies, all the elves and ghosts and werewolves and poltergeists and everything. Good and bad, the Families are on both sides of everything. There's no good or evil with them. Just . . . whatever they feel like doing, and have the power to do it."

"That sounds like as good a definition of evil as I've ever heard," said Pat.

"Well, look what I just did," said Danny. "I felt like attaching a gate to a stone, and when Xena suggested that I really focus on it, then I could do it. Was that evil?"

Pat shrugged. "Depends on whether you throw the stone at some other high school's quarterback and jump him ten yards back and drop him on his ass."

"That's just a prank," said Wheeler. "Can you do it?"

"He wouldn't need a stone," said Hal. "He could just do it."

"And it would be evil," said Pat. "Hurting somebody else just for the fun of it."

"So was it evil when I messed with Coach Lieder?" asked Danny.

"A little bit maybe," said Pat.

"But mostly funny," said Hal.

"And he deserved it," said Wheeler.

Danny remembered the men he had terrified into submission out over the Atlantic, and then stashed in a jail. They were murderers, or meant to be. They deserved worse than he had done to them. But it didn't make him feel all that great about the fact that he had the power to torture them like that. And that he had just *done* it, the moment he thought of it.

"Something you already carry with you," said Danny. "And I'll try to put the gate on it in such a way that you don't just accidentally pop through it. So don't give me your wallet."

"Wheeler can give you the condom he always carries," said Hal. "He's *never* going to use that."

Wheeler glared at him. "They gave it to me in fifth grade. It's like a rabbit's foot, I'm not going to *use* it, it's older than my dick by now."

"Ew," said Laurette. "You made me think of your weenie."

"Said the girl with the constant cleavage," said Wheeler.

"Please," said Danny. "Something you carry but you don't touch, but you *could* get to it in an emergency."

Pat already had a tampon out of her purse.

"Our turn to say 'ew,'" said Hal.

"Every girl carries them and nobody thinks anything about it," said Pat.

"I don't," said Sin.

"I carry extras," said Laurette, getting two tampons out of her purse.

"Then I *am* using my condom," said Wheeler, reaching into his pocket.

"I don't carry a purse," said Sin. "What am I supposed to do, tuck it behind my ear?" She handed the tampon back to Laurette.

"You don't carry a spare just in case?" asked Laurette.

"I'm never early and I'm not afraid of a little blood anyway," said Sin.

"Are you afraid of a little vomit?" asked Hal. "Because this is making me sick."

"Welcome to girlville," said Pat. "But since you're never going to have a girlfriend *or* a wife, it won't matter if you're squeamish."

"What if I'm rummaging in my purse for something else and I brush against it?" asked Xena, looking doubtfully at the tampon she was holding. "And should I unwrap it?"

Danny took it out of her hand.

"He's touching one," said Hal.

"Girl cooties," said Wheeler.

Danny studied the thing. Squeezed it. Pushed his finger against the end. "Just give me a second," he said.

He made a really tiny gate completely inside the end of the tampon. He tossed the tampon around on his hand and nothing happened. But when he pushed his finger into the end, he jumped through the gate—this time only a few inches away. But it still made him lose his balance.

"Oh, a three-inch gate," said Pat. "That'll show 'em. 'Better be nice to me or I'll move another three inches!' "

"I'm just testing," said Danny. "You have to push your finger into the end before the gate will work."

"What happens if you forget which one is the gate and you use it?" asked Hal.

"I thought you didn't like talking about messy girl stuff," said Laurette.

"I can't help what pops into my head," said Hal.

"Please tell me you're not picturing *me* using it," said Pat.

"Well *now* I am and thanks so much," said Hal.

"I don't have anything that isn't hard and shiny," said Sin.

"Your lip gloss," said Pat.

Sin pulled a tiny canister out of her pocket. "It's hard and shiny," she said.

"The stuff inside is black and squishy," said Pat.

"I can put the gate down inside," said Danny.

"If you hide a gate in here I can't use it and my lips will get pink," said Sin.

Laurette pulled a stub of black licorice out of her purse. "Here, it's black. And it's squishy."

Sin took the licorice and studied it. "What century was this made in?"

"It's old, it's black, and it's gross," said Laurette. "Nobody will be surprised that you have it in your pocket. Or does your mother wash your jeans?"

Sin gave a disdainful toss of her head. "Washing is so bourgeois."

Ten minutes later, they all had something flexible with a tiny gatemouth inside it. Three tampons, a licorice stub, a condom package, and a lion-shaped eraser that Hal had in his pocket.

"Why a lion?" asked Sin.

Hal shrugged. "Got it as a prize at the dentist one time."

"And you carry it with you," said Sin.

"Lost a tooth, got a lion," said Hal.

"It's Aslan," said Wheeler.

Hal looked really angry.

"Stop it," said Danny. "Have some loyalty, Wheeler."

"He told about my condom," said Wheeler.

"So if one of us pisses off another one of us, then suddenly we're all about getting even?" asked Pat. "Oh, that'll work."

"We don't tell each other's secrets," said Laurette. "And we don't make fun of each other."

"Does that mean I can't mention your cleavage, *ever*?" asked Danny.

"We don't make fun of things that matter," said Laurette.

"Making fun of my cleavage is just another way of telling me that it's working."

"I think that's a good rule," said Danny.

"We all make fun of how Laurette shows her boobs?" asked Xena.

"We don't make each other feel bad," said Danny. "We don't tell each other's secrets to outsiders."

The others agreed.

"All of your gates," said Danny, "they'll take you here. But there's a chance one of the Families will find out about this place, so when you get here, if it's an emergency, just reach out to this tree." Danny showed them the one. "And here under this branch, there'll be another gate. Can you all reach it?"

They all proved that they could, even Xena, whose arms weren't all that long.

"Where will that gate take us?" asked Pat.

"Someplace far away. Someplace where I'll put a stash of money and a weapon. You'll never have to use it, but it'll be there, in case somebody's following you through the gate."

"So you don't have any idea yet where it'll go," said Pat.

"I'm thinking Disney World," said Danny.

"A weapon in the Magic Kingdom?" asked Sin. "That's just wrong."

"I'll find someplace safe, where I can stash a weapon and nobody will find it," said Danny. "For now, though, I'll make it lead to a place in DC. And then I'll make another gate there and show you all where it is, so you can get back to Buena Vista but in a different place."

"So we can try it out? It'll just be sitting there and if we want to go to DC we can use it?" asked Wheeler.

Everybody looked at him. "Once," said Danny. "You can try it once, to show that you know how to use it. But if you do it any other time, somebody might see you and then they'd know. It only works as an emergency escape if nobody knows, and that means you never use it. If you want to go to DC I'll send you there."

Wheeler laughed nervously. "This is really, like, serious and all."

"I thought you already understood that," said Danny. "If you stay friends with me, if you help me, you're going to be in real danger. And you'll need a real escape route. But if you want to beg off, then do it now. Let's not go any farther. I can leave this school any time. Without me here, you're safe. You haven't been seen *doing* anything yet."

"No," said Xena.

"We'll be good," said Hal.

Only Wheeler said nothing.

They all waited.

"I feel like I've already totally screwed up and you won't ever trust me no matter what I say," said Wheeler miserably.

"I'll trust you until you do something that shows me I shouldn't," said Danny.

"But I'm an idiot," said Wheeler.

"I told you he knew it," said Sin to Pat.

"I mean, I forget stuff. I blab stuff without thinking."

"Well, don't," said Danny. "That's all."

Wheeler nodded miserably. Then he suddenly disappeared and there he was over by the tree. He put his finger up where the next gate was going to be.

"Wheeler," said Danny. "You can't get away from *me* that way. Every gate I make is a part of me. I know where they go, and I know when people go through them. I also haven't put a gate in that tree yet."

"I just wanted to see if you had taken away my gate," said Wheeler.

"If I ever do," said Danny, "I'll tell you. Or I'll take away the condom." At the thought, he made a small gate that swallowed the condom even though it was in Wheeler's hand. He made it plop onto the ground in the middle of the group.

"Wow," said Wheeler. "You can take it right out of my hand?"

"No, I did that," said Xena.

"Really?" asked Wheeler.

"He really is an idiot," said Pat.

"Wheeler, I trust you," said Danny. "Now trust me, too." But in his heart, Danny knew that he would never really trust Wheeler. Would never send him out to deliver a message or run an errand more serious than buying sodas or picking up pizzas. Because his first instinct had been to use his gate carelessly. To test Danny. He doesn't know how to keep a promise.

They're all young. Maybe none of them do.

But he was in high school. These were the friends he had.

And it was cool that he could attach a gate to an object. I've made enchanted amulets, even if they are just tampons, licorice, a condom and a little-kid's eraser. No magic writing on them, nothing but a tiny gate embedded in them. It made him feel clever and powerful.

And there was Xena's hand on his arm again. He liked it there. He didn't pull his arm away.

Then he remembered that he didn't actually feel any attraction to Xena.

That was before she was attracted to *him*. Now she was very attractive.

I'm such a teenager myself, thought Danny. He remembered Lana, Ced's wife back in DC. How she made him feel. Xena was much nicer than Lana, and a lot less crazy. What if Danny had a girlfriend for a while? Not somebody who would seduce him and mock him for succumbing. Not a *succubus*. An actual girlfriend.

Then he remembered the stories of Zeus raping women all over the Aegean. And Hermes—how many women did the old myths have Hermes seducing? There was no lock on a bedroom door that could keep him out.

Xena's basically saying I can have her if I want. I could go into her bedroom tonight and sleep with her and her parents would never see me come in or go out. And she'd let me. She'd think it was cool.

Until we'd done it. Then she'd think we were together. And we would be. What if she got pregnant? What if she thought it made her cooler than the other girls and it caused a rift in the group?

Keep your pants zipped and your brain out of Xena's bedroom, Danny told himself.

She leaned her head on his shoulder.

Danny turned his body to face Xena. She put a hand on his chest. He took the hand and held it between his. "We're friends, Xena. And fellow soldiers in a war. Let's see what happens when the war is over."

Xena tossed her hand and stepped to Pat. "I told you he was gay." Then she laughed as if it had been a joke. Which it was. Mostly. Maybe.

I have no business trying to lead a group of any kind. I should take back all these gates and leave right now and never come back. Everybody will be better off it I do that.

Everybody but me.

He'd been lonely his whole life. This was the first time he had friends. And he couldn't give them up. He didn't want to give them up, and he could do whatever he wanted, and so he was going to stay here with them. Because they thought he was cool. They liked that he was powerful. They weren't trying to kill him. And they liked him before they knew he could do this thing with gates.

And he was going to be thinking about Xena in spite of the fact that he wasn't attracted to her. Or to any of the girls. He was sixteen now, so any offer was going to make him obsess for a while. Knowing that it was just his hormones making him feel this way didn't make the feelings go away. Might as well enjoy the feeling. As long as he didn't *do* anything about it.

That night Danny went to DC and Stone agreed to let him put the tail of the emergency gate in his attic. "But no gun," said Stone.

"What if someone's coming after them?" asked Danny.

"Be creative," said Stone.

What Danny came up with was a stack of pennies with gates on both sides. As long as you handled them by the edge, you didn't go anywhere. But if you touched heads or tails, you found yourself someplace interesting and public. Just inside the gate of the White House. The middle of the Capitol rotunda. Lincoln's lap. On the nose of the giant in the Awakening statue. If one of his friends was getting chased through the gates, they come to Stone's attic closet, grab a penny, and throw it at whoever comes through the gate after them.

"Weaponized money," said Stone. "But if one of your friends comes through just for fun, I get to throw a penny at them."

"They're nice," said Danny. "I don't want them getting treated badly just because they're drowthers."

"You know me better than that," said Stone. "I'll treat them badly because they're teenagers."

When Veevee and Hermia heard about the portable gates, they both demanded some of their own. Veevee had a charm bracelet, which she loaded up with rings, each one a gate leading to a useful place—her condo, the Silvermans' farm, Danny's house, Danny's school, Stone's bedroom. "I'm his wife, I don't have to use the attic," she said.

"What if somebody steals the bracelet?" said Danny. "I suppose if Hermia locks them for you and you only open them when you—"

"While you were playing with your little friends," said Hermia, "we were working."

"We can't make gates," said Veevee, "but now I can lock them and Hermia can unlock them. We both have lock and key now."

"We're working on moving gates," said Hermia. "I think I moved one. Just the tail."

"But she can't do it again," said Veevee.

"So then it doesn't have to be a ring," said Danny. "I can attach a gate to anything, and it only works when you want it to."

Hermia handed him a euro. "Put a dozen or so gates on this," she said. "I'll only open the ones I need, when I need them."

Her list of destinations was longer than Veevee's, but she had to stay a jump ahead of her Family. Danny attached two dozen gates to the coin. At first he tried to arrange them in some orderly way, but Hermia just laughed. "Danny, I can see them all, I can tell them apart, I know where they go, and I can keep them all locked except the one I want to use. Go ahead and pile them on in a jumble."

He gave her Paris, New York, Dubai, Singapore, Katmandu, Accra, Brisbane, São Paulo, a dozen other cities—not to mention the Greek Family's office building in Athens, the North Family compound in Virginia, and the Library of Congress. "It's practically the whole atlas," said Veevee admiringly.

"I'll add as many gates as you want," said Danny.

"No, I'm not jealous, and I know you'll open a gate to anywhere I want. What I'm worried about, Danny, is that there's no gate that takes me to *you*."

Hermia nodded. "We have all these gate *mouths* with us. But we need a gate whose tail always leads to wherever you are."

"I can't have you popping out of my pocket," said Danny.

"I know," said Veevee. "Have us come out of an old-fashioned oil lamp. We can be your genies."

"Amusing as that sounds," said Danny, "I don't want you popping up when I'm on the john."

"What if you need our help?" asked Hermia.

"I'll always know where these gates are. If I need to, I can move the tail of one of your portable gates to a place near me."

"Unless you're unconscious," said Veevee.

"I'll think about this," said Danny.

"You can lock it," said Hermia. "And then unlock it if you need us. We aren't going to intrude on your privacy."

"We unlock it ourselves only if we think something is really wrong," said Veevee.

"We peek through ahead of time," said Hermia.

Danny hated the whole idea. It was one thing to give them the power to go anywhere by using their amulets. But to give someone constant access to *him*—that wasn't going to happen. Even if they promised not to use it.

"I don't think he sees a difference between peeking through a gate and coming through it," said Veevee. "He doesn't want to be spied on."

"You have to trust us," said Hermia.

"I said I'd think about it," said Danny.

"Meaning the answer is no," said Veevee.

"It's really unfair," said Hermia. "*You* can make a gate anytime you want, no matter what we're doing. We can't hide from you, but you don't think we can be trusted not to spy on you or intrude when you're kissing some girl."

"We won't take pictures," said Veevee. "Or at least we won't post them online."

"I *said* . . ." Danny began.

"He's getting testy now," said Veevee.

"I don't spy on you," said Danny, "and I know you won't spy on me. But that's how power is—just because you have a power doesn't mean you want other people to use their power on *you*. Fairness only seems reasonable when the other person is more powerful than you."

"As it seems to us," said Hermia.

"I hate to sound like one of the Family," said Danny, "but . . . you're just going to have to live with it till I get used to the idea. Maybe someday I'll wish I had made gates that follow me around like puppies, so you can always find me. But right now I don't know how to do that, and I don't think I even want to, and so . . . I won't."

"Tough guy," said Veevee.

"He's not so tough," said Hermia. "He sounds like he's apologizing. Real assholes don't even pretend to be sorry."

"True," said Veevee. "It isn't in his nature, so he's not good at assholery yet."

"Thanks," said Danny. "I think."

"Well," said Hermia, "I'd better go, or the Family will track me here."

"You've got to get those trackers out of her," said Veevee.

She was right.

Danny studied Hermia, and then passed a gate over her, one that left her exactly where she was.

"What was *that* about?" asked Hermia.

"I didn't know what I might have gained by going to Westil," said Danny. "For all I know, I might always have had the ability to attach gates to portable objects. And maybe going through a Great Gate doesn't affect the mage who made it. But I think there *is* a difference. When you went through the gate I just made, I could feel a difference in you—the places where the gate was trying to heal you and meeting with resistance. Maybe that's what it was, anyway. I counted five places like that."

"You should just send her through an airport scanner," said Veevee. "They'll show you exactly where the trackers are implanted.

Danny laughed. "Of course. Veevee, will you come along and make a distraction?"

He took them to the Roanoke airport. Veevee got to the end of the security line and then started wailing. "Where's my ticket? I had my ticket right here!"

Her noise drew everyone's attention, and in the moment, Danny put Hermia right in front of the security gate, ahead of the person at the front of the line. Then he opened a peephole over the shoulder of the TSA official working the screen.

Veevee, seeing Hermia in place, took off on an elaborate charade of searching for her lost boarding pass. The guard waved Hermia into the machine.

Danny had been right about the trackers. Five of them, exactly where he had felt the gate trying and failing to heal her. The trip to Westil *had* given him more power. A sharper focus, a greater awareness.

He moved the porthole to a spot an inch from Hermia's ear. "Gate to my house in Buena Vista," he said. Then he gave the same message to Veevee.

In a moment they were all there. "I spotted all five trackers," said Danny. "I think I can gate them out."

"'Think'?" said Hermia. "This is my body we're talking about."

"I'll have a nice big gate ready for you to pass through so when I get each one out, you can heal yourself instantly. What can go wrong?"

"Famous last words," said Veevee.

But after another minute of dithering, Hermia said, "Oh, just do it."

"Are you sure?" said Danny.

"Do it, gate boy," said Veevee. "Can't you tell when a woman's saying 'yes'? You really are young."

In about ten seconds, Danny was done. There were five chips on the table, and Danny had passed the healing gate over Hermia after removing each one. It was very quick.

"It did hurt," said Hermia. "Surgery is surgery."

"Sorry," said Danny.

"I was just reporting, so you'd know," said Hermia. "I never thought it would be painless, so it wasn't a complaint." She picked up one of the chips. "So my parents thought it would be a good idea to put these things in their baby girl."

"The question is, what do we do with them?" said Veevee. "I say gate them to an incinerator."

"Or implant them in somebody else," said Hermia.

"That wouldn't be nice," said Veevee.

"I was thinking, what about the President? Or Prince Charles?" said Hermia. "Or some dictator somewhere. Make my Family go chasing them."

"Or five different people," said Veevee. "Make them go crazy trying to figure out which one is you."

In the end, Danny gated one tracker under the skin of each of the Hittite-Armenian assassins and sent the other trackers about a mile deep in the Atlantic. Then he gated the two assassins from the jail to the Greek Family's offices in Athens. "Let my folks deal with them," said Hermia.

"Are you going to tell them what the bastards tried to do to you?" asked Veevee.

"No," said Hermia. "Let them try to talk to each other. They'll know we picked these clowns to receive exactly two of the trackers for a reason. They'll know it wasn't random. But if I tell my family, they'll just kill them. Even if they're seriously angry at me, they won't approve of assassins from another Family going after me."

"So you think the assassins won't talk?" asked Danny.

"My family won't dangle them upside down over the ocean," said Hermia. "Or maybe they will—but they won't do it as cleverly and magically as you did."

"We *are* gatemages, aren't we?" said Veevee with some satisfaction. "It's so much *fun* to prank everybody at once."

They went to Veevee's favorite gelato place—Angelato, on Arizona Avenue in Santa Monica—and ate their gelatos on the Third Street Promenade. Then all three of them gated away to wherever they were going to spend the night. Veevee laughed in delight as she prepared to stick a finger into one of her rings. "Oh, I feel so *powerful*. Like the first time I got the keys to the family car." Then she was gone.

Alone in his little house in Buena Vista, Danny could hardly believe what he had done in a single day. Went to Westil and met the Gate Thief. Created portable gates for his friends. Removed the tracking chips from Hermia. Ate dessert in California and got back before bedtime.

Botched a Great Gate.

He really wanted to think about Xena as he went to sleep. But all he could think about was the angry gate that Marion and Leslie were tending now. How could he do something that stupid?

And then, inexplicably, he thought of Coach Lieder's daughter, Nicki. How was she doing? Had they realized yet that she was healed of her cancer?

That, at least, was something Danny hadn't screwed up.

Search

It should have been easy for Wad to find the windmage from Mittlegard whom Danny North had called Ced. Not only was there a swath of destruction across a long stretch of Hetterwee, making it easy to narrow down his location, but even if he tried to blend into the local population, even if he had acquired local clothing, his foreignness had to be obvious from his language.

Hetterwee was a broad plain that got heavy snow in winter but scant rain in summer. The grass was fast-growing and the sod was thick, but the whole world turned brown by midsummer and the grazing herds now stayed close to the many streams that flowed down from the Mitherkame, the High Mountains.

Mitherkame was high and thickly forested, a place where mages of stone and water, tree and eagle prospered and grew strong. Wind could whistle and whine through canyons and narrow passes.

But Hetterwee was a wide-open land where the wind made waves in the high grass, rippling for miles. There the wind could dance.

Deep in the grass, insects abounded, eating fallen seeds; birds and rodents came to eat the seeds as well, and to eat the insects too; and great grazing animals came in vast herds to slice or tear off the grass well above the matted sod. The predators—wolves and great cats—came to cull the lame and old and unprotected young from the herds. Here a mage of herding beasts and a mage of predators could equally find a home.

It was a place where a traveler could walk for days without any certainty that he had come any closer to his destination, or escaped any distance from the place where he began.

Yet somehow in this dry grassy wilderness, small villages of drowthers found a way to make their homes of cut-up sod, scratch their tiny farms out of the clay that they exposed, and one way or another eke out a living and store up enough strength to spawn a next generation, and then another. They did not hunt the herding beasts, for fear that they were watched over by a beastmage; nor did they wander alone, for fear that a mageridden predator would hunt them down for sport. They kept to themselves; they watched the weather on which their precarious lives depended; wariness kept them alive.

Wad gated from village to village, coming in as a stranger, but one who knew the language—for Wad could speak all the variants of Westil spoken in this world, or at least he never found one he couldn't pick up in a few minutes. He dressed himself in clothing that made him seem to be a journeyman in search of work. He should have been far more acceptable than Ced in these little villages, yet Wad could see that they were lying to protect the windmage from Mittlegard.

"My friend would have come soon before or soon after the storm that stripped your fields and blew down your houses," Wad said in village after village. "I have to find him—his wife is ill, and I must get him home for the children's sake."

But they never answered him except with a shrug or, if he forced the issue, a defiant stance, brandishing a stout stick and daring him to ask another question.

Somehow, though gales had torn roofs from houses and hail had ravaged the already scanty fields, these people took Ced as one of them instead of seeing that he was the one who had caused their misery.

Despite the help of the drowthers, Ced could not hide from a Gatefather forever. If the people would not talk to Wad openly, he would open a tiny window in their houses and listen to their conversation. They told him all he wanted to know, and more: They knew that Ced was the windmage who had harmed them so; they knew he came from another world; Ced had told them all of this himself. He was the god of the wind, come in person to apologize for the harm his mighty gales had wrought, and to make amends as best he could.

At last a window revealed Ced himself, asleep in the place of honor near the fire, in a house with a chimney, marking it as the richest in the hamlet.

Wad gated him from the house so gently that he didn't wake up. It was the cold that woke him, half an hour later; the wind itself, cold and thin at the top of a high crag in the Mitherkame.

Ced awoke shivering and knew at once that a gatemage had him, for how else could he have been taken out of the warm house and out into the cold? The wind told him he was in an open place, the lightness of the air that he was very high up. And when he opened his eyes, the starlight showed him that he lay on a patch of ground not more than ten strides in every direction before a drop-off that hid the rest of the world from view.

"Sorry to take you from the fire," said the young man who sat watching him. Ced recognized him at once—the mage who had come to meet Danny North at the tail of the Great Gate. The Gate Thief. The enemy.

"I'm not the one you want," Ced warned the man at once. "He went back to Earth."

"I know where Danny North is," said the Gate Thief. "He has most of my outself with him. Is the captive ever unaware of the boundaries of his prison?"

"Is that where I am now? A prison?" asked Ced.

"A place for undistracted conversation," said the Gate Thief. "No one will interrupt us. But a mage of your power—no, I could not keep you here, if you wanted to be gone."

"A mage of my power," Ced answered scornfully. "A monster power that harms everyone and helps no one."

"And yet you keep using it," said the Gate Thief.

"The air calls to me," Ced whispered. "Day and night, I hear it singing. I feel it on the hairs of my arms, my legs. It wakens me and I can feel the motion of all the airs of the world. Faraway winds and gales, nearby breezes, the passing of a running deer, the wings of a butterfly. This place is too much for me."

"It isn't the place," said the Gate Thief. "It's you. Passing through the Great Gate was what woke you. The air has been calling to you all along, as much in Mittlegard as here in the shadow of the Mitherkame."

"I don't know those words, sir."

"Mittlegard is the word for Earth, as you know quite well. And this is the Mitherkame," said the Gate Thief. "These mountains are the spine of the world called Westil among the mages of Mittlegard—though Westil is only one of the languages here, and also the ancient half-forgotten name of a kingdom that once included all the Hetterwold and the forests of the north."

"I'm a stranger here," said Ced. "If the wind hadn't called me with such strength, I wouldn't have missed the passage back to Earth. Can you send me home?"

"You know I can't," said the Gate Thief. "You know that Danny North took my gates from me, all but a handful, too few for me to make a Great Gate even if I wanted to. And I don't want to. Bad enough to have you here; worse for Mittlegard if I returned you there."

Ced understood. "So here I am, alone and friendless."

The Gate Thief looked at him quizzically. "Friendless? When they let you sleep in the place of honor near the fire?"

"They're kind folk, and forgiving, but they don't know who I am. They only know the power of the wind, and they're afraid of me."

"If they treat you well, and don't seek to kill you or control you, then they're your friends. Don't set so high a standard for friendship, Ced, or you'll have no friends."

"So what are you?" asked Ced. "You took me here without my consent. I hear the winds that whine around this crag, far below me—if I stepped to the edge I'd fall and die. So I'm a prisoner."

"Do you think the winds you're hearing would let you fall? They'd bear you up if you asked them to, and land you gently anywhere."

Ced felt a thrill of joy at what he said. "You mean that I can fly?"

"I mean that the wind you serve so well and rule so weakly has no desire to let you die."

"I suppose if you wanted me dead, you could have plunged me into the middle of the sea."

"There's air in the sea, and it would find you instantly, gather around you, make a bubble for you, and bear you up to the surface, where the wind would dry you instantly and again, you would fly."

"Then into the heart of a mountain—you could kill me if you wanted to."

"You've figured out my secret," said the Gate Thief. "I would like to be your friend."

"What form would such a friendship take?" asked Ced. "I had a friend once who provided me a home and food, and let me make my own mistakes, and figure things out for myself."

"I'm the kind of friend who would like to prevent your mistakes from killing people—either directly in the storms you raise, or afterward, when their ruined crops lead to famine and death this winter."

Ced reached out and took the man's hand and gripped it. "That's what I want, too, with all my heart."

"You seem to mean it," said the Gate Thief. He looked relieved.

"I do," Ced answered. "I'm not a violent man. I don't like breaking things. But when the wind starts . . ."

"It takes on a will of its own," said the Gate Thief. "It grows and grows, stronger and tighter, whirling and dancing. Do I have it right?"

"Yes!" cried Ced.

"And the ecstasy you feel—it's overpowering. You want to scream with joy. Do I have that right as well?"

Ced nodded, ashamed now, because the Gate Thief had caught out the secret Ced had been keeping even from himself. "It's a drug. It's heroin and coke and ecstasy and methamphetamine all at once—it's way more powerful than pot, which is the only drug I ever actually tried. Once it starts, I don't even want it to stop. Even though I know the terrible things that are happening, I can feel the tearing and breaking at the edges of the wind, but I can't stop."

"Meaning that you choose not to stop," said the Gate Thief.

That, too, was true, and Ced felt the shame and guilt burst within him, and in front of this powerful stranger he broke down and cried. "You should have killed me in my sleep," he said.

"I have so much blood on my hands. Not soldiers' blood from a war—the blood of children who died in the collapse of roofs or were swept away from their parents in the wind and dashed into trees or rocks or plunged into ravines. The blood of the parents who died reaching for them, or later, searching for their little bodies. I should be dead—I owe a hundred deaths already."

"Twenty deaths, in fact," said the Gate Thief. "Your shame makes you exaggerate."

"Twenty," Ced repeated, and he wept again.

The Gate Thief's hand was on his shoulder. "I take it that you tried to stop."

"The voices of the wind won't leave me alone. How do I make them still, so I can think?"

"You don't," said the Gate Thief. "You sing with them, so the voice becomes your own, their movements a part of your own breath. What you feel, when you feel all the winds of the world, is your own outself, spread as thin as air, and because you're the only windmage who has passed through a Great Gate in this age of the world, you meet no other there to challenge you. The winds are yours. If you love them, Ced, the winds are *you*."

"How does a gatemage know so much about how windmagery works?"

"Because all the magics of the world are one," said Wad. "And because I loved a windmage once."

"Your wife? I had a wife." Ced thought of poor broken Lana, and how grief and relief warred within him when she left.

"My mother," said Wad.

He had a mother. He was once a child. He's a human being, like me. And also a monster—like me.

"What are you going to do with me?" asked Ced.

"I want you to learn how to use your power to protect this world," said the Gate Thief.

"Protect it from what?"

"From the monsters. From the gods."

"Gods?"

"You called them the Families, there on Earth. They'll be here soon, and they'll be every bit as strong as you, and every bit as unprepared to control it. But unlike you, they'll have no consciences. They won't care what their magery costs the common people of this place."

"My caring doesn't bring them back to life," said Ced.

"But if you learn to master your power, you'll be far stronger than they are—at least for the first while—and perhaps you can protect the people. Prevent a little of the horror that would otherwise come. Would you like to do that?"

"I can't even prevent my own damage."

"You prevent it every day, every hour that you aren't raising a wind. You prevent it when you go among them, not to threaten them with storms if they don't obey you, but to help undo the damage that you've done. Why do you think they love you? Because you don't think that you're a god. Or maybe because you think that godlings should be kind."

"They love me?"

"This is a world long ruled by gods. When I closed the Great Gates, I weakened them, and as the old mages died, the new ones had only a fraction of their power, and life got better here. Now what counts as a great mage is a person of relatively petty power. But the mages of Mittlegard will come here with power unseen in this place for fourteen centuries. They'll bring their wars and rivalries with them, and then provoke more, as the mages here attempt to resist them, and fail. Only you can stand before them as an equal. As their master, if you prepare, if you're readier for war than they are."

Ced remembered an old line from a movie. "I'm a lover, not a warrior." He thought it might have been Rodney Dangerfield who said it. The man who got no respect.

"If you love something, then there's something to fight for," said the Gate Thief. "I think you've come to love these people."

Ced wasn't so sure. Guilt was surely not identical with love. But maybe there was a little overlap.

"But this is a different kind of war," the Gate Thief went on. "The lover has to stay alive inside the warrior. Because I don't want you to destroy them, Ced. I want to master them, but then to win them over to our side."

"Our side?" asked Ced. When had they become allies? Aloud, he said, "If the mages from the Great Families join us, who would we be fighting against then?"

"Someone worse," said the Gate Thief.

"The Families are monsters," said Ced. "They train their children to be monsters, and I can't imagine anybody worse."

"I can," said the Gate Thief.

"Who?"

"Mitherkame and Mittlegard are not the only worlds with people on them, and not the only mages capable of becoming monsters."

Ced felt tired. "I don't want any part of it."

"I know," said the Gate Thief. "What you wanted was to pass through a Great Gate and find out what it would do to your power."

"And it made me a monster."

"It made you a great mage," said the Gate Thief. "Your inexperience and lack of self-control led to the monstrous things you did. You *can* learn to control them. You can help the Families learn to control their greater powers. Only then will we have a chance against the Eater of Souls."

Ced thought of how Danny and Hermia had spoken of the Gate Thief—the legendary enemy, the Minotaur, the terrible monster that they would have to face.

"Why are you laughing?" asked the Gate Thief.

"You said 'Eater of Souls' exactly the way people say 'Gate Thief.' "

The Gate Thief nodded. "I was the thing that Danny North feared most."

"You destroyed every gatemage you found for a thousand years."

"No I didn't," said the Gate Thief. "I never touched a gatemage until he tried to make a Great Gate. All they had to do to stay safe from me was to confine their gatemaking to their own world. Why wasn't that enough? Why couldn't they be content to gate from place to place, to heal anyone who passed through their gates? Why wasn't such a wonderful power enough for them?"

Ced thought of his own experience with power. "Because if it's there, you have to reach for it."

"Monkeys in the trees," said the Gate Thief. "Always hungry for the fruit that's out of reach."

"What's your name?" asked Ced. "I think of you as the Gate Thief, but that's only your job title."

"They call me Wad, in the place I lived most recently."

"And what did your mother call you?" asked Ced.

"She called me Loki—but that was a job title, too. It's the name given to the most powerful gatemage of the North family. It was under the name of Wad that I last tasted hope. It's the name that my friends call me."

"Tell me about this monster worse than the mages of the Families," said Ced. "Tell me about the Eater of Souls, so I can decide whether I'm qualified to call you Wad."

"I don't know if it's one being, or one of many. It could be the same one, coming back again and again, because if I understand correctly what it is, then it never dies and is very hard to kill."

"But what *is* it?"

"A manmage," said Wad. "But not the kind we're warned against. Not like the manmages of Dapnu Dap, who once ruled the world of Mitherkame by seducing and flattering and eventually riding men and women as their heartbeasts."

"They sound bad enough."

"You can still find their bodies, when a manmage's outself is riding a heartbeast. You can kill them. But from what I learned before I closed the gates, the god Bel doesn't do this. He takes over the man's body, and it isn't his outself that comes to control it, it's his inself."

Ced tried to understand it. "So he has nothing left in his own body?"

"I don't know if the Belmages ever had bodies. I don't know what life is like in the world they come from. But they passed through gates into our world, never in large numbers—and as I said, it's possible that it only happened once, and there's only one. Because when one body dies, it doesn't kill his inself. He simply jumps into someone else, displacing their inself, *becoming* that person."

Ced understood now what the threat was. "If he takes over the body of a great mage . . ."

"Then he has all that mage's power. That's what the Belmages did, before we understood and began to fight them. A great mage of our kind would suddenly change, become more powerful and yet more ruthless. Systematically evil, that's how it looked. But when we fought against a mage who had become so terrible, we simply . . . won. Killed him sometimes. But sometimes we were able to imprison him, talk to him—and he wouldn't remember a thing. Not a thing. He didn't remember the way heartbeasts remember their jaunts together with their mage inside. He never felt controlled. He was simply—absent. Cut off from his own body. Asleep in some deep sense. One of them said that he was wandering, but he couldn't say where, or anything that happened to him."

"So the mage you had imprisoned—he really hadn't done the terrible things that made you go to war with him."

"There was a thing that took over his body, but when we got control of him, made him powerless, the thing was no longer interested in staying inside him. It left. The Egyptians discovered the danger first. That's why they cut the organs out of the bodies of great mages and put them in separate jars. So there'd be no way for the Belmage to use their body for evil after their own in-self was gone."

"But how do you even fight something like that?" asked Ced.

"Another Loki faced him once, and won. He gated the body containing the Belmage into the Sun of Mittlegard. We always assumed that the Belmage died there, along with the body, because there was no other human close enough to jump into. But now I wonder if the Belmage didn't simply wander for a long time, lost. If that's the case, then there's only the one. But he came back, and in my time he was too clever to be fooled again. I couldn't use the trick that other Loki used. So I took all the Great Gates from the world, so that no matter what body he took, it would be a weaker one, and he could never get from there to here."

"So if I went back . . ."

"Everyone that Danny North brought here to Mitherwee—to this world, to Westil—is now more powerful than any other mage in Mittlegard. The Belmage will know. It will crave that power. They're all in terrible danger, and none so much as Danny North himself. Because if the Belmage takes him, he can make all the Great Gates he wants. And if there are many of them, and not just one, they'll all be able to come here, to the heart of magery, and make their bid to rule the universe."

Ced nodded. "Displacing all the gods. Becoming the permanent, immortal, unkillable gods."

"If they really are unkillable. If we don't stop them."

"What if this Belmage really did take over Danny North? What could we do?"

"Kill Danny," said the Gate Thief. "What choice would we have?"

"Why didn't you kill him already? You were there with him at the Great Gate."

"Because Danny North hasn't done anything that makes him deserve to die."

"He made a Great Gate."

"When people made Great Gates, I took the power to do it away from them," said Wad. "But I didn't kill them. I'm not the Belmage. I refuse to be a monster."

"I refuse to be a monster, too. But it doesn't mean that I'm not one."

Wad smiled. "I know. But I can help you get control of your power. To become master of the wind, instead of the wind ruling you, as it's doing now."

"It *feels* as though I'm controlling it. And yet I can't stop, because I want whatever it wants."

"That's right," said Wad. "You're like the wick of a candle. The flame could not survive without the wick to concentrate it—but the wick is not the master of the flame. The flame consumes it, bit by bit."

Ced knew at once that this was true. He nodded. "I wouldn't have said it that way, but it's the truth."

"I'm glad that you're aware of it—it's the beginning of wisdom. It's the hardest thing for a mage to learn."

"And you'll teach me, Wad? How to control my power?"

"Me?" Wad laughed. "How, when I never learned the lesson all that well myself? I'm the tool of spacetime in just the way that you're the tool of the wind. No, I'll take you to the best teachers. The ones who can help mages of every kind, because they have almost infinite patience and understanding, or they could never become masters of their own magery."

"Who?"

"Treemages. Not all of them. Just a few. The best of them, the master teachers. The ones who understand that the tree is in the root. It was a treemage of fourteen centuries ago who saved me alive to do the work I'm doing now. He persuaded a great tree to open itself to me. Inside its living wood, I made a tiny gate that drew me upward through the tree, a tiny fraction of an inch every day, so little movement that I almost wasn't moving at all. But I passed through the gate each day, healing all the ills of my body. And it also healed the tree, so that limbs never broke off without regrowing. The tree lived those fourteen centuries in perfect health, as I did. Until I felt a shuddering in the All. I felt Danny North coming into the universe—coming into his power. I didn't understand it at the time. I only knew it was time to come out of the tree. I hardly knew who I was. I couldn't speak. I had to learn to be human again, instead of being a part of the tree. But I learned. All too well. I'm human now. And Danny North is in the world. He bested me and has my gates. I'm nearly helpless to fight the Belmage, or even the Families of Mittlegard. That's why I need you to become master of yourself, so you can stand beside me."

"I'm not a brave man," said Ced. "I don't know what I'll be like in war."

"No one ever does," said Wad. "And the answer is never the same on two different days. Will you come with me to the treemages of Gos in the Forest Deep, and see if one of them will take you on?"

"I think you've already asked one, and he's said yes, or you wouldn't have come to me," Ced answered.

"I've asked," said Wad, "but he won't say yes until he meets you, and you have to come of your own free will."

"I'll go with you and learn what I can learn. And if I find that everything you said is true, I'll stand with you as best I can."

"If it isn't true," said Wad, "it won't be because I lied. It will be because I'm only guessing at half the things I know about the Belmage, and I might be wrong. I hope I'm wrong. I hope we can defeat him in the end."

9

Visitors

Danny wrote out the message and rehearsed it with his friends until they had it memorized. He didn't want them to read it. He wanted them to look at the Families face to face, eye to eye. Not challengingly, but calmly, easily. They were the messengers of a Great Mage. They had to act like it.

"I come from Loki," the message began. "He has made a Great Gate. He has faced the Gate Thief and defeated him. He has passed through the Great Gate to Westil and returned. He will allow each Family to send two mages to Westil and return at once, but only if you agree, individually and as Families, to these three promises.

"One. You will not make war on or cause harm to any other Family or any individual mage.

"Two. You will not take the lives of drowthers or enslave them, but will respect their laws and customs.

"Three. You will cease the killing of gatemages or suspected gatemages. Instead, you will send them to Loki to be trained.

Gatemages will never belong to any Family, but only to the company of Gatekeepers. I will return tomorrow for your answer."

Danny sent them one at a time and watched carefully through a peephole in case someone tried to harm them. He made peepholes for Veevee and Hermia as well. The messengers held on to their amulets. Danny was determined that no one would be harmed.

Hal and Xena stumbled over the memorization a little, but corrected themselves and went on. No one else made a mistake. They appeared in each Family's meeting room, in front of whoever happened to be present in response to the anonymized email they had all received.

Then Danny brought each of his friends back the moment the last word was spoken. It wasn't a press conference. It was an offer and an ultimatum, both at once. He didn't have to explain that failing to agree to the terms would put any Family outside the peace that Danny was establishing. That meant that when the other Families sent their two mages through to Westil and back, they would be free to use their vastly increased power to make war on the noncompliant Families.

"They'll all agree," Stone had said. "The question is whether they'll keep their word."

"That's why they won't know where I am," said Danny. "So they'll never know where their punishment is coming from."

He spoke boldly of punishment, but he had no idea what he would actually do if someone broke their word. It depended, he supposed, on what form their oath-breaking took. If they tried to get someone to the Great Gate without permission, he would put them somewhere inconvenient. If they mistreated drowthers or started a war, he would let the peaceful Families send more and more mages through to Westil until the oathbreakers were outnumbered and defeated.

If they killed somebody, he would . . .

Put them in Hammernip Hill?

He didn't want to think about killing people with his power. But if they harmed one of his friends, he'd do what it took to make sure they never did such a thing again. His messengers were under his protection, and that had to mean something if it was going to work.

But he knew they would measure his intentions by what they themselves would do with the kind of power he had. They would be ruthless, even cruel. So they would assume that he meant to do the same, and would fear him.

Which means, thought Danny, that I really am exactly what I'm trying to prevent them from becoming—a power-hungry tyrant, determined to bend everyone else to his will.

But if I don't keep them under control until they can see how much better this new order works than the old ways ever did, then the experiment can never work. The world will have no peace. So I must be the tyrant over the tyrants, to keep all the drowthers, the orphans, the weaker members of the Families—to keep them safe.

Safe from Uncle Zog and Grandpa Gyish. From whoever the other Families' equivalents might be.

After each messenger came back to Danny's tiny living room, Hermia and Veevee continued to watch the Family that had just been visited, to see what they'd say. Most of them were so naive that it didn't seem to occur to them that just because the messenger was gone, no gatemage was listening. Only Hermia's family seemed to be speaking artificially, with exaggerated sweetness and willingness to comply. "They know we're listening," said Hermia. "They won't say anything real."

"They have to eventually," said Danny. "But there's no reason to spy on them any further. They'll agree because they have no choice, and they'll keep their word because they fear what will happen if they don't."

"But Danny, my darling," said Veevee, "you haven't sent a messenger to your own dear Family."

Danny didn't bother saying something petulant, like "they're not my family." Like it or not, they most definitely *were* his kin, the Family he knew better than any other.

Xena raised her hand. "I'll go," she said. "I want to meet your real parents."

"No you don't," said Danny.

"You think I'll embarrass you?" asked Xena.

She apparently had the idea that she was some kind of girlfriend of his, and that he simply didn't want to bring her home to meet the parents.

"I have to talk to them myself," said Danny.

"But you don't have an amulet," said Sin.

"He doesn't need one," said Hermia. "He can make a gate to any place on Earth faster than he could possibly reach an amulet."

"I knew that," said Sin.

"I just want my Danny to be safe," said Xena possessively.

She's embarrassing herself, thought Danny. Doesn't Xena see how obvious she's being?

Then it occurred to him that high school girls, as a tribe, weren't exactly subtle about who they liked and who they didn't. Nobody was going to act like Jane in *Pride and Prejudice,* so nobody can tell whether they like the boy or not. Xena had decided to be in love with the guy who could take her anywhere in an instant, and so she didn't care who knew it. In fact, being obvious about it might be her way of staking a claim so none of the other girls thought of trying for him.

"You really don't know what mages are like," Veevee said to Xena with exaggerated kindness. "That's because Danny is the only one you've ever met, so you don't understand. If you make an obvious offer to any other mage from one of the Families, they'll jump your bones without a quibble. Then they'll walk away, leaving whatever bastard they've conceived inside you."

"I'm not offering anything," said Xena. "I just *care* about him."

"Tone it down, darling," said Veevee. "You're scaring the boy."

"He's not gay, you know," said Xena. "He isn't scared of me."

Great, thought Danny. She knows that I'm sort of interested. How can it be so obvious?

"If he ever sleeps with somebody," said Veevee, "he'll doubtless get all conscience-stricken and marry the poor girl, and then where would you be? Stuck with a man who will come to hate you, one you can never be equal to in any way. The permanent magically retarded wife, always dragging him down. Is that how you want to spend your life, darling?"

"I get it now," said Pat. "When you say 'darling,' you mean 'idiot.'"

"I'm glad *somebody* speaks Catty-Bitch-ese around here," said Veevee. "I'd hate to be the only one."

"I don't speak it," said Pat, "but I understand it. I learned it in school."

"Oh, don't be modest," said Veevee. "You speak it like a native."

"Neither of you knows my mother," said Hermia. "She could take you both to school."

"So you're one-upping each other about who's the bitchiest?" asked Hal.

"It's not a competition," said Laurette.

"You just think you automatically win because you've got the biggest knockers," said Xena.

"Does anybody really say 'knockers'?" asked Laurette.

"You have to talk to your Family, Danny," said Hermia.

"I know."

"Tonight. Now. They're going to hear about the terms you offered everybody else and if you haven't talked to them, they'll think they're not getting a chance at a Great Gate. Then they really will be determined to kill you."

"Oh, they've only been kidding around up to now?" asked Danny.

"Up to now, half of them have been protecting you," said Hermia. "Or at least your own parents have been. But if you make it seem that they're shut out . . ."

"I know," said Danny. "I know I know I know."

"So do it," said Hermia.

"Later."

"Now."

Danny grinned. "You're not the boss of me."

"I am," said Veevee. "The school has me down as your legal guardian. Go talk to your family."

"I didn't make an appointment the way I did with the others," said Danny.

"And you can be sure they know about it by now," said Hermia. "They're already thinking the worst."

She was right. Everybody was right. Danny gated to the library in the old house in the compound.

The walls had been rebuilt since they tore them out looking for Danny on the day Hermia had pointed out that there was a spy inside the wall. There were new carpets. Everything was all nice and clean for company. All the aunts and uncles were sitting around the table. Baba and Mama at one end of the table. Gyish and Zog weren't there at all.

Danny looked at each of them in turn. Aunt Lummy and Uncle Mook, the two he knew best and trusted most. They looked worried and stern. Auntie Uck and Auntie Tweng and Uncle Poot and Uncle Thor seemed much more relaxed, but Danny imagined that was because they didn't actually care what happened to Danny—or they had such rage toward him that they felt a greater need to disguise their feelings.

Baba and Mama were smiling. And oh, yes, there were Danny's half-brother Pipo and half-sister Leonora. They weren't important in the council, so they must have been brought in to create some kind of cozy family atmosphere. As if they had ever given Danny the time of day.

"If Zog and Gyish don't sign off on this, it won't happen," said Danny.

"Hello to you too, Son," said Baba.

"I'm not here as your son, sir," said Danny. "I'm not here as a North. I'm here as the only person in Mittlegard who can make gates."

"Is that still true?" asked Mama. "Your Keyfriend and Lockfriend haven't picked up any new skills?"

"I'll be back when Gyish and Zog are here," said Danny.

"Wait," said Baba. "We didn't think you'd want to see them, but they're just outside, you don't have to go."

"Of course he wants to see them," said Auntie Tweng. "He wants to rub their noses in it."

"In what, exactly, do you think I want to rub their noses?" asked Danny.

"In the fact that you're a mage," said Auntie Tweng, "and we all know that the reason you didn't send one of your little drowther friends as a messenger was so you could come here personally and gloat."

"*Do* you know that?" asked Danny. Of course it was true, at least a little bit, but it wasn't the whole reason and it galled him that anybody in this room thought they knew Danny. "I can't imagine why any of you thinks you know me at all. With the possible exception of Uncle Mook and Aunt Lummy, none of you ever cared enough to find out what kind of person I was when I lived here."

"Yes, this is just the tone we expected from you," said Uncle Poot. "Self-centered and arrogant as always."

"We know what power does to a person," said Thor.

"And how would you know that?" asked Danny. "None of you knows what power *is*. There hasn't been any real power in any of the Families for fourteen centuries. And as far as I'm concerned, it can stay that way."

He thought of disappearing right then, leaving them to stew on it for a while. But that would be childish, and Veevee would tease him and Hermia would yell at him and so he stayed where he was.

"You can't hear the arrogance in your own tone?" said Auntie Tweng.

"He's always been like that," said Zog as he entered the room. "Vain about his schoolwork, vain about everything, even when he had nothing to be vain about."

"Shut up, Zog," said Baba.

"Oh, you think you're still head of the Family, is that it, *Alf*?" said Zog. He stressed Baba's original name instead of calling him Odin.

"Of course he is," said Mama.

"No," said Zog. "*He* is, now." He thumbed toward Danny.

"The only way I could be head of this Family," said Danny quietly, "is if I were a member of it. But I'm not. I never was."

Mama began hotly: "Our blood runs in your—"

"The best of your blood is buried in the dirt of Hammernip Hill," said Danny. "Whatever genes I have can't be helped. But as you made very clear, blood means nothing if I don't have some tangible value to you. And right now, the only way to keep the whole world from erupting in war is for all the Families to know I don't belong to any of them. Nor am I one of the Orphans."

"Those drekka," said Grandpa Gyish. "Bastards and foundlings."

Danny wanted to make a tiny gate to make him trip and fall on the floor, but he restrained himself. "Making bastards has always been a favorite sport of the Westilians," said Danny, "but the genes tell true, and the Orphan mages are as powerful as you."

"Are you sending Orphans through the Great Gate, right along with the Families?" asked Thor, sounding alarmed.

"Oh, come on now, don't you understand how this works? I send whoever I want through the Great Gate. I've already sent four Orphans through a Great Gate."

"It already exists?" said Zog eagerly. "The new gate?"

"Not for you it doesn't," said Danny.

"So you aren't going to let me through, is that it?" demanded Zog. "Even if the Family chooses me."

"With only two places to fill," said Danny coldly, "there is no chance that they'd send a Clawbrother like you. They'll send Mama and Baba for exactly the reasons you made Baba the Odin and let him marry Mama. Because they're the most powerful mages in the Family. All the Families will send their most powerful mages." It took all Danny's self-restraint to keep from reminding Zog just how far down that list he was.

From the hatred on Zog's face, Danny knew he didn't have to.

"The little boy is still pissed off because you bruised his shoulder," said Grandpa Gyish.

"That injury healed the moment I went through a gate," said Danny. "Just because you base all your choices on spite and vengefulness and fear, Grandpa Gyish, doesn't mean that I do. You never had the power to cause me any pain that lasts."

Then Danny pointedly looked at Baba. "But you did," said Danny. And he looked at Mama, too. "So I want you to know that I'm past all that. I'm giving the North Family equal access to the Great Gate, when I make it. No more than any other Family, but no less, either. If it's the two of you who are chosen to represent the Norths in the passage to Westil, that's fine. But if not, so be it. I don't really care."

"Of course it will be them," said Auntie Uck. "It's already decided, as soon as we learned of the terms you were giving the other Families."

Danny looked at Thor, who was head of the Norths' network of spies.

"No, I didn't find out," said Thor. "Do you think the other Families would let my drowther informants get close enough to know anything? They all contacted us at once. To find out whether we'd gotten an invitation from you and to see if you were treating us equally."

"What did you tell them?" asked Danny.

"We told them nothing!" said Zog savagely.

"Telling them nothing," said Danny, "was the same as telling them everything—that I hadn't spoken to you yet, that you didn't know yet what would happen."

"We knew," said Uncle Mook. "Zog and Gyish guessed wrong about the motive, but we all knew you'd come here. Because however much you may hate and resent us, you don't want us dead."

"Don't count on that," said Gyish. "Spiteful little bastard."

"If he wanted us dead," Aunt Lummy pointed out gently, "we'd be having this meeting inside Hammernip Hill. He could have put us there whenever he wanted."

"Do you accept the terms?" said Danny. "Assuming you've heard the three promises I'm demanding from everybody."

"We've heard them," said Uncle Mook. "For some of us, the terms will be easy to swear to."

"Which is why Zog and Gyish had to be here," said Danny. "They not only have to say the words. I have to believe them."

"Or what?" asked Zog. "You're not sending *me* through the Great Gate anyway, so what can you do to hurt me?"

Now it was time for a demonstration of power. Danny made a gate that swallowed Zog and dropped him from the ceiling. He landed sprawling on the table, the breath knocked out of him.

The sheer surprise of it shocked everyone, and most of them jumped up or pushed back. Thor tried to do both and ended up knocking down his chair and then falling over it.

"What can I do to hurt you, if you break your oath?" asked Danny quietly. "Why, anything I want."

Danny rose to his feet. The others sat down, except for Tweng and Uck, who were helping Zog get off the table and back to his chair. "As with all the others, I'll expect your answer tomorrow."

"At what time?" asked Thor.

"At the time I return," said Danny.

"And when will *that* be?" demanded Gyish, who was apparently unhumbled by what Danny had just done to Zog.

Danny didn't bother to answer. He just gated back to his living room, where the others were waiting.

"That went well," said Hermia dryly.

It took a moment for Danny to realize that Hermia had been watching—and Danny had not made gates for her and Veevee this time.

"Oh, don't get all uffish about it," said Hermia. "I've been working on trying to do *something* besides lock your gates."

"You made a gate?" asked Danny eagerly.

"I wish," said Hermia. "But I moved the other end of the last viewport you made for me."

"You moved it all the way to the library?"

"No," said Hermia. "I attached it to you, and *you* carried it with you. I was essentially looking and listening through the top button of your shirt."

Sin giggled. Xena glared at her. "Woah, cool," said Wheeler.

This was a huge breakthrough. Hermia could move the end of a gate and attach it to an object.

"Can you do it, too?" Danny asked Veevee.

"I haven't tried," said Veevee. "This is the first I've heard of it. I didn't even realize she was listening while you were gone, or I would have been angry at you for not making *me* a viewport. I may not be as young and pretty as Hermia, but I love you more than she does."

"Will you teach her how to do it?" Danny asked Hermia.

"Of course," said Hermia. "I only succeeded for the first time just now, and I only had to move it a few feet. I have no idea how far I can reach with it. Probably not very far."

"So the messages are delivered," said Pat, "and Hermia thinks you handled it well with your family."

"Actually, I think she was being sarcastic," said Danny.

"No, I wasn't," said Hermia. "I really think it went well. You made your point with that bully Zog, and everybody else you treated respectfully. I don't know if I could have done that."

"He's so ni-i-i-ice," said Wheeler.

"He is!" insisted Xena.

Please get off my side, Xena, said Danny silently. Especially because I don't even *have* a side.

"My point is," said Pat, "the messages are delivered, so isn't it time you took *us* through a Great Gate?"

"You?" asked Hermia in genuine surprise. "What's the point?"

"To see what it does to us," said Pat. "There's a lot of bastard mageblood in the world by now. Who knows whether we might not have some latent abilities?"

Veevee laughed. "You don't have to invoke all those happy impregnators among the corps of minor gods. Magery is certainly latent among the entire human race. Or so Danny thinks, since he's so sure that humans began here in Mittlegard and only became mages when a tribe stumbled on a naturally occurring gate and got carried to Westil."

"If there were such a thing as naturally occurring gates," said Hermia, "don't you think there'd have been one during the centuries since Loki ate all the gates?"

"The Gate Thief got any gate that opened," said Danny. "And maybe they only happen when the planets are aligned somehow. Maybe there are cycles."

"Or epicycles," said Hal.

"Danny's a Virgo," said Xena. "I'm not sure how the planets lined up for him, though."

"It's just a theory," said Danny. "And it has nothing to do with astrology."

"Let's test it," said Veevee. "Take these little *darlings* through a Great Gate and see what it does to them."

"If you're going to do it at all," said Pat, "you need to do it before you send any of the Family mages through. Once there are other great mages loose in the world . . ."

Danny thought of his father coming home with his power over metal and machinery multiplied by two. Or ten. And for that matter, what would his mother be able to do? There were gods in the past who really could hurl lightning. No doubt a mage of light and heat like Mama would be able to make lightning, after passing through the Great Gate.

Pat was right. The Family mages would be godlike, and if they weren't quite scrupulous about keeping their word to Danny, he'd be busy dealing with them. He wouldn't have time to work with his drowther friends to find out just how permanent their drowtherhood might be.

Well, he hadn't told the Families exactly *when* he'd make this Great Gate he was promising. Obviously he couldn't delay forever. If they became impatient, there *was* a Great Gate in existence, one that was not in Danny's control.

And that night, as Danny was undressing for bed, he couldn't stop himself from playing through in his mind a not-terribly-unlikely scenario in which he delayed far too long, angering the Families, which then united against him and attacked the Silvermans in order to show their displeasure.

Powerful as Marion and Leslie now were, because of their passage through a Great Gate, they could not stand against the united Families. Perhaps not even against one Family in a concerted assault. Yes, Leslie could detach all the beastmages from their heartbeasts. Yes, Marion could break up the earth under them.

But there would be threats they couldn't see. There would be winds and water that they couldn't stop. There would be fire.

And even if the whole farm in Yellow Springs was burned to the ground, there that public Wild Gate would be, waiting. As the victorious enemies gloated, walking over the burnt-out ruin of the Silvermans' farm, their refuge, their lives, someone would accidentally step through the Great Gate. Wouldn't that be the kind of prank that spacetime looked for?

No, Danny could not delay forever. But if he took his drowther friends through a new Great Gate right away, perhaps there would be time enough to train them a little. Maybe they would have latent mageries that bloomed into sudden life. Maybe . . .

Maybe pigs could eat with knives and forks. Even powerful mages born in Families took years of training in order to master their abilities. What fantasy was this, that Danny could bestow on his friends what his Family had as their inheritance?

I am not all-powerful. I may have the most useful magery in the world right now, the one that can change everything. I may have other people at my mercy. But I can't even control a Great Gate that I made. I didn't know the consequence of weaving into it the lingering outselves of long-dead rage-filled mages—but the fact that I'm not to blame doesn't mean that I'm not compelled to live with the consequences of my foolishness.

How much more foolishness will I have to bring about because of the things that I don't know? It isn't my drowther friends who need training. It's me. But the only person in either world who can possibly help me is my most dangerous enemy. The Gate Thief.

I have most of his gates under my control right now, but who knows what tricks he knows that I am not aware of? Who knows what danger I would be in if I went to him for help? He's a Gatefather—he can lie to me as easily as he can breathe, so even if he promised to help me, how would I know that he meant to keep his word?

And that image of the Silvermans' farm as rubble and ash kept coming back to his mind.

There was a knock at his door.

He felt a thrill of terror, his heart leaping with sudden adrenaline. The Families had found him!

Then he heard Pat's voice. "It's me," she said. "I need to talk to you."

Relieved, his heart still racing, Danny took the five steps to the door—the house was so tiny—without remembering that he was in the middle of undressing for bed. When the door opened, Pat looked him up and down.

"I see you were expecting someone else," she said.

Danny was wearing his tighty-whities and his socks.

"I was in the middle of undressing for bed," he said. "And I wasn't expecting anybody."

"I would have waited for you to put on a robe." She stepped through the door and Danny closed it behind her.

"I don't own a robe." He walked into the bedroom, picked up his jeans, and came back into the living room.

"Don't bother," said Pat. "I won't be here long."

"Long enough to sit down?"

Pat looked around. "On what?" she asked.

That wasn't really fair—the house had come with an old tatty sofa, and there was a kitchen table with three wobbly chairs. But Danny always tossed his dirty clothes on the couch and the chairs were stacked up with books.

Danny gathered up the clothes from the couch and dropped them on the floor.

"Tidy," said Pat.

Danny put his hand on her back to usher her to the couch.

Pat shied away. "What are you doing?"

Danny pulled back his hand. "Offering you a seat?"

"I can find my way to your couch without your hands on my body," she said coldly. "I'm not Xena, I don't want your hands all over me. And for what it's worth, she isn't, like, in love with you."

"I didn't think she was," said Danny.

"Oh, *she* thinks she is," said Pat, "but it's not you she wants, it's to have a god's baby inside her belly."

"I'm not a god," said Danny. "There *are* no gods, just people like me."

Pat faced him with fire in her eyes. "On the contrary, buddy-boy.

People like you are proof that there *are* gods. Dangerous powerful beings who can do terrible things to people who don't obey them."

"What terrible things have I done to you?"

Pat touched her face. "Oh, isn't it wonderful, my kind master! You have bestowed smooth skin upon your pock-marked servant! Now at last she's worthy to have your hands placed upon her body!"

Danny was completely flummoxed. He hadn't meant anything at all by touching her. He didn't know why he had even done it. He didn't go around touching people.

There was nothing he could say to change her false impression. "Have a seat while I put my pants on," he said.

"I told you I'm not staying long." But she sat down and watched him pull up his jeans. "I don't even know why I came."

"Well, we've settled that you aren't here to have sex with me," said Danny. He meant it as a self-mocking joke.

"Right, just because I don't want your hands on me, you think I'm some kind of cold frigid bitch."

Her words were so out of proportion to anything that had come before that Danny couldn't imagine what was going through her mind. "Is that what I think?"

"For your information, no, I wasn't molested as a child, no, I wasn't abused, no, I don't have any repressed memories of terrible things that now interfere with the natural development of my sexuality. I'm just a private person who doesn't like to be touched."

Danny just stood there for a couple of seconds. "It's so good of you to come all the way over here and tell me that," he finally said.

Pat sat there, looking at him in surprise. It was as if she was only hearing now what she herself had just finished saying. "That's not what I came here to say," she said. Her face turned red and she looked away. "I can't believe I went off like that, I don't know what I was . . ."

Danny pulled up one of the kitchen chairs across from her—he didn't even have to take a step to do it, the kitchen being the other end of the living room—and sat on it. "Let's pretend I didn't touch you and so you didn't react the way you reacted for whatever reason you reacted that way, and let's just say that I asked you to come in and take a seat and here we are." He put on an air of jovial welcome. "Pat, my good friend, what brings you here so late at night, considering that you don't want to sleep with me or have my babies?"

Pat was not amused at his humor. "My parents made me see a shrink because I like to be left alone."

"Well, that explains the 'repressed sexuality' thing."

"She had an M.D. and a Ph.D., but that just shows they'll give those degrees to any bonehead who puts in the time. She was a fake who wanted to hypnotize me and put false memories into my head. She actually thought she *had* hypnotized me and started suggesting all kinds of sexual things my father had snuck into my room and done to me when I was three. She was, like, a volunteer hypnotic pornographer. Serious child porn. Ugly." Pat shuddered. "My parents kept making me go back until I finally told my dad what that bitch was trying to get me to 'remember' he had done to me."

"But you hung on to the vocabulary."

"Whenever people go off on how I don't like to be gladhanded or stroked, she comes to mind. Being an introvert isn't a pathology, you know."

"I know," said Danny. "I don't like to be touched either." He thought back to the way Lana had accosted him when he first came to Stone's house, and he realized that he hadn't spoken the actual truth. He hadn't liked Lana touching him at the moment, because it was such a surprise and because he didn't like her having control over him. But his *body* very much liked being touched, and he still remembered that encounter with Lana. He remembered it a lot, and he had imagined several different endings to the event that he much preferred to the way it had actually ended.

But he knew that was nothing more than the impulse of his DNA to replicate itself. In fact, like Pat, he didn't like to have people touch him. At least not without an invitation. "I have no idea why I did that," said Danny, "and I'm sorry. I'm also sorry your parents didn't get you, and I'm sorry the shrink was a schmuck. Can we please get on to whatever you actually came for?"

Pat turned red again and curled up onto the couch, turning her body partly away from him. He had never seen her look vulnerable before. "What am I doing? Why am I saying these things?"

"Really. Please," said Danny. "Tell me what you came for."

"I'm worried about you," she finally said. Still not looking at him. Still embarrassed. "You're so. So."

"Stupid?" Danny prompted.

"Yes," she said. "Not school-stupid, not even people-stupid. I mean, you're actually very clever and kind of sweet and I think you don't have a malicious bone in your body, though your sense of humor is sometimes kind of on the mean side."

"Senses of humor usually are," said Danny. "But I see your point. Thanks for the counsel."

"See?" she said. "You're joking, but you're also making fun of the fact that I came here at night, alone, and I've said everything wrong until I feel so stupid I could die, and yet you're also sitting there waiting so patiently for me to finally say what I came to say, because you *are* sweet, and that's why I'm so afraid, because I don't think you know how evil some people can be."

Pat had no idea what it was like to live inside a Family. "I know a little more about evil than you think."

"I'm not talking about your family," said Pat. "You're the expert on mages or gods or whatever you people are. I'm talking about—people in general. Regular people. Even people who mean well. You're so trusting! You came here to Parry McCluer and you decide you're going to be friends with us, and why? Because the principal assigned Laurette to be your guide on your first day, and you just had to tease her and sit down with us and how *did* you choose us?"

Danny had no answer to that. "I was going with the flow. If I hadn't liked you guys, I wouldn't have stayed around."

"But you didn't like us," said Pat. "I mean, how could you? We're a *mess*, every one of us, weird on the outside and certifiably insane underneath that repellent exterior."

"But Laurette has nice cleavage, and I am of the heterosexual persuasion," said Danny. "Maybe that's all it is."

"You're *not* one of those panting morons," said Pat. "And in fact we really *are* pretty decent people, so you could have chosen a lot worse friends. My point is that you didn't know, you had no idea who we were, but you plunged right in as if we were friends and. And."

"And then we became friends," said Danny. "But isn't that how it's done?"

"No!" said Pat. "It takes time!"

"I didn't have time," said Danny. "I've only got a couple of years of high school and look, don't you know how I was raised? I've told you—I never met anybody outside the Family. When I went to DC I only met a handful of people and one of them became a dear friend, one of them was a user who thought I was his ticket to easy street, the perfect burglar. One was a girl who really has the memories that your shrink tried to implant in you, and so she was completely unpredictable and selfish. One was her husband, for reasons I never understood. And then there was the convenience store owner who tried to murder me and my burglarizing partner, and the store owner's assistant who I talked into murdering him and—am I boring you?"

Pat was covering her face with her hands. She shook her head without uncovering. "I'm so stupid," she said. "I want to die."

"Please don't," said Danny. "The police would wonder why my fingerprints were all over your back."

She laughed in spite of herself. "I'm coming to warn you and you know more than I do. You know more about everything."

"No, I don't know anything at all. Really, I just gave you a complete list of *all* the people I knew in DC, my complete resume as a friend-maker. Unless you count the Silvermans and Veevee, but they kind of had an introduction to me and believe me, I didn't do all that good a job of making friends with them, either. But I had to, don't you see? I was on the run, my Family was after me to kill me, I had no idea how to live outside the Family compound. I had to make friends with people and only find out later whether I could trust them. Like Hermia, at first I thought she was out to kill me, but—"

"That's my point," said Pat, uncovering her face. "That girl. She is not your friend."

Danny shook his head. "You don't know anything about her."

"I know nothing about her. But she. Is. Not. Your. Friend."

"This is about Hermia? You came here to warn me about Hermia?"

"I came here to beg you to be careful. You trust people that you shouldn't trust."

"I trust *you*," said Danny. "I let you into my house late at night. I listen to you because I believe you really are my friend. Why should I trust you and not her?"

"What could I do to you?" asked Pat. "But she—she can hurt you."

"I'm not falling in love with her, if that's what you think," said Danny. "She's older than me. But she's like Veevee—a fellow gatemage. She taught me how to lock my own gates—she took terrible risks to follow me and we teach each other. We help each other."

"See, that's it," said Pat. "She's using you."

"And I'm using her."

"No, she's *using* you. It's all calculation, it's all—"

"And you know this how?"

"I just do! She needs you right now, but the minute she doesn't, the minute she sees some advantage in betraying you—"

"But that might be true of anybody," said Danny.

"No," said Pat.

"Yes!" insisted Danny. "People are human, even people like me. You can trust people until you can't. They mean what they say until they don't."

"That's where you're wrong," said Pat. "People aren't all like that. There are people you can count on because they'd die before they'd betray you or even let you down."

Danny thought about that. It was a strange way of looking at the world. "I've read a lot of history," said Danny. "It filled the time when the other kids were learning magery. And I don't think I remember ever reading about anybody who wasn't human, with all the normal failings."

"Then you better go back and read again," said Pat. "Joan of Arc, for instance."

"What about her?" said Danny.

"She was absolutely true to her voices. She never denied them."

"Well, actually, she did."

"She was tricked and trapped and she recanted and died for it because in the end she was *true*. There are people like that."

"Lunatics?" said Danny.

"Don't joke, buddy-boy," said Pat, "because I'm serious. Your cynical attitude about people is mostly right, but there really are good people who can be counted on."

"My attitude isn't cynical, it's realistic. Who else is on your list, besides the girl who heard voices?"

"And led armies, and created France as a nation."

"I apologize to dead Jeanne d'Arc for speaking of her so lightly."

"There was Jesus," said Pat.

That took Danny aback. "What about him?"

"True to his word. A true friend."

"To whom?"

"To everybody," said Pat.

"You're a Christian," said Danny.

"What about it if I am?" said Pat. "Even if you don't think he died for your sins, *he* thought he did. And he went ahead with it, he was true to his word."

He didn't bother explaining to her that the Families just thought of Jesus and Mohammed and Moses and Elijah as Semitics. Mages, but not from the Families, not from Westil. "Jesus and Joan of Arc," he said. "Not a very long list."

"They're famous, that's all," said Pat. "The list is very, very long. There are millions of people who gave their word and then kept it, even at the cost of their own lives, at the cost of terrible agony. Soldiers who did brave things and died. Businessmen who kept true to bad contracts and lost everything, but they gave their word. There are people like that!"

"All right," said Danny. "I believe it." And when he thought about it, he wondered. "Am I one of them?" he asked.

"I think you are," said Pat.

"I'm a prankster, I lie all the time, I'm good at it, I conned people out of their money all the way to DC. But I also try to keep my promises. This is so weird. Is it possible that I'm actually an honest man?"

"I don't know," said Pat. "That's not my point."

"I know," said Danny. "You didn't come to tell me that *I'm* virtuous. You came here to tell me that *you* are."

Pat sat very still, thinking. "Yes," she said. "That *is* why I came."

"To tell me that you're not Xena, who just wants to have a baby with the most powerful man she's ever met," said Danny. "And you're not like Hermia, who's just using me and letting me use her because by helping each other we both gain. With you it isn't a bargain or a trade, and it isn't because you want to get something from me."

Pat was crying now. "Yes."

Danny got up and sat on the couch beside her and she nestled against his shoulder and he put his arm around her and she cried. "You came here to tell me that you're my true friend and that I can count on you in a way I can't count on anybody else."

She nodded against his shoulder.

"You came to tell me that you love me."

She pulled away, turned and flopped down against the other arm of the couch and cried even harder. "I'm so stupid," she said. "If I'd known that was what I came to say I wouldn't have come!"

Danny put his hand on her back and she did not recoil. He stroked her gently and said, "You came to tell me that you're the best of my friends, that you're the truest, the most reliable. That you don't think this magery is cool, you think it's dangerous, and I'm in danger, and you don't want anything bad to happen to me, because what you care about isn't power or coolness. It's me. You care about me."

She nodded, and she wasn't crying now. His hand was stroking her back, and when she sat up his arm stayed around her and she turned her tear-soaked, red-eyed face to him and he kissed her.

It wasn't like with Lana. Yes, it was, in that his body approved of what was happening. But he wasn't afraid. He took her at her word. He trusted her. And he realized that in all his conversations with his friends at high school, Pat was the only one he actually listened to with any expectation that her words would matter to him at the level of reality rather than entertainment.

Which wasn't strictly true, he realized. He respected Hal and liked him and he thought Hal was also worth listening to. But he wasn't like Pat. He didn't see as clearly and harshly and truthfully as Pat did. Hal told the truth as far as he knew it—but Pat was far more likely to know true things, so her honesty was more valuable. More reliable.

Meaning I can use her.

Danny hated the thought as soon as it came to his mind. It was an ugly bit of self-knowledge. He broke off the kiss.

"Please," said Pat, and tried to resume it.

"No," said Danny.

Pat nodded and sat back, facing forward, like a scolded schoolgirl.

"Oh, I want to kiss you," said Danny. "You're the only woman I've actually felt this way about, though I didn't realize it until just now. I really do trust you and respect you and you're my true friend, which is what you came to say and you said it and you're right and I believe you. But here's the thing. I'm not as good as you. I use people. I can count on you, but can you count on me?"

She gave a little shrug. "I can't control that," she said. "I can only control what *I* do."

"Well, I can control what *I* do," said Danny. "My body wants you right now. Tonight. You understand me? And if I hadn't stopped kissing you just now, you would have let me sleep with you, am I right?"

She bent forward and hid her face in her hands again. "I'm a terrible Christian," she said.

"But I don't want to be that guy," said Danny.

"What guy?"

"The guy who sleeps with a woman because he can. Like most of the guys in our Family history. Those gods who got women pregnant all over mythology. I'm not as good as you are, Pat, but I'm better than *they* are. Loving me is going to do nothing but make you miserable."

Pat got up from the couch.

"Please," said Danny.

"I have to get home to bed," said Pat. "My folks will worry. They're worriers."

"But you would have stayed the night with me."

"Because then *you* would be my family. But you're not. They are. I have to go."

"I didn't lie to you," said Danny. "I could have."

She stood at the partly open door. "I know that," she said. "You've been straight with me. You're even better than I thought you were. I love you more than I thought I did. You love *me* more than either of us thought you could. We're never going to sleep together, I'm not going to be the woman in your life, and yet right now I'm as happy as I've ever been in my whole life. Go figure." Then she went through the door and closed it behind her.

I am the stupidest guy in the whole world, thought Danny. I let her go out that door without saying a single word more.

But Danny also knew that his decision was the right one. His desire for her was far more than the fleeting interest he had had in Xena, which was based entirely on Xena's eagerness. What he didn't know was whether his desire for Pat was also based on her availability. Maybe Pat was simply more the kind of woman that he was attracted to—quiet, smart, truthful, a little sharp-tongued but also kind-hearted. Sort of like Leslie. Sort of like Mama. Maybe that's the kind of woman he would always fall for, and she simply happened to be the first.

He was about to do the most dangerous things in his already-dangerous life. Whether his attraction to her was just momentary or he really loved her in a stay-true-your-whole-life kind of way, this was not the time to complicate things. Besides, what if the Families had spies watching him? What if she had stayed the night? Then he'd be putting her in danger of being used as a hostage. Or of being tortured or killed because that would be a way to hurt him, the Gatefather that was always out of their direct reach.

He was right to break off that kiss and she was right to leave and that was how it had to be.

And how did it begin? With him touching her as he ushered her to sit down.

Did he unconsciously know even then where her visit to him was going to lead? Did he know deep inside that he felt something stronger for her than for any other woman he knew?

No.

He touched Pat because that's what Marion did when he was bringing a guest into his house. Always the hand on the back, guiding them in. Marion was something of a toucher. Danny wasn't. But without realizing it, he had picked up the idea that when you have a guest, and you want to bring them in, you put your hand on their back to guide and accompany them.

Danny had never had an actual guest at his house before, and so when Pat showed up alone, unexpected, Danny, in his nervousness, unconsciously followed the pattern he had observed with Marion Silverman.

That's all it had been.

But where it led was to a place much deeper than that. Pat was the smartest of his friends, the most mature. Her caustic nature partly came from the fact that she stood outside everything, observing. The way Danny had always been a permanent outsider. She was the one who was most like Danny, at least in the way she dealt with people. Always detached. Always cautious, analyzing.

Except I'm not cautious. And where she's silent, I talk, I say things. In fact, Pat is nothing like me and I'm nothing like her, but I'd be a better person if I were.

Then again, she'd be a happier person if she were a little more like me. Wouldn't she? She always seems so sour.

Stop thinking about it, he told himself as he took his pants back off, and his underwear and socks, and slid into bed to try to sleep. Stop thinking about it.

But he didn't stop. Pat was all over his thoughts before he

slept, and while he slept, and he woke up thinking about her in the morning, cursing himself for a fool as he prepared to head over to Coach Lieder's house. The last thing he needed was to have a woman on his mind.

10

Confession

Wad gated to the farming village in the high country of Iceway. He appeared near the public well, so that there was no chance that his manner of arrival would go unremarked. He came showing his power: A gatemage is in the world, and he came here, and he walked from this well directly to the house where the strange woman and her two damaged, terrified sons were brought only a few days ago.

It was the house of Roop and Levet where Wad walked. Inside, he found—as he expected—that the eldest daughter, Eko, was tending to Anonoei, the onetime concubine of King Prayard, and her two sons, eight-year-old Eluik and six-year-old Enopp.

The boys had spent the past two years in total isolation, living like tortured animals. For Enopp especially, the two-year imprisonment had been more than half his life, for who remembers anything before the age of three? Their imprisonment had ended in terror and violence, with soldiers stabbing at them; and then they had been magically gated to this high mountain place, to be cared for by strangers, and their wounds healed, and their mother restored to them, and her children restored to her, and all was . . .

Not well. Wad did not expect things to be well at all.

The boys did not speak, but they saw him come in. They did not fear him. If they thought of him in any way, it would come from the fact that they had seen him magically heal wounds, that he had arranged for them to be fed and kept warm. They would think of him as the great mage who had rescued them from hell. If they were capable of rational thought at all.

Wad was looking at the boys, who were looking at him. Anonoei was looking down at the table, where she was chopping an onion. Chopping it very, very fine.

It was Eko, the eldest daughter of the house, who spoke first. "The man in the tree," she said. "Have I done well with them? Do they look strong to you?"

"Yes," said Wad.

"The boys don't speak to me or anyone but their mother and each other. The younger one doesn't speak even to them. The mother speaks to me now and then. I haven't pressed them. I think something terrible has happened to them."

"It has," said Wad.

"He saved us," murmured Anonoei.

"Yes," said Wad. "I did. But before we can proceed any further, I have to make sure you understand everything that I did, and why I did it. Only then is there a chance that we can work together to try to undo some portion of my crimes."

Anonoei looked up then. "*Your* crimes?"

"I know you remember me," said Wad. "I know you saw me spying on you from the rafters, back when you were King Prayard's mistress and lay with him in the castle where another woman was the queen."

"That *was* you," she said.

"You winked at me," said Wad.

"You saw us, and you said nothing, though I knew not and know not why. But I winked at you, to show you that I knew you were there, and that I, too, would say nothing. That's why I recognized you when you snatched us out of our prison cells when the soldiers were trying to kill us. When you brought us to the snow, I thought I knew you, but I couldn't think when or how we met. I thought you were a strange kitchen boy. But you were really a great mage, a gatemage, all along."

"I was, though at the time I barely knew it myself," said Wad.

"A gatemage," whispered Eko. "But living in a tree."

"That's one story," said Wad to Eko. "But I'm here to tell another. About how some men came to murder Queen Bexoi and I, appointing myself as her protector, warned her and saved her life. I showed her then the kind of mage I was, and she showed me the kind of mage *she* was."

"Bexoi?" said Anonoei with contempt. "A Sparrowfriend!"

"That was her disguise. She's a Firemaster at least, if not a Lightrider. And she has the power to make a self-clant so perfect that not only could it speak in her voice, but also when the assassin stabbed it, it bled, and the blood spilled onto the sheets."

Anonoei touched her fingers to her lips.

"No one knew but me. I saw it with my own eyes. I was proud that she trusted me. I became her lover. She bore my son and pretended it was Prayard's."

"The baby was yours?" said Anonoei. "So Prayard didn't lie when he told me that he never put his seed in her." She looked away.

"He was faithful to you," said Wad. "And you joined in plotting against him and against the Queen. I know you were guilty of that, and you know what the penalty would have been, had you been caught."

"Never against *him*," she said. "And I was part of no plot. They told me to pack for a journey, for myself and my sons."

"You knew what it meant."

She did not disagree.

"Bexoi wanted me to get you out of the way. I loved her and I did her bidding. But I also distrusted her even then, and so I didn't kill you. What I did was worse. I took you and your two dangerous sons, and I put you in the mouths of old slag tunnels in the face of the cliff, and I made gates that caught you if you fell and put you back at the top of the cave, so you lived in constant torment, always about to fall, never able to end your captivity by leaping from the cell. That was my idea, my plan. That was how I saved you alive. How I punished you and your innocent sons, because you posed a threat to the woman I loved, and to my son that she was bearing."

"That's a poor excuse," said Eko boldly.

"It's no excuse at all," said Wad, turning to the girl. "It was a monstrous crime against the three of them, and I did it. I thought of it and I carried it out and no one knew that they were there except for me. I stole food and gave it to them. As time went on the food grew better and I made their imprisonment more bearable. When the Queen learned that they were still alive and demanded that I kill them, I disobeyed her. There are a few things in my favor."

Wad turned back to Anonoei. "But nothing makes up for the evil that I did. I tormented you and your sons. Whatever terrors and dark visions inhabit their minds, I caused."

Wad looked at the boys, for his eye caught some motion. It was the younger one, Enopp. He had broken his gaze at Wad and was now looking at his brother and then his mother. His face showed some animation for the first time. But Eluik remained dead-eyed, his gaze still riveted on Wad.

"Whomever you blamed and whomever you hated there in your prison cells, and whomever you feared, I was your captor, your jailer, your torturer. What does it matter that I despised myself for what I had done to you? I continued to do it.

"So let me give you some consolation. Queen Bexoi got the King to sleep with her. You were gone, and so were your sons. He believed that my boy was his own, and now he came to love the Queen, and he wanted to give her a baby. So he begot a child upon her. And then she didn't need my little bastard anymore.

"My son, whom she called Oath and I called Trick, was now a danger to Prayard's true son. He was also the only person that I loved, once I understood that Bexoi had used me, had never loved me. So she murdered my boy and tried to murder me. On the day I released you from the cells where I had kept you, that was when she killed my son.

"If she had killed me as she meant to, I couldn't have saved you, and you'd be dead as well. But I escaped from her, and I rescued you. But don't imagine that I had repented of my crimes against you. I meant to let you out someday, and I tried to make your imprisonment more bearable, but I was not about to let you go. It was Bexoi's monstrous murder of her own child, of *our* child, and her open try at killing me that finally made me let you go.

"You see that I don't pretty up my actions. Bexoi is a monster, but so am I. If I'm better than her it's only because I kept you alive and didn't murder you right out. But is that really better? Weren't you just the prey that the spider binds up and hides away to devour another day? I kept you as a tool to use against her, when the time came."

Wad fell silent. Eko looked at him in a kind of fascinated horror. He doubted that the boys understood, though the younger one at least seemed interested. Anonoei, though . . . she understood all.

"This is that time," she said. "The time to use us as tools against her."

"No," said Wad. "You're far too weak, and so am I. I was once the greatest gatemage that the worlds had ever known, but now there is a greater one than I. He took all but a few of my gates. I am no match for Bexoi now, and you are most certainly no match for her. I came here to set you free of me, since I'm no use to anyone. I came here to tell you the truth so you would know your enemies. So you would hate the right people, when it was time to hate. Prayard had no hand in what happened to you. He searched for you and he grieved for you, but you were beyond his finding, and when he came to love Bexoi it was only in the firm belief that you were dead."

Anonoei shook her head and laughed bitterly. "Foolish boy—or are you older than you look? Don't you know that Bexoi was not the only one to hide her magery? Like you, I am a mage, but of a kind forbidden."

Wad had to think for a moment, because if she had been a gatemage, she could have gotten herself and her sons out of prison any time she wanted.

"A manmage," he said.

"Not a great mage by any means," she said. "But yes, I realized my power when I came of age. When I could flatter people into doing anything I wanted. I began to realize that once I owned them, they were mine. I owned Prayard. Do you understand me? He didn't fall in love with me. I decided to own him and I did."

Wad thought for a moment and then he laughed. "Well, it doesn't make any of my actions better than they were, but it's nice to know that I'm a monster among monsters. These boys, then—the sons of two mages and not just one."

"I imagine they'll have some talent for this or that when they get older," said Anonoei. "Maybe even the much-sought-after seamagery. Or maybe one of them will be a gatemage by and by."

"It'll be me," said the younger one, Enopp. "I'll be a gatemage!"

Eko clapped her hands together. "He spoke!"

Anonoei rushed to her younger son and embraced him. "Oh, my baby, no, you can't just decide, the power chooses you, it's already inside you and someday you'll find out what it is."

But Enopp kept looking at Wad. "A gatemage," he said. "Because you can go wherever you want."

It was in that moment, in those words, that Wad first realized what he had to do. He had come to this place with no plan other than to tell the truth and then take them wherever Anonoei decided they should go. But he heard Enopp's innocent words as if they were a recipe for how he might possibly redeem himself. How he might really help Anonoei. How he might get the power to undo Bexoi and destroy her root and branch.

Go wherever I want, the boy said, but Wad knew that he could not. He did not have gates enough inside him now to make a Great Gate, so he could not go to Mittlegard. But then he realized that he could. That there *was* a Great Gate, a wild one, controlled by no mage now. Danny North could not lock it and so anyone who knew of its existence could make use of it. Wad could pass through that Wild Gate and go to Mittlegard and back again, restoring what power he had left to its full strength. It would not get him back his gates—Danny North still had those safely locked inside a place where Wad could never go against the young Gatefather's will. But it would sharpen his faculties, bring him back to the state he had once been in, when he saw all the gates in the world, even the gates of the Semitic gods, and he ate them all.

Unlike Danny North, he had not been fool enough to try to *use* the captive gates, but he had found them and held them. He could make himself that strong a mage again. He could restore his own vision, the range of his seeing.

And if he could take himself to Mittlegard and back again, he could take Anonoei as well.

But perhaps not. Wad was a gatemage who knew how to rule over the lost and disobedient outselves that were woven into the Wild Gate. Anonoei could not resist them. Manmage that she was, she would know that they were there, but not the form they took. They might entice her out of herself. They might entwine her in the Great Gate. And because she was a manmage, they would only be fulfilling the law by taking away her power.

No, if Wad were really to strengthen her so she might be a

match for Bexoi, he would have to get Danny North to help him hold the Great Gate open for her. He would have to *teach* him what to do, to train the man who bested him so that he could never be defeated and Wad could never get his lost gates back.

How could he give even more power and wisdom to the mage who had shattered him?

Because I deserved the shattering, thought Wad. He was an instrument in the hands of spacetime and so I got what I deserved. I misused my power and so I lost all but a tiny shred of it. And I will have to go as supplicant to Danny North, to get him to help me make amends for how I raised the monstrous Bexoi to be mistress of Iceway.

All of this came to him between Enopp's words and Wad's answer to him.

"I see that your outself may indeed be divisible," said Wad. It was true enough—the outselves of all children might be divisible, and those that were going to be gatemages would be the most divisible of all. But there was no way to tell at such a young age. "But things like that take time. No one knows what you'll become."

Anonoei looked at Wad. "For you he speaks," she said.

"He sees my power," said Wad. "He's too young to understand my wickedness."

"The wickedness of all the mages," said Anonoei. "What did I ever do but seek to advance myself?"

"And love your children."

"Look at the danger I put them in," said Anonoei.

"Their very conception was dangerous," said Wad. "But all children are born into a world of danger, where they're bound to die."

"Listen to the two of you," said Eko.

They looked at her, surprised that such a quiet, mousy person would speak to mages of their kind.

"Bragging about who is most monstrous," said Eko.

Was I bragging? Wad asked himself.

"Monstrous or not," said Anonoei, "I want revenge."

"I came here so you could have it," said Wad. "Against me, if you choose. I will not gate away."

"And what then?" asked Anonoei. "Without your help, what vengeance can I have on *her*?"

"Promise me this," said Wad. "That you will not harm her baby."

"This from the man who—"

"I know what I did to your sons," said Wad. "I'm telling you now that if you harm her baby, you will not be able to live with it. I know what I'm talking about. No matter how you rage against her, her baby has done nothing. Your children did not deserve to suffer, even though their existence posed a danger to my son. My son did not deserve to die, even though his existence posed a danger to this new child of Prayard's and Bexoi's. And their son does not deserve to die."

"So this is the root you've found for your morality?" asked Anonoei. "Do what you want, just don't hurt the children?"

"For lack of any deeper root, that will have to do for now," he said. "Agree to that, or kill me now, because I'll never help you get revenge against a child. I've gone down that road and it's too terrible to travel on again."

"There's no way that we could hurt her more," said Anonoei.

"But what good is it to hurt her, if we destroy ourselves in the process?" asked Wad.

"Listen to the two of you," Eko said again. "All your power, and all it is to you is a means to get revenge."

Wad looked at her sadly. "I tried to save the world, once upon a time, but what I was saving it *for* I still don't know, and in the end I failed."

"Then try again," said Eko. "The world's as much in need of saving as it ever was, and somebody ought to try."

Anonoei put her arms around her sons. "This is all the world I care about now."

"If that were true," said Eko, "you wouldn't be plotting vengeance on a queen, a firemage. You'd be looking for a place to take your sons where they'd be safe."

"I thought I had that here," said Anonoei.

"We're in Iceway, and your enemy's the queen," said Eko. "And by the way, Man-in-the-Tree, thanks for bringing the king's missing mistress to our house. That will help us prosper, you can be sure."

"I didn't know anywhere else to take them," said Wad.

"Well, I've done what you wanted. And I'm not turning them away even now, though if it's discovered who they are, her enemies will happily kill me and my whole family, don't you think?"

Wad slumped down to sit on the floor of the tiny house. "I think that I'm the puppeteer, pulling strings, but then I trip on them and find that someone else has hold of *my* strings."

"Who?" asked Enopp.

"Fate," said Wad. "Unintended Consequence. That's the only god that's real."

"Do you have an actual plan?" Eko asked Wad.

"Yes," said Wad. "As of this moment, yes, I do."

11

Reunions

Danny hadn't had enough sleep, but his inner clock woke him at exactly the time required for him to make it to Coach Lieder's house for a special practice. Now that Danny had capitulated and ran his fastest for Lieder's stopwatch, he found that he enjoyed it. Showing off, not competing.

Danny was human enough to like being admired, and one thing about Lieder, when he was working with an athlete who was really trying, he knew how to show respect and give encouragement. It was a side of Lieder Danny had never seen, and never would have seen as long as he was with the slackers and geeks.

He was still with the slackers and geeks, but he was also running for the Parry McCluer track team, and even though it was a while before any of the meets would begin, and for all he knew he wouldn't live long enough to compete in any of them, it was fun to get to Lieder's house before sunrise, running the whole way in the dark, and then see how Lieder had laid out fixed courses for him on the streets of Buena Vista, so that he would know just how far Danny was running in a given amount of time.

Now that his friends were all enlisted in the Great Gate project, the only way that Danny still connected with high school life was his running. He had come here to get away from magery and live a normal life; he had brought the magery with him, and running was the only normal thing left for him to do.

This morning, though, Coach Lieder wasn't alone. Nicki, his daughter, was with him, and though she seemed a little sleepy, she didn't have that wan look. That dying-nymph appearance. Her passage through a gate had healed her of whatever she was dying of. Lieder may not know it, but Danny had prepaid him for all the private track coaching. And yet it had cost Danny nothing. The effortless gift of a god. Need healing? Well here it is, because why not.

But just because it cost Danny so little didn't change the fact that she was dying, and now she would live. Maybe that had something to do with why Lieder was more encouraging than Danny had expected. After all, he had so much less to feel angry and bitter about.

"Do you mind if Nicki watches?" asked Lieder. "She was up anyway, so . . ."

Did he think he was good at lying? Danny knew that Nicki must have asked him to waken her especially for this. And maybe Lieder was simply indulging his little girl. Or maybe he thought Danny would perform better with a girl watching. Or maybe he hoped something might happen between Danny and his daughter, though why Lieder should wish for such a thing Danny didn't know.

It had to be the first one. Nicki liked Danny—and what's not to like?—and when a daughter who had been *this* close to death now had a crush on a boy, what father wouldn't indulge her? Especially when he was right there to supervise any interaction between them.

Danny felt her eyes on him the whole time. He ran short sprints today—Lieder was keeping him close to the front porch so he was never out of Nicki's sight. And if the idea was that Danny would work harder to impress a girl, it wasn't exactly wrong. He certainly made his best times in the various dashes. And this despite having run the whole way here, and not having had enough sleep the night before.

Last night I was this close to pledging my undying love to Pat, and this morning I'm showing off for Nicki. I'm such a teenage boy. Which is to say, I'm such a fickle jerk.

Well, running in front of a girl wasn't kissing her. There was a difference and he'd keep it well in mind.

Even in the cool of an autumn morning, Danny was dripping with sweat. He had really given it his all, and he knew that sweat wasn't unattractive to girls, not when it had been earned by real exertion, not when the guy doing the sweating had an athletic build. It was only sweaty fat kids and geeks that turned high school girls off. Danny had learned this from his reading of young adult novels during the years he was studying to prepare to be a normal high school student.

"Hi," he said to Nicki when Lieder beckoned him to the porch. She gave him a little wave and a shy smile.

Lieder ignored the exchange between them and began reading off the times. "And you ran here, right?"

"Yes, sir," said Danny.

"So the idea is to have these sprints in you at the end of a long race. To pace yourself so that you stay in contention but you don't have to lead."

"You know that I don't care about leading," said Danny.

"But the team needs you to win. To rack up points. So not for yourself, but for the team. You stay close enough to be in contention, but sprints like these are still inside you."

"Why not just have me run the sprints?" asked Danny.

"I've got guys who can do the sprints. They're not as fast as you, but they win enough. I need you in long distance. You're a coin I can only spend once or twice in a meet. I'm not going to use you up on the short stuff."

"You want me to be a quarter, not five pennies, is that it?"

"Yeah, smart guy," said Lieder. "I want you to be a damn Susan B. Anthony dollar."

"But fifty cents will do," said Nicki. "He wants you to try for the dollar so you might make the fifty cents."

Lieder reddened. If any other kid had said such a thing, he would have been angry. But it was his daughter, so the redness went away quickly. "She thinks she sees through her old man," he said with a smile. "But I want the buck. I want a buck fifty."

"Well, I better get home and shower," said Danny.

"Oh," said Nicki. She looked disappointed. Then, realizing that Danny was looking at her curiously, she stepped back and turned away, embarrassed.

"Nicki's going back to school today. She was kind of hoping you might ride with us."

Danny indicated his dripping shorts and tee-shirt. "I can't go like this."

"You could shower here," said Nicki. Then she covered her mouth as if to keep more words from coming out.

"And put these back on?" said Danny, laughing.

"Look," said Lieder, "Nicki's right. I've worn you out with sprints. Now if you run all the way home and shower and change you'll be late to school."

It was true. They had gone long.

"You shower, and throw on something of mine. It'll be baggy on you, considering that you're made of toothpicks, but we'll swing by your house and you run in to change. We'll wait."

Danny considered for a moment. It was a very generous thing. But could he afford to arrive at high school in Lieder's car?

"How about if you drive me home and drop me off? Then I can walk to school on time."

"Well, I'm not letting you get in my car as sweaty as you are right now," said Lieder. He laughed, but . . . was it really so important that he shower at their house?

Danny shrugged and stepped up on the porch. "Whatever I do, I gotta do it now."

Nicki rushed ahead of him and showed him to the house's one bathroom. It really was an old place. But the tub was modern enough—it wasn't sitting on claw feet, it was molded to the floor, and instead of a shower curtain there was a glass door.

He turned on the water and heard Nicki close the door behind him. He got his shoes and clothes off as soon as the door was closed and by then the shower was steaming a little. He got in and was washing his hair with regular soap when he heard the door open.

"Not looking not looking," said Nicki. He couldn't look because he'd get soap in his eyes so he'd have to take her word for it.

When he got out there was a towel laid out for him, and a pair of pants and a shirt in a style no self-respecting kid would wear. No underwear. His own clothes were nowhere to be seen. She must have taken them.

She was going to wash them for him. She was showing him how domestic she was.

No, she was trying to do something nice. Give her credit for being kind. Don't assume that girls want your body just because Xena does. Xena knows you're, like, a Norse god.

The only way the pants would stay up was if he held them with one hand while he held his shoes with the other. He went barefoot out of the bathroom. "Somebody stole my clothes," he said, "but we'll have to search for the thief later, when I'm wearing pants I can run in."

Lieder laughed. "I didn't think anybody could look worse in those clothes than me."

"He doesn't," said Nicki. Then blushed. Then laughed.

"Can I make it to your car barefoot? There's not any, like, gravel or hot coals or anything?" Their driveway was gravel, but it ran around the back of the house.

"It's all paved," said Lieder. "Back door."

Danny followed Nicki out the door, catching the screen with his shoulder because both hands were occupied. Only after he was through the door did she remember and turn back to hold it open for him, and so her reaching hand smacked him in the chest.

"Ow," she said. "Your chest is hard!"

"Sorry it got in your way," said Danny. "Like your dad said, all toothpicks."

Then she led the way to the car, which stood on a paved carport pad. There was loose gravel all over, though, so Danny had to pick his way carefully to the back door. Nicki ran around and got in the front passenger side, and Lieder backed them down the driveway and out into the street.

Only now did Danny realize that they didn't know where he lived—nobody knew that except his friends. Unless they had looked up his school records. Which they must have done, because Lieder drove right there without any directions.

Of course, in the days when Lieder was spying on him to try to catch him running and time him, he might have seen where Danny ran to after school. Surely he hadn't planned this out far enough in advance to consult the school records.

"Thanks," said Danny as he got out of the car. "I'll bring these clothes back to you at school."

But they didn't drive off. They followed him up the short walk into his house. That bothered him. He hadn't invited them in. In fact, he had made it clear he wasn't inviting them in. So he had to gather up his clothes that were scattered in the living room and retreat into the bedroom to change.

When he came out, there was Nicki, washing the dishes that

had stacked up by the sink. "You know, if you rinse them right after you use them, they're easier to wash."

"But I don't mind scrubbing," said Danny.

"Now you won't have to," she said, drying her hands. "At least, not the ones I washed."

Danny looked around for the coach.

"Daddy went back to the car. He said this place was too messy for him to find a place he trusted enough to sit there."

"Yeah, well, I wasn't expecting company." Though in fact it had looked just like this when Pat came over last night. Hadn't expected her, either. "We'd better get to the car," he said.

But she didn't get to the car. She walked up to him and put her hands on his waist. Shyly. How does a girl *shyly* do something as bold as that? But she radiated shyness even as her hands rested on his waist just above his jeans, so that her hands were right on the stems of his hips. Her touch was just exactly perfect. And she looked up into his eyes and said, "Danny North, I don't know how you did it, and I haven't dared say this to Daddy, he's just calling it a miracle, but I know you healed me. I don't know how or why, but I felt it that day you visited. I felt it wash over me, and I felt stronger. Every hour, every day since then, stronger. I know you did it. I made Daddy take me to the doctor right away and he said it was all gone. The cancer. I was clean of it. He'd never seen anything like it. He actually asked me if I'd been to a faith healer."

"Had you?" asked Danny.

"No. My healer came to me," she said. "I don't expect any explanations. I don't want to know how you did it. I just know it was you, and thank you." Then she tiptoed to kiss him on the mouth. Full on the mouth. It hadn't even been twelve hours since he kissed Pat, and here he was getting kissed again. Only this girl didn't even know he was a mage. Though she did know, somehow, that he had power, so it amounted to the same thing. Apparently you show a girl you can do real magic, and she's got her mouth on yours as soon as possible.

Are you complaining, you idiot? Is this bad? Do you hate it?

Not really, he had to admit to himself.

And she was still kissing him. And now her arms were around his waist instead of on it, and she was pressed against him, and—

The car horn tooted outside. A house this small and so close to the street, it sounded like the car was right in the living room.

"Thank you," she said again. Whether for the kiss or the healing Danny wasn't sure. For the kiss, he wanted to answer like a store clerk: "Thank *you*."

Instead he just followed her out to the car.

Shy? She showed not a speck of embarrassment when she got out of the front seat and climbed into the back beside him. "It's not right to make him sit alone in the back," she explained to her father.

"But it's fine to leave me alone in the front?" he asked, but he was joking.

Have I got me the coach's daughter for a girlfriend? I'm trapped in a young adult novel. A *girls'* novel, so it's all about the love story instead of the death squads coming to get me.

I already had a triangle with Xena and Pat. What does Nicki make it? A square? No, this is solid geometry now: a tetrahedron.

But at school the strangest thing happened. Nicki made no effort to follow him in. She just waved at him, and it was Lieder who explained, "Got to get her all signed in."

And when Nicki showed up in his first period class partway through—was that arranged on purpose? To have some of the same schedule as him?—she gave no sign that she recognized him. One of the guys near Danny whispered, "Hubba hubba," and for the first time Danny realized that Nicki, now that she wasn't sick-looking, was quite attractive. Not that he had thought she was ugly, but he hadn't realized that she was attractive in general, and not just a nice-seeming person to him in particular. Her shape was high-school-girl slender, but with unmissable breasts, though she wasn't Laurette—there was no cleavage showing. How did I not notice this before? Even when she was kissing me and those breasts were pressed up against me, how did I not notice how they give her a pretty nearly perfect shape?

Nicki turned toward the hubba-hubba guy and gave him the shy smile. What a tease, she can turn it on and off whenever she wants. The come-hither, I'm-so-shy smile that she must have practiced in front of the mirror.

Has she been playing me?

She spent the whole rest of the period *not* playing him. Unless ignoring him *was* the game. She certainly had him thinking about her most of the period. She had spent the morning on the porch in her nightgown and lacy robe watching him sweat, she had come into the bathroom while he was naked in the shower and taken away his clothes, she had come into his house and washed his dishes and then *kissed* him long and with her body pressed to his and now, in this class, she didn't notice he existed?

Two can play at this game, he thought.

But a moment later he realized, no they can't. Girls can play it on guys, but guys can't play it on girls. At least I can't play it, because I keep glancing at her and she never looks at me, it's like I had gone through a gate and was now watching invisibly through a porthole in spacetime, and why would I do that? Because I can't take my eyes off her. She's playing me and it works, I'm just a fish dancing on the line.

He made it a point to eat lunch with his friends, but that was worse, because while everybody else was normal—Xena flirting with him had to be regarded as the new normal—Pat was also playing the I-don't-see-you-you-don't-exist game.

The difference was that he and Pat were friends, and the kiss last night had been his idea probably more than hers.

Or had it? Girls were all manmages, when you thought about it. They wrapped guys around their fingers and dragged them any way they wanted.

First time I've ever envied the gay, thought Danny. But then he had to admit to himself, being honest, that he felt nothing of the kind. This was all kind of exciting. Complicated, yes. A little dangerous. But what *had* he come to high school for, if not for the fact that this was where they kept the high school girls?

Just before P.E. in the afternoon, a freshman doing office time for some freshman sin brought him a note from the principal. "Come see me right now," it said.

"What did you do without asking us along?" asked Wheeler.

"Nothing," said Danny. "I'm on Lieder's team, why is he bothering me?"

"Want company?" asked Hal.

"Looking for an excuse to ditch P.E.?" asked Danny.

"Always."

"Don't worry. Lieder's in a better mood. His daughter's all better and she's even back in school."

"I didn't know he had a daughter," said Hal.

"Or that she was sick," said Wheeler.

"Somebody mated with Lieder?" asked Hal.

"He has a job," said Danny. "There's always some woman who wants a man with a job."

"Really?" asked Wheeler. "That's the first time anybody ever gave me a reason why I should graduate from high school. So I can get the kind of job that will make a woman want to mate with me."

"Naw," said Hal. "No way. You're going to have to swim upstream and spawn."

With that Danny left them and jogged to the office.

Mama and Baba were sitting on chairs across from the principal's desk. Baba at once rose to his feet. "Danny," he said, "we're your Uncle Alf and Auntie Gerd. I know you haven't seen us in a long time, but when we heard you were living here with your Aunt Veevee gone half the time, well, we had to look in on you."

"We had no idea his guardian was absentee."

"She's not," said Danny. "We see each other nearly every day. It's these people that I don't know. Did you ask them for I.D.?"

Baba chuckled. "We just want a chance to talk to you, Danny."

"We didn't know how else to do it," said Mama. "You don't answer your phone."

"I don't *have* a phone," said Danny.

"You see our problem," said Baba. "But Principal Massey kindly offered us the use of his office for our conversation."

"No," said Danny, walking back out of the office.

"Come back here, young man!" demanded Massey.

Mama followed him. "Please," she whispered. "Please, I beg you. If you have any feeling for me at all."

"I spent most of my life with feeling for you," whispered Danny. "It almost led to Hammernip Hill. Should I tell the principal to ask the sheriff to do some excavating there?"

"Please," she said.

Principal Massey had followed them out into the corridor by then. "Danny North, that was the rudest thing I've seen you do—and that takes some doing."

"I don't remember a single act of kindness from these people," said Danny. "I'm settled in here now and I don't know what they want from me. Don't you have rules about letting strangers have access to the children in this school?"

"But . . ." Principal Massey reached his hands out helplessly, one toward Danny, one toward his parents. "It didn't occur to me that they might be strangers. I still don't believe they are. They look so much like you."

Danny had no answer to that. It had never crossed his mind that he could not deny being his father's son, let alone his nephew. He looked just like Baba. Except for the fact that he also had a strong resemblance to Mama. Both resemblances in the same face, at the same time. If Principal Massey had half a brain in his head, he'd wonder why anybody looked so much like *both* his aunt *and* his uncle, one of whom, presumably, was not his blood relative.

"We'll talk out in the parking lot," said Danny. "We'll talk where I can walk away if I feel like it." And where nobody can listen through a door. And nobody can sneak up unobserved.

"Well, that's all right then," said Massey.

"In fact, we'll talk out on the street, which isn't school property. Then you won't get in trouble, Principal Massey."

"Very . . . thoughtful of you."

They left him behind and walked in virtual silence until they were beyond the parking lot and across the street. Virtual silence, because Mama kept trying to talk and Danny gave her a sharp *sh!* and walked faster. Finally they were so out of breath from keeping up with a young man who was, after all, a sprinter that they couldn't have spoken if they tried.

"I told you the terms," said Danny. "I told you that I'd come for your answer. I told you not to come for me. As far as I'm concerned, there's no Great Gate for you. You'd have been too dangerous, anyway. The two of you."

"We aren't the ones the Family chose," said Baba. "I'm not Odin anymore."

"They took back Gyish? Or was it Zog?"

"It was Mook," said Baba. "They couldn't trust me to make an unbiased decision because I was your father and because they all know now how we plotted to keep you even after we knew you were a gatemage. We're lucky we aren't in Hammernip, for putting the family at such a risk."

Danny wanted to say, Boo-hoo. But he realized that Baba was telling the truth. He and Mama *had* taken a risk, knowing about him but not killing him. They had risked everything.

"So Mook will have an answer for you. We're not invited to the councils," said Mama.

"Why are you here, then? To ask for a private passage through the Great Gate? Here's news for you—it hasn't been built yet, and I meant what I said. No special favors for anyone, no extras."

"It's not about the Great Gate," said Baba impatiently. "It's about us. As your parents. What did you expect us to do? We hoped you'd be a gatemage. All right? We didn't hope for any baby at all, we hoped for you, very specifically. A tricky, mouthy, linguistically brilliant brat with no loyalty to anyone, because that's what gatemages *are*. We hoped you'd open a passage to Westil, yes. Of course we did. Before we knew you, we expected to be able to use you."

"And you still do," said Danny.

"Because we're not insane," said Baba. "You exist. Everybody wants to pass through a Great Gate. What do you expect, that we alone, of all the Westilians in Mittlegard, would care only about our beloved boy, with not a thought about the gates that we created you to make?"

"I don't expect anything from you," said Danny, "which is a good thing, because 'anything' was what I never got."

"Danny, we gave you all we could," said Mama. She came closer. "And I don't just mean life itself. We had Mook and Lummy look after you. Feed you when you stayed late. Listen to your questions and answer them. Watch out for you to give you warning if you did something dangerous. We made sure that Thor was in charge of the watchers, so that if you needed to get away, you wouldn't be caught."

"If we stayed close to you," said Baba, "then the Family would never trust us to be impartial when it came time for decisions about you. We could either have the power to protect you, or we could be your loving affectionate parents. Not both."

Danny knew that this was true. He had always known it.

Mama interpreted his silence as a kind of victory, and she pressed the advantage. She placed her hand on his upper arm, not gripping it, exactly. Just holding him.

But he had been touched by enough women in the past

twenty-four hours. He was done with being betrayed by his natural reaction to physical touch. A bit of physical affection from his long-absent mother? It sent a thrill of relief through him. He wasn't having any of it. He shrugged away and backed up a step.

"Touch me again and you're out of here," Danny said.

Mama gave something like a sob and stepped away, holding the hand that had held him in her other hand, as if she had been devastatingly wounded, as if the hand were pumping out blood and the injury could not be healed.

"We were proud of you," said Baba, not even glancing at his wife's reaction. "You were so clever. You understood your danger—not gatemage danger, but drekka danger. You kept your head down. You kept trying to find ways to survive. We saw it and admired you and respected you. I don't know if I would have had the self-control to handle myself as you did. The trickster boy you were as a child disappeared completely, swallowed up in the careful, careful young man who finally found his power and used it to run away and save his life."

"How nice of you to admire me from such a distance," said Danny. But his father's words of praise filled him with light and brought tears to his eyes.

We human beings are such *machines,* thought Danny. All the emotions are available at the flip of a switch. Predictable as robots.

"Danny," said Mama. "I get it that you hate us. I do understand it."

But Danny didn't hate them. He was angry with them, had been hurt by them, but no, he didn't hate them. After everything, all he really wanted was his mother's affection and his father's approval. Now they were offering exactly what he wanted. Only these things had been so long withheld that Danny refused to trust the fulfillment of his longing.

"Whatever you want from me," said Danny, "I don't have it. Or if I do, it's not for you, not anymore."

"That's what I was afraid of," said Mama.

"I told her not to expect anything better than this," said Baba.

For a moment, hearing such finality in Baba's voice, Danny believed that this whole meeting had been a trap. That, having failed to win him over, they would now unleash whatever assassination they had planned for him.

So he gated fifteen feet away.

Mother burst into tears.

"We aren't going to betray you," said Baba coldly. "How could we, even if we wanted to?"

"Let's go, Alf," said Mama.

"Yes," said Baba. He led her away toward the family pickup—which looked even more beaten-up now, having spent a short time buried in a crevice in the earth.

Watching them walk toward the truck, Danny saw them for the first time, not as the crafty leaders of a group of ruthless mages, but as a middle-aged man and woman, weary of everything, having been repudiated by the ungrateful son who blamed them for having done only what was possible for him, and nothing more.

Danny passed a gate over them. He did it smoothly, carefully. They did not miss a stride. If they felt anything, he would have been surprised. But their steps looked younger, not so tired as they continued to the truck and got inside. He did not wish to punish them. He had thought he did, but now he felt no such desire. He just wanted to stop wanting them to love him. Because now they were saying that they did, and he was hungry to believe them; but they had so many motives to lie that he could not trust a word they said or a thing they did.

12

Mittlegard

Wad and Anonoei were back and forth about what to do with the boys. Eluik and Enopp were young and powerless, but they were the most valuable prize. Without these two sons of King Prayard, potential heirs, Anonoei herself had no leverage in the kingdom. Her personal powers were unsuspected, a necessity for a manmage who wished to stay alive. Only the boys mattered.

Anonoei wanted them kept safe at all costs. So, for that matter, did Wad. But what constituted their safety was where they disagreed.

"You say it's not even your own gate, not under your control," said Anonoei.

"It's not under anyone's control at the moment," said Wad, "but it exists. It works. There is no danger from the gate. Do you think I'd deceive you about such a thing, when I mean to make the passage with you?"

"When they're needed, we'll need them *here,*" said Anonoei. "Who is King Prayard in Mittlegard? What protection will being his sons offer them there?"

"More to the point," said Wad, "their father's nothingness in Mittlegard will *be* their protection. No one in Mittlegard has any reason to want them dead, or any motive to capture them. They'll have the safety of being nobody. While here, everything depends on your being able to trust whomever you leave them with. Who is that person?"

Anonoei named several, but Wad had spent too long as the castle monkey, seeing what everyone did in their private moments. He told sadly true tales about every man and woman that she mentioned. She was soon near tears. "I never had friends," she said.

"No one has friends," said Wad. "I was as true a friend to Bexoi as anyone has ever had. But I kept you alive when she wanted you dead."

"For reasons of your own," said Anonoei.

"I made no claim of generosity," said Wad. "I make none now. But I want your sons alive, and I will trust strangers on Mittlegard more than anyone known to you in Iceway or anywhere on Westil."

"Then I'll stay here myself, watch over them, and wait for you," said Anonoei.

Wad rehearsed the facts to her yet again. How their magical arrival in this high mountain village could not have gone unnoticed. The story would spread, had already spread, would soon float down the Graybourn until it came to the capital city, Kamesham, and then to the castle, Nassassa. There would be no lack of wits in either place, and soon they would put together the woman and two boys who appeared in the high mountains at just the time when a woman and two boys vanished from caves in the cliff face below the castle while soldiers of Prayard attempted to kill them.

"I'm not leaving you here to die," said Wad. "I'll need to move these people who took you in as well, or they'll surely be tortured to find out information that they do not have."

"By 'here' I didn't mean I would stay in this very village. I meant here on Westil, here where we don't have to pass through any gates."

"Stop wasting my time with fears as ridiculous as this. If you were really afraid, you'd try to use your manmagic on me, to get me to comply with your will. But you don't, so clearly you don't mean it."

"Would my manmagic work on you?"

"Until I realized what was happening and gated away, of course it would. I appreciate your showing me the respect of not trying. Likewise, if I wanted to I could gate you and your boys against your will to the mouth of the Great Gate and push you through, and you couldn't do a thing about it. Instead, I'm *talking* to you, because I've treated you as pawns and captives long enough."

"I've heard what happens to gates," said Anonoei.

"What have you heard? How could you hear anything? There hasn't been a gate on Westil, except of my making, for more than fourteen centuries."

"There *have* been gates," said Anonoei. "Everyone knows the stories. A gatemage learns to go from here to there, and then suddenly the Gate Thief comes and takes them all away. What if that happens while we're—"

"Haven't you understood anything, woman?" demanded Wad. "*I'm* the Gate Thief. Me. That's why I could keep you locked up behind my gates for more than a year, and no one took the gates from me."

"If you're the Gate Thief—and yes, I understood you, but why should I pay attention to such ridiculous brag?—then you must have been alive for more than a thousand years. *You,* a mere boy—"

"Why would anyone bother to become immortal in an *old* body?" asked Wad. "But I'm not immortal. I was in a tree. More precisely, a treemage persuaded a tree to let me gate into the living treeflesh between the bark and the dry wood. There I made the tiniest of gates, which moved me slowly upward through the tree, rising with me, rising far more slowly than a fingernail grows. Passing through a gate heals you. I healed myself, I healed the tree, minute by minute, day by day, year by year. The tree lived and I lived, never aging, never ill. And I watched. Every gate that was made, I sensed. At first my powers were magnificently strong, as yours will be if you ever make up your mind to go through a Great Gate. But that boost in power fades with time. I had to watch ever more closely, concentrate ever more tightly. My outselves roamed the world, alert, watching. After the first five hundred years, I sensed nothing from Mittlegard; after the second thousand, gates on Westil were like a distant whisper, except for the making of a Great Gate. That was like a shout, as the gates entwined and roped and rose into the sky. Then I reached out and swallowed them. That's your Gate Thief. The husk of an ancient man, kept alive within a tree, seeing nothing, hearing nothing, only an endless watchfulness for the making of a Great Gate, with only the captured gates of long-dead mages to keep me company."

"So you're not as young as you seem," said Anonoei. And then she smiled, so he would know that she understood the bathos of her own remark.

"I came out like an adolescent orphan, hardly remembering anything of my life before, not even understanding that I was the Gate Thief, and for a time not knowing what a gate was. I ate gates by reflex then. I made them the same way. A kind woman took me in and I made a mother of her, until someone murdered her for refusing to cooperate with an attempt to poison the queen."

"You're talking about Hull?" asked Anonoei.

"Please don't tell me that you knew beforehand about the killing of that good woman," said Wad. "Unless it's true. If you lie to me we can't be friends."

"So many rules you have," said Anonoei. "I lie to you all the time, and you lie to me. We're human and we lie, because that is the only way people can possibly get along with each other."

"You're wrong," said Wad. "We can tell each other the truth, as far as we know it. We might be wrong about what we believe is true, but we can speak our best understanding to each other. Hull did that with me, and I with her."

"She knew you were the Gate Thief?" asked Anonoei. And when Wad didn't answer, she smiled. "I see—you told her the truth, except when the truth might make her like you less."

"So what is it that *you* aren't telling me?"

"That I think you're right, the boys will be safer on Mittlegard, and if I can't take the risk of trusting you to get me through a Great Gate and back again, I might as well give up. If you're not trustworthy then I've got nothing, but if I refuse to trust you then I've got nothing. So I might as well trust you and hope that you amount to something."

"A fair gamble."

"I trusted a king once," said Anonoei.

"He never let you down."

"But he did," said Anonoei. "He may not have meant to, but he failed to find me and set me free."

"My powers were too much for him," said Wad. "What could he do against a gatemage?"

"Queen Bexoi did something," said Anonoei.

"She murdered a baby when I was distracted. That was the limit of her power." He said it calmly, as if the mention of Trick had not caused emotion to rage upward from his belly to fill his heart with grief and his mind with rage. "And she knew what I was. If Prayard had known, he would have suspected me, and if he had suspected me in your disappearance, he would have had me tortured to find out where you were."

"You? Tortured?"

"He would have tried."

"Did he even ask you?"

"I told him that I had looked at every inch of the castle and you weren't there. Nor had I seen anyone carrying you out. All true, you'll note."

"And also lies," said Anonoei. "I'm such a fool to believe in you."

"I'm all you've got, and you're all I've got."

"All you've got to use against Queen Bexoi?" said Anonoei. "Why not just pass her through a gate to the bottom of the sea?"

"She has to lose and know that she has lost," said Wad. "She has to see you in her place, and your sons in the place of her son."

Anonoei laughed and nodded. "*Now* I can trust you. *Now* I know your heart."

But she did not know him, not his heart, not his mind. Yes, he meant to wreak his vengeance on the queen, and so he spoke that way because Anonoei would understand that motive and believe him. But his real reason was that until he had put Anonoei back in her right place, beside the king, with her sons as his heirs, the guilt of his own crimes would be unbearably heavy, more than he could bear.

I spent fifteen centuries trying to save the world, and I would sacrifice it all for mere vengeance? Bexoi would never be brought to justice. She played the same game as all the royal people of the world; should she be called a monster because she was better at it?

No, Wad's chief purpose was still and always would be to keep Bel from walking upon the face of Westil, taking its reins into his hand. If he could redeem himself for his crimes against Anonoei and her children, without discommoding that main purpose, that would be well and good. But for vengeance and retribution he would not cross the street.

Hearing such a thought in his own mind, he laughed bitterly. Self-deception always works—it has such a willing audience.

"What are you laughing at?" asked Anonoei.

"Myself," he said truthfully.

When they explained the purpose of their upcoming journey to the boys, the younger one, Enopp, seemed to understand. Eluik, as usual, looked at the face from which the talking-noises came, but there was no sign that the language registered in his mind at all.

Then he talked to Roop and Levet.

"I did you no kindness bringing this woman and her children here," said Wad. "I realize that now. The soldiers will be here soon, and if they don't kill you outright, they'll have you brought to the castle of Nassassa and torture you to tell them things you do not even know."

Levet understood and her face flashed with anger, though she said nothing. Roop showed no anger. He merely bowed his head in resignation. "What must I do?" he asked.

"There is a windmage from Mittlegard named Ced. He's being trained by a treemage at the southern end of Mitherkame. The treemage refuses to have a name, since trees have no language. I asked the treemage if he would object to having the meadows near him cultivated, and he did not mind at all. Fell no trees and he will be your friend. Until you have a harvest, he will teach you how to let the trees provide for you."

"So we leave everything," said Levet.

"Again," said Roop.

"You've moved before. This time it will be a warmer place, with richer soil and a growing season long enough that it isn't over before the seeds have pushed up stems and sunk roots fully into the earth."

"What service will we owe the man?" asked Levet.

"None," said Wad. "Not even the hand of your lovely daughter as his bride."

They looked alarmed.

"I say he *won't* require it," Wad reassured them.

"Are there people in the world who would demand such things?" asked Roop.

"Kings require it of each other all the time. It's how Queen Bexoi came to Iceway. She was forced on Prayard against his will."

Roop reached out his hand to hold Eko. "You say we must do this."

"Or leave your children orphans. Or watch them tortured before your eyes, if they believe you really know where I and this woman and her two sons have gone."

"You're a terrible friend to have," said Eko.

"I am," agreed Wad. "But then, I could have left you to your fate, not caring."

"You'd never do that," said Eko. "That is not the man you are."

You don't know the man I am, thought Wad.

As if she heard him, or guessed from his face, Eko said, "I know you better than you think."

"Because you saw him crawling from a tree?" her little brother Bokky teased.

"Because he *did* bring them here," said Eko. "He remembered us."

"I wish he hadn't," said Levet.

"He remembered we were kind to him," said Eko, "and so when he needed kindness for someone else, he came to us."

"Yes," said Wad.

Eko faced him boldly. "If you said that I would need to marry someone to save my family," said Eko, "I would do it."

"But I won't say that to you," said Wad.

"You'll keep us safe," said Eko. "From everyone?"

"I'll take you to a place that I believe will be as safe as anywhere on Westil. More than that I can't promise. I won't be there to watch. It's the best I can do."

In the end, had they a choice? They gathered their few possessions, and Wad made a public gate for them, and they stepped through it, one by one.

Anonoei watched them do it, she and her sons.

Wad turned to her, when the last of Roop's and Levet's family had gone. "Now you know what it looks like," he said.

"Going through a gate?" Anonoei asked. "I have fallen through the gate of my prison a hundred times."

"What trust looks like," said Wad.

"They're not mages," said Anonoei. "What choices do they have?"

"I don't know what powers those children might have, and for all I know the father has some power with vegetables, or the mother a way with snakes. They have choices, as many as you have."

Anonoei laughed. "I have as few as they, you're right," she said. "Perhaps they seemed weak to me because they love each other."

It was such a shocking thing to say that Wad had no answer for her.

"I lived too long at court," said Anonoei. "I have seen people owned, desired, and coveted, and I have seen people used, but few were loved, and few were loving."

"You love your sons," said Wad.

"I barely know my poor broken children," said Anonoei, resting one hand on Enopp's head, the other on Eluik's shoulder. "Aren't you going to follow those farm folk, and introduce them and the treemage to each other?"

"He'll know who they are because they came through the

gate, and they'll know him because the gate has led them straight to him."

"What if they come back through the gate?" asked Anonoei.

"The gate is gone. I took it back. I husband my gates carefully these days," said Wad. "A few are all I have. You see, the Gate Thief got the rest."

She looked at him sharply. "You said that you—"

"I was the Gate Thief for a thousand years or so," said Wad. "I burgled one hearthoard too many. I am punished now, and the punishment is just."

Wad turned to Eluik, who was not looking at him. "Whatever you are or might become," said Wad, "passing through a Great Gate will strengthen you." But the older boy gave no sign of hearing.

"He's still singing to himself," said Enopp.

Wad and Anonoei waited for the younger boy to explain.

"Alone in the cave, with all the falling," said Enopp. "We sang to ourselves."

Wad wondered if Enopp had some connection with his brother that allowed him to know what he was doing during their many months of isolation.

"That's what *you* did, is it?" asked Anonoei.

"Of course," said Enopp. "I sang every song I knew. You should have taught me more of them, Mother."

"I'm glad you're not still singing them now," she said.

"Oh, I am," said Enopp. "I hear them all the time. I just don't listen to them. Eluik does, though. He's still trying to understand the words."

"But they're all in plain language," said Anonoei.

"Not the words of the *songs*," said Enopp impatiently. "The words beneath the songs."

"What words are those?" asked Wad.

"I didn't understand them either, not at first, but I was little. There were many words I didn't understand, when I was little."

The words beneath the songs. Wad thought he might have some idea what words those were, and who spoke them. The gates that held the prisoner, that surrounded them—they were connected to Wad, to his hearthoard. To the place where the thousand gates of other mages were imprisoned. They had shouted all the time, Wad hardly heard them. But it was possible that these voices carried with the gates. That an isolated child, with nothing else to occupy him, might have heard something. Especially if there were gates in his own hearthoard, gates that he was yet too young to use. But the captive gates cried out to the captive boy, and if he was a gatemage himself, he would have heard them in the same way that Wad, at the height of his powers a millennium ago, could sense the location and the owner of every gate in two worlds.

Wad took the boy by his hand. "Would you like to come with me and your mother now?"

"And my brother," said Enopp.

"Him too," said Wad.

"Of course," said Enopp. "It's good to be out of the cave. Eluik is even happier than I am. He's eager to go with you."

Again Wad looked from the younger boy to the silent elder one. If Eluik objected to his little brother's speaking for him, he gave no sign.

Enopp took his older brother's hand, and Anonoei held him on the other side. Wad passed a gatemouth over them, and they were standing in the stone circle where the Wild Gate now shone plainly, obvious for anyone to see and use. It was good that the place was scarcely inhabited, that people shunned it. Stone circles were shrines no longer. Since the Great Gates were taken, they were regarded as dark places of ill fortune. They were avoided. All to the good. But that could not last forever. Someone would figure it out.

"Don't let go of hands," said Wad. And then, after a breath, he stepped through.

The Great Gate swallowed up the four of them, and they were standing in a barn, with cows around. A woman was attaching a machine to the udders of a cow.

"Is someone expecting you?" she asked politely, in a heavily accented version of the ancient language of West Ylly Way. Wad understood her, because he had already spoken to Danny North and Ced. There was no hope that her words would mean a thing to Anonoei.

"I wasn't expecting *you,*" Enopp answered her, imitating her accent.

Another sign the boy might grow into a gatemage, to have a knack for languages.

"I've come to speak with Danny North," said Wad.

"He isn't here," said the woman, turning her back.

Angry at this stranger for such treatment, Wad gated to the other side of her. But before he could speak to her, a cow kicked him hard in the leg. He cried out and fell, then passed a gate over himself.

"The only way to punish a gatemage," said the woman, "is to take him by surprise."

"Punish me for what!"

"I know who you are, Gate Thief," said the woman. "I told him never to bring you to Mittlegard, yet here you are. Do you think because you have these darling children with you, I won't hurt you? Especially the damaged one—why did you bring him here, except to protect you from me?"

"I didn't know you were here," said Wad, "and I don't know who you are."

"She's my wife," said a man's voice. And in that moment, Wad was falling into a crevice in the Earth. Not a wide one, but it was enough to swallow him.

Wad gated to the loft of the barn. "I'll never die by falling," said Wad.

"Didn't my wife inform you that our stepson is away?"

"He'll be here," said Wad.

"How can you be sure of that?" asked the woman.

"Because he's been sensitized by passage through a Great Gate. He knows when someone passes through any gate in the world."

That was when Danny North strode through the open door into the barn.

13

Trust

Danny was getting dressed for another morning practice when he felt it: Something had happened at the Wild Gate.

He stopped pulling on his running shorts, froze in position. The feeling didn't come again. He tried to think what he had actually experienced. It came from that portion of his outself that was entwined in the Great Gate in the Silvermans' barn.

It felt like when Veevee or Hermia passed through his gates. Only far stronger.

Why? Because it was a Great Gate?

Because it was more than one person going through a gate at once.

He had felt it before when his friends went through his first Great Gate, but had not been able to think about it then because he was immediately engaged with the Gate Thief.

Now he even knew the direction they had passed. It was a group of four people, and they came from Westil to Earth.

Whoever it was had arrived in Silvermans' barn. It was milking time. Leslie would be there.

Danny even knew who it was. Because lingering after the sensation of the Great Gate being used there was another feeling—a quickening in the gates that Danny held captive inside him. The strange gates were saying—not in words, but deeper than words—"He is coming, he is coming." And the gates that belonged to Loki himself were brightening because their true owner was now in the same world with them. "Let us go home," they were saying, straining ever so slightly against the restraint of Danny's hearthoard.

The Gate Thief had brought three people with him through the Wild Gate.

Danny pulled off the shorts and put on pants and a shirt, socks and shoes and a jacket. He would not be running this morning after all.

Once he was dressed, he stepped through the gate in his house that led to the Silvermans' upstairs hall, then walked from house to barn through the biting cold of this autumn morning. The trees were dazzling with color. There was a trace of frost on the grass.

Inside the barn, Leslie and Marion were standing side by side, looking up at the loft where Loki stood with a woman and two young boys.

"Took you long enough," said Marion.

"I was mostly naked," said Danny. "I stopped to dress."

"Thank you for that," said Leslie.

"Danny North," said Loki.

"I don't want you here," said Danny in Westilian.

"I need your help," said Loki. "But it will be hard to converse with your friend prepared to make the ground swallow us up."

"Only swallow," said Marion, in his heavily accented version of Westilian. "Not chew."

"His mercy is noted," said Loki. "That's why I didn't gate him to the bottom of a convenient river. Or into a tree."

"You didn't harm him," said Danny, "because you are afraid of me."

"I didn't harm him," said Loki, "because I am an intruder, and he is protecting his home and his friend."

"And you didn't leave, because you wanted to be here when I arrived."

"I promise not to do anything to anyone here," said Loki. "I will not try to take back my own gates, or swallow any others'. In return I hope you will not try to take the few that remain to me."

Danny turned to Marion and Leslie. "May I invite them into the house?"

"Guest law will apply then," said Marion.

"I know," said Danny.

"It will bind you as well as us," Leslie reminded him.

"It will bind us all," said Danny. "Aren't you curious to know about the woman and the children?"

"Anonoei, onetime mistress of King Prayard of Iceway," said Loki. "And the unofficial but potentially useful sons of the King, Eluik and Enopp."

Danny nodded to them formally. It was a ritual greeting that all the children learned very young, to be used on important and solemn occasions. Only as a child, Danny's bow had been deep, and from the waist; the nod he gave now was that of a ruler toward subordinates—the nod that Baba bestowed on those saluting him as Odin. No one could mistake what he was asserting, and indeed they did not. The return bow of the woman and her sons was deep, though not so deep as to imply worthlessness. And Loki also bowed slightly from the waist rather than merely nodding in return. The hierarchy had been asserted and agreed to.

"May we enter your home?" Danny asked the Silvermans again.

Leslie sighed. "Gate me to the kitchen, please, Danny."

He did.

"I'd like to walk with our guests," said Marion.

Loki understood, and instead of gating down from the loft, he descended the ladder, Anonoei and the boys after him. Then Marion drew Loki with him, and walked beside the ancient yet youthful gatemage toward the house.

Danny knew that Marion would make dire warnings about what would happen if Loki broke his word. Danny also knew that Loki would agree cheerfully, knowing that in a pinch, he could always gate away, so Marion's threats were more symbolic than practicable.

Meanwhile, Danny looked at the woman and smiled. "You're a mother. I had one once."

"I hope a mother that you loved."

"Devotedly," said Danny. "Why don't you and your older son walk ahead, and let me talk to the young one. Enopp, is it?"

Anonoei took Eluik by the hand and walked from the barn, whose smaller door was still standing open after Marion's and Loki's departure.

"These are cows, aren't they," said the boy Enopp.

"They are," said Danny.

"They're huge," said Enopp.

"Cows may be bigger here than in the place you came from," said Danny. "But these are particularly well-fed and healthy cows. Leslie takes good care of them. Though at this moment I believe they still want milking. Would you like to help me?"

The boy nodded. "I'm only little," he said. "And I'm not very strong. I've been in prison, you know."

"I'm sorry to hear that," said Danny. "Did you do something very bad?"

"No, but I'm dangerous, because there are people who think my brother or I should be king after my father, and not the child of Queen Bexoi. She's from Gray, and her brother is our enemy."

"I'm glad you're out of prison, since you didn't do anything wrong."

Enopp shrugged. "I'm glad to be out, too, but it's dangerous for me even to exist. I don't have to actually do anything."

"I know the feeling," said Danny. "I was older than you, though, when people made the same judgment about me."

"Did they put you in jail?"

"I'm a gatemage," said Danny. "They couldn't if they tried. All they can do is kill me or leave me alone."

"Or kill someone you love," said Enopp.

"Ah," said Danny. "I see you understand how power works."

"I'm son of a king," said Enopp. "I think I'm going to be a gatemage, too."

Meanwhile, Danny had attached the milker to a cow. "Do you see how I did that?"

"Does it hurt the cow?"

"It's designed to fit her teat exactly right," said Danny. "She likes it."

"What does it do?"

Danny spent the next fifteen minutes explaining the milking machines and letting Enopp help in whatever way he was large enough and strong enough.

"What do you think of Loki?" asked Danny.

"Who?" asked Enopp.

"The gatemage who brought you."

"Wad," said Enopp.

The word made no sense to Danny in this context. "You want bread?"

"His name," said Enopp. "That's what Mother calls him."

"Wad," said Danny. "Not a noble name."

"He used to be the castle spy. He would climb everywhere, watch everything. Hull named him. The chief baker. She's dead, somebody murdered her because she refused to murder the Queen. It would have been better if she had done it. The Queen is an evil bitch."

Danny was amused at the way Enopp echoed what he must have heard. "What about Wad? Is he evil or good?"

"He kept us in prison," said Enopp. "But when Queen Bexoi said to kill us, he didn't. After a while he gave us better food. And he got us out just when soldiers were trying to kill us in our caves."

"That sounds frightening."

"It was," said Enopp. "They were my father's soldiers."

"Did they know who you were?"

Enopp thought a moment. "I don't know," he said. "But they knew I was little."

"You have a point," said Danny. "Enopp, why did your mother and Wad bring you here?"

Enopp shrugged. "It isn't safe for us in Iceway. I think they want us to be safe here."

"This world isn't safer. People die on both worlds, just as easily."

"When I'm a gatemage, I'll hide where they can't find me."

"Are you sure that's what you'll be?"

"I'm already good with languages," said Enopp. "That's a sign."

"It is," said Danny. "Are you also a devilish little brat?"

Enopp gave that more thought than Danny had expected. "I don't know. I have only been free of my prison for a few weeks."

"We'd better watch carefully then," said Danny, "so we don't get taken by surprise when the pranks start."

They kept milking till the job was done. Only then did Danny take Enopp by the hand and walk with him across the yard to the house.

In the kitchen, Leslie had the table spread with small plates and a big platter of warmed-up sliced bread and an array of butter, jams, and honey. Everyone was eating. Enopp ran right to the table beside his brother and started jabbering to him. Danny saw that Eluik did not answer him, or even show a sign of listening.

But Enopp was undiscouraged by this; and it wasn't as if Eluik were inert, for he was eating steadily, though without any visible pleasure in the food, which Danny knew from experience was extraordinarily good.

"Did my son bore you?" asked Anonoei. "He chatters as if he thought himself a great philosopher or statesman, with the world eager to hear his words."

"I could not have been more eager," said Danny, adopting the arch-formal tones he had only overheard when spying on the adults meeting in the library of the old house in the North Family compound. "Your son is surprisingly happy for one so recently a prisoner."

"He is resilient," said Anonoei.

Danny could not help glancing at Eluik, but then looked at Loki, as if he had only chanced to look at Eluik as his gaze passed from Anonoei to the Gate Thief.

"You have achieved your first purpose," Danny said to Loki. "You have passed through a Great Gate."

"My first purpose was to see that no such gate existed," said Loki. "But having failed in that, it is true that I thought it wise to refresh such small powers as are left to me."

"You know more than I about how these powers work," said Danny, "but it seems to me that while our brute force depends on the number of our gates, our dexterity depends on knowledge and experience. I have the brute force, it's true, but you have the deftness of long practice."

"Long practice followed by far longer disuse," said Loki. "I have spent fourteen centuries and more drifting upward through a tree, aware of little but occasional flashes of gatemaking, which I quickly extinguished."

"Yet you did come out of the tree," said Danny, "and apparently some time before I attempted a Great Gate."

"But not before you made your first few dozen gates," said Loki. "Your first few hundred, I should say."

It was the Gate Thief's admission that he had been aware of Danny for some time. That he had sensed, however dimly, that Danny was alive, a great mage in potential if not in accomplishment.

"I didn't even know I was making the gates," Danny admitted.

"Be careful what you say," said Marion.

"He knows," said Danny. "He has been watching me even before he knew that it was I whom he watched."

"Aren't we the lofty speakers now," said Leslie. "I feel as if I'm in a school, studying Westilian style."

"These gatemages and their linguistic show-offery," said Marion in English.

"I am learning your English a little," said Loki, and while his words were slow and stilted, his Ohio accent was nearly perfect.

"How?" demanded Leslie in English. "Who in Westil could possibly teach you? Do you have spies here?"

"He does," said Danny, also in English.

Leslie stood up and paced to the kitchen counter, then turned around, as if somehow the sink had been besieged, and she were its sole defender.

"Me," said Danny. "His spies are inside me—the gates I took from him. Thousands of them, and through them he can glimpse a little. He can hear."

"How much?" demanded Marion. "What does he know?"

"I don't know," said Danny. "All his gates ever do that I know of is demand that any working gate be eaten up. If he had succeeded in swallowing my gates, then I could tell you just how much a mage can learn through his captive gates. But I'd rather have my ignorance than his knowledge."

"If I could hear more, I'd speak better," said Loki, reverting to Westilian. "In truth, I see nothing. I hear nothing. I am inside the womb of his mind. But there is where his language dwells, and his memory. I cannot search at will; but I can overhear his thoughts, when he makes them into language. I can see his memories, when he concentrates on them. I am *not* spying. Where he has imprisoned my outself, I have no choice but to see and hear what he shows me."

But Danny didn't believe Loki. The trouble was he didn't know in which direction the lie was leaning: Did Loki see and hear far more than he admitted? Or had he seen and heard nothing at all until he passed through the Wild Gate, enhancing his powers and coming so much nearer to Danny himself?

"What did you come here for?" asked Danny. "You came with these three, so your purpose was more than your own enhancement."

"Their lives are in danger," said Loki. "Here they will be safe."

"That's absurdly false," said Marion. "All the mages of the world would be assaulting us, if they knew this Wild Gate existed in our barn. There's no more dangerous place on Earth."

"But who would tell them?" asked Loki. Then he raised a hand. "That was not a threat."

Marion did not relax, his posture even more alert. "How else can we hear that statement?"

"An observation," said Loki. "This Wild Gate has existed for days now, and yet they leave you alone. If your secret were out, they would not wait."

"They're afraid of our power of defense," said Leslie. "Marion and I have passed through a gate. No beastmage can hold on to his heartbound, if they come against us. The ground surrounding us is under Marion's control. Danny could gate them away, even if they got past our defense."

"So you think they do know, and bide their time?" asked Loki.

"What do you want," demanded Marion. "I don't believe you brought this woman here for her protection. I feel a great power in her."

"I felt it first," said Leslie. "She's a mage in her own right, and passing through the Great Gate made her dangerous."

"It did," said Anonoei. "But the very fact that you mistrust me shows that I have used none of my power on you."

It took only a moment for the implications of her remark to sink in. Marion rose to his feet and joined Leslie by the sink. "Danny, she's a manmage," Marion said in English.

"I got it," said Danny. "But as she said, she hasn't used it."

"Or she's so powerful that we can't *feel* that she used it on us."

"So you think she's making you so suspicious of her?" asked Danny.

"If she tried to use it I would gate her away myself," said Loki. "*I* gain nothing if she irritates you, and neither does she. We face a deadly enemy on Westil, a Firemaster at least, if not a Lightrider."

"Queen Bexoi," added Enopp helpfully. "Our father's true wife."

Danny looked from Loki to Anonoei, and saw that Bexoi was, indeed, Anonoei's objective here. The grim determination in her face, the hand that rested on Enopp's nape, the little toss of her head, all these testified to Enopp's having said the truth.

But Loki was another matter. His approval had come a fraction of a second late, and looked too much like an imitation of Anonoei's. He had a very different goal.

"You want Anonoei empowered," said Danny. "You want her battling this Bexoi. But that's not why you've come."

"Ced," Leslie suggested. "That windmage who stayed on Westil."

"I've befriended him and stopped his storming all over Westwold," said Loki. "I have him studying with a treemage to learn how to still his inself so he can control his powers and use them with finesse."

Still only a partial truth, Danny saw. "Do we have to talk alone?" he asked Loki.

Loki studied Danny for only a few moments, but in those moments Danny felt the Gate Thief's gates stir within him. "You have something that I need," said Loki.

"Take them back if you can," said Danny. "But I warn you that I know enough now, and have power enough, that I can take the rest whenever I want." Danny was telling the truth as far as he knew it, but he also had no idea of what defenses Loki might retain, especially now that he had passed through a Great Gate.

"You misunderstand me completely," said Loki. "And I have no desire to hide from your friends the thing I came to get, the thing I need so desperately."

"If not your gates, what?" asked Danny.

"Your trust," said Loki.

Danny looked at Anonoei. "Is that why he brought you? To use your manmagery to make me trust *him* and not you?"

"If that were his plan," said Anonoei, "is it working?"

"No," said Danny.

"Then I think you can safely conclude that this is not his plan. Whatever he wants from you, he hasn't told me anything."

"Trust isn't a prize in itself," said Danny. "What do you need my trust *for*?"

"There is a war much older than you, much older than myself," said Loki. "A war as old as humankind. Between the Belgod and the Mithermages."

Danny waited.

"I need you to take over my work," said Loki. "I know you don't trust me, and the very fact that I said this much has raised your suspicions even higher. Yet the war must be fought or lost, and I don't have the gates to do it. The job of protecting against the Belgod is yours now."

Danny thought again of the runes he had read in the Library of Congress. "Hear us in the land of Mitherkame, hear us among the great ships of Iceway, among the charging dunes of Dapnu Dap, among the Mages of the Forest and the Riders of the Wold."

He was reciting in the old language of the inscription, a language Loki had to know: Fistalk, or something near it. The language of the Norse as it had first been bent and twisted by the Semitic language of the Carthaginians.

"This is very old," Loki murmured. "Where did you learn it?"

Danny went on reciting. "We have faced Bel and he has ruled the hearts of many. Bold men ran like deer from his face, but Loki did not run."

"I am not that Loki," said Loki.

"You know the tale, then?" asked Danny. "Is this the war that you're still fighting?"

"He thought he had won, just as I thought I had won. But we never win. He can't be killed, and he outwaits any wall we raise against him. Eventually it wears down. He keeps returning."

"Was he dropped into the sun?" asked Danny. "Did he somehow live through that?"

"His body died, of course," said Loki. "But his inself can't be killed, any more than yours or mine can die."

"But we do die," said Danny.

"Our bodies die," said Loki. "But you know our outselves can outlive the body—those are the ancient gates that I kept captive for so long. They're still alive in that Wild Gate."

"But without an inself," said Danny.

"Don't be a fool," said Loki. "They only live because the inself also lives. Wherever it is, the outself draws its life from there. The Wild Gate is filled with the rage of those inselves, so angry that I took their gates from them."

"So the inself of Bel did not die with the body."

"It took him a thousand years to return to Mittlegard, and his rage was terrible."

"What did he do?" asked Danny.

"Not as much as he intended," said Loki. "He conquered everywhere, but I closed all the gates against him. He couldn't possess any of our mages and follow them to Westil because there were no gates. And so our mages were able to defeat him."

"How would you know?" asked Danny. "After the gates were gone, you were gone as well."

"If he had not been prevented, you would not be alive to talk to me. The language of Westil would have died in this world. There would have been no Gatefather from any Family to create a Great Gate. I knew, because you existed, that for fourteen centuries I had kept him trapped in Mittlegard."

"And you fear that now he will break loose and come to Westil through the gates I make?"

"I know he will," said Loki. "And since I can't prevent him, and you don't know how, then I beg you to trust me. Let me teach you how to do the things that in all of history before me, no one learned to do. You alone can learn them."

"The eating of gates," said Danny.

"The poem you were reciting to me," said Loki. "That Loki ate gates, as did the Persian Gatefather whom Belgod had captured and turned to his purposes."

"What is it that you do, then, that you would teach me?" asked Danny.

"Don't believe him," said Marion. "He's promising you power. It's like the temptations of Christ."

"It's exactly like the temptations of Christ," said Loki. "Only not the way you think."

"You've heard about the Christian god?" asked Leslie, incredulous.

"I exiled myself from Mittlegard in 632," said Loki impatiently. "The Roman Empire had fallen, Christians were all over Europe, Byzantium ruled the East, of course I know about the Semitic gods. I studied in Egypt, I had all the gospels, I had the ancient Coptic lore. What do you think I want to teach this boy?"

"How should we know?" said Marion. "If we knew it, we would have taught him ourselves."

"Teaching you is the most dangerous thing that I can do," said

Loki, "because once you know it, if the Belgod captures you then all is lost and Westil is undone."

"Don't teach me, then," said Danny.

"But only you have the power to stand against him. Look at me! Think what I did! If I had the power to stand against him, do you think I would have eaten all the gates and run away?"

"I have no more power than you," said Danny.

"You have a thousand times my power," said Loki, "and that is what it's going to take. My knowledge and your power. But you have to trust me, and I don't know how to win your trust, because you know better than anyone what liars we gatemages *always* are."

"I don't *always* lie," said Danny.

"Only when you speak," said Loki.

"I'm not just like every other gatemage," said Danny. "I made the choice *not* to lie."

"Too bad," said Loki. "Because unless you can lie, with the expertise at lying that comes from long practice, you will lose against the Belgod, because he is the father of lies, and yet you must deceive him or you are doomed."

"Do the job yourself!" cried Danny.

"I couldn't do it even if you gave me back my gates!" Loki answered him. "Even if I ate this Wild Gate, as long as you are alive in the world, he'll lay his traps for you until he has you and then you can make a thousand gates to let him through, and he'll use your millions of gates to rule both worlds and none will ever stand against him, not in a thousand years, not in ten thousand, not in a billion years."

Danny didn't know whether to believe him or laugh. So he made a joke. "Well, there *is* the heat death of the universe."

"I have no idea what that means," said Loki.

"The ultimate result of entropy," said Danny.

Loki looked at him blankly.

"The end of everything."

"Fool," said Loki. "There is no 'end of everything.' What you call dying or ending is nothing but changes in the shapes of things. Who told you such nonsense? Only Belgod benefits from telling such a lie."

Danny leaned on the table, burying his face in his hands. Even as his body spoke of weariness, though, he remained alert, in case Loki tried to do something sneaky while Danny was thinking about the distracting things that Loki was telling him.

And in that moment, Loki struck.

Danny could feel it inside himself, in his hearthoard, the place where he held captive all but eight of Loki's gates. A shifting of the hundred thousand gates that were Loki's outself, for now he could feel them all and knew the number without counting them. A hundred forty-three thousand, nine hundred and ninety-four gates, and every one of them moved within Danny and became . . .

Danny's servants.

The shouting stopped, except the feeble struggles of the remaining prisoners that Loki had captured long ago. All of Loki's own gates, the ones that were a part of Loki's outself, fell silent. No, not silent at all. They turned attentive. Alert to Danny's own will. As alert to him as Danny's own gates were.

"I give them to you," said Loki.

"What does that mean?" asked Danny.

"They're yours to build with," said Loki. "Yours to weave. If you use them, they won't turn wild. They can't."

"You can't give me something that's a part of yourself."

"Yes I can, and yes I did," said Loki. "How else will you trust me?"

"But they're still a part of you."

"That's true," said Loki. "The ones that are still inside you will continue to show me what you think and remember, what you see and do. I can't help that, it's how the world works. But believe me, they're yours now. I couldn't take them back, unless you freely gave them back to me. Which I hope someday you will. But if you never do, they're yours forever."

"Or until I die," said Danny.

"Or until the Belgod takes you, and it all belongs to him," said Loki. "This is the only way that I can earn your trust. To show you how completely I trust you. The only reason I withhold the eight gates you left to me is because without them I can't help Anonoei or Ced on Westil. I'm going there now, if you permit it. I'm taking her back there with me."

Enopp had been listening, rapt, but now he looked worried and spoke up. "Taking *her*?"

"Yes," said Anonoei. "And leaving you here in safety, if we can."

"No!" shouted Enopp, jumping up, knocking his chair backward, though it didn't fall. "You can't leave me here!"

Then, to Danny's surprise—to everyone's surprise—Eluik's hand shot out to rest firmly on Enopp's shoulder and push him back and down into his chair. The older boy said nothing, but Enopp fell silent and looked at him. Then he burst into tears.

"He says I have to stay," said Enopp. "And he does too."

"He didn't say a thing," said Anonoei.

"It's his outself," said Loki. "I can see it now. Hiding inside Enopp. It's where he went when I held them both in prison. He must have sent his outself to comfort his brother through their captivity. He's been riding inside his brother all along."

Leslie immediately stepped forward to put her hand on Eluik's head. "I should have seen it, but it never occurred to me. Yes, he's riding him like a heartbound."

"So you can break the link?" asked Marion.

"I've never tried with a manmage," said Leslie.

"He's a manmage?" asked Anonoei.

"No," said Loki. "Not necessarily. He's too young to know what he is."

"He's too young to have sent his outself," said Marion. "But he did."

"He didn't know what he was doing," said Loki. "He couldn't have. It isn't magery, not with any kind of skill. And if you tear them apart, against his will—"

"How do we know what his will is?" demanded Anonoei. "He was taking care of his brother, but maybe he didn't know how to get back."

"Like an outself trapped in a bagged-up clant," said Danny, remembering when he tied up some of the cousins.

"Exactly like that," said Marion.

"This boy took such care of his brother," said Leslie. "Completely forgetting himself. I never heard of such love."

"You want us to take care of these boys," said Marion.

Loki said nothing.

Danny understood now. "He wanted *someone* to take care of them. He and Anonoei have work to do, and they want the boys out of danger. But he didn't know you existed."

Loki looked at Anonoei. She buried her face in her hands. "I don't want to leave them."

"But you also don't want them with you," said Loki.

Danny looked from Marion to Leslie, the two of them now standing behind the boys. "You want them, don't you?"

"They started doing magery far too young," said Marion. "Who knows what that does to a child?"

"I did this to them," said Loki. "I had no idea *this* could happen, but at the time I didn't care. And now they're still in prison."

"Eluik's fine," said Enopp. "He says to leave him alone."

"Nobody's going to do anything to him," said Marion.

"Not me, anyway," said Leslie. "I think he has to learn how to bring home his own outself." She looked to Loki. "He's just lost, right?"

"No," said Loki. "It's not that simple. His outself and inself aren't fully separable. He's too young. He sent his outself before it was safe to send it. So it's still bound to his inself. Both parts of him, the ka and the ba—he's as much inside his brother as inside himself. It might *kill* him to separate him from his brother. His inself might also be lost."

"He's not lost," said Enopp. "He's right where he wants to be."

"That's because he's young and stupid," said Loki. "What he did was kind. No, it was noble. But his body can't last like this. His ka has to come wholly back inside his body. As it is, he's in very grave danger of losing his body. And then he would only live inside you, Enopp."

"He can stay as long as he wants."

"It doesn't work that way. Right now the only reason he hasn't taken you over is because he's still partly connected to his own body. But if he ever lost that, then the two of you would fight for control of *your* body."

"No we wouldn't," said Enopp.

"Right now, Enopp," said Loki. "Who said that? Was it you, or was it Eluik talking through you?"

Enopp fell silent. Thinking.

"Exactly," said Loki. "Eluik sent himself partly into you in order to protect you, to watch over you. But if he doesn't get back inside his own body, then his body will die, sooner or later, one way or another. And when that happens, Eluik will become like the Belgod. A loose ka, attached to another person's body."

"You keep saying 'ka' and 'ba,'" said Danny.

"If you trust me, I can teach you," said Loki. "Meanwhile, these boys are bound together and they don't want to change. For all we know, Enopp is silently begging his brother not to leave him. He might not even know he's saying it."

"I'm not," said Enopp. "He can go if he wants, I'm not afraid anymore."

"Eluik may not believe that," said Loki. "Or he may not know how to leave you. Or he may be even more afraid than you ever were, Enopp. He might have been coming to *you* for comfort. I don't know. You don't know. He doesn't know. But somehow he has to sort it out and get back entirely inside his own mind and outside of yours, or he will become something terrible."

Enopp got a stubborn look on his face.

It was identical to the stubborn look on Eluik's face. The only difference was that Enopp was looking at Loki, and Eluik wasn't looking at anybody.

"Nobody's going to force you to do anything," said Loki. "Isn't that right?" Loki looked at all the adults.

Anonoei showed grief and fear on her face. "I can't leave them."

"You aren't with them," said Loki. "Not as much as they're with each other." Loki spoke to Marion and Leslie. "Danny trusts you. He loves you. He has enough of me inside him that I can see how deep it goes. You're good people, as far as he knows. Is he right? No absurd modesty here—you mean no harm to these children, right?"

"I would never let them come to harm," said Leslie.

Marion nodded. But he looked worried.

Danny understood. "You can't watch over the Wild Gate and these boys at the same time."

"We can watch over anything here on our farm," said Marion. "But I can foresee a circumstance when the things we have to do to keep other people away from the gate would be the opposite of what we would need to do to keep these boys safe."

"You have to watch the gate," said Loki.

"Screw the gate," said Danny. "Protect the kids."

"You say that because you don't know what you're talking about," said Loki.

"He says it because he's a better man than you," said Anonoei.

"I don't deny that," said Loki. "But Danny North doesn't understand the monster that we're at war with—not the Families, but Belgod. I would rather see these two boys torn apart by dogs than let Belgod pass through a Great Gate." Before anyone could do more than gasp or groan at his heartlessness, Loki raised a hand. "If you knew what I know, you'd feel the same. A terrible enemy is poised to rule both worlds with irrevocable power, forever. It would never, never end. Do you understand me? Especially if he ever got control of Danny. To keep that enemy from achieving that kind of mastery, that *infinite* evil, I would let any of you die. I would die myself, if by dying I could be sure of stopping him."

He looked so fierce that the others remained silent.

"That's hypothetical," Danny finally said. "You want the boys safe, *and* you want the gate safe. So do we all. But you don't get to decide what Mom and Dad do, if push comes to shove. They decide. So the question is—are you going to trust them with the boys? Or not?"

Loki put his hand to his forehead. "I can't expect any of you to understand what I know. How could you believe it, even if you understood?" He rose to his feet. "Anonoei, if I can give my gates to Danny North, you can give your sons to these good people."

"He *took* your gates."

"I did," said Danny. "But then he gave them to me. I'm not sure how he did it—but they're obedient to me."

"Either give your sons to Marion and Leslie, or stay here with them," said Loki. "With you or without you, I'm returning to Westil now."

"If I let you," said Danny.

"You couldn't stop me if you tried," said Loki.

"I could eat that Wild Gate," said Danny.

"If you could, you already would have," said Loki.

"Can you?" asked Danny. "Because if you can, do it."

"Three-fourths of that gate is yours," said Loki. "I don't have the power to swallow any gate of yours. But the quarter of that gate that isn't yours—you don't know how to disentangle it. You don't know how to swallow an active gate that isn't your own."

"Teach me," said Danny.

"It can't be taught," said Loki. "It can only be learned. I can't even demonstrate, because I don't have enough outself to make a

Great Gate and show you, and besides, I would never be so arrogant as to make a Great Gate with angry captive outselves bound up in it."

"In other words," said Danny, "you never thought of it, you never tried it, and now you want me to feel stupid for doing it."

Loki stared at him for a long couple of seconds. "Gatemages all think they're so smart," he said.

"You'd know," said Danny.

Loki reached out a hand to Anonoei. "Are you coming with me or not? I've been in the same world with the Belgod longer than I should. He knows me. And I'm in no shape to meet him now. So I'm not waiting any longer."

Anonoei gave her sons one more agonized look. "Eluik, Enopp, I love you," she said. "I promise I'll come back. Please obey these people. And above all, find a way to separate and become yourselves again."

"Now," said Loki.

Anonoei took his proffered hand.

In that instant, they were gone.

Danny felt the gate that Loki made, and felt it disappear the moment they had passed through it. Loki had gated to the barn, and no sooner had he and Anonoei got there than Danny felt them pass once more through the Wild Gate, back to Westil.

"Is Mother going to die?" asked Enopp.

"No," said Leslie.

"Let's not start by lying to these boys," said Marion. "We don't know what she and Loki are going to do or how well they'll do it. But I believe she does mean to come back for them, if she possibly can."

"I wasn't lying," said Leslie. "I was *encouraging*."

"Loki is the oldest, wisest mage in either world," said Danny. "And he's looking after your mother."

Enopp nodded. "And are you going to teach me how to be a gatemage?"

"If that's what you turn out to be," said Danny. "Which we won't know for at least a few more years."

"Is that a promise?" asked Enopp.

"It's an honest statement of my intentions at this time," said Danny. "But since I don't know the future, I'm not going to make any promises I might not be able to keep." Danny spoke over Enopp's head, to Marion and Leslie. "I have to get to school. Are you all right?"

"Our lives just got a little more complicated," said Leslie. "But what could possibly go wrong?" She gave him her sweetest, most sarcastic smile.

"That's why I love you," said Danny.

He gated back to his little home. Only as he looked at his own kitchen did he realize that he was so stupid, he hadn't taken any of Leslie's bread with him to eat for breakfast.

14

Loyalty

Keel was as loyal a servant as a king could have, or so it seemed to everyone but himself. But Keel knew that it was mere coincidence that created that illusion.

In his twenties, he had been called Plank, because he was master of refitting of the King's ships. His own father trained him to the task, for he was Plank son of Plank son of Plank, three generations of master shipwrights, who could heal a damaged ship and make it whole again.

Unlike his father, who was a grumbler and griper, Keel-when-he-was-still-Plank had never uttered a word of complaint. After the war with Gray ended badly, and the treaty forbade Iceway to have more than six small fighting ships, suited only for subduing pirates, Plank never criticized the treaty, nor said a word against King Prayard's father for having started and then lost the war.

Instead, he quietly set about repairing all the ships that managed to limp home from the war. Five of the smallest and fastest he refitted for speed, to skim lightly across the water in pursuit of pirates.

The others—the great warships—he refitted so that even the most suspicious inspectors from Gray would see nothing but cargo vessels, suitable only for trade, ships that wallowed in the water, sluggishly lurching from port to port.

When Prayard became king, he came himself to see what Plank had done. He stood on a tower overlooking the harbor and watched the clumsy cargo vessels that once had been proud warships, as they bumbled up the Graybourn to the docks, or yawed their awkward way downstream, barely manageable from the helm. Prayard did not complain, either. "You have kept my father's word," he said to Plank. "It is a good servant who preserves the King's honor."

"I am the King's true servant," said Plank. Then, most softly, he said, "Return at night and see my obedience."

Five days later, Plank was wakened by the hand of his youngest son, Knot. "A visitor who has no name," said his son, and Plank knew it had to be the King.

No word was spoken, and only the most shaded lamp was used, casting a tiny bar of light whenever Plank raised the shield. He led his hooded visitor onto the most sluggish of the former warships. He dismissed the watch and took the King down into the belly of the ship, one deck above the bilge.

Then Plank lifted a hatch, handed the lantern to the King, and plunged down into the bilgewater. Rats squealed and scurried, but Plank paid them no attention. "Cast the beam here," he said softly.

The King raised the shield and aimed the beam at Plank's hands. Plank gripped a lever that was snugged up under a deck joist and pulled it toward himself, moving it through an arc that was one-eighth of a circle. Where the lever had been invisible, now it was plain to see.

"What does it do?" asked the King softly.

"This lever is attached to a baffle under the hull. When the lever is parallel with the joist, the baffle is extended. It catches the water and makes the ship move slowly and awkwardly. It's a home for barnacles. But at sea, far from shore"—he did not say, Far from the observing eyes of the Grayfolk—"a captain could send a trusted mate down into the bilge, to wade his way along the whole length of the keel, turning all these levers one-eighth of a circle, and then the baffles are drawn up snug against the bottom."

The King nodded. He was a seamage. He understood that this would make the ship move much more smoothly through the water. The sailcloth, with its load of barnacles, would still be a drag on the ship, but it could be managed now.

"But the mate must be careful," Plank continued. "For if he turns the levers forward instead of aft, the baffles are completely released and fall away from the ship, leaving the hull smooth and clean. That would be a tragic accident, for the ship would then move as swiftly and surely as a warship, and some might think that the treaty had been violated."

"An awkward design," said the King softly. "What madman would think of such a thing?"

"I fear it was my own invention, sir. I'm glad the King will never know how clumsily I obeyed his command."

"You must be sure to acquaint every captain of this mechanism, and make sure they know which way to turn the lever," said the King. "We would not want to find ourselves, quite by accident, with a war fleet of a hundred ships, where the treaty binds us to no more than five fighting vessels."

"On your advice, sir, I will train the captains," said Plank.

Every time a ship came into port, Plank would send his divers down to replace the sailcloth in the baffles, and to make sure the mechanisms worked smoothly. But only those divers saw how the baffles were made, and only the captains of the ships understood how the mechanisms were controlled.

It was up to the King to decide how large a crew these wallowing merchantmen would carry, and how well the men might have been trained for war.

Two years later, when Plank's overseer, the steward of the royal factories, retired, it was Plank, and not the man's own son, who was appointed to the post. "Because you serve me so loyally," said Prayard, "doing for the King what the King cannot even think to ask."

That was how Plank became Keel, master of shipyards, wagonyards, smithies, road graders, armorers, and all other manufactories that served the royal will. As Keel, he did all that the King expected, preparing Iceway to be constantly ready for war while seeming to be committed to peace, and keeping the secret of it from all but a handful of the men who labored under him.

But the deepest secret of all was this: Keel was not loyal to the King at all.

Keel was loyal to Iceway. Not to the rocks and canyons, the fertile mountain valleys fed by icy streams, the great fjords that cut their way into the bitter coast, the islands where Icewegians kept their trading posts and fishing villages.

Keel was loyal to the people, one by one and all together, the nation of Iceway. As long as the King acted in the interest of the Icewegians, Keel obeyed and served. But if the King betrayed them, Keel did what was right for the survival and the freedom of the Icefolk.

That's why, as Plank, he had never shown the levers to King Prayard's father, for he was the man who had lost the war and betrayed Iceway with a humiliating treaty. Prayard, though, seemed to Keel to act in the interest of the people, and so he showed him the fleet that was ready for his use, should he choose to use it.

But King Prayard did not use the fleet. He was grateful enough—Keel's advancement to a place of greater trust and authority, not to mention wealth and status, was proof of that. But the King did not *use* the hidden warfleet. He stayed married to the Birdbrain of Gray, the useless Bexoi. He allowed the men of Gray to strut through the streets of Kamesham unkilled, he allowed the ambassador and his spies to have the run of the castle Nassassa without a taste of poison or the cold bite of a dagger in the ear.

King Prayard did not suspect that Keel was the center of a plot to kill Queen Bexoi and assassinate every Grayman in Iceway, because Keel was careful with his plans. No one understood the whole plan; no one knew any part but his own.

It was to have begun with the poisoning of Bexoi, but the nightcook of that time, the woman Hull, discovered the plan and blocked it. Keel arranged for her to die that night, and began again. He knew of a much more foolish plan to murder Bexoi outright, one that originated among the Graymen; he was content to have the bitch from Gray be murdered by the hands of Gray. But that plot, too, was blocked, though this time Keel did not know how.

A third time he planned, and this time he understood that King Prayard himself would have to die. But not before his concubine, Anonoei, and her two sons were safely out of Nassassa and hidden where no one from Gray could find them.

That was when Anonoei, in the midst of preparing for a journey she had only learned about that morning, simply disappeared, along with her sons.

Keel understood then that even plans that no one knew about were somehow known. There was a manmage in the castle, he realized. Someone who could peer into the thoughts of his heart—or someone's thoughts, someone's heart.

Ever since the disappearance of Anonoei, Keel had bided his time, making no new plans, watching to see who it was who had kidnapped or murdered Anonoei and her boys.

He had watched as Bexoi gave birth to a darling child that everyone loved, hailing the brat as true heir, even though Bexoi was no mage and the child would surely be drekka, or weak if he was a mage after all. He had watched as Prayard trotted Bexoi out before all the people, and they began to love her instead of hating her as the symbol of their enslavement to Gray.

He had rejoiced when that baby died, accidentally smothered by a pillow in his bed; the nurse who had been careless was promptly killed. Keel would not have lifted a finger to save her—fools deserve whatever comes to them—but at the same time he was glad of her foolishness.

But that same day, there had been a flurry of activity among the palace guards, some business about rappelling down the face of the cliff below the castle and bringing out—dead—some squatters who had apparently been living in some of the ancient caves. How the squatters had got there, and how they had been supplied with food, no one explained, and when Keel set out to learn more, he found that all the guards who had been involved in the operation were gone. Sent away the same day. It was very strange, and Keel did not like it when he did not know what was going on in Nassassa.

He made no complaint at being kept ignorant; indeed, he never showed interest in anything but his own duty. He was the perfect servant, the embodiment of loyal service to the King. But with Queen Bexoi so pregnant that she seemed about to burst with the next baby—the next heir whose succession to the throne would mean Gray's perpetual domination of Iceway—Keel knew that it was time to act, and perhaps not subtly this time.

What stayed his hand was the knowledge that he did not know enough. He still did not understand how the earlier plots had been detected and blocked. These days Queen Bexoi took great care never to be alone.

Prayard also had her well guarded, too many guards at once. One man could be enlisted, another man bribed—but five? Six? Someone would blab or boast. Keel had to find another way to kill her.

Perhaps it would be enough to kill the King himself. What could Bexoi do, with her child unborn?

It was too uncertain, though, for Keel to feel ready to act. Too many things could go wrong. Gray might leap into action, using the death of Prayard as a pretext to seize power. Keel's war against Gray might die before it had well begun. There was no point in creating chaos, if he was not prepared to turn it into a strong new order that would regain Iceway's freedom and power.

If only Anonoei had not been taken. If only one of her sons were still alive. Someone to be a focal point for Icewegian patriots. Keel would not be regent himself, but it would be someone that he trusted—perhaps even Anonoei. Since she was no mage at all, and a compliant woman, she would be easy to guide.

But she was gone, and so were her sons. It was a terrible time for those who loved Iceway. If only King Prayard were a better king, and not the doting lover of that Sparrowgirl Bexoi.

It was one of Keel's talents that he could conduct his ordinary business while plotting his plots; he did not have to talk his plans out with anyone, nor did he need to draw maps or doodle words and notes. He seemed to others to be busy all the time; they did not know what was going on behind his eyes.

His meeting with the heads of two quarreling merchant families ended—he had almost, but not quite, grabbed them by the hair and banged their foolish heads together. They were both young, too young for so much responsibility. Only men who were old enough for their temper to be cool were fit to lead in matters of commerce.

Or revolution. Or war. Sometimes Keel even wondered if *he* was still too young.

It hardly mattered. Since none of his plans worked out, he would be old soon enough. Maybe he needed to be more hotheaded, and not so careful.

Then again, hotheads were quickly caught and killed. Keel got where he was by being methodical and silent.

As he was silent now, alone in his small office overlooking the armory yard. He strode to the window and looked out over the hum of activity. He knew the purpose of every man and woman who crossed the yard, knew what was in every wagon, what was being forged by every fire.

"Do not turn from the window. Do not show any sign that you are not alone."

It was a woman's voice. He knew the voice. It was Anonoei.

But he did not turn. If she was alive, if she was here, then something powerful and dangerous was going on.

So he said nothing, did not turn. He waited.

"Now, as if you were weary of watching, close the shutter, my old friend."

Wordlessly—for he did not want anyone below to glance up and see his lips moving, and thus conclude that he was not alone—he closed the shutters and then turned.

There she stood, looking exactly as she had the morning when he told her to pack for herself and her sons, only the smallest bag of the least clothes, only what she needed for two days. Instead the foolish woman had made a big production of packing a trunk, and someone must have seen, must have said what she was doing, and so she had been taken.

But she was still beautiful. Still warm and comforting in the way she looked at every man. As so many times before, Keel thought: I can see why the King loves this woman.

He certainly forgot her quickly enough when she was gone.

"I'm sorry I could not send you word before now," she said softly.

"I feared that you were dead."

"So did I, sometimes," said Anonoei. "And other times I wished that I could die. But now I am glad to be alive, and glad of my friends. Are you my friend?"

Keel shook his head. "I am the loyal servant of—"

"Oh, my dear, my dear old friend," said Anonoei, "I know what you are the loyal servant of."

"Who?" he asked.

"Some say you serve only your own career. Some say you serve the factories as once you served the shipyards. Some say you serve your family's ambitions. Some say you serve the King like his faithful dog."

"Dogs turn on their masters; when the master falls, when he dies, the dog will drink his blood and tear his flesh."

"Always a cheerful man," said Anonoei. "I know you serve something higher than your own career, higher than your family, higher than the King. I know that you are loyal to Iceway."

"Are you going to pretend that you share this loyalty?" asked Keel.

"Are you going to ask where I have been?" asked Anonoei.

"No," said Keel. "If you don't want me to know, then your answer would be a lie; if you want me to know, you'll tell me without my asking."

"My loyalty is to my children," said Anonoei, "but thanks to a trusted friend, they are now safe, in a place where no one can find them, let alone harm them."

"One might suppose that you are saying they are dead," said Keel.

"Not dead. Very much alive, and ready to inherit the kingdom, if the need for that arises. But I hope it does not arise."

Keel wasn't sure how to hear her words. With anyone else, he would assume that it was all a sham—that she was telling the truth by denying it. But there was something about her that made him think she might be honest.

"You hope the Sparrow Queen's wombling will take their place?"

"Those sons were born from love, not ambition," said Anonoei. "I think they will be happier not to be kings, or to be used by those who want to make them kings. But if they're needed, they're alive and safe. I thought you should know."

"It was kind of you to tell me," said Keel. He let the tone of his voice say, If that's all, then go away.

"You're an amazing fellow, Keel. A woman that you thought was dead shows up in your cell and you seem utterly unsurprised."

"If I showed what I feel then all men would know my heart," said Keel.

"Instead, only I do."

"Your new friend is a gatemage," said Keel. "Or else you could not have entered this place. Be careful—gatemages have a way of running afoul of the Gate Thief and losing all their magery. You wouldn't want to be stranded somewhere inaccessible. I hope your boys are in a place they can walk away from, when the gates are gone."

Anonoei smiled a thin but pleasant smile. Keel was a clever man. He knew what the smile had to mean.

"The liar told you that he *was* the Gate Thief, didn't he? Don't you know that gatemages can never tell the truth? It's against their nature."

"Let's talk about what we're going to do now," said Anonoei.

There was nothing overtly sexual or even ironic in her tone, and yet "what we're going to do now" made Keel's thoughts suddenly turn to the rumpled bed in the corner of the room.

"Not now," said Anonoei, as if she had read his thoughts. It seemed some women could always read such thoughts, when men had them. Or perhaps men *always* had such thoughts, so it took no great cleverness to read them. "I know you plan to kill the King, but I wish that you would not."

"You do me no favor to say that," said Keel. "I have no such plan."

"That was your plan when you told me to pack. I obeyed you, but made it obvious enough that surely someone would notice me and tell the King, so he could prevent my going."

"Did he?"

"Someone else did," said Anonoei. "I will not let you kill the King."

Keel shrugged. "Since I do not plan to do this awful crime," he began.

Then he found himself outside the door of his room. He had not moved, or rather, he had made no effort to move. Yet he had been inside the room, and now he was outside it.

The door opened. "Come in," said Anonoei. "Do you believe me now when I say that you will not kill anyone I tell you not to kill?"

"So you're a mage after all," said Keel, reentering the room.

"Am I?"

"Or that gatemage friend of yours is listening, sending me here and there at your command."

"Oh, no one commands him, dear Keel. You have the magery of iron. It does what you command, your machinery never needs oiling, your iron never rusts. That is what you do."

"And what do you do?" asked Keel.

She reached out and touched his hand.

All at once his body filled with a bright longing for her to wrap her arms around him.

And then, just as quickly, she shifted her hand and he felt himself to be unworthy of her love. He did not want her to embrace him, he wanted her to overlook him entirely.

She took his hand between both her hands and all those feelings fled. Now between them there was only a deep, abiding friendship. The most important friendship of their lives.

"Manmage," he whispered.

"I did not want you to think I was untalented," she said. "Or that my sons were only half-mages by their birth."

"How can I trust anything I think or feel or decide, if you can make me swing from one longing to another in a moment?"

"Don't base your decision on how you feel," she said. "You

never have; why start now? I came to you because you're the steady one. You chose your loyalty and never wavered. I have no desire to change that loyalty—only to explain why your perfect loyalty should lead you to another course of action."

"Another?" asked Keel. "I have no course of action, so I can hardly change it."

"I will not attempt to control your decision," said Anonoei, "but do remember how useless it is for you to try to lie to me. You're a subtle man, Keel, and you tell your secrets to no one but me."

"I have no secrets."

"It will not be good for Iceway if King Prayard dies. Yes, my sons are alive, but I will not bring them back until they're old enough to stand up for themselves. This is a bad time for the chaos of a dead king without an heir, or with only an unborn baby to inherit. The jarlingmoot will insist on electing an adult as king, breaking the line. But there's no one ready to stand as king. Not even you."

He knew that she was right.

"I want Queen Bexoi's baby to be born alive," said Anonoei. "It's good for Iceway if Gray believes that a half-Gray child is next in line for Iceway's throne."

Because she was communicating with him at levels deeper than speech, he understood exactly what she meant. "You think the child can be controlled?"

"I think the mother means to kill the King herself and rule Iceway through him."

"And you think this is a reason to allow the sparrowbitch to live?"

"I think this is a reason to keep the King away from her."

"I'll take her to an island far from here and strand her on the shore—will that do?"

"She would burn the ship to the waterline before she'd let it take her anywhere," said Anonoei.

"A firemage," said Keel. "Not a Feathergirl."

"A Firemaster at least," said Anonoei. "And so powerful she can make a clant that bleeds."

Now Keel understood why Luvix had been so sure that he had killed Bexoi.

"I should have guessed it," said Keel.

"No one else did," said Anonoei.

"Except you," said Keel.

"I don't guess," said Anonoei. "You must be more patient than you have been so far."

"What if I choose to ignore your warning?"

"Then I'll find someone else to help me," said Anonoei, "and you can watch the people suffer as you destroy Iceway. As I said, my loyalty is not to Iceway, though our plans can help each other if you choose."

"What do you want me to do?" said Keel, believing her but also knowing that his belief was probably the result of her magery.

"Give me time," she said. "Give me a chance to go work my plans in Gray. Let me shape events so Gray's ambitious heir grows impatient with his father. Let it be Gray that collapses in chaos, while Bexoi is here, nursing and protecting her second son. Let's see whether her motherly love is stronger than her ambition. Either she'll stay here and remain safe, or she'll go—and leave her son behind."

Keel did not have to say all that immediately came into his mind. That Anonoei wanted Bexoi's son, and not one of her own, to be the pawn in the game of succession. That if Bexoi left her child behind, the child would be under Keel's control. That if she took the child with her, King Prayard would be without an heir if something happened to Bexoi and the boy. That if she remained here in Nassassa, under Prayard's protection, then Anonoei would have a free hand to work whatever mischief she and her gatemage friend might be planning for Gray.

It was a much better plan than anything that had been within Keel's power.

"I wish I could trust my approval of your plan," said Keel.

"I'm not that strong a manmage," said Anonoei. "I can't make you want what you do not want. I can't make you fear what you do not fear. I can't make you think of what you do not already know."

"Then what *can* you do?"

"I can work on weak-minded people who don't know what they want, who aren't smart enough to fear what they should fear, and who think they know already what they do not know. That's the drawback of manmagery—all our forced servants are weak and dull. So I come to you, not to be my servant, but to be my friend and ally."

Keel thought of how, at a touch, she had made him want her.

But he must have shown on his face that he was thinking of this, because she shook her head. "I did not make you feel what you did not feel," she said. "I made you aware of what you had always felt."

And he knew that it was true. That all the time the King had loved Anonoei, Keel had also longed for her. He had such self-control that he had concealed his desire even from himself. But it was always there.

"Let's be clear on one point," said Anonoei. "I know you have that desire, and I am specifically *not* exploiting it. Whatever you do, you must do it in the full knowledge that I will *never* be yours. I have all the sons I need and want, and all the husbands, too. Do you understand?"

It was as if she had erected a wall of ice inside his loins. "I do not act for such reasons," he said.

"That's why you're worth dealing with," she said. "You're good at what you do, and I am good at what I do, each within our limitations. Mage against mage, neither of us is a match for Bexoi. Perhaps no one is in all the world. But we won't stand against her. In fact, we will stand *with* her, protecting her, protecting her son. As long as she and that boy are alive, Gray will be torn apart by conflicting ambitions. And by her choices, she will reveal herself and expose herself and, in the end, betray herself."

"You have a plan far deeper than the one you're telling me," said Keel.

"And you will have plans within plans. But know this: I keep my word. I know that you keep yours. So if you promise me that you will act together with me, then I know that you'll be my ally until you give me fair notice that our pact is over."

"Yes," said Keel. "You understand me well enough, and I make that pact. I will not take the King's life. I will protect Bexoi and her baby. I will give you time to work your workings in Gray."

Anonoei smiled. "I always knew you were the natural king of Iceway. Because only you act for the good of all, and not just for your family or your own ambition."

"I have no ambition."

"You have the large ambition of a patriot," said Anonoei. She took him by the shoulders and kissed him on the mouth—not a woman's kiss, but the kiss of a sister, a friend. "Count on me, and I will count on you."

And then her hands were not on his shoulders, her breath not on his cheek. She was gone from the room, vanished in an instant. Her gatemage had taken her.

And Keel was left there alone with the deep longing for her that had never caused him pain before, because he had not known that it was there. He would die for her, kill for her. He loved her more than he loved his wife or his children, more than he loved his own life. More than he loved Iceway.

If only she would use her power to take this powerful desire away from him.

Yet if he lost that desire, who would he be? What would be in his heart then, if she were gone from it?

15

Running on Automatic

It wasn't a real track meet. Officially, it was an "exhibition" between two high schools, Rockbridge County and Parry McCluer, months before the actual season began. More like two boxers sparring to keep in shape. Like pre-season football. Like *nothing.*

Only you'd never know that from the way Coach Lieder was taking it. Apparently the future of the human race depended on the outcome of every event. If a Parry McCluer athlete won, the human race was safe for another year. If one of the kids from Lexington won, then the alien assault ship was that much closer to landing and enslaving all of human life. Lieder didn't get angry at the losers, he got *despondent.* He even said, "We're doomed, we're doomed." Even though his team was doing a little better than the other guys.

When the manager—a sophomore that Danny barely knew—pointed this out, Lieder looked at him with pity. "Oh, we don't suck as bad as Rockbridge. That's like going out with an ugly girl and saying, 'Well, at least she's breathing.' "

Since Danny suspected the manager had never gone out on any date, "breathing" would have been an improvement for him. But the kid wisely said nothing.

Danny won the 1600 and 3200 meters easily, but Lieder glowered at him and pointed out that he was nowhere near his best time. "It was a race," said Danny. "I won it."

"But you didn't *try*," said Lieder.

"I didn't have to," said Danny. And then inspiration struck. "You want to show these guys my best? In November?"

Lieder thought about this. "So you think you're our secret weapon."

"I've only been running competitively for a few weeks," said Danny. "If I'm a weapon, it's still secret from *me*."

Lieder turned his back and walked away. Which, for Lieder, was like an apology.

But then Lieder got the bright idea of tossing Danny into the 200 meters with no prep.

"I'm tired," said Danny.

"You don't get tired," said Lieder.

"Of course I get tired," said Danny.

"Ricken is limping like a big baby. If you're in the race, he'll try harder."

Danny had committed to the team, which meant obeying the coach, even when he was pushing his athletes too hard in an event that meant nothing. So he said, "Sure thing," and went to take his place at the starting line.

The 200 was almost a sprint, like running a football field from one end zone to the other and back again. But it was Ricken's big event and Danny wasn't going to shame him in it. Even though Ricken was glaring at him as if jumping into his event had been Danny's idea.

Danny passed a gate over Ricken, just in case he really had hurt his ankle like he said. Then, to be fair, he passed all the other runners through gates that took them no distance at all, but got rid of any fatigue or stress injuries or cramps they might be suffering. Let's have an even playing field, thought Danny. Everybody do your best.

It turned out that Ricken's best was better than Danny's after all. Of course, Ricken actually cared and Danny was tired. He hadn't passed *himself* through a gate, so he was still fatigued from the two longer races. Truth to tell, though, he might have been able to stay ahead of Ricken when he made his move at the end. But Ricken wanted it, it was his event, and Danny didn't want to be an asshole.

"You asshole," said Ricken, still panting after the race. "You let me win."

"You mean I didn't trip you?" asked Danny. "I didn't shove you?"

"You didn't *sprint*."

"I ran the thirty-two and the sixteen already today. I didn't *have* a sprint in me."

"You moron!" shouted Lieder as he approached.

"He talking to me or you?" asked Danny.

"Must be me, because you're not a moron, you're an asshole," said Ricken. But he punched Danny lightly in the arm and moved off. They both knew it was Danny that Lieder was yelling at.

"I send you into the 200, you run the 200!"

"Ricken and I left all the Rockbridge guys licking our sweat," said Danny. "And Ricken didn't show injury, did he?"

"I don't send you in to inspire the other guys," said Lieder. "I send you in to win."

Danny stood there.

"You got anything to say for yourself?"

"Besides how I already won two races?"

"Without trying."

"But without losing."

Again a silence.

"You're still at war with me, aren't you?"

"No sir," said Danny. "The 200 is Ricken's distance. He trains for it. He's better than me."

"Bull pucky," said Lieder.

Danny leaned close and talked softly. "I told you I don't compete. I hate competing. Ricken competes. He cares."

"Start caring," said Lieder.

"If I cared about track," said Danny, "would I be at Parry McCluer, with you as my coach?" Danny turned his back and walked away. Not toward the stands. Not toward the team. But toward the fence, which he scrambled over almost like a hop, and then across the road. To the untrained eye, it might have looked like he was walking off the team. But to Danny's more discerning perceptions, he was merely walking off the field because his last event was over.

Lieder must have seen this too, because he didn't yell at Danny to get his butt back with the team, and all the usual abuse.

Or maybe it was because Nicki was there talking to her dad. Calming him down maybe. Or telling him that she liked putting her tongue in Danny's mouth and so he'd better not piss the boy off. Whatever.

Danny didn't go to the parking lot where the team bus was waiting. Instead, he started running up Greenhouse Road, away from Highway 11. Let it look like he was blowing off steam.

What he was really doing was following the voices.

He had learned to ignore the clamor of the captive gates; they were not so much voices as inchoate longings that did not speak to anything in Danny's experience. They felt distant to him, though in the abstract he felt bad about their long captivity. That vague compassion had been, he supposed, the reason he had included the most eager of them in the Great Gate he made in Silvermans' barn. Hadn't that turned out well.

The voices that had been Loki's own gates, however, were a different matter. At first their nagging chant had been like the pulse of a large beast, another heart beating somewhere in his body. Gate, gate, gate, they intoned; and when he made the Great Gate, they had seemed to panic. But them, too, he had pressed down and kept at bay, so that he could concentrate on other things. He thought that it must be rather like tinnitus, the unceasing whine that some people hear constantly in their ears. You just learn to blank it out.

But in the days since Loki had *given* his gates to him, everything had changed. The constant throb of gate, gate, gate was gone. At first, what remained had seemed to him like silence, except for the distant clamor of the captives that remained inside him.

It was not silence, though. It was something different. These gates that had once seemed almost insane in their monomania were now attentive, observant. Danny felt himself being watched. But not in an unfriendly way, not by a stranger. Rather it was as if his own inmost mind, the part of his mind that watched his conscious thoughts and responded to them, had been joined by others. They did not judge him, but they had suggestions.

That was what had taken him a while to understand. They did not speak in words. Even the gate-gate-gate of the past had not been in actual language. It was deeper than language. He knew the meaning of the pulse of desire. But he could not have named the language it was being spoken in, and then concluded that it was no language at all. It was self-speech. As was their conversation now.

Voices, then, but not words. And yet remembering their suggestions, even a half-moment later, he thought of them as words. His own words. His own language. Just as his conscious mind translated the impulses that came from his deep observer-mind into language the moment they surfaced into consciousness. When Loki gave his lost gates to Danny, they had become, if not an actual part of himself, the most intimate of friends. They were on his side. Their suggestions were designed to help him do better.

They did not care much about what happened with Coach Lieder, because Danny didn't actually care that much. It was a part of the high school life that he had desired, but since arranging to come to Parry McCluer, things had become quite strange, and the whole enterprise of American public education seemed a little pointless to Danny. Homework? Really? A track team? He was going through the motions now.

To him, the only thing real about high school was his friends. His feelings about them—and Loki's gates agreed. About *them* they had suggestions, though mostly they reinforced his own intentions. Don't let Xena think for a moment that you return her imaginary affection—check. Pat might be something real; don't mess with her or hurt her if you can help it. Check. Trust Hal, because he can be counted on, but recognize that Wheeler is the slave of impulse and doesn't know how to keep his word. Right, right.

Now, as he ran from the grounds of Rockbridge High, up to the crest of Greenhouse Road and then down the steep slope toward the nursery that gave the road its name, he found that Loki's gates were the music giving meaning and rhythm to his running.

Education, that was the idea they were talking about. Learning. He needed to learn. But they were not talking about calculus or social studies. There were things that Loki's gates thought that he absolutely had to know, and didn't know.

So he asked them, silently: What should I know?

Belmage. Danger of the Belmage. The danger that made us close all gates, prevent all Great Gates. Danger of the Belmage.

Immediately Danny remembered the Fistalk inscription quoted in that book in the Library of Congress. "Here Loki twisted a new gate to heaven. . . . Here Odin crushed the might of Carthage until the survivors wept in the blood of their children." Nasty stuff. An earlier time.

Oh, like Hitler and Stalin and Pol Pot and Osama bin Laden were any better.

That was not Loki's gates talking—what would they know of that? It was an interruption from Danny's own observer-self, criticizing his own conscious thoughts. "Nasty stuff, earlier time" had provoked his deep self to push a thought to the surface, refuting his own foolish conclusion. Of course, the moment the thought came to the surface, it *became* his conscious thought, while the observer-self continued to lurk in the background.

But now he felt the prodding of Loki's gates. Yes yes yes, they were saying. Think about that. That's what you need to think about.

What? Danny demanded. What was I thinking about?

That's how Loki's gates differed from his own deep self—he never didn't know what his observer-self was responding to. But Loki's gates were still not himself. They were his, they served him, but they were not truly a part of him.

Yes yes yes, they said again. Think about this.

So they wanted him to continue this self-examination as he ran down the hill, staying on the right, the outside, as he went around the blind curves, because people took this road too fast and he had to make sure he was visible to them. They wanted him to think about the difference between his deep observer-self and his conscious mind and the gates Loki had given him and . . .

Where were his own gates?

Oh such a good question. It was as if they applauded him.

If Loki's gates talk to me, then why don't my own gates?

And then he thought—or did Loki's gates put the thought into his mind?—The reason my gates don't talk to me is that they *are* me. For all I know they *do* talk to me, but I hear them as myself, as . . .

No no no.

It was like playing hot-and-cold as a child, the cousins all yelling "Warmer, warmer, hot, hot, *cold* now!" as the child who was It searched blindly for the hidden object.

This memory had come unbidden. Did that mean it came from his own gates?

No no no.

"Then what are my gates doing?" he asked aloud.

And then, as he came to a stop at the bottom of the hill, where a complicated three-way intersection with Furrs Mill Road was too narrow and dangerous for him not to pay attention, he realized: Who has been operating my body as I ran down this hill, thinking all these thoughts?

It wasn't my observer-self—that was listening to my ponderings. It certainly wasn't my conscious mind—it was *doing* the pondering. I have no memory of anything I did, any choices I made coming down the hill, and yet I was making them. I was passed by several cars—now I can remember, vaguely, that they came from behind and ahead, several of them—but they never interrupted my conscious thoughts.

My gates were operating my legs and arms. Keeping me on the road. I had a mindless task to perform—keeping myself alive while running—and I turned it over to someone else while my conscious self and my deeper observer-self were engaged in this inner conversation.

And it all came together. While Loki had been asleep in a tree for a thousand years or so, he had set most of his gates to carrying out a simple but urgent task: watching the world for gatemages. And they had stuck with that task the way his own gates—his outself—had taken care of his running body while his mind was otherwise engaged.

But Loki had freed his captive gates from their old, unceasing assignment, and given them to me. They weren't watching the world anymore, they were . . .

No, they *were* watching the world. They were still doing what Loki had set them to do. But they were reporting to me. Or rather, preparing me to be ready for battle.

And he realized that *this* realization had come from the voices.

Or at least it had been confirmed by them. They want me to learn about the Belmage because now that there are Great Gates in the world and a Gatefather capable of making more of them—me—I am the person that the Belmage will come after.

The words of the inscription came back to his mind. "We have faced Bel and he has ruled the hearts of many. Bold men ran like deer from his face, but Loki did not run." Of course this wasn't the Loki whose gates Danny now had within him. It was a much earlier Loki, one who had defeated Bel in his day.

"Loki found the dark gate of Bel through which their god poured fear into the world and through which he carried off the hearts of brave men to eat at his feasting table." What did that mean, actually? Was it something like what the Gate Thief did?

But more of the inscription came to mind and his observer-self realized that it was the voices that were pushing it to his attention. "The jaws of Bel seized his heart to carry it away. Loki held tight to his own heart and followed the jaws of the beast."

Wasn't that the very passage that Danny had used to guide him in overcoming the Gate Thief? That had to be what it meant, didn't it? That Bel was a gate thief, too?

"Loki tricked Bel into thinking he was captive, but he was not captive. His heart held the jaws; the jaws did not hold his heart." Yes! That's what I did to Loki! That's how I defeated him!

"And when he found the gate of Bel, he moved the mouth over the heart of the sun. Let Bel eat the sun and drag it back to his dark world! He has no more home in Mittlegard."

That was the end of the inscription. What am I missing? It sounds like Bel is a gatemage, not a manmage at all.

Then it dawned on him. Just because the inscription was ancient didn't mean that the person who wrote it knew what he was talking about. Was it written by that earlier Loki himself? Doubtful. It was written by somebody later, repeating what he had heard. Had he heard it from the Loki's own lips? Maybe. But would that even matter? If the writer was not himself a gatemage, would he understand anything that a Gatefather said about what he had done in fighting the Belmage?

He was at the top of Furrs Mill Road, where it intersected with Highway 11. Danny turned right onto the bridge and ran along it as the light turned green and cars and trucks set the whole bridge to vibrating like an earthquake. It always did that. It was nothing.

Once again, Danny had no memory of coming up the hill. Only when something different came up did his running come to his conscious attention.

I have been following that ancient inscription because it gave me the idea that helped me overcome the Gate Thief. But the Belmage is definitely *not* a gatemage, and the inscription sounds as if it's a battle between two gatemages. That's what the writer probably thought it was. But Loki—*this* Loki, the one I know, the one whose gates are inside me—he realized what the Belmage really was.

If the Belmage had been a Gatefather, it would have done no good to take all the gates.

So the inscription accidentally taught me how to fight another gatemage, but it taught me nothing about how to fight a manmage.

And not an ordinary manmage anyway. The Belmage.

Belmage Belmage Belmage, echoed the voices.

Who in the world can teach me about the Belmage? Danny asked.

Nobody in the world today, that's who, Danny said to himself. For fifteen centuries and more, gatemages and manmages have been killed whenever and wherever they were caught. How can anybody possibly tell me about the Belmage?

Loki, that's who.

Yes yes.

But he doesn't tell me anything. If I'm supposed to learn from him, why isn't he here teaching me?

He won't he won't.

Then how can I learn? Who knows?

Silence.

You know, Danny said silently to the voices. You know. Loki won't tell me, but you know everything he knows and you serve me now, you're mine now. So instead of obeying him and keeping silent, you're going to teach me.

Silence.

So teach me.

He was off the bridge so the vibration under his feet stopped. Solid ground felt almost boring after the bridge.

He stopped and waited till traffic cleared so he could make the dangerous crossing of Route 11 to get on McCorkle Drive, which was far safer to run on than 11.

You're not going to teach me, Danny said to the voices.

Silence.

But you want to teach me.

Silence.

Danny thought about how he couldn't remember much about the running that had been controlled by his own outself. He realized that the voices had brought that memory to his mind. A memory of what he had failed to remember just a few minutes ago.

But it hadn't been *their* memory, it had been his. They didn't *have* memories, they could only prompt me to remember what I already knew.

Well, that's a dead end. I can't remember what I never learned.

Remember.

How can I remember? I never knew!

Re. Member. We. Re.

It was so vague. No words. He had no words to explain to himself what they were trying to say.

You do remember.

Remember.

But you can't *tell* me what you remember.

Almost. Warmer. Warmer.

He thought again about how he had been able to think back and remember the cars that had passed him. Cars that he hadn't been conscious of when they passed him, and which he had forgotten until he *tried* to remember them, but then the memory had surfaced. Sort of. Vaguely.

You remember, he said to the voices, but you don't *remember* that you remember. Something has to call up the memories. You have to be tricked into remembering. You have to be reminded in order to remember.

The voices flooded him with relief. He was right.

He was also standing on the edge of Highway 60, directly across the road from the combination McDonald's and Citgo station. How could he possibly already be here? No way had that much time passed.

But it had. He could think back now and remember every curve of McCorkle Drive, every uphill and downhill. He could even remember what thought he had been thinking at each stage along the way. The distance he covered had nothing to do with how much thinking he got done.

And now he remembered that he had been distracted repeatedly by other thoughts. He had thought about Pat and wondered what it would be like to sleep with her. Had thought about Xena and realized how dangerous it was to let himself think about *her* much more powerful sexuality. Thought about Nicki Lieder and wondered what her game even was and wondered even more how she had figured out that he had done something to heal her.

Yet he also remembered thinking a clear chain of thoughts about the Belmage and Loki's gates and how they put thoughts in his head and whether they could remember things and . . .

This was their demo. They were showing me how they held together a clear, continuous chain of reasoning even though I actually got distracted by thoughts of women and also by some of my anger at Coach Lieder—I had been thinking of that when I actually crossed 11, about what an asshole he is, trying to get me to stick it in Ricken's face. I thought about so many things, I wasn't concentrating on one thing at all.

But something kept pulling me back, something held on to the thread.

It isn't just running that the gates, the outself, can take care of for me. It's also my thinking. They have no language, they can't *tell* me any memories, but they can prompt me to think back and recover the memories . . .

There's still the problem that *I don't have Loki's memories* so you can't prompt me to recover them!

Silence.

But you didn't prompt me to remember anything, Danny said to them as he realized it. *I* prompted *you* to remember it and then *you* fed the memories to me.

That's what you want to do. You want me to somehow prompt *you* to tell *me* what Loki learned.

Yes yes yes.

How?

And then, for a long moment, he became profoundly stupid. Completely lost. He stood there looking blindly at the road, seeing nothing, and thinking absolutely nothing. A complete stupor.

A police car pulled up in front of him. The window came down. Danny walked over to the window, bent down to look inside.

"I couldn't tell if you were trying to cross the road or what," said the cop.

Danny realized that the "or what" might have something to do with throwing himself in front of a semi-truck.

"Just deciding whether to go to McDonald's or just run back home to BV."

"You're going to run to BV?"

Danny indicated his clothes. "I was at the track meet at Rockbridge."

"They have a team bus."

"Coach Lieder pissed me off," said Danny.

The cop grinned. "OK, I get that. Just . . . if you cross the street, be careful. You looked like you were about to cross, but you somehow froze in mid-step. You know? Like a freezeframe in a movie."

"I had no idea," said Danny. "Just got caught up in an argument I was having with Bleeder. Inside my head."

"Well, just remember, nobody ever wins an argument with the coach." The cop gave him a little wave and drove off, the window rolling up as he went.

Nice guy.

Danny turned to face south on 60. Stay on the left side. Don't cross the street.

He didn't run. He jogged. Shambled, really.

What was that about? he asked the voices. What had he been thinking about when he suddenly got so stupid?

He was asking the voices how he could prompt *them* to tell him about things that only Loki would remember.

And then he realized. They had demonstrated something. That had disconnected him from the moment. Or they had disconnected his own gates, or distracted him—something. They had done something so that his body *didn't* just keep on doing what he told it to do, the way Loki's gates had kept on following his instructions while he lived in a tree, the way Danny's outself had kept on running his body while he thought about other things.

He thought about how he remembered what he had been thinking about during each stage of his run along McCorkle Drive. He had mentally gone back to the process. Going up this hill, making that turn, passing this driveway, going down the hill, looking at the highway onramp, seeing the McDonald's sign.

He had mentally retraced all the steps.

But he couldn't *re*trace steps that Loki had taken, and he had not.

But he could *trace* them.

Do you know where Loki learned the nature of the Belmage?

A sort of vague approval.

You can't *tell* me where.

Yes yes yes.

But can you take me there?

Again, vague approval.

Danny jogged left into a driveway, past a building, to the back of the parking lot, behind a tree and some bushes, and made a gate.

He had no idea where the gate was leading. He left it up to Loki's gates. Don't tell me where I need to go, because you can't, you don't know. Just *take* me there because what you have is not word memory or even picture memory, it's kinetic memory. You remember what you *did*, and then the other kinds of memories come popping back.

Yes yes yes.

There was the gate. He stepped through it.

And found himself in a bare stretch of desert, and it was nighttime, and it was cold. But there was a lot of moonlight, and there wasn't a cloud in the sky, so he could see just fine.

His first thought was: Mohave Desert? Death Valley?

Then he realized: America hadn't even been discovered when Loki lived in Mittlegard.

And this was *too* bone dry.

And—duh—in the Mohave Desert it would be three hours *earlier* than it was in Virginia, and so it would be even earlier in the day. Here it was night. He was on the dark side of Earth.

He looked at the position of the moon. The stars. He wasn't a fanatic about it, but he knew how to locate himself, roughly, if he did a little thinking.

Plus, he also knew where all his gates were. They were far beyond the curvature of the Earth, but he was at just about the same latitude as the gates at Veevee's place in Naples. That meant, going due east, and figuring from the time of day . . .

He was somewhere in the Sahara.

He remembered how he had made a gate that took him and his entire P.E. class a mile above the high school. Maybe he could get an aerial view of this desert and maybe guess why Loki's gates had brought him here.

But instead of using a gate to go vertical, he climbed a rise to the east. When he reached the crest, he looked down and saw that the bone-dry desert went right to the edge of a river in a deep valley. Lots of lights—a city across the river, and some of it on his side, too.

The river ran north-south. He was on the west side. Upstream—to his right—there was a lake. And a huge dam.

Then it became obvious. He was in Egypt. Within sight of the Nile, just downstream from the Aswan Dam. Across from Kitchener's Island. Thousands of people all around. A tourist with no visa—no passport—and not a word of Arabic.

But when Loki came here, if he came here, nobody spoke Arabic. That was the language of obscure barbarian tribesmen across the Red Sea. The language of the common people here was Coptic; the educated spoke Greek. The religion was Christian.

What now? he asked the voices silently. And then, out loud: "Are you remembering anything yet?" It was vaguely comforting to hear his own voice.

He knew as he asked the question that this isn't how he would get the answer. He had to walk through the memory. He had to take his own body where Loki had gone, and then let the memories wash over him. Not his own memories, Loki's. He had to become Loki, act out Loki's part, and then he'd be able to remember what Loki had seen and heard, just as he had remembered, just a moment ago, his run along McCorkle Drive—and everything he had thought about and noticed as he ran.

So it was a kind of time travel.

There is no way this is going to work.

He felt the need to make a gate, and, assuming that feeling came from the voices, he made the gate and stepped into it.

He was standing in a wadi. Sand had flowed like a river through here. Carried by wind, though, not water. And so it would have piled up, not washed down. Building up like snowdrifts, not fanning out like silt in a stream.

He walked where it felt right to walk, trying to let memory wash over him, and failing.

Because it was wrong. Something was wrong.

He needed to walk somewhere that didn't exist.

Only it did exist. It was just buried in sand.

He needed a shovel.

He gated back to Lexington, where it was still afternoon, though starting to get a little darker. He popped out behind the Lowe's on the far side of the Walmart. He walked in and bought a shovel and a pick. Then he thought of a better plan and went back and bought two more shovels.

A minute or two later, he interrupted Hal and Wheeler playing some game on the Xbox at Wheeler's house. "This couldn't wait?" asked Wheeler.

"Got to do it while it's dark," said Danny.

"So we've got a couple of *hours,*" said Hal.

"While it's dark *in Egypt,*" said Danny.

They were smart guys. They got it.

They just didn't like it.

"I don't even like digging in the sand at the beach," said Hal as he dubiously eyed the sand-filled wadi.

But Danny set to work without insisting they do anything. "Just help as much as you want to. And if you want to go home now, the gate's right there." Danny didn't even look at them. Just started digging.

Pretty soon they were digging beside him.

If they had been archaeologists, they would have proceeded methodically, slowly. But they weren't archaeologists, and this probably wasn't even an excavatable site. Because as Danny and Hal and Wheeler dug into the sand, Danny began to remember the place. Not his own memories, of course. But he knew without knowing how he knew just who had lived here. A monk. A Christian ascetic, not one of the ones who collected disciples, but one of the few who avoided them. Only Loki had gone to him.

There was the cave. Or rather, the depression in the cliff. It's not like he had to stay out of the rain—and since he had chosen a south-facing cave, he wasn't even staying out of the sun.

No, he was staying out of the sight of people who came looking for him. He really didn't want to be found.

Did he want to die?

Suicide would be a sin. This was a holy man. He didn't want to die. He had a friend who brought him water, and he shielded his face, his whole bald head, from the sun. Under a little awning.

I came here—Loki came here—and brought his own water and then just sat here. Day after day. Saying nothing. Danny remembered it, the silence.

After a few days—on Sunday, actually—the hermit said, in Greek, "Go away."

In that instant, Danny remembered gating away. Right in front of the man. Letting him see that he was a gatemage.

Of course, it was Loki who had done that. Whatever he wanted from this man, it depended on the man knowing just what Loki was, what he could do.

"You've stopped digging," said Hal. "Are we done?"

Danny broke out of his reverie. Out of the memory. It had been so real. Even though it was dark here right now, and it had been broad daylight when the hermit told Loki to go away.

This was going to work.

"Yeah, we're done. With the digging."

"Cool," said Wheeler. "Now I get to explain to my mom why I'm covered with sweat and sand."

"Just go shower," said Danny. "I'll gate you right into the bathroom if you want."

"Somebody will be in there," said Wheeler. "Every hour of the day and night."

"My house," said Hal. "You can shower at my house."

"My clothes?" asked Wheeler. "It's not like any of yours will fit me."

Without another word, Danny gated with them to Wheeler's bedroom. "Pick out some clean clothes," said Danny.

Wheeler did.

Danny gated with them to Hal's house. "Shower here?" he asked.

"Fine," said Wheeler.

"I don't know why you were sweating," said Hal. "It's not like you actually did anything."

"I worked my ass off," said Wheeler.

Hal just looked at him.

"Compared to regular *me* I was digging my ass off," said Wheeler.

"I'm going back now," said Danny. "Thanks. You saved me a couple of hours of solo digging."

"Not to mention how we got to see all the sights of Egypt," said Hal.

"I'll take you back there someday," said Danny. "In daylight."

"No way," said Hal. "It's just a desert. I'll look at pictures on Google Images. Give me a break."

Danny gated back to Egypt and sat down in front of the hermit's cave and let Loki's memories flow back through Loki's gates.

16

Frostinch

Anonoei had never been in Gray, though the shadow of that kingdom had darkened her entire life. Or perhaps brightened it. If Gray had not defeated her homeland of Iceway and imposed harsh terms upon it, including the loveless marriage of Bexoi, the sister of the Jarl of Gray, to Prayard, the heir to the throne of Iceway, would she ever have become Prayard's mistress and mother of his sons?

No. She would have become his wife.

Once she understood that her power over men was far greater than the ordinary allure of women, she knew she could pick any man in the world to be her husband and win his undying devotion. Prayard—handsome, kind, intelligent, powerful in magery, and heir to the throne of the only kingdom she knew—would have been her choice.

But he was already tied to Bexoi when Anonoei came to understand her power. So yes, it was due to Gray that she became Prayard's mistress instead of his wife.

Prayard's former love for her might have been achieved through her illegal, immoral, indecent manmagery; but her love for him was genuine, and still was. Anonoei wanted her vengeance on Bexoi, of course—enough that she would use the power of her cruel captor Wad to achieve it. But she also truly wanted what was best for Prayard, despite the fact that once he was torn away from her influence, he fell in love with the Gray bitch.

And Anonoei had learned enough about men in general and Prayard in particular to understand that his true happiness did not depend on which women inhabited his bed and bore his children. For him, happiness would be the liberation of Iceway from Gray.

And since that would also happily coincide with Anonoei's vengeance on Bexoi, she was content.

That was why she had watched through the tiny windows Wad made for her, spying on the Jarl of Gray and on his son and heir, the beautiful, conniving Frostinch. With him, no sexual allure would be believable—he seemed to have no interest in sex of any kind. If Anonoei knew anything about manmagery, it was that whatever she got other people to do had to be the kind of thing they already tended toward, or other people would suspect some kind of ensorcelment.

It was power Frostinch hungered for, and so she would use his lust for domination as the tool to bring Bexoi down.

She was ready now. She knew enough about Frostinch to speak the language of his heart. And now that her magery had been so vastly magnified by passages through a Great Gate, he would be unable to doubt her.

So it was that as he sat on his chamberpot—one of the few times he was ever alone—she appeared in his closeroom. She wore nothing magnificent or revealing. She had dressed herself carefully in undyed homespun, with her hair drawn back in a severe bun. It was the garb of what passed for holy women in Gray.

As she expected, Frostinch took her presence in stride. The only sign of his surprise was that his bowels loosened in that instant, filling the small room with the fetor of his troubled digestive system.

"So there is a gatemage in Westil," said Frostinch softly.

"There is," said Anonoei, "but I am not that mage."

"What are you, then? My assassin?"

"If I were here to kill you, I would have come in behind you, or simply pushed a knife through the gate," said Anonoei. "I am the enemy of your most dangerous enemy."

"Yet you speak with the accent of Iceway," said Frostinch. "And Iceway is my most dangerous enemy."

"Neither of us is fool enough to believe that your most dangerous enemy is a land your father subdued years ago, a land that lies under his heel," said Anonoei. "Your greatest enemies are Grayish by birth, and of the royal house."

"My father is not my foe," said Frostinch, "and there is no one else in Gray powerful enough to aspire to be my enemy."

"Pay attention," said Anonoei in her most contemptuous voice. Instead of letting him be angry at her, she turned his immediate resentment into a grudging respect. If this woman spoke to him with contempt, then perhaps he deserved it. Perhaps she was wise. Perhaps she could be used. And if she regarded him with contempt, then perhaps he could turn that against her.

Let him think he was superior to her, and simultaneously wonder if she might be superior to him. That would keep him listening, weighing all she said.

"Born of Gray, I said, not *in* Gray."

Frostinch gave a single contemptuous laugh. "If you mean my Aunt Bexoi, then your gatemage has chosen the wrong emissary."

"Your disdain for her is proof of your stupidity," said Anonoei, "if more proof were needed. All your plotting, and it never dawns on you that she has outmaneuvered you at every step."

"My aunt the Sparrowtwit? She got pregnant by Prayard, that's all. It complicated things but it didn't change anything important."

"She blocked all your father's spies from access to Prayard—which means that the spies that secretly served you are also blocked."

"She did nothing," said Frostinch. He washed his backside—something his father used servants for, but Frostinch trusted no one enough to allow them to stand in that position. "You're wasting my time."

"No, you're wasting mine. I told my friend you were too arrogant and stupid to save. He won't listen to a woman, I said."

"I won't listen to a fool," said Frostinch.

"You don't even know your aunt," said Anonoei. "She left for Iceway before you were fifteen."

"I sat with her while she told me stories, and watched how she couldn't even get sparrows to obey her, no matter how much she fed them."

"And it never occurred to you that the disobedience of the sparrows was proof that she was not a birdmage at all?"

"Why would anyone claim to have such a pathetic power if . . ."

His voice trailed off. It was a pleasure to see him realize that he had indeed been stupid. He dried his buttocks. "You claim that she had so much foresight that she thought a child was worth deceiving?"

"The heir to the Jarl of Gray? A boy who had already shown himself to be an ambitious little monster? No offense intended, of course."

Frostinch smiled. Anonoei had understood him well—"ambitious little monster" was no insult to him. "So she was deceiving me then in order to blind my eyes today."

"And until this moment, it worked, didn't it? You thought she was a tool you could use, and that when that tool was taken from you, it was Prayard's doing, not her own."

"You have no evidence of anything like that."

"Fool," said Anonoei. "I'm here, am I not? After spying on your every conversation for days. And you think I wasn't able to spy on her before? That I do not know exactly what I'm speaking of? That I don't know how she arranged to deceive your agent Luvix when he tried to murder her?"

In that instant Frostinch's pose of languid unconcern evaporated. "What do you know of that?"

"I know that your aunt has the power to create a clant so vivid that when he stabbed the clant, it bled. He believed he had succeeded."

"No one can make a clant that . . ." Then he concentrated on refastening his breeches. "You saw this?"

"My friend saw it. After he stole the poison Luvix had intended to use and gave it to Bexoi."

Anonoei watched him process the fact that she had known of the poison.

"And you have been spying on me?" he asked.

She repeated his conversation of the day before with one of his agents, whom he met in a garden, pretending she was a woman he desired. He did not understand that no one believed any more that he had the slightest interest in women.

He listened, nodding. "So either you have been spying through a gate, or my dear and trusted friend has betrayed me."

"She has not betrayed you," said Anonoei. "But by all means have her killed. Destroy another of your own weapons. Make yourself weaker. I'll wait till Bexoi has trapped you and made you her puppet, and then you'll be ready to listen to me. But alas you'll also be completely useless to me by then. So you'll betray me, in order to curry favor with Bexoi, hoping she'll drop you a crumb of power. Only she'll laugh at you. 'Anonoei is dead,' she'll tell you."

"You?" asked Frostinch. "Anonoei? Prayard's mistress?"

"Not as dead as everyone assumes," said Anonoei.

"And your sons?"

"Alive and out of your reach," said Anonoei. "Just as I am out of your reach."

She knew before she said it that he already had his hand on the dagger he kept in the back of his trousers. Now he whipped it out to slash it across her body. But she stepped back into the gate Wad had prepared for her, reappeared directly behind him, and shoved him forward. Already overbalanced by his own lunge, he toppled over. It gave her time to pick up his chamberpot and pour it out onto his body, spoiling his clothes.

"You are nothing, Frostinch, compared to mages with real power. I have passed through a Great Gate."

"Impossible," he said. "The Gate Thief allows no—"

"Don't you know how to *think*?" she demanded. "It does not occur to you that my friend *is* the Gate Thief?"

He laughed nervously, getting up, reaching for something to brush the foulness from his clothing. Then he pulled off his tunic and unfastened his trousers, standing naked and completely uninterested as he regarded her. "My body is washable," he said, "and I can get my clothing cleaned. These efforts to humiliate me are pointless."

"So was your attempt to slash me with your dagger," said Anonoei. "I came to offer you our help against your aunt. But you remain too stupid to realize how much you need our help."

"Has Bexoi passed through a Great Gate as well?"

"If she ever does," said Anonoei, "she will rule all of Westil. Without passage through a Great Gate, she is the most powerful mage of our time. Even *with* my passage through a Great Gate, I doubt that I alone am any match for her."

"If she's no Sparrowfriend, what then is her magery?" asked Frostinch.

"Why should I tell a fool?" asked Anonoei. "You are the Sparrowfriend, the weakling. Couldn't you see how she mocked your pathetic magery?"

"I'm a Hawkbrother," said Frostinch.

"Hawk?" asked Anonoei. "Oh, so I've heard. But the birds that come to you, the birds you ride, the birds who spy for you—all I've seen you use are crows."

He grinned. "Crows are little noticed. Alone, they steal whatever I need them to steal. In a pack, they can tear the meat off an enemy in minutes."

"I don't disparage the many talents of crows," said Anonoei. "What I despise are people who pretend to be nobler than they are. *Hawkfriend*."

"I have ridden hawks," said Frostinch.

"They shuddered at your presence, and tried to kill themselves to be rid of you."

For the first time, he was genuinely angry and humiliated. "How could you know that! It was years—"

"*I* have spied on you for days, but the Gate Thief has watched you for years. When you're dead, who will be Jarling of Gray?"

His face went ashen. "Is that her plot?"

"She has high hopes for her son by Prayard. Your father and you think you have nothing to fear from the baby, because you imagine that she has no talent to pass on to him. Here is the power she has: power to rule in his name. Once you are dead, have no doubt that your father will name this baby in her womb to be his heir. Then, when he is born, both your father and Prayard will die—very differently, but die they will—and she will rule in the baby's name. Have you any doubt that such a plan would work?"

Frostinch walked to the window. His skin was covered with gooseflesh, though it might be the bitter cold from the window.

He kept his closeroom cold, the windows uncovered. To kill the stink perhaps. Or to make him feel that he was strong and hardy, a true man of war, instead of the man of crowlike cunning that he was.

"What do you hope to gain from me?" he asked. "If she's so powerful and clever and dangerous, then she'll succeed and I can't stop her."

"True," said Anonoei. "She has already blocked you at every point. But there are things you could do that would prevent her plot."

"I already tried to have her killed," said Frostinch, "though not because I feared her."

"No, you merely thought your father was coddling Iceway for her sake, and you wanted to have another bloody war and kill Prayard and wear the crown of Iceway on your own head."

"Why should I be a mere Jarl when I might be a king?"

"Fool to care about the title," said Anonoei. "Power is the only fact. Titles are decorations. Names are lies. Do you finally understand that until you see things as they truly are, you can accomplish nothing?"

"How are things, really, then!" he said defiantly.

"You're naked and cold at the window," said Anonoei. "I could push you out."

"And then you'd have no use of me."

"Exactly," said Anonoei. "And Bexoi has not killed you yet because until she has a child that she can show your father, and use to win his heart, you are more useful alive. Only when he is already the doting uncle, impressed with Prayard's loyalty to him, and his devotion to your father's younger sister, only *then* will your tragic death lead to him naming his nephew as his heir."

"So I have time."

"A little," said Anonoei, "if you know how to use it."

"And what do you and your friend the Gate Thief—if that's who he really is—intend for me to do with this time you say I have?"

"Isn't it obvious?" said Anonoei. "Kill your father now and become the Jarl yourself."

Then she stepped through the gate and returned to Wad.

The Gate Thief shook his head. "He used to be clever," said Wad. "You made him stupid."

"I made him believe that he was stupid," said Anonoei, "and then told him how to be clever. I hardly need to be a manmage to do *that*—learned people do it all the time."

"But I saw your manmagery all the same," said Wad. "He practically worships you."

"Most men do, if I want them to," said Anonoei.

"*Will* he kill his father?" asked Wad.

"He'll try," said Anonoei. "And because he really is clever, he'll probably succeed even without our help."

"But you intend to help him."

"Kill the man who defeated and humiliated Iceway? Yes, I think I will, unless you stop providing me with gates."

"Remember how few of them I have," said Wad.

"So passage through the Great Gate didn't increase their number?"

"It increased how long they last, how strong they are, my ability to manipulate them, my sense of other gates and where they lead. But no, passage through a Great Gate does not add any new gates to my store."

"Nor, apparently, does it make people any smarter."

"It didn't improve your intelligence or mine," said Wad, "but we were already as clever as we needed to be."

"As is Frostinch," said Anonoei.

"Yet it didn't occur to him that he should find out what *your* magery is."

"I didn't let him think of it," said Anonoei. "That's elementary. Whenever he became curious about me, I distracted him. Again, I barely needed magery to control him."

"When he is Jarl of Gray, he won't be any smarter."

"I don't want him smarter," said Anonoei. "I'm not going to use *him* to defeat Bexoi. Manmagery doesn't let me add new powers to my clients—they are what they are. He will be my puppet, but no match for Bexoi."

"Who *is*?" asked Wad.

"You," said Anonoei. "But I don't expect you to face her down, either. You're still too much in love with her."

Wad recoiled at that. "She murdered my son."

"The son you made with her. Remember what I am, and believe me, Wad. However much you hate Bexoi, you still have love enough for her that it will make you hesitate at the last moment, and she'll destroy you."

"How will you bring her down, then? How will you defeat her? Do you think that you're manmage enough to make her *your* servant?"

"Watch and see," said Anonoei. "When it's over, you'll be the only one who knows what I have done. But you'll agree that my victory was perfect and complete. I could find no better way to punish her."

"And you won't tell me now?"

"You would prevent me," said Anonoei, "even though you think you wouldn't. I'm not controlling you, but I *do* need to use your talents. Not knowing, you'll continue to help me, even though you know that if you knew my plan, you wouldn't."

Wad smiled. "Or so you think."

"You think that you *would* approve, and so you help me," said Anonoei. "I don't have to use manmagery on people who are sure they're wiser than they are."

But of course she did use manmagery on him. She used it on everybody. She used it all the time. But part of the power of manmagery was the ability to make its victims believe that they were freely doing what she manipulated them to do. That would be her vengeance on him, for those years of torment in captivity. For the damage that he did to her sweet son Eluik. But because he had also saved them, and because of all his help to her, she would never *tell* him of how she controlled him. So he would not suffer. She could enjoy her triumph over him, and enjoy the fact that he so ignorantly enjoyed it too.

17

Ka and Ba

How do you learn anything with your brain switched off? Yet Danny quickly realized that this was exactly what he had to do here in the Egyptian desert. Loki's gates didn't actually know anything, or remember anything, except at one remove: They remembered where Loki had been when he learned powerful secrets about the Belmage, and they remembered what he had been doing.

So Danny had to be where Loki had been, and do what he had done, and then let memory flow into his mind. Memory that was not his own, of things he had not done. And the memory included no language. It only included what Loki came to know, at a level below language.

The moment Danny tried to make sense of the memories, his conscious mind took over. And his conscious mind introduced language. Language drove out the inchoate, wordless Loki-memories.

So he could not make sense of anything, while it was happening. He had to let it wash over him. It required a sort of trance. His conscious mind had to be off in space, not concentrating on anything.

It is so hard to concentrate on not concentrating.

So at first the memories were jagged. They flashed in and out like lightning. There was no coherency. Images of a scrawny, sunburnt Egyptian man, small in stature, bald, his shoulders tented by thin white linen, a dusty linen kilt around his loins, but otherwise naked. The memory included heat. And then cold, and darkness.

The man was talking, but Danny heard no words. He did not want the man's words, though this man was the teacher—some kind of hermit that Loki had consulted. A man who knew ancient lore of Egypt, knowledge older than Christianity, though he was certainly a Christian ascetic. But the memory of his words could not be recovered this way. Instead, Danny had to recover the memory of the story that Loki had built up in his own memory.

When words came to mind, then, they were not the hermit's words, they were the words that mattered to Loki as he listened. *Ka. Ba.* But as soon as Danny attached to the words, their meaning in this context fled away.

Fortunately, the memory could be endlessly started over, repeated again and again. The gates were patient. What else did they have to do? So as Danny gradually mastered the art of meditation, at least well enough for this purpose, this day, the memory began again, and now it washed over Danny and became his own.

Later, he told himself. I will remember remembering the memory, and that will become the story. For now let it flow. Let it fill you.

He had no idea of the passage of time. Captured by the memory, he did not know if it was day or night where he sat alone in the desert, in front of the cavelet that he and Wheeler and Hal had cleared of sand. He only knew what the time was in the memory, as it flowed through a long, long conversation.

A couple of times, breaking the memory flow, he despaired. Loki had placed all the things the hermit told him into a context of Loki's own experience with gates, with mages of every kind, in a world where magery was far more common, where a gatemage was educated in his Family's history and knowledge and skills. How could Danny, in his ignorance, possibly make sense of any of this?

He let it flow.

He let it flow.

And then a hand touched his shoulder.

That had not happened before in the memory! Who was it who interrupted Loki?

Danny waited for the memory of Loki turning, to see what he saw, to know what he knew.

Then the hand touched him again, more sharply this time, shaking him, and Danny realized: This is not in the memory. This did not happen to Loki. This is happening to me.

"Please," he whispered. His voice was a feeble croak. "Please wait."

The hand shook him again. Very hard. It almost knocked him over.

Danny felt like weeping, did weep one great sob, and then the intruder's work was done: The trance was broken, the memory fled.

His own memories rushed back. He was in Egypt, a nation for which he had no passport or visa. He was caught.

He almost gated away. But then it finally dawned on him that the person was talking. The sunlight was dazzling. He could hardly see. And he must have been deaf, for now the voice swelled and faded. It was English. He knew the voice. He squinted. He shaded his eyes.

The face came down to be directly in front of his. She was angry. Hermia. Hermia had followed him here.

Stupid stupid stupid! Didn't she know he was doing something important, something *vital*? How did she dare to interrupt him?

"Drink this!" she was saying.

He looked down and saw that she was holding a bottle of water. Evian. He didn't like Evian.

She had the cap off. She jammed the mouth of it against his lips. It hurt. His lips were dry and chapped. Split. He looked at the top of the water bottle. There was blood on it.

"Dehydrated." That was one of the words she said.

He opened his mouth and tipped his head back and let her pour water into his mouth. He had to work at swallowing. It was as if he had forgotten how to do it.

No, he was simply waiting for Loki's kinetic memory to kick in. He was waiting for Loki to remember drinking. But Loki hadn't drunk anything.

That's because Loki's whole conversation had only lasted an hour. But Danny's attempt to remember it had lasted much longer, starting over again and again.

He succeeded in swallowing. The water came down his throat so painfully that he realized: I have gone a long time without drinking.

Hermia was gone. But he still held the water bottle in his hand. He tried to lift it to drink more. He couldn't remember how. He bent over and touched his cracked and bloody lips to the plastic lip of the bottle. The water didn't come upward. But he was able to hold it against his lips as he straightened his body. This brought the bottle up with him. Water flowed from it over his lips. He made his lips and tongue work and swallowed some of it. This time it felt better. But then it went down wrong and he coughed. Choked. Dropped the bottle. Even as he continued to try to cough out the water that had gone down his windpipe, he felt around for the bottle. Why can't I see it? he asked himself. Everything's so bright.

Then there were hands again, hands on both sides of him, picking him up, raising him to his feet. It hurt to unwind his body, to stand up. His legs would not support him. His legs had no feeling. How long had he sat in the same position without moving?

They were talking to each other. Two women. Hermia again. Veevee. The other gatemages. His friends. They were both angry. They were both worried. But they were speaking in language, and he was avoiding language. He didn't want to hear language because that would distract him from . . .

No, no, he wasn't remembering anymore. He was no longer in the trance. It was good to have language now. He needed to hear what they were saying and understand them.

"He's not hearing us," said Veevee.

"Tell me what I don't know," said Hermia.

"We have to get him to Naples," said Veevee.

"There's no gate to—oh, Naples, Florida. Let's just concentrate on getting him back through this gate to the house he left from."

Danny staggered. His legs were beginning to get feeling again. An ecstasy of pins and needles. An agony of pain in his long-unmoved joints.

"He's trying to walk," said Hermia.

"He was just staring at the cave?"

"Makes the Narcissus story make sense," said Hermia. "Forced to stare at the same spot forever."

"Only not his own reflection."

"How do we know what he was seeing?"

What was I seeing? Can I remember anything? Was this all wasted, because it didn't enter my own mind in a way that I have any hope of making sense of?

They got him down the sandy, rocky slope to the gate and suddenly they were indoors. Hal's bedroom. Was that really the last place he had been? It didn't matter which had been last. There was *a* gate from Hal's room to the cave in Egypt, and that's all that mattered. Hermia had found it. Then she had gone for Veevee to help her. Chaining from gate to gate.

Hal was there. He swore, tried to help.

Danny should have been able to walk easily. He should have been healed of everything by passing through a gate. Certainly the physical pain was gone. The feeling in his legs was back. But he was still having trouble walking.

"We're getting him back to his own house, dear," said Veevee. "You were a great help, but we've got it from here."

"You're sure that nobody *made* him do this?" asked Hermia.

"He was completely normal," said Hal. "For Danny, anyway. He had this project he was doing. It had something to do with Loki. He had to go to the desert and we had to dig out the cave. It didn't make a lot of sense."

"But you don't think anybody else was controlling him?" asked Hermia.

"How would I know?" said Hal. "For all I know, somebody's controlling *you*." He was standing between them and the gate back to Danny's house.

"You're such a dear," said Veevee. "Please don't worry. The gate already healed him. But he's still not functioning properly, so we're not sure what's happening. If we take him to a hospital they'll find nothing wrong and we'll have to explain why we brought him in."

"I'm OK," said Danny to Hal. "I'm just having trouble . . . using my body."

"He's like a beastmage who got lost in his heartbound," said Veevee.

"Apparently, judging from his motor skills, his heartbound is a drunken slug."

Hal stopped blocking the way. They got him to and through the gate.

Back in his own house, Danny wouldn't let them take him to Naples. "No reason to go there," said Danny.

"We have to rehydrate you," said Veevee. "Going through a gate doesn't replace the water you lost. A day and a half in the desert sun. Not to mention a *night* in the desert. What were you thinking?"

"I was doing research," said Danny.

"Into near-death experiences?" asked Hermia. She was tasting water from a glass in Danny's kitchen. "You drink this stuff?"

"Buena Vista's finest," said Danny. She handed him the glass and he drank it down in one long sloppy draught.

"I can't believe that your third-degree sunburn has turned into a *tan,*" said Veevee. "I think of all the lotions and hours in tanning booths and . . . all I needed to do was get a savage sunburn and go through a gate."

"Do you have any idea how you terrified us?" demanded Hermia. "Suddenly nobody can find you. Marion and Leslie have no idea. Nobody knows. Until Veevee finally thought of asking your high school fan club."

"My friends," said Danny.

"You are the world's only Gatefather," said Hermia, "and you don't have the right to disappear without telling anybody."

"I told my friends," said Danny. "And I was only going to be gone for a few hours."

"At least thirty-six hours," said Veevee.

"I didn't know," said Danny.

"You could have died," said Hermia. "Do you understand that? What drug did you take?"

"No drug," said Danny.

"Don't lie," said Hermia. "It took forever to get you out of that trip you were on. Were you hallucinating?"

"Not half well enough," said Danny. "Instead of being mad at me, do you want to find out what I was doing? I warn you—in order to do that, you'll have to actually listen to me."

"Oh, you're telling *me* off?" said Hermia. "You do a foolish, stupid—"

"Hermia," said Veevee, "let's listen to him and *find out* whether he was foolish or stupid."

"Now you're on his side?" demanded Hermia.

Danny and Veevee looked at her in silence.

Hermia stood up straight, took a deep breath, and flopped down on the couch beside him. Veevee pulled up a kitchen chair. "So the old woman gets the straightback chair."

"You just went through a gate, you feel fine," said Hermia.

"You know I have Loki's gates inside me," said Danny.

"You captured them, yes," said Hermia.

"But now he's given them to me. So we . . . talk."

"You and Loki?" asked Veevee.

"In a way. Maybe. But I think I'm just talking to his gates. They obey me now. But they're still part of him, so maybe he knows and maybe he doesn't. It doesn't matter. There are things in his memory that I need to know, and he's not here. Plus, if I asked him I don't think he'd tell me. He doesn't seem really eager to teach me."

"But you can talk to the *gates*?"

"I don't know how it works," said Danny. "Have you ever heard of anybody *giving* their gates to somebody else?"

"That would be like giving away your outself," said Veevee.

"Yes, I've heard of that," said Hermia. "Old family legend. Two friends who were so devoted to each other that they became each other's heartbound."

"But it isn't like that," said Danny. "He's not riding me, and I'm not riding him. He isn't controlling me. He isn't a manmage."

"Can you *make* his gates?" asked Hermia.

"After what happened with the Wild Gate, I wouldn't dare to try. But please, please let me tell you what I learned while I can still remember it."

"Learned?" asked Veevee.

"I was there to act out the kinetic memory of the time when Loki learned some great secret from a Christian hermit in Egypt.

A Coptic-speaker, but a scholar all the same. A collector of ancient Egyptian lore. Secret stuff that isn't in the inscriptions, it isn't in the books of the dead, it isn't anywhere. It's just *known*, and he told it to Loki, and the gates can't give it to me in language, they can only help me recover Loki's mental state when he learned it. Do you understand?"

"I don't think *you* understand, sweetie," said Veevee.

"I don't," said Danny. "But let me talk it through. Because it was working. There at the end when you shook me, I was finally getting it. After starting over again and again."

"Sorry I saved your life," said Hermia.

"Please, please let me tell it." He almost cried with desperation.

"He's asking you to shut up, dear," said Veevee.

"I know what he's asking."

"If you don't want to listen," said Veevee sweetly, "then will you please leave and let him tell *me*?"

Hermia buried her face in her hands.

"It's going to be a jumble," said Danny. "I feel it slipping away like a dream. It's about the ka and the ba. The ka is the inself, the ba is the outself."

"Everybody knows that," said Hermia.

"I didn't!" said Danny.

"Shut up, please, Hermia," said Veevee. Her voice sounded so sweet that it was clear she was murderously angry.

"And it's *not* the same. That was what was so hard," said Danny. "We think of the ka as being tied to the body, *part* of the body. So we send out the ba into our heartbeasts, into our clants, into our gates. But neither ka nor ba is part of our body. Neither one."

"That's absurd," said Hermia. Then she clapped her own hand over her mouth.

"This is what Loki heard that made him so excited and frightened," said Danny. "I *remember* how he felt about it. I remember him understanding this. The ka and the ba are bound to each other. Together, they're both the thing we actually *are*. The body is just—a dwelling place. A tool set. It has a life of its own, a mind of its own, but it isn't *us*. Any of us. Mages and drowthers alike. We are ka, we are ba, we are not these animals that we wear."

"We're listening," said Veevee.

"Sounds very gnostic," said Hermia.

"No it doesn't," said Danny. "It doesn't sound gnostic at all. Or Coptic. It sounds like the thing that made Loki close all the gates."

"If the ka and ba aren't part of our human body," said Veevee, "then where do they come from?"

"From the world of the Belmages," said Danny.

"In other words," said Hermia, "from 'heaven.' "

Danny clamped his hands over his ears. "Please, please don't pollute this. Let me say it first. Let me say it before you start trying to bend it to fit whatever shit you Greeks think you already know. Did any of you go closing gates? No? Loki did. So shut up and let me *try* to remember why."

"Sorry again," said Hermia.

"From the world of the Belmages," said Danny. "It was a gate from their world that first turned these hairless apes into humans. But it was also these bodies that gave them the powers we turn into magery."

"No," said Veevee. "I mean, I thought the powers came from the ka and ba."

"That's the thing. Everybody has a ka and ba. It comes into the body when we're born or . . . whenever. It comes in. But in the process, the body has a . . . a . . . an *interface* with the ka and the ba. When mine came into me, when Loki's came into him, that's what I mean, that's what I remember, when Loki's ka and ba entered his body, it fragmented his ba into all his gates. That's when he became a gatemage. Body plus ka and ba. You see? There's no magery without the body."

"So far this is so exciting I can see why you nearly died to learn it," said Hermia.

"I haven't gotten to the exciting part yet," said Danny. "It's in the book of Revelation. 'And there was war in heaven: Michael and his angels fought against the dragon; and the dragon fought and his angels, and prevailed not; neither was their place found any more in heaven. And the great dragon was cast out, that old serpent, called the Devil, and Satan, which deceives the whole world: he was cast out into the earth, and his angels were cast out with him.' "

"I thought you said this was ancient Egyptian lore," said Hermia.

"Sounds like the King James version to me," said Veevee.

"The devil. Satan. That's the Belmage. He was cast down—that means he was sent through a gate to Mittlegard. But he wasn't put into a human body. He and his angels were sent here as naked ka and ba."

They pondered this. So did Danny. "I feel so much of what Loki understood slipping away from me. Now I don't even know how much of this is what he concluded and how much of it I'm making up right now, trying to make sense of it."

"Just go ahead," said Veevee. "I'm finally beginning to see why this matters."

"I'm not," said Hermia.

"Belmage is *not* a manmage. There *are* manmages, and what he does is very similar to manmagery, but he isn't in a human body. He's bodiless. But think what the devil keeps doing all the way through the New Testament. He possesses people's bodies. He and the other devils. His angels, you see? Jesus was always casting them out."

"I thought that was just schizophrenia," said Hermia.

"Or multiple personality disorder," said Veevee.

"That's the only thing today that *looks* like what the Bible describes. But there are all these bodiless kas and bas around. The Belmage is their boss. The big guy. The main enemy. That's all 'satan' means—"

"Don't bother telling gatemages what words mean," said Hermia.

"So the Belmage hates us all, because our ka is joined to a body and it changed us. Gave us these powers. If we learn how to use them. The ability to use magery is hereditary. Tied to the body. But that's why he wants to take possession of the bodies. Take over, get the power."

"But they aren't joined to our body the way *we* are, are they?" asked Veevee.

"No, they aren't. They don't get magery of their own. They get inside us and boss us around and get the use of *our* magery. That's the danger of the Belmage. He's not a guy who sends his ba into other people the way a manmage does. Persuading you, changing your perceptions. No, *his* whole ka and ba climb into you. He wears you like a puppet. He makes you use your powers to do his will. But when you die, *he* doesn't die. In fact, he loves it when your ka gets separated from your body, because then he's in sole control."

"So why doesn't he just kill you and take over?" asked Veevee.

"That's the thing. The ancient Egyptians believed the Semitic gods could animate dead bodies. That's why they emptied out the brains and internal organs of the people of great power, and put them in the canopic jars. So that the body wouldn't work. So that the Belmage or his minions couldn't animate your corpse and continue ruling in your place. Embalming wasn't about living forever. It was about making damn sure you stayed dead."

"But *can* they?" asked Veevee. "That would be—zombies."

"No, no," said Danny. "The hermit called that superstition. The Belmage can't control a dead body unless he's already in control when the ka leaves. People believe what they believe, right? But the Belmage needs to take control of a living body, and he wants powerful ones. He wants mages. Then he uses their magery."

"So when he possesses somebody, you have to kill the person he possessed?" asked Veevee. "That seems really final."

"It doesn't even work," said Danny. "The Belmage isn't dead. You can't kill the ka or the ba. They don't die. I mean, the ones truly attached to human bodies die, but that only means they're cut loose from the body. The ka and ba are still alive. That's why we can still hold on to the gates of these mages who've been dead for a thousand years. They're severed from a ka that's still alive . . . somewhere. But the Belmage—he didn't really *have* a body, so he's not changed by the death of the body. He just goes on to another."

"You're saying that these Belmages are the only ones who reincarnate."

"I don't know, that's not the way they discussed it. I don't know what happens to regular people who die in the regular way. This is a memory so I couldn't exactly ask questions," said Danny. "And here's the thing. The Belmages were really *bad* at this at first. They aren't manmages. They aren't any kind of mage. So they don't have powers the way we do. What they have is a *lot* of practice. They've been diving into people, getting whatever control they can, for *ten thousand years*. Even Loki hasn't lived that long. So the smartest, the best of them—*the* Belmage. The Enemy. The great Dragon. *That* one is the most powerful, the one that has acquired the greatest skill. He's *learned* ways of getting inside people that are far more powerful than any of the other castoffs."

"So what Loki realized," said Hermia.

"What made him close the gates," said Veevee.

"Was the realization that the Dragon had finally figured out how to attach himself so firmly to a person that he could ride him through a gate."

"Oh my," said Veevee.

"Think about it. The presence of a Belmage inside you, being possessed—that's a disease. Isn't it? Passing through a gate should cast him off."

"But people holding hands with other people can take them through a gate," said Hermia.

"Holding hands. Two people *with their own bodies.* But this extra, this rider, this possessor, he gets cast out. What do you think Jesus was? Healing people, casting out devils."

"Oh, you're saying he was a Gatefather?" asked Veevee.

"This isn't from the hermit, we're away from what Loki learned, the hermit wasn't going to say anything that denied the divinity of Jesus. Let's get back to what Loki knew. He realized that the Belmages were learning how to attach to people in such a way that they could go through gates. I think that's what's really going on with that passage from the Library of Congress. That Belmage had taken possession of a gatemage. The Loki of that time didn't realize what was going on. He thought that the gatemage he saw in the body was his enemy. But it was the Belmage *inside* him. So when the Loki of that ancient time fought the Belmage, he actually killed the poor sap of a Gatefather that the Belmage had possessed. The Belmage himself never left this world. He couldn't actually pass through a gate. He could use the power of the Gatefather he was controlling to *make* gates, but he couldn't go through them. And sending him through one threw him out of the body."

"This isn't what you remember from Loki," said Hermia.

"No, sorry, no, it just makes sense now, that's all. And I don't remember—I mean, I didn't find out why Loki knew that the Belmage of his time was getting ready to go through gates. The Dragon was probably riding a Gatefather at the time, so Loki ate all that Gatefather's gates—*not* killing him. That made the Gatefather useless to the Dragon. He'd leave him then, see? Because he was powerless. But he would just have found another gatemage. Or he would have gotten into *anybody* and then gone through a Great Gate and magnified his power and so—"

"So Loki ate all the gates, and kept eating them," said Hermia. "Until we *brilliantly* came along and made a Great Gate after all."

"And put a Wild Gate out in the world," said Danny. "I have so totally screwed up."

"No, *Loki* screwed up," said Veevee. "He should have realized that someday there'd come along a Gatefather who was even more powerful than he is, and he'd eat *his* gates. He had to know it."

"Maybe that's why he woke up from the tree he was living in, because he knew I existed." Danny stopped himself. "More speculation, more guessing. What we know is this. Loki realized he had to close all the gates to keep the Dragon and his followers, these loose kas and bas, from taking over everything."

"I'm still not getting it," said Veevee. "So they can use gates."

"I get it," said Hermia. "As long as using a gate stripped them out of you, all you had to do to cast a devil out of somebody was to pass him through a gate. But if they can *stay*, then nothing casts them out except death itself. Whoever they take over is possessed till they die. And the Dragon or his devils, they don't die when the human dies, they just find another powerful mage to possess. Human life is ruled by these guys *forever*."

"Human life is over," said Danny. "Only the Belmages have a life. Everybody else is forced to be their puppets. To be spectators in their own lives."

"So all these years that Loki has prevented Great Gates," said Veevee, "these Belmages have been possessing people, and because there were no gates, nobody could get rid of them."

"True," said Danny. "That's why it's all about the Great Gates. When Loki did it, Westil was still free of the Belmages. They had never been able to make the passage—till then. So Loki kept Westil completely free of the Belmages. And even here, he kept all the mages weak by preventing their passage between worlds. So the Belmages could never get control of any *real* power. For all we know, they've been leaving mages like us alone, and concentrating on the people who actually run this world."

"Stalin, not Odin," said Veevee.

"Hitler, not Jupiter," said Hermia.

"But now imagine Hitler with the power of a Tempester or a Tidefather or a Stonefather—one who's passed through a Great

Gate. Because just supposing Hitler was really a Belmage possessing this Austrian painter dude, then Hitler didn't really die in that bunker in Berlin in 1945. The poor sap he was riding died. But the Dragon just cut himself loose and went in search of somebody else."

"So maybe we're fighting all the monsters of history here," said Veevee.

"No, *Loki* was fighting them," said Danny. "And I just wrecked everything. I just lost him his war."

"Nothing's lost yet," said Veevee.

"And there's also this," said Hermia. "I think it's all merde."

Danny looked at her blankly. "What are you talking about? You think I got the memories wrong?"

"I think you probably got them exactly right," said Hermia. "But just because one ancient man said it to another ancient man—and let's remember, one was a crazy Christian hermit living in a cave, and the other was *Loki,* for heaven's sake—just because they believe it doesn't mean it's true."

"But just because you *don't* believe it doesn't mean it's *not* true."

"Look at how you got all this information," said Hermia. "You put yourself into a hallucinogenic trance. You were sitting there in the Egyptian sun, baking, not drinking, not eating, not moving, just locked in place, having hallucinations while conversing with—whom? Why, crazy Loki's outself! Do you see how absolutely unreliable this is?"

"No, I don't," said Danny. "Loki's a smart guy."

"Being smart and being a loon aren't mutually exclusive," said Hermia. "*You're* smart and *you're* a complete loon."

"No he's not," said Veevee.

"We just saved his life in the desert because he was catatonic in the hot sun. Please find me a definition of 'lunatic' that doesn't include that!"

Danny had no answer to that. He knew she was wrong. He knew that what Loki learned was right. Or at least he *trusted* that it was right.

But maybe he only believed it because he had worked so hard to get at the memory.

"Don't let her talk you out of this," said Veevee. "She doesn't know anything."

"No, but I *am* attached to the rational universe," said Hermia. "Not meaning to give offense, but Veevee, you spent your whole life convinced you were a gatemage without any evidence at all."

"But it turned out that I was," said Veevee.

"But you believed without evidence," said Hermia. "It doesn't make you a reliable judge of weird theories like this. Don't you get it? Danny's probably completely right about what Loki learned. Only he was a loon learning from a loon, and Danny's a loon using a lunatic process to recover their lunacy, and we'd have to be loons to take it seriously."

"Since you're the expert on lunacy," said Veevee, "just what do *you* think should happen?"

"I think it's time to let the Families use the Great Gate," said Hermia. "There's *no* reason to keep people from passing between worlds. There are no kas and bas that take possession of people's bodies. There's no Dragon waiting to pounce. He doesn't exist. It's from the craziest book in the Bible, for heaven's sake."

Danny pressed his palms against his eyes. "I'm so tired," he said.

"You just put yourself through torture, nearly to the point of death," said Hermia. "I'd say, yes, you need a nap."

"I missed a whole day of school," said Danny.

"That's why we knew something was wrong," said Veevee. "Your friends got worried and so they had the girl with the cleavage look up your records in the office and call me."

"I thought you guys were already looking for me," said Danny.

"I was," said Hermia. "I just didn't know where to look."

"You mean that it didn't occur to you to ask a drowther," said Danny.

Hermia shrugged.

"But my drowther friends, *they're* the ones who actually took action," said Danny. "*They're* the ones who saved me."

"What are you doing in high school, Danny?" asked Hermia. "What is your *obsession* with drowthers? It's time to let the Families through the Great Gate, and restore the proper order to the world."

Danny looked at her, filled with dark despair. "That's not how you used to talk."

"Maybe I finally realized that the world was no more screwed up when the gods were running the show, using the power they got from passage back and forth with Westil, than it is now, when scientists and engineers put the instruments of slaughter into the hands of drowthers."

"Let me think," said Danny.

"I don't mean to be rude," said Hermia.

"Yes you do," said Veevee.

"I don't want to be rude," said Hermia, "but sometimes truth is rude. You've been playing at high school. You've gotten all sentimental about drowthers. But look at your friends, Danny. They're appalling human beings. And now they worship you, yes? You rule over them, only what a pathetic little band of worshipers you chose for yourself, don't you think? Was that really the best you could do?"

Danny could hardly bear it. A part of him was furious that she would judge his friends like that. And a part of him saw her perspective and wondered if she was right, if he wasn't just like all the other mages, exploiting the worship of drowthers. If that was true, then they weren't friends at all. Just . . . tools. He was just using them.

The way he had used Hal and Wheeler to help him dig a cave.

As if he had a right to *command* them to take hours out of their life to go to Egypt to dig sand. Just because Danny was a Gatefather.

I've reinvented all the worst features of the snobbery of the Families, and I did it in the name of trying to be a regular high school kid. On the first day, I'm putting people through gates and taking charge of their lives as if I had a right. I'm as bad as any of them.

Hermia was looking at him with a weird combination of concern and smug superiority.

She is not my friend, Danny realized.

But Hal and Wheeler, Xena and Laurette and Sin and Pat—*they're* my friends. Even if I'm a lousy friend to them, they're good friends to me.

Screw the Families. Screw the Great Gates. Whether Loki was right or wrong about the Dragon or Belmage or Satan or whatever, he was definitely right to close all the gates and keep them closed for a thousand years.

"You know what, Hermia?" said Danny. "I like my friends. They don't try to get me to treat other people badly just because they're not as powerful."

"You're such a drowther," said Hermia.

"You used to feel the same way," said Danny.

"I grew up."

"In the past couple of weeks?" asked Danny.

"Oh, I see where we're going with this," said Hermia. "You think I've gone through a sudden personality change. You think I'm possessed by the Dragon."

"What an interesting suggestion," said Veevee. "I never would have thought of that, but now that you bring it up . . ."

"You do realize," said Hermia to Danny, "that if you now start thinking that anyone who disagrees with you must be possessed by Satan, that is the road to genuine lunacy."

"It never crossed my mind that you were possessed," said Danny. "Not by the Belmage. I think you've been talking to your

Family. I think they found you even though we removed the tracers. I think they've talked you into being with them."

Hermia's silence, along with a slightly reddened face, were enough of a tell for Danny to know that he had hit it aright.

"I'm sorry they got to you," said Danny, "and I'm sorry that you agree with them now."

Hermia regarded him in silence.

"Well, this is awkward," said Veevee.

"Not really," said Hermia. "He's saying that if I had held my current views when we first met, he would never have accepted me as his partner in this project."

Danny shook his head. "You *didn't* have these views, that's all I know. But you also helped me learn to control my abilities. I haven't forgotten that."

"But we're not friends now," said Hermia.

"We're friends who disagree about something important," said Danny.

"No, I think that by talking down your drowther friends, I actually elevated them in your estimation, and lowered myself."

Danny couldn't disagree. That summed it up pretty well.

Hermia walked to the sink and refilled Danny's glass. As she did, she spoke. "See, Danny, you hate your Family. And Veevee doesn't really have one. But I love my Family. I can't erase my old loyalties. I can't turn against them."

"You did, though," said Danny.

"Because I was excited about finding real gates in the world," said Hermia. "Now I'm over the first rush of excitement. I'm back to my true self."

"Back under the thumb of your Family," said Danny.

"Whatever," said Hermia.

"I made a deal with all the Families," said Danny.

"No, you imposed a diktat on them," said Hermia.

"Which you agreed to."

"Because you're the Gatefather and I'm not," said Hermia. "But I always thought you were wrong."

Veevee gave a quiet little hoot of laughter. "You really have a talent for revising history, kiddo," she said.

"I've gone from 'dear' to 'kiddo,'" said Hermia. "I'm in a death-spiral here, aren't I."

"I'm sticking to the deal I offered the Families," said Danny.

"You think you're so egalitarian, but look how you're treating me, because you're the Gatefather and I'm just a Lockfriend."

"Maybe you're right," said Danny. "But that's the system you prefer. By that system, yes, I'm the Gatefather and you're the Lockfriend."

Again the silence as she stared at him.

She dashed the glassful of water in his face.

Then she walked to the gate that led to Washington DC and went through it.

Danny wiped the water from his eyes. "Think I'm rehydrated yet?" he asked Veevee.

"She'll change her mind, Danny."

"I don't think so," said Danny. "To her I'm just a kid. A kid from the North Family. The Illyrians think they're better than everybody—especially Norths. I don't think she's going to change her mind and come crawling back to try to put things back the way they were."

"Well, so what? She can't make gates, and you can."

Danny wanted to cry. "I kind of like to keep my friends."

"Like you said, sweetie. She never was your friend."

"Yes she was," said Danny. "She was a great friend. But she changed her mind."

"All right. But love is not love if it alters when it alteration finds."

"That is one of the most convoluted lines of poetry ever written," said Danny.

"But *Sense and Sensibility* made me cry and cry," said Veevee.

"Dead squirrels in the road make you cry."

"You're taking this all very calmly," said Veevee.

"Because it doesn't matter what Hermia says, Veevee. The Belmage is real. Loki is right—that's the real war. All this bull about the Families going through Great Gates, that's just stupid. I need to learn how to eat gates the way Loki did. I need to get to Westil and pull the gates up after me, just as he did."

"Please don't tell me that this will involve another trip to Egypt," said Veevee. "At least bring somebody along to pour water over your head from time to time."

"You know what?" said Danny. "I'm going to eat a couple of peanut butter sandwiches and go out for a run. I've got to make sure my legs still work."

"So you're going to stick with the high school thing a while longer."

"It's either high school or figure out how to save the world, and whom to save it from."

"I like it when you say 'whom,'" said Veevee. "You actually know the rules."

"I don't know any rules," said Danny. "I don't know anything."

Inside him, Loki's gates were murmuring to him. It's all true, they were saying in their wordless way. Don't doubt it. True true true. The Dragon is real. The Dragon wants to go through a Great Gate to Westil. Keep him out of the Great Gate.

"All I can do is muddle through as best I can," said Danny.

"It's what we all do," said Veevee.

18

Clear Memory

What no one knew about Wad, what he barely knew about himself, was how lost he was. You don't live a thousand years inside a tree without losing something, and what Wad had lost was his own story.

Once he had been driven by a terrible purpose, something so important it was worth locking himself away from human life and devoting everything to the single task of taking away from any gatemage in Westil and Mittlegard the power to make a Great Gate. In doing this, he diminished all the mages, and consigned generations of human beings to suffering and death for lack of the power of healing that the gatemages had held.

But, waking from the tree, called from it by something he did not recognize or understand, Wad had wandered with no purpose at all. A girl had fed him and given him clothing, so he did not freeze to death or starve. A bakerwoman had taken him in and so he had dwelt in a castle and learned to care about the things that castle dwellers care about—kings and dynasties.

He had followed his body's inclinations and fallen in love with a woman of beauty and ruthless power. Only gradually had he discovered that he had some moral principles, things he would not do. He would not murder King Prayard's mistress and their children. He would not rip the baby from Bexoi's womb in vengeance for her murder of the child they had made together.

It implied that once upon a time, Wad had been a man who thought deeply about right and wrong, and came to conclusions different from those that were common among the mages. That man had learned much about the workings of power, had acquired never-before-seen skills in gatemagery.

Above all, he had strength of will. When he set his mind to a purpose, he accomplished it.

Yet was there any sense in which Wad was still that man?

If he was, what purpose did he have now? Anonoei had her plans, and Wad helped her, as once he had accepted the purpose King Prayard assigned to him, and then had become the willing tool of Bexoi in her plotting.

When Wad came upon Danny North, he had acted according to what was left of the driving purpose of the man that Wad had once been. But when Danny North fought back and ate most of Wad's own gates, Wad had backed away, beaten, and now even this feckless boy in a faraway place had more purpose in his life than Wad.

No, it was Wad who was feckless. Danny North had accomplished everything he set out to do. His mistakes had been mistakes of ignorance. Even Wad had not known what would happen to a Great Gate made of the captive outselves of other Gatefathers, for the very good reason that few mages had ever *had* captive gates to work with.

It was Wad who had no sense of responsibility.

No. He could not lie to himself, even in self-loathing. He had far too great a sense of responsibility. When he adopted someone, he took absolute responsibility for them—even when they were his captives, like Anonoei and her sons during their many months in prison; even when they were using him without conscience, like Bexoi and, for all he knew, Anonoei.

Wad especially took responsibility for his failures. Even when he had no idea what the right thing to do might have been, he blamed himself for not having done it.

As he watched Anonoei manipulate everyone whose life touched Bexoi's, Wad understood quite clearly that Anonoei's purpose was dark and destructive, and she showed him over and over again why manmagery had always been feared and banned, why manmages were destroyed whenever they were caught at their work. When her plotting came to terrible fruition, just as with Bexoi's, Wad would bear the terrible guilt of having helped her accomplish it. And yet he had no will of his own to give him the strength to say, Enough, we will do no more.

Or was it that his will was every bit as dark and evil as Bexoi's, as Anonoei's, as anyone's, but by letting them make the decisions, he left himself an excuse? Yes, I share responsibility, but it was not my plot to do this terrible thing.

These were the thoughts that he brooded over, whenever he was not actively doing something else, and sometimes even when he was. Watching Ced raise a tiny dust devil and whip it into such power that it became a blade that could cut through stone, Wad could not stop his mind from wandering back to his own troubles, his own mistakes.

Where is the teacher who can help me know *when* to use my power, and whom to trust, and whose plans are worth fulfilling?

I don't even know if my own former plans are the ones I should support, or if I made a terrible mistake fifteen centuries ago.

At that moment, on another world, Danny North took the gates that Wad had given to him—and why not, since he already *had* them?—and used them to bring back a memory.

Wad had no idea what Danny North was seeing, hearing, experiencing. But to Wad it was all so clear and powerful that he could not escape from it. He lost all contact with the present moment. He could not see Ced or the ancient treemage who was teaching him. He could not feel the sun on his back or the grass in the meadow where he lay.

He could only see the old hermit Kawab, sitting in the mouth of his cave on the rocky plateau west of the Nile.

Wad knew him instantly, knew that he had sought this man for a year, once he discovered that he existed. Knew that he had come to him for guidance, for the answer to his question.

What was the question?

He heard himself in memory, explaining why he was there.

"She was possessed by a Belmage, and so I passed her through a gate, to drive the Belmage away," Wad remembered explaining. "I knew enough to take her to a place far from him, so the Belmage didn't dive right back into her and rule her again as if she were his clant. Only it didn't work."

Wad remembered now the terror of that realization. When he followed the Illyrian Clawsister he had just freed from possession, she laughed at him. "Fool," she said. "Fool! You have no power over *me*."

"What is this Belmage?" Wad remembered asking Kawab. "You are the last of the Enemies of Set; you are the only one who can tell me why my gate did not drive this one away."

Kawab said nothing, did nothing. But a single tear streaked the thick dust on his face.

"What is it?" demanded Wad. "You know what this means, and it grieves you."

"It was no Belmage," said Kawab. "Not one of the Sutahites, the followers who were cast out of heaven with the Dragon. It was Set himself, the Dragon, the Enemy of all souls, and your story tells me that he has gained the power to hold onto a body beyond the power of any man to drive him out."

"How do I fight him, then? How do I free this woman from him?"

"You can free her only by killing her," said Kawab. "And yet it will not harm Set himself. He cannot be killed. He will simply find another man or woman to possess, to control. And none can heal her, none can drive him out. He is the devil of devils."

"Don't tell me the dogmas of Christians," Wad insisted in that memory. "I came to you for the lore of the Enemies of Set."

"They are the same, the same," murmured Kawab. "What do you think John the Revelator was talking about in the Apocalypse? War in heaven—that was the battle in the world of Duat, which Michael won, which Osiris won, it was the same war. Set was cast down to the Earth, the great Dragon, Satan, the devil, Baal, Bel, the Enemy. Only fools think that truth disappears when the boundaries of belief are crossed. Set is the enemy, the slayer of Osiris, the possessor of souls. His followers are weak, pathetic creatures. You can drive them out with your gatemagery, you can trick them, frighten them. They have no power except what people give them. But Set and a very few of his disciples, *they* are the most terrible manmages ever to live—or not-live—here upon the Earth."

"I don't understand what you're talking about," Wad had answered him. "What is Duat? Who is Michael or Osiris or whatever you call him? What was the war? And who is this Set, this great Dragon, this Satan?"

Over and over this memory played through Wad's mind, starting over whenever Danny North lost the thread of it back in the Egyptian desert on Mittlegard. Again and again Wad heard himself ask and ask and ask and yet for hours there was no answer. Danny North could never get him to the answer.

This much consciousness of the present moment Wad retained: He reached to his own gates, the ones he had put under

Danny's power, and he calmed them. Slowed them. Kept them tied to the memory. He tied them to his own inself, not taking back control of them, but giving them cleaner, clearer access to himself, to his memory. And through them, he was able to calm and soothe Danny North himself. Stop him from losing the thread of the memory. Help him hold to it, follow it, allow it to reach fruition.

Finally the voice of Kawab went on, the soft voice, the urgent voice. "We are all creatures from another world."

Yes, from Westil, thought Wad-who-was, his old self there in the desert.

"Not from the world you call Westil or Mitherholm, and not from the world you call Mittlegard or Middle Earth. Where do you think that name comes from? Terra stands in the middle, between two worlds. The world of the mages who call themselves gods, and the world of all souls, Duat, where every human comes from."

"How can I come from there, if I don't remember it?" said Wad-who-was.

"Because we are tied to the body. Ka and ba, both parts of the soul, what you call inself and outself—they are tied to the body, to this hairless ape, this featherless biped, this tribe-dwelling louse-picker, and in that moment all access to the ancient memory is lost. Yet you remain yourself, for all the decisions of the body are made in the ka, the bonded mind, the inself, and the body has no choice but to obey. New memories are made, by ape and ka and ba together, a new self, a whole soul. It is why we were sent to Mittlegard, to get this body, to learn to control it."

Then Wad-who-was asked the question that immediately occurred to Wad-that-is, lying unconscious in the meadow on Westil: "In what part does the magery lie? Is it of the body or the inself-and-outself?"

"Both," answered Kawab. "It is the body that gives shape to the powers inherent in the ka and ba. Because the ka is rooted in the body, the ba is free to roam and act out the will of the self.

Because of the abilities inherited from your parents' bodies, your ka and ba expressed their powers as gatemagery; your ba is divided into ten thousand parts, more than the ba of any other man I have seen, a ba like grains of sand. Because of this, you can make ten thousand gates, or a thousand Great Gates. Because of this, you have the power to eat the gates of any other living mage, for you can take their gates into yourself and overwhelm them. But without this body, you are a ka and ba like any other."

"And without my ka and ba?" asked Wad-who-was.

"Then the body is only a tool-making monkey," said Kawab. "The natural man. A beast with lips that make words, but no mind to understand the deep meaning of anything."

It was clear to Wad-who-was, and so it became clear again to Wad-that-is.

Now Kawab could explain who it was that Wad-who-was had failed to drive from the body of the beastmage he had tried to save.

"In the world where every ka-and-ba was born, there was a war. Set was the evil one, and he persuaded many to follow him. But they lost the war and were cast out of Duat, down to Earth, through a gate that only worked in one direction."

"But you say we are all cast down to Earth from Duat," said Wad-who-was.

"We are not *cast* anywhere," said Kawab. "We are born, one by one, created as body-and-ka, with a ba to do their bidding. The ka joined deeply to the ape. We are *born*. This did not happen to Set and his followers, the Sutahites, the ones you call Belmages. They cannot become part of the ape, as we have."

"And yet they take possession anyway," said Wad-who-was. "One or ten or a hundred Belmages or Sutahites, however many it takes to do it, they force their way into the body and rule it. We gatemages drive them out, until now, until this Set."

"They only take possession as your manmages do—they persuade the ka-and-ba to see the world the way they see it, and then to act within the world according to their will."

"It's the same thing."

"It is *not* the same thing," said Kawab. "They feel nothing of the body—they only watch us feel it. They do not cause a single finger to curl, a single eyelid to close or open. They cannot taste the food we eat, or make the jaws chew. They have only the power that comes from our obedience."

"Except for Set."

"Not even him," said Kawab. "Not even the great Set. He rides the ape-brain like a man on horseback, but he never *becomes* the horse."

"Not even the way a beastmage becomes the heartbeast?" asked Wad-who-was.

"It is the ba that goes into the beast, but it is the ba of a mage who is attached to a living body of flesh and blood. The ba knows how to become a part of the body. The ba feels what the beast feels. Yet doesn't it also persuade rather than rule?"

"The will of the mage is much stronger than most beast-minds," said Wad-who-was.

"But the strongest beasts can disobey the ba; is that not true?"

It was true, or so Wad had heard from the beastmages.

"Even Set?" asked Wad-who-was. "Even he cannot bind himself inside the human body?"

"Even when he rides the woman through your gate and laughs at you. He may have power to stay, even through the gate, but he has not *become* the woman. She is still there, a ka-and-ba inside the body, but completely subject to him. Feeling her limbs move in obedience to the will of Set, hearing her mouth speak his words, powerless to stop him. And yet she is the one who owns the body; Set is and always will be an interloper. That's why he hates us all. That's why he wants to destroy us."

"Then he is all-powerful," said Wad-who-was. "Because he can take possession of the most powerful mages, and they can never get free of him, and must always do what he says, and he cannot be killed, but they can be killed."

"I did not say that," said Kawab, "because that is not known. What we do know is this: The ka-and-ba of the Sutahites, these wandering souls, cannot be divided. Even when they possess a body such as yours, which caused your own ba to divide ten thousand times, their ka-and-ba remains a single thing."

"What does that *mean*?" demanded Wad-who-was, frustrated with the strangeness of Kawab's teachings.

"It means that Set can only possess one person at a time. And most of the Sutahites are so weak that they cannot possess even one person—they have to join together, two or five or ten or more, in order to get control. They drive their victim mad with a chaos of voices, and even when his ka has retreated deep into the mind, and the wanderers have control, they can hardly agree among themselves. No one of them is master. We think the man is mad, because his behavior is not guided by a single will."

Wad-who-was had seen this, and now he thought he understood. "Set himself, this great Dragon, can rule over a person by himself, needing no allies."

"He and the mightiest of the Sutahites. We call these devils by many names, but we don't know if any of them is the true name of the Master Sutahite. We only know that only a fool calls upon one of the great ones, for they can take possession far more easily when they are called. The fool who summons one *believes* that he is the master over the Sutahite, but he is deceived; it is the Sutahite who rules."

"So the pentagons they draw—"

"Decorations only," said Kawab. "They have no power, these fools who call themselves wizards and necromancers. The power that you Mithermages have, *those* are real. But when a Master Sutahite has power over a man, then the Master calls many lesser Sutahites. They obey him then, and gain great power from their obedience to a Master who rules a human body. They can easily influence the minds of many other people, so they think that the one possessed by the Master is a great wizard with mighty powers. All illusion."

"So they are not as powerful as we think they are," said Wad-who-was.

"I said 'when a Master Sutahite has power over a man.' But when he has power over a Mithermage, then the mage will do his bidding, and his powers belong to the Sutahite who rules him."

"Until a gatemage comes and drives out the possessor," said Wad-who-was.

"Which works with every Sutahite, but not with Set himself, or so your story tells me. For if he has the power to resist *you*, there is no gatemage among all your kind who can drive him out."

"But as long as he rules a mage, he has that mage's power," said Wad-who-was.

"And when he takes possession of *you*," said Kawab, "he will be master of all. Because only those who obey him will be permitted to use any Great Gates, and all others will therefore be weaker than he is. He will rule both worlds, passing back and forth between them. He will summon ten thousand, a hundred thousand Sutahites to Westil, and take possession of all the mages, there on that world where few have strength enough to resist them. For humans here on Mittlegard have developed strength in the ape-brain, to resist possession; those who have this strength are far more likely to have children than those who are easily possessed. On Mitherholm, there is no resistance. All the power of all the Mithermages will be in Set's hands, through the Sutahites who will be unable to resist his will. Then they will return to Earth and conquer all. When that work is complete, they will challenge Duat. But even if that fails, they will still have this: possession of all the bodies that were reserved for the ka-and-ba who obeyed the law and fought against Set in the war in Duat. Is that not a victory? Is that not the triumph of the devil?"

Those words rang in the ears, in the mind of Wad-that-is. He would have leapt to his feet, finally understanding what he had forgotten during his centuries in the tree.

But Danny North had not seen with such clarity, because of course he had no personal memories of the interview with Kawab. And so he started it over, every word of it again and again. And Wad lay trapped on the meadow in Mitherkame while Danny sat dehydrating in the desert of Egypt, replaying the same memory over and over, struggling to understand it.

Then, at last, it ended. Hermia wakened Danny North in Egypt, and Wad's eyes flew open and he cried out in relief to have his mind finally clear of the memory.

"Who held you?" demanded Anonoei.

"When did you come here?" asked Wad. "You weren't here."

"You lay here unmoving an entire night, and then a day. Ced came for me, through a gate you left for me to use, and we came back by another gate you left for me."

Wad remembered now that Anonoei had been visiting one of her toadies who was working against Bexoi in the castle of Nassassa. He had sent her through a gate, and had already made the gate that would bring her back. He had made them overlap perfectly, so that it remained public for her to use for her return. That way he didn't have to watch and bring her back herself. He was tired of watching her flirt with men and turn them into jelly.

But a public gate is public in both directions, unless Wad locked it, which he hadn't. Ced must have noticed where Anonoei stepped through from this meadow. And when Wad fell into the trance of memory . . .

What had Danny North learned?

Would it be good or bad if he understood?

It was certainly good that Wad now understood completely what once he had guessed at. For now he remembered how he had gone at once to the beastmage he had failed to save. Only she fell to her knees before him this time, instead of mocking. "Thank you, Loki!" she cried out as soon as he appeared. "You saved me."

"I did not save you," Wad had said.

"But he's gone," she said.

Gone, but of his own free will. Not cast out by my power. He simply didn't want me to find him.

That was a good sign. That meant that the Belmage—Set, to use Kawab's name for him—still feared Wad enough to want to avoid him. Set had given the beastmage back to herself so that Wad would not know where to find him.

It was in that moment that Wad began to eat the gates. It took him a little while to figure out how to do it, but hadn't Kawab told him it was possible?

And it worked. Wad ate all the gates. All the Great Gates but one. Then he passed through it, ate it behind him, then ate all the gates on Westil.

But it was not enough. The other gatemages saw what was happening, felt their own gates consumed, and immediately began to create new gates where the old ones had been.

It was not enough to eat the made gates. He had to reach into the other mages and eat the gates they had not yet made.

It took him days to learn how to do it, and during that time he could hardly sleep, because he knew that the other gatemages were searching for him. They could find him because he was holding their gates captive. He had to block them by eating every gate as soon as it was made.

That was when he trained his outself, his ba, to watch for any gate at all and cry out to him with strength enough to waken him from his exhausted sleep. Gate gate gate, they cried, and he awoke and ate whatever gates the mages searching for him had created.

Until at last he was able to reach inside them, find their gatehoard—their ba—and gather it all in. The more they resisted, the easier it was to snap off the connection. All the gates they would ever make, and he took them and held them, ruling over them, controlling them.

And then there were no gates left in the world, and no gatemages left to make new ones.

Only then did Wad go in search of the ancient treemage—now long dead, though this one who was training Ced was a disciple of a disciple of—who got a tree to let him inside its bark, to feed on its sap and keep both himself and the tree vibrant and alive forever.

Forever, that had been the plan.

But the tree expelled him. Or he unconsciously pulled himself out of the tree. Or both. And Wad had no idea why. The system had been working, and now it was broken.

It was broken because he—or the tree, or spacetime—knew that Wad had no power to resist or control Danny North, let alone steal from him.

It had to happen, Wad supposed. If there were two mages, one would be greater than the other; and, given time enough, you could find a third who was greater still. Powerful as Wad was, there was bound to come another, eventually, who was stronger than he was. One whose gates could not be eaten.

"Please talk to me," Anonoei asked.

Whether it was because he was dying to talk to someone about all that he had just remembered, or whether she used her manmagery to cajole him or control him into telling, he told her all of it.

"You saved the world," she said.

"And Danny North has it in his power to unsave it. Now there is an open gate, and if the Dragon—Set—can find someone, some mage, to ride through it, he'll be here, along with as many wanderers as he can bring, and this world is lost."

"I can see how you'd think that was a bad thing," said Anonoei.

"You think it isn't?" demanded Wad.

"I was being ironic," said Anonoei. "It's the worst thing that could happen. All the power of all the Mithermages, under the rule of a monster? I'm against that."

"I'm glad to hear it."

Ced and the treemage had listened to all of Wad's account. But now the treemage said, "Time to return to work, Ced."

"But after hearing all of this, how can I concentrate?" asked Ced.

"It is precisely at such times that you must have the power to concentrate. So now you'll make a whirlwind small enough to use a single grain of sand to bore through a block of wood, a hole that is only one sandgrain in diameter."

"Impossible," said Ced.

"Two sandgrains, then," said the treemage. "The single-grain tunnel will be tomorrow."

They went back to work.

Anonoei had only one question for Wad. "These Sutahites, these Belmages. Are they manmages, then?"

"No," said Wad.

"But they work in the same way. What my outself does, reaching into a person, persuading him—that's what they do, only using their whole ka?"

"They can't separate ka from ba, or so Kawab said."

"Why can't you just say yes or no?"

"Because I don't understand all the ramifications of the things Kawab told me. He isn't—wasn't—a mage himself, so he doesn't even know the ramifications. It's lore that he learned and memorized and then intended to pass on. To other disciples of the order, but they were being persecuted at the time, so there were no others. They had been killed or had fled or had obeyed when Kawab commanded them to go into hiding. There was no one left to teach."

"Only you," said Anonoei. "But you were enough."

"For sixteen hundred years or so," said Wad. "Until now."

"And now?"

"Set is surely still alive somewhere. Waiting for a chance to get control of Danny North."

"If he can," said Anonoei.

"Danny is a strong-willed boy," said Wad. "Stronger than me. So maybe he can resist. As long as he doesn't do something stupid, like inviting Set in."

"What form could such an invitation take?" asked Anonoei.

Now that his memory had been awakened, Wad could think back to the lore of possession that, as a gatemage, he had been required to learn. "Words, of course. Calling the Belmage by name, if they have names—maybe the name didn't matter, just the fact of calling."

"And no other way?"

"A Belmage could jump from one person to another if they had some kind of physical intercourse."

"Sex."

"Or a deep kiss. Or a common flow of blood—two wounds pressed together. There were some people so weak-willed that a Belmage could jump between them with only a steady gaze connecting them. But few Mithermages are so weak as that."

"That's how it is with me," said Anonoei. "A weak person, my voice alone is enough. A little stronger, and I have to have them in gaze before I can send my outself into them and turn them to my will. If I'm going to ride them like a heartbeast—well, before passing through the Great Gate, I didn't have the power to do that. And even now, I can't do it without consent. Without . . . the kiss."

Wad understood the hesitation. It wasn't kissing she had used. She had doubtless slept with several of her toadies in order to be able to ride them as heartbeasts.

"So you're saying that they *are* like manmages," said Wad.

"Or manmages are like . . . Sutahites?"

"Like Set. Like the devil and his angels. Yes. Like that."

"No wonder everybody fears and hates us," said Anonoei.

"Including me," said Wad. "Not hate, but fear. I always wonder if you've used your magery on me."

"Not deliberately," said Anonoei. "I've never *sent* anything into you. But I do this by reflex. I'm sure that I've probably had some influence I wasn't even aware of. But never enough to control you. Your choices have been your own."

"So the powerful desire I have to sleep with you," said Wad. "That's not of your making?"

"I think it has more to do with—what did Kawab say?—the apewoman that I'm riding in."

"In other words, I just think you're pretty," said Wad.

"You're male and I'm female," said Anonoei. "You think any willing female is pretty."

"You're willing?"

In answer, she kissed him.

"But is it safe for me to sleep with you?" he asked her, when the kiss was over.

"Doesn't that depend on how strong your own will is?" she asked.

"It's a foolish thing to do right now," said Wad.

"You're right," she said. "But what if we gate somewhere that Ced and his teacher can't see us."

That sounded good to Wad, and so he moved the end of the gate she had just used so now it led to a room in Nassassa, a locked room. With a bed.

After all, I've slept with a queen, thought Wad. Why not with a king's ex-concubine?

Vaguely he thought: Shouldn't I have the strength of will to resist this desire?

Clearly he answered himself: It is my will to have this woman, right now. And she's willing. So shut up.

19

Treachery

This is high school, Danny reminded himself. This is what you wanted.

Supposedly he was helping Laurette study for a precalculus test that was coming up. Danny thought of calculus as a game—sometimes tedious, but usually enjoyable. To Laurette, however, it was a perpetual mystery. Danny explained in words that he *knew* were clear. He demonstrated over and over.

Laurette concentrated hard, echoing his words, even tracing the operations he performed, yet she still didn't really understand it. Once she got an answer right but instead of being thrilled or relieved, she almost wept in frustration. "I don't know what I did," she said.

"You did the operation and entered all the right numbers in the calculator and I didn't do any of it. You got it right."

"But *why* did I get it right? I thought I did all those things with all the other problems that I screwed up!"

"Laurette, are you planning any kind of career that's going to need math?"

"I just don't like being stupid," she said, and then she did weep.

"You're not stupid," he said. "You're just not interested in math." He put his arm across her shoulders.

She melted into him, weeping onto his shirt. "I'm interested in A's," she said. "That's always been enough before."

And then he realized that instead of just clinging to him, she was stroking his chest.

And that's when he decided that he hated high school. Nothing was ever what it seemed to be. Laurette seemed genuinely frustrated by her math class. And yet here she was, turning it into something romantic. So how much of her crying was real? How could he know?

They're all manmages, girls are. Every damn one of them.

Not Pat. Give her credit—she played no games.

But she also didn't need any help with her homework.

Danny took Laurette's hands in a brotherly way and set them on the table. "You just need to do it again. On the next problem. I'll watch. Do the steps. You can get it right every time, Laurette. Just concentrate on the operations, not the numbers you're plugging in."

"I know you like Pat," said Laurette. "But I just don't see why."

"Fortunately," said Danny, "you don't have to."

He got up from the table and headed for the refrigerator. "Is there anything off limits in the fridge?"

"Everything in the fridge is off limits," said Laurette. "My mom micro-menus. She calculates the family diet down to the microgram."

"So doubtful," said Danny. "You don't own a scale that reports micrograms."

"You can eat anything from the cookie jar," said Laurette.

"But your mother's vegan wheatless cookies are inedible," said Danny. "None of you has a gluten allergy."

"She read somewhere that wheat is bad. It's just a phase, she's probably already sneaking bread herself on the sly. Then she'll feel guilty, confess to us all, and we'll get bread again, too."

"It's amazing that your whole family doesn't look like concentration camp victims."

"We all cheat," said Laurette. "Though in my case, it's not for flavor or even hunger. It's all about keeping the cleavage."

"Yes, well," said Danny.

"You never look anymore."

"Don't have to keep reading a book I've already memorized. Wasn't Sin coming over, too?"

"No," said Laurette.

"She said she was."

"It's my turn tonight," said Laurette.

"I hate high school," said Danny.

"I don't want to have sex with you," said Laurette. "I just want you to be *interested* in it. I know you're not gay, because of what Pat said."

Danny's heart sank a little. "What did Pat say?"

"I asked her, 'What was it like to kiss him?' And she said, 'I wonder whether we're really going to Grandma's for Thanksgiving or if my parents are going to call it off again this year.'"

"Oh," said Danny.

"And then I said, 'So you slept with him, is that it?' And she said, 'My parents always have these big plans but then they don't do any of the jobs you have to do to make the plans come off.'"

"Her parents are very frustrating to her," said Danny. "But I think if procrastination bordering on laziness is the worst thing wrong with your parents, you're doing pretty well."

"I don't actually care about Pat's parents, Danny," said Laurette.

"Boys are supposed to be constant horndogs. And mythological gods are supposed to be even worse."

"Some of them are," said Danny. "Maybe most of them."

"Maybe you are, too, if you find girls you think are attractive." She was crying again.

"What *is* this?" asked Danny. "We're friends. You're attractive. And funny and nice and I like you fine."

"But you don't *want* me."

"Is that the only measure of . . . anything?" asked Danny. "And you need to get your homework done so I'm leaving."

"Please don't," said Laurette. "Please just . . . can't you just kiss me and *see* if you like it?"

"I'd like it just fine. I'd like it a lot. That's why I'm not going to do it."

"You can't possibly be *Christian,*" said Laurette. "Why can't you ever do something because it's *fun*?"

"I do things for fun all the time," said Danny. "But I don't like hurting people."

"Pat doesn't own you! You're not *married*."

"Actually, I lied. I do like hurting people. I spent my whole childhood thinking up malicious pranks and playing them. Really nasty stuff. Involving poo and pain and bad smells and minor injuries. Plus a lot of humiliation. But that's because I detested everyone in my family, and they detested me back. And my pranks were funny. There's nothing funny about kissing you when I don't mean it and when I know you'd talk about it and it would hurt Pat and it would also hurt Xena and Sin because I *didn't* do anything with them."

"What if I didn't talk about it?" asked Laurette.

"I'm going now," said Danny.

"You said that before, and yet you're still here." She got up from her chair and put her arms around him and leaned her head on his chest. "You really are physically fit, you know. Good health is so attractive."

"Now you're just being idiotic," said Danny.

"And you're still here," said Laurette. She slid a hand down his back, under the waistband of his pants.

"All that's down there is my butt," said Danny. "You have one, too."

She used her other hand to grab his wrist and plant his hand on her backside. "*That's* a butt," she said, "and you *don't* have one. That's what I'm looking for. To see what holds your pants up."

This had gone far enough. Because it was working exactly as she intended and he just didn't understand why she was doing this. It seemed like a game among the girls, but they also seemed to mean it.

He gated back three paces.

She burst into tears. "I'm that repulsive."

"The opposite. You won't leave me alone and you are *not* repulsive and I'm grimly determined not to be that guy."

"What guy?"

"The guy who thinks he's a god and impregnates women left and right."

"I'm on the pill, if that's what worries you. And I know you don't have AIDS so you don't have to use a condom."

"I can't believe you said that," said Danny.

She was back in front of him, fiddling with his zipper.

"What happened to 'No means no'?" he said, removing her hands from his jeans.

"That's so eighties," she said. "I wasn't even born then. And it's about *girls* saying no, anyway."

But he had no snappy retort, because in that moment he felt something that could not be real.

He felt somebody using the Wild Gate.

He knew it was that gate because there were a dozen of his own gates woven into it in one direction, two dozen in the other, so the feeling of gate-use was that much stronger.

Hermia and Veevee used gates often and he knew what that felt like. It was part of the background noise of his life—though it was far more noticeable now, since he'd been through a Great Gate himself. This, though. This was someone he didn't know. And then another person. And another.

"Excuse me," said Danny. "Something's happening. Nothing to do with you. Got to go."

"What's wrong? You look—"

But he didn't get to hear how he looked. He had already gated to the Silvermans' barn.

There was no one there.

There was also no Wild Gate. Someone had moved it. And he hadn't even felt it.

No, he *had* felt it. That's part of what drew his attention to the use of the gate. Someone moved it and then people started using it.

Someone? There were only two gatemages in the world, besides Danny. Unless it was the Westilian kid that Loki had dropped off with the Silvermans.

Danny gated to the house. The boys were sitting in the living room. The younger one was playing a videogame. The older one was staring into space. Both here, nothing changed.

"Danny," said Leslie. She stood in the doorway that led to the hall. "What's wrong?"

"Somebody's using the gate." He didn't need to specify which one.

"No!" said Leslie. "Nobody's come in here!"

"Somebody moved this end of the gate," said Danny. "It's not in the barn anymore."

"Hermia," said Leslie.

"I didn't know she could do it," said Danny. "But who else? Veevee?"

"What are you going to do?"

"She's already sending people through. Her Family, no doubt. So much for my two-from-each-Family rule."

"You realize that you have no time at all," said Leslie. "Without the advantage of having been through a Great Gate when they haven't, Marion and I aren't such great shakes as mages. They'll blow us away."

"I suppose you're right—they wouldn't be doing it this way if they had peaceful intentions. I can't believe she did this."

"She thought she could get away from those Family ties, and she was wrong," said Leslie. "You can talk to her about it later. Right now, what are you going to do?"

"I've got to get you and Dad and these boys somewhere safe."

Leslie nodded, and there were tears on her cheeks. "I'll get Marion in from the quarry."

"No," said Danny. "I will." He walked to the boys on the couch and peeled the headphones off Enopp's head. "Take my hand," he said.

Enopp did, then took Eluik's hand. Danny reached for Leslie, and as soon as they gripped each other he gated them all to the pit at the north end of the farm where Marion quarried simple granite from the bedrock. The pit wasn't deep. He quarried by sending his outself deep and drawing up the stone, floating it to the surface. The pit was just so the neighbors and passing cars couldn't see the stones rise through the soil without the aid of human hands.

Marion grasped the situation as soon as Danny said, "Hermia moved the gate and she's using it."

He gated them to Veevee's condo. Veevee wasn't there.

"She's at the beach," said Danny. "I'll be right back." And in a moment he was. Veevee was dripping and furious. "I can't believe that little Greek bitch would betray us all like that."

"Family," said Leslie.

"That doesn't excuse being a traitorous bitch," said Veevee.

"But it explains it," said Marion. "Besides which, I think the way *they* see it is, she's finally *stopped* being a traitorous bitch and now she's a loyal Family member again."

"Or they held her dog hostage," said Leslie.

"What's happening?" asked Enopp.

"Join hands and at the next place, they'll explain it to you," said Danny.

He took them to DC, to Stone's house. "Hermia's been sending people through the Wild Gate. Turns out that passing to Westil and back gave her the power to move other people's gates. Specifically, the Mittlegard end of the Wild Gate."

"And you didn't stop her?"

"I didn't know what I was feeling until she was already sending people through," said Danny. "I didn't know you could move a Great Gate."

Stone bowed his head. "Have you gathered up all the gates she knows about?"

"All of hers. All the ones that connect our houses. That was practically a reflex. Like clenching your sphincter muscles when you're scared," said Danny.

"What an ill-raised child you are, Danny," said Leslie. "We don't talk about sphincter muscles in front of impressionable children."

"They're going to attack all the other Families," said Danny. "Mine first, I'm sure. But at this point, the only thing I can do is make a Great Gate and send everybody through. Or the Illyrians will kill everybody else and rule the world. Am I not right?"

"Oh, if history teaches us anything," said Stone, "it's that gods with a sudden increase in power instantly remember how much they hate their enemies."

"We're all so good at grudges," said Leslie.

"What are you going to do to Hermia?" asked Marion.

"Nothing yet," said Danny. "Unless she forces me. Where do you want to go?"

"Hermia doesn't know about my place in Maine," said Stone.

"Neither did I," said Veevee.

Stone ignored her. "There isn't even running water, but it's between two very cold lakes, clean water, plenty of firewood, and an outhouse. These boys aren't used to indoor plumbing anyway, am I right?"

"*I* am," said Veevee.

Leslie smiled sweetly. "Does a mage poop in the woods? I think *so*."

"Any mages in residence here?" asked Danny.

"I'll call them," said Stone.

There were three, all women, one in her fifties and a pair of twenty-year-old twins. No time for introductions. Danny made a public gate, made it open and obvious, and they all passed through. Danny didn't go with them—they'd all get acquainted at the lake and Danny would join them later. He took back the gate and then headed for the North Family compound.

He arrived in Mook's and Lummy's kitchen. They weren't there.

He found them on the front porch. "Bring everybody," he said.

"What is it?" said Aunt Lummy, looking scared.

"The Greeks got into a Great Gate that I thought was safe. They're passing through it now and you know they'll come here first."

Uncle Mook was already running to the old house.

"I'm taking us all to a safe place," said Danny.

"How long do you think we can hide from them?" asked Lummy.

"Long enough for me to make a Great Gate and pass you all through it."

She burst into tears and embraced him. "I knew you'd forgive us."

"You and Uncle Mook never did anything that needed forgiving," said Danny. "And I haven't forgiven anybody. I'm just not going to let the Greeks rule the world."

"It was that Greek girl, wasn't it?" asked Aunt Lummy. "You can't trust a Greek. Homer said so and he was right."

"It was Laocoon who said it. Homer was just quoting him," said Danny.

"Actually, what Laocoon said wasn't printable. Homer cleaned it up for him," said Lummy.

The bell was ringing. It was never rung except when there was war. Danny took Lummy's hand and gated to the gathering place.

"You!" shouted Great-uncle Zog, looking furious.

Danny gated him to the kitchen of the big house. "I don't have time for any shit," he said. "I was betrayed and the Greeks are going to Westil and back right now."

All the adults knew what that meant, and they kept the children silent.

"I'm gating you to a place where I can make a Great Gate. But I'm telling you right now. I'm letting *everybody* use it. Not just the North Family. Anybody has a problem with that, then that's a person who isn't going through. Is that clear?"

"What do you mean by 'everybody'?" asked Auntie Uck. "I'm not disagreeing, I just want to know."

"Everybody who isn't Greek," said Danny. "Families and Orphans. And there's a truce at the new Great Gate. Do you understand me? A total truce. As soon as I make the gate, Hermia will know where it is and they'll head for it."

"Then as soon as *we* get through it, we'll head for *them,*" said Grandpa Gyish. He actually looked happy. Thrilled, even. Also evil. Definitely he looked evil. Danny remembered why he hated some of these people.

"You've never been through a Great Gate," said Danny. "It takes time to figure out what you can do. So no, I'm not sending you off to war. I'm going to gate off anyone who approaches. I can do it. When they see that everybody else has gone through a Great Gate, too, and they have no advantage, *then* I think we can work out a truce."

"Don't be absurd," said Uncle Poot. "You weren't here for the last war. There'll be no truce."

"I don't expect it to hold," said Danny. "Where's my father?"

Thor answered. "In town. Your mother and your brother and sister, too."

"A family outing," said Danny. "How sweet. I'll come back for them. The place we're going to belongs to a good friend of mine. My friend, do you understand me? Everyone there is my friend, but it's Stone's house and in that place *he rules.*"

At that moment Zog rejoined the group, even angrier than before. "You filthy little drekka, I'm not going to—"

This time Danny gated him to the parking lot of the Lexington Walmart.

"He's horrible, Danny," said Aunt Lummy, "but you can't leave him out. They'll kill him. They hate him most of all."

"I'm not going to leave him out," said Danny. "I just don't have time to deal with his assholery. I'll gate him through and you all can tame him." Danny made a public gate, a big one. "Before you step through this gate," he said to everybody, "you look me in the eye and tell me that you'll obey Stone and harm no one."

"That'll take too much time," said Uncle Mook.

"Look me in the eye and say *yes,*" said Danny. "Because if you don't keep your word, I will be ruthless. Do you understand me?"

They all said yes as they passed through the gate.

Danny followed, and took back the gate behind him.

Stone's cabin was too small for everyone to sleep there, and it was bitterly cold on this November night, but it wouldn't matter. They wouldn't be there long. Danny ignored everybody's questions and headed for the narrow isthmus between two jewel-like lakes.

No rope this time. He began turning around and around. Immediately he spun out gates—his own gates, not the ones Loki had given him, and definitely not the captive gates. He took his time and wove it strong and true.

By himself, Danny would have had no idea how to build it so it wouldn't lead to the same circle of stones on Westil where his previous two Great Gates had led. But Loki had known many good places on Westil for a Great Gate to lead, ancient places, secret places that only Loki knew.

So at Danny's urging, the gates that Loki had given him used their kinetic memory to guide him as he threw the thick-woven gates upward.

He felt the approval of Loki's outself: a ten-thousand-year gate, they told him. Danny wasn't sure he was thrilled to know that the gate would outlast him by hundreds of lifetimes, but . . . it meant that it was well-made, and it would do the job.

Then he wove another gate, just as strong, leading back to a spot on the other side of the cabin. "Stone," said Danny. "You and Veevee first."

"We've already been through a Great Gate," said Veevee.

"Not this one," said Danny. "So go and come back again. Veevee can show you the return entrance. And Veevee, I need you there to shepherd everybody through—and so you can lock the gate if somebody on Westil tries to interfere or use the thing. And if Loki shows up, explain it to him. Though maybe he knows. Maybe he knows whatever his gates know."

Danny could feel that the Greeks had stopped going through the Wild Gate. "They're done," he said. "That means they're coming. Hermia knows where this gate is. She may try to interfere. I have to concentrate on watching for her and protecting this place. So when you get back, Stone, you're in charge of this end."

With that, Danny went off by himself, into the cabin, up into the loft.

The two Westilian boys went up the ladder after him. "You can watch," said Danny. "But do not speak to me." Not that the older boy needed the warning. And if the younger boy was really a gatemage, maybe he'd be able to follow what Danny was doing.

Danny looked for Hermia, though not with his eyes. She was

easy to find. She only had a few divisions of her outself, her ba, but since her passage through the Wild Gate she glowed so brightly that she could not escape his notice.

She was trying to lock the Wild Gate.

Fool, thought Danny. The time to lock it was before you sent your entire Family through it.

Danny began unweaving his own gates from the Wild Gate. He knew what would happen—the former captives would remain, and he would no longer be able to feel when people passed through it.

But it would be a far weaker Great Gate without his ba woven through it. And the return gate was entirely his. That one he simply took back. There was no return now, if anyone used the Wild Gate. Hermia would know what he was doing. Let her watch.

He had thought of doing this while they were still passing through the Wild Gate. But he didn't know what half-unweaving the outbound gate would do to anyone using it at the time. Danny wasn't prepared to do murder, and for all he knew, that's what it would be.

As for the return gate, yes, he could have closed that at any time. Removed it and brought it back. But that would have left Illyrian mages on Westil, stranded and angry—and far more powerful than any mages on Westil. It would be irresponsible to send such an affliction to the other world. Better to let them all come back here and *then* weaken the outbound gate and close off the return permanently.

Hermia was angry, no doubt. Poor dear. What did you think would happen? Did you think I'd be understanding? That I'd do nothing?

Yes, angry indeed. For now he felt her trying to take hold of the end of the outbound gate that the Norths were all passing through.

Danny didn't even bother fighting her. He could have

overpowered her easily. But then he would have had to do it again and again, whenever she felt like making another try.

So he took her gates.

As a Lockfriend, she had only three divisions of her outself. But she had to send them out in order to manipulate his gate. Without passing through a Great Gate, she would never have had power to reach this far. But now two of her three gates were here, trying to move his Great Gate.

Danny ate them.

Then he followed them back to her gatehoard and ate the last one, too. All three now, everything she had, was inside his hearthoard. He could feel their terror. But no anger. Hermia was not angry. She was afraid, but she knew she deserved this. She knew that he could easily kill her, gate her to the bottom of the ocean and have done with her. Her treachery deserved no less. It had been the opening salvo in a war she could not win.

But he wouldn't kill her. She must have known that about him, though clearly he did not know *her* at all. However, she would understand that rendering her blind and crippled to gates was actually a mild punishment, compared to the rules of war. Now he would not have to stay awake, waiting for her next move.

Indeed, this attempt to move his new Great Gate might have been intended as an offering. She must have known he would detect the attempt and block it. She was giving him the chance to punish her in this lesser way. Still terrible, but there was always the chance he might give her gates back to her.

The chance, perhaps. But he could not think what she might say or do to win back his trust.

There were nowhere near as many Norths as there were Illyrians. They were already done, and all the Orphans, too.

"I want you to go through the Great Gate, too," said Danny. "And come right back. This is a better gate. It will make you stronger than you are. Will you do that?"

"Yes," said Enopp. "Who was it that you ate up?"

"A friend who betrayed me," said Danny.

"But you didn't gate her anywhere," said Enopp. "Wad gates people places. He kept me in prison for more than a year."

"I'm not . . . Wad," said Danny. "I'm a different man and I use my magery a different way."

"Are you a weakling?" asked Enopp. "Eluik thinks you are weak, to be afraid to hurt people."

"When someone is dead I can't bring them back," said Danny. "And if I hurt them too terribly, I can never win their trust."

"Weak," said Enopp. "That's what Eluik says."

"When he takes back his own body and speaks for himself I'll take notice of what he says," said Danny. "Meanwhile, are you willing to go through the gate and come back?"

"Yes," said Enopp.

And Eluik nodded.

Danny gated them down to the isthmus where the outbound gate was. Stone would send them through.

Then Danny gated himself to Lexington and found Zog. He was still full of rage, but he spoke politely. Fawningly. "The Lord Danny has subdued this vile old bird," said Zog. "I know who holds the power here."

"There is to be no violence at the place where I've made the Great Gate," said Danny coldly. "My friend Stone owns the house. You will obey him while you're there, or I'll make you pay."

"I understand the Lord Danny's mercy."

"I am Loki to you," said Danny.

Zog looked stricken. "You would *use* that vile name?"

"I have met the Loki who took the gates. He acted with wisdom and courage, and I share his purpose. It's a far higher purpose and far more terrible war than any *you* have ever fought."

"What do you know of war?" asked Zog contemptuously.

"I know that you lost every one you fought in," said Danny. "I know that by obeying me and treating me with respect, you will earn the right to have your powers greatly increased. You've already had all your body's pains and weaknesses healed, haven't you?"

Zog nodded.

"That was a gift I gave you, even as I gated you away so you didn't waste my time with your petty hatred."

"The Lord Loki is generous." He said "Loki" as if he were spitting out a cockroach.

Danny gated him to Maine.

He found his parents in the upstairs room of a sandwich restaurant in a fine old house. With them were their children from their first marriages—Father's son Pipo, nine years older than Danny, and Mother's daughter Leonora, who had just turned twenty. Pipo's mother and Leonora's father had both been killed in the last war, but it wouldn't have made any difference. Once it was decided to let Father and Mother mate in order to try to make Danny, the old marriages wouldn't have mattered. Families made their decisions, and people obeyed. Even the heads of the Families obeyed.

Mother looked happy to see him. It was her first response and it touched him a little. Father, however, knew that he would not be there if there were not something terribly wrong, so his response was dread. Dread, but *not* fear of Danny himself. They knew him well enough not to fear that he was there to attack them.

As for Pipo and Leonora, they had never been awful to him, but they had also never protected or helped him in any way. They were nothing to him, and he was nothing to them. But that meant they had a better relationship than the one Danny had with most of the Family.

Danny sat beside them and crisply told them what they needed to know. "I'll pay the bill," he said, and then gated them to Maine.

When the waiter came back, Danny asked for the check. There was no reason for a drowther waiter to have a bad night just because the gods were starting a war.

With the bill paid, and a good tip given, Danny went outside, stepped into the gap between two buildings, and gated himself away.

Family by Family, he spent that night going through the world, gating everyone to Maine, leaving them for Stone and Veevee to guide them through the gates, and then going on to the next Family.

The land around the cabin was getting crowded and people were cold, though a couple of fire mages had warmed the house, and windmages were keeping the air still. At one point Father tried to talk to him. Danny interrupted him. "Stone keeps a pickup truck on the other side of the lake," he said. "Now that you've been to Westil, see what you and Mother can do with the machinery and electronics. With all the Families fairly evenly balanced, and the Norths outnumbered, the only possible advantage is your abilities with machines. Drowther machinery. Who knows how you might be able to use it now?"

Father nodded. "Does this mean you're with us now?" he asked.

"No," said Danny. "But if you have any brains, you'll forget about this Loki and set out trying to create an alliance with the Orphan mages. There aren't enough Norths to fight this war, and they, too, will have to survive in a world dominated once again by powerful gods."

"That's wise counsel," said Father.

"No, Father," said Danny. "It's a demand. I'm going out now to find all the Orphans I can and bring them back. Stone has to go with me because I don't know who and where they are. So I'm setting you to greet them and send them through the Great Gate. Thor can prepare defenses, if they come against us after all. I'm beginning to think Hermia *didn't* tell them where I made this gate, but I might be wrong. Use this opportunity to treat them decently and *as equals*. That means keep Zog and Gyish away from them."

Father nodded. "Your plan is a good one. I see that it's our best chance to survive the coming war. I will bring all the Orphans into our Family and—"

"No," said Danny. "They are not to be adopted. They are not to be put under your authority. You're going to have to do something much harder. Treat them as allies. As equals. Let them *agree* to accept North leadership in battle, but *not* North hegemony. Is that clear? They remain independent."

"I didn't mean to rule over them," Father protested. "I just—I assumed they would want—"

"Assume nothing," said Danny. "Treat them as equals. Now I have work to do."

"Will you ever stop hating us?" asked Father.

"At this moment, I hate nobody except one, and he's not a North."

"Who is it? That Greek girl?"

"It's the Dragon. Set. You haven't heard of him."

Father looked blank.

"That's the war that matters. This thing among you gods—it will be terrible and I'm afraid of how you'll make the drowthers suffer with all your arrogance. But I have to find Set and figure out a way to keep both worlds safe from him, and even Loki doesn't know how to do that."

"Zog said that we have to call *you* Loki now," said Father.

"No, *Zog* has to call me Loki. I'm Danny North to everyone else. 'Loki' still means the Gate Thief, though he uses another name on Westil."

"I thought the Gate Thief was the enemy of all gatemages."

"We all thought that, but it isn't true. The Gate Thief has kept Westil safe for centuries, and by closing all the gates he has sharply limited the power of Set here in Mittlegard. But now there are Great Gates again, and the danger is terrible, and all of your magery is useless against him. Now get to work, please, Odin, and send Stone to me. I wish you well with your war."

Father went away.

Stone joined him and together they spent the entire day going to every Orphan that Stone knew, or knew about. A dozen or so refused to go with them. Two score of them agreed to go to Westil and back, but insisted that they would then go home and fend for themselves. The rest, though, agreed to try, at least, to work with the Norths, to train with them, to cooperate if it really came to war with the Greeks.

None of the other Families even considered allying with the Norths. But they all kept the truce while they were at Stone's cabin; then Danny gated them all back to their homelands to prepare for war. They knew that war would come. And by the time he had met them all, Danny had lost all hope that it might be avoided. They would all bide their time while they mastered their greatly increased powers. But the espionage would start at once, and the collisions would follow, sooner rather than later. They would escalate into combat. People would die.

When Danny and Stone returned to the cabin, it was late afternoon. The day had warmed up a little. Danny saw that Father was making an effort—he and Mother were talking with several of the Orphans, and others were paired up with Norths, practicing magery in some rather spectacular ways. The waters of one lake were churning. Large stones were falling from a nearby cliff, then stopping and sliding back up to resume their place. There were whirlwinds underfoot. But everyone was being careful and polite. Zog and Gyish were nowhere to be seen.

Danny found Thor. "How many of your informants are Mithermages?" asked Danny.

"All the ones who are mages, you've already brought here. The others are drowthers."

"Is there any chance of the Family surviving this war?" asked Danny.

"Oh, a very good one," said Thor. "If we have the greatest Gatefather in history fighting beside us."

"Don't count on it," said Danny.

"Well, then, our chances aren't so good," said Thor.

"See what Father and Mother can do with the machinery of war," said Danny.

Thor seemed puzzled.

"Tanks and fighter planes, Thor," said Danny. "I don't think any other mages know how to deal with them. What Father can do with machines, what Mother can do with electricity—that's where you put your money, Thor. The Norths get there first, and if you play it right, the others won't have any hope of catching up."

Thor grinned. "You care about us after all," he said.

"You're my damn family," said Danny. "Even if you never made me glad of it for a moment." Danny turned away.

"What will *you* be doing, Danny?"

"I'm creating a public gate to take you back to the farm. But it's a one-way gate. Once you leave here, you aren't coming back, at least not by gate. There will be no gates leading to this Great Gate. But for anyone who tries to come here without my permission, there'll be plenty of gates. They just won't go to desirable places. Understand?"

"Danny, do you know what war means?" asked Thor. "Do you understand that someday you're going to have to kill somebody?"

"I've had a man killed before," said Danny, "and I've seen death."

"When?" asked Thor.

"I've had a busy time since I ran away from home." He paused. "Here's the gate back to the compound. Get people back there before they eat up everything Stone has."

Then Danny went back to Buena Vista. He had missed a whole day of school. He was exhausted. But he had to make sure that Hermia, who knew all his friends, was not arranging some kind of mischief. The Mithermages could take care of themselves, now that they had passed through a Great Gate. But Danny's friends would be easy targets for his enemies. So far they were safe—he had checked on them several times through the night and day just passed.

Now, though, Danny had to sleep. He would be safer if he slept here at the cabin, and the Great Gate would be better protected. But if Danny was in Buena Vista, alone, then any attack would probably come against him personally. That's what he wanted. He could take care of himself. He wasn't going to let anything happen to Pat. Or any of them.

20

Worries

In so many ways the boy is the opposite of me," said Wad.

Anonoei was brushing her hair in front of the mirror. "You mean he's tall? Or he's a terrible lover?"

"Taller than I am," said Wad, "but we may never know what kind of lover he'd be, since he seems grimly determined never to give or get pleasure of that kind."

"You're spying on him?"

"Yes," said Wad. "I could hardly believe he didn't realize that by giving him my gates—which he already had—I was given a window into his mind. Well, his perceptions, anyway."

"Taking advantage of an untrained child. Shame on you."

"He even knows that he can use my gates to access my memories. Yet it seems not to have occurred to him that I can use those gates to access his present actions."

"Maybe he has nothing to hide," said Anonoei.

"Nobody has nothing to hide," said Wad. Then he thought better of it. "No, I think you're right. This Danny North really is exactly what he seems."

"Unlike Wad the kitchen boy," said Anonoei.

"Equally unlike Anonoei, King Prayard's drowther mistress," said Wad.

"Manmages have to hide what we can do," said Anonoei. "Fortunately, our magery makes it fairly easy to do. That's one of the main reasons for the drastic penalty. If you manage to recognize manmagery, you rarely get a second chance to strike."

"Quite the contrary," said Wad. "I think the death penalty for manmages was created as an all-purpose excuse for murder. 'I had strange compulsions whenever I was near him, so I knew he was a manmage, so I killed him.' "

"I have strange compulsions when I'm near *you*," said Anonoei.

"Those are normal compulsions," said Wad. "Everybody has them."

"But few would feel them toward *you*."

"But you know what I am," said Wad. "Godlike powers are such an aphrodisiac."

"You're not half the mage you used to be."

"Still mage enough to port you around from place to place," said Wad. "What I'm wondering is, how much of my eagerness to serve you in this way comes from my natural generosity and how much from the arcane influence of your magery."

Anonoei paused in mid-stroke. "Now, now. We've had this conversation before, and we agreed that it's circular. No matter what you desire or think, you can always say, 'I wonder why she's making me feel this desire.' Or 'this revulsion,' or 'this compulsion,' or whatever comes to mind."

"It's in the nature of circular arguments that you can never quite escape them. You didn't have to charm me into helping you seek vengeance on Bexoi. I have reasons enough of my own."

"And don't forget your powerful guilt over imprisoning me and my sons," said Anonoei.

"I know that didn't come from you," said Wad. "I felt it long before you knew who your captor was."

"Even if I *had* known, my abilities at that time depended on being present with the person I was influencing."

"And now that you've been through a Great Gate?"

"I can divide my outself, rather the way you can. Perhaps I always could and didn't know it. But now I can leave a bit of myself inside my clients, to keep my influence fresh and strong, and to see what they're experiencing."

"Sounds distracting. I actually have to pay close attention to see what's going on with Danny North."

"You're not a manmage," said Anonoei. "They all float in the back of my mind. Or rather, the back of my mind floats in *them*."

"And have you given *me* a piece of your mind?" asked Wad.

"If I had, would I tell you?" asked Anonoei.

"It depends on your motive," said Wad. "What if you're so devoted to my happiness and well-being that you leave a bit of your ba inside me so you can be sure that everything you do pleases me?"

Anonoei got up from her chair and went to the window. "Why shouldn't I use my abilities while I'm making love?"

"I'm not suggesting that there's anything wrong with it," said Wad. "But you are far, far too aware of *exactly* what pleases me from moment to moment for me to believe that you're not using your magery."

"Am I hearing a complaint?"

"You're hearing a question," said Wad. "When the lovemaking is finished, my lovely one, how much of you remains inside me?"

"More of you is inside me right now than there is of me inside you," she said.

"Not a clear answer."

"If I were the sort to spy on you, I would deny it, and I would make you believe me. So what's the point of your asking?"

"Because I want to hear the words."

Anonoei sighed. "I leave a bit of my ba in you exactly as I do in everyone else. It's hard not to. I care about you. I also need you and depend on you. It's important for me to know how you feel about me, what you want, what you fear."

Wad couldn't help but smile. "Honesty—the cruelest deception of all."

"You know that I'm not deceiving you."

"Or you're using honesty while disguising the fact that you're *making* me take such delight in it."

"Will you send me to Keel?" asked Anonoei. "I have to deal with his fear of discovery. He thinks Bexoi has set spies on him."

"Of course," said Wad. "But tell me, first: Have you ever placed your ba inside Queen Bexoi herself?"

"I've never been in her presence," said Anonoei. "Both Prayard and I saw to that. So no. I've seen her from a distance, but never close enough, in my pre-gating days, to get inside her devious mind."

"So the one person it would be most useful to watch, you can't see."

"But *you* can," said Anonoei. "Through your little spy-gate."

"That only shows me what she wants me to see," said Wad. "I think she lives her entire life as if she expected me to be watching. She undresses and dresses as if she had an audience. She knows what I can do."

"She has that kind of self-control? Every action is a performance, all the time?"

"Absolutely," said Wad. "She plays her roles every moment, waking and sleeping."

"Sleeping!" Anonoei scoffed.

"I think even her dreams are lies that go along with the

persona she's adopted. I think she believes her own lies as she tells them, and keeps on believing them."

"If she believes them, are they lies?" asked Anonoei.

"A question I once asked Pope Boniface the Fourth," said Wad. "He was busy converting all the pagan temples in Rome into Christian churches. I tried to explain to him how resentful the Greek and Roman Families of mages were about such treatment, and he told me that the gods didn't exist. I considered myself proof of the contrary, and I showed him what I could do. I gated us both up into the Alps—very high mountains in Mittlegard. There we stood in the bitter cold of an Alpine winter, with him still dressed in his lightweight sleeping gown, and he informed me, even as he was freezing to death, that my existence was a lie. That I was tempting him as Satan tempted Christ."

"I have no idea who you're talking about," said Anonoei.

"I realized that he really did believe that what he was actually experiencing—the cold of the mountain wind, the sight of high mountains and snow all around him—was a delusion, a vision I had created to deceive him. I told him that the snow and the wind and the mountains were real, that he was lying to himself, and I wasn't even from the same planet as the person he called 'Satan.' He informed me that *I* was the liar, and that's when I pointed out that I couldn't be lying, because I believed what I was telling him, while *he* knew perfectly well that the cold was real, so *he* was lying to *me*."

"Another circular argument."

"He told me that this only proved I was a better liar than he was. He admitted he felt the cold, which showed how powerful the illusion was. My obvious shivering from the cold did not change the fact that it was a delusion. 'If you lie to yourself, it's still a lie,' says he, 'even if you do it so well that you believe it.' A very wise man, for a Pope."

"I take it 'Pope' is like 'King'?"

"More or less," said Wad. "I can meet with anybody I want. I can always get past the guards and bureaucrats."

"Speaking of which," said Anonoei, "I'm a bit concerned about Keel. He seems to be quite urgently afraid at this moment."

"Then maybe that's an excellent reason for you *not* to go."

"Keep an eye on me, my castle-monkey, and extricate me if there's any real danger."

At that moment, however, Wad sensed that someone was coming to Westil through the Wild Gate. Several people. More and more. Yet Danny North seemed oblivious to the fact. Certainly he wasn't sending them.

"This is actually a very bad time for me to send you anywhere, especially anywhere dangerous," said Wad. "Someone's coming through the Wild Gate."

"What is the boy thinking? I thought you said he fully understood the danger of accidentally letting this Dragon through to Westil, hidden inside the body of some traveler."

"Danny North isn't doing it. Ah, now he's finally noticed it, and he knew at once what was going on. One of his friends moved the gate." Wad was impressed. "Clever girl, that Hermia. It's very hard to move someone else's gate without their noticing."

"What are you going to do about it?"

"I have to go watch this end of the gate. As long as everyone turns around and goes straight back to Mittlegard, there's no danger. But if somebody tries to stay . . ."

"That young windmage stayed," said Anonoei.

Wad got out of bed and began to dress. "By the time Danny North helped me remember with clarity who our enemy is and what he can do, Ced was already here. I knew him well enough to be reasonably sure he was *not* possessed by Set."

"And if some other arrival *is* possessed by Set—how will you know?"

"I won't. So anyone who tries to stay, I get him back to the return Gate and push him through."

"Aren't you afraid he'll possess *you*, if you come so close?"

"By 'push' I didn't mean *push*," said Wad. "Any would-be immigrant, I'll gate him to a point where he'll stumble directly into the Wild Gate the moment he emerges. I will never be near him. And Set can't jump so easily from one person into another. Especially someone with a powerful inself. A ka that won't just move out of the way."

"You flatter yourself," said Anonoei.

"Possibly," said Wad. "But it's not the same as what you do. He jumps in with his whole ka. But never having *owned* a body, worn the ape as his very self, it's harder for him to get in. So I think I could keep him out."

Anonoei rolled her eyes. "Send me to Keel now, please," she said.

"It's too dangerous," said Wad. He was fully clothed now. "I'm going to be distracted, watching all these people come through. I need to see them so I can remember them later, if they get past me somehow."

"I'll be fine," said Anonoei.

"Is Keel a timid, fearful man?"

"A very bold and courageous one."

"So whatever he fears, the danger is probably real."

"But my beloved Wadling, I'm *me*. Nobody can hold on to a notion of hurting me; I change their minds. I need you for transportation, not for rescue. Please respect my abilities as I respect yours. I'm not your prisoner anymore."

"That is such a manipulative thing to say," said Wad.

"If I were using magery to control you, I wouldn't *need* to manipulate you with guilt."

"Unless my conscience is entirely of your creation."

"Alas, no," said Anonoei. "There are times I wish I could put out your conscience like a sputtering candle." She began turning around and around. "Please send me through a gate into Keel's office. There's no one there at this time of day."

Wad still had his misgivings, but she was right—she could take care of herself. It's not as if she was going to face someone as strong-willed as Bexoi or, for that matter, Wad himself.

He sent her, still spinning like a child dancing. If she tripped, it would be her own fault.

Then he went at once to a place near the stone circle where the Wild Gate lay. Sure enough there were people milling around on the top of the hill. No one had left the circle yet—but too many of them were gazing around them instead of going back. And some of them were trying to use their powers. From inside a circle with an active gate! Didn't they know anything?

No, of course they didn't. And apparently the Greek girl who stole the mouth of the Wild Gate didn't think to come through herself and make sure everyone returned.

So Wad retrieved the gate he had used to send Anonoei, made it into a large public gate, and placed it directly in front of the inbound gate, setting it so it would transfer people immediately to the outbound one. That used up four of his eight gates. He used another gate to pop each of the loiterers to the mouth of the outbound Great Gate.

Just a matter of tidying things up.

It was fortunate that no one on Mittlegard had the slightest experience with gates. They would no doubt think that any glitches were just a part of the process, and if they suspected someone caused them to return immediately with no chance to look around, they would doubtless blame the Greek girl, and if they were angry it would serve her right.

If he still had even a serious fraction of his original gatehoard, he could have swallowed up the whole Wild Gate himself and had done with it. But he didn't have the power, and Danny, who most definitely did, lacked the knowledge and skill to overmaster the formerly captive gates. Nor was Wad interested in teaching him—the last thing he needed was for the boy to acquire serious deftness. He was dangerous enough as it was.

Through it all, he kept feeling a nagging worry about Anonoei. It got more and more intense. You're just being a fool, he told himself. She really *can* take care of herself.

Only when it was clear that there were no more mages coming through the Wild Gate did it finally dawn on Wad that it was not *like* him to worry overmuch about someone else's safety. Not with the kind of nagging, pestering concern that had been bothering him.

If Anonoei wanted to call for his help, and if she really did have a slice of her ba inside him, wouldn't it feel *just* like that? What if that worry was actually Anonoei screaming for help?

But the feeling was gone now. So apparently she *had* dealt with it.

He gated back to the room they had shared, in a house whose owner was away for the season. It was only as he stoked the fire to warm the room for Anonoei's return that he realized that there was another reason why her calls for help might have stopped.

The sickening dread he felt now was nothing like the feeling that had nagged him while he supervised the transfers at the Great Gate. It was so obvious, when he had genuine personal dread to compare it with. She really had been nagging at him, *shouting* at him to get her out of there.

Wad made a gate to Keel's office and nearly went through it at once. Until he remembered that Anonoei, too, had been confident that she could deal with any problem that might arise.

He shrank the ends of the gate until it became a mere viewport, and brought it to his eye to look through it.

There was no one in the room.

He looked around twice until he thought to lower his gaze to the floor.

It was the gown Anonoei had been wearing when she left. It lay on the floor, discarded.

No, not discarded. It was filthy.

No, it wasn't filthy. It was soaked in ash and bodily fluids, which also extended out from the gown where the head and hands and feet should be.

She had been burned to death. But not by an external fire, for the dress wasn't even singed. In his life on Mittlegard before he closed the gates, Wad had seen what murder looked like when a Firemaster heated someone's body from the inside until it was utterly consumed. It was Anonoei's dress, and what was left of her dead body was still wearing it.

Keel had been partly right, when he thought he was spied on. When Anonoei went to talk to him, it wasn't a spy who waited to intercept her. It was Queen Bexoi herself. Bexoi the Firemaster.

21

Intimacy

Danny knew that his parents expected him to come back to the compound after everyone got back from their instantaneous trip to Westil. There was a war about to start, using magery with a scope and intensity that had not been seen in Mittlegard since the seventh century.

But Danny had no intention of taking part in the war—not the way they would expect him to. They would hold councils and plan strategies. They would be practicing to see what they could do with their newly enhanced magery.

Danny also knew that he couldn't just go back to high school and sit it out. He would have to be involved in this war, like it or not.

But war or no war, he was *not* going to drop out of high school.

He had not slept in thirty-four hours when he came back to Parry McCluer just as school was letting out. Nobody noticed him, in their rush to get to the buses or the parking lot or just plain *out*.

That is, they noticed him enough to not bump into him, but few of them realized, as they passed him in the halls, that he had been absent all day. Whatever their normal response would be to seeing this normal kid on a normal day, they did. A wave, a nod, nothing.

He didn't see any of his friends. Had they all ditched? Had something happened to them?

"Danny," said a girl. Someone touched his back.

Danny turned. It was Nicki Lieder.

"Dad was so worried when you didn't come to practice this morning and then you weren't at school and nobody answered your phone."

"Sorry," said Danny. "Family emergency."

"I was sure it was something like that." Her hand was resting on his waist. He almost hadn't noticed it, the move had been so subtle. But it was a girlfriend thing, he knew that—a possessive gesture that communicated to anybody passing by, "He's mine, I have the right to do this."

He didn't want to hurt her feelings by removing her hand. So he turned partly away, then back again; it broke the contact. "I should have called," he said.

"I understand completely. So will Dad. He's so gruff, people don't realize that he's really very concerned for all his athletes."

Yeah, and he's a complete asshole to anybody who isn't one of "his athletes." But Danny didn't say it.

The hand was back, except that because he wasn't facing her, she was touching his waist right at the top of the zipper, her thumb hooked onto the waistband. It was a surprisingly intimate place to touch him. Maybe if he didn't wear his jeans so low—but he had always worn hand-me-downs that were a little small on him, or way too big. The former had to ride low so there'd be room in the crotch; the latter rode low because they were on the verge of falling off. Now that was where pants felt comfortable to him. But it also put her hand very low on the front of his body and for a long moment that's all he could think about.

And in the silence between them, he knew that's exactly what she intended.

Innocent little Nicki wasn't all that innocent. Whatever it was that had led her to kiss him that time, it was still there. She hadn't given up. She was still offering.

Or was she demanding?

This didn't seem like the same girl he had talked to that day in the Lieders' kitchen, when he had healed her and changed her life. By not letting it end, of course, but also by restoring her to strength and health, and by talking with her like a normal person instead of an invalid. Apparently he had made much too great an impression on an impressionable girl.

He could just remove the hand, but the lingering presence of her hand so near his groin was obvious enough now that he felt the need to say something aloud. "There's only one woman who has the right to touch me there," he said, "and it isn't you."

She didn't remove the hand. What girl wouldn't remove her hand when the guy said something like that?

Instead she answered, "Who is it, then?"

"My wife," he said.

"But you're not married."

Now, at last, he took her by the wrist. He couldn't understand why he felt so reluctant to move her hand away. Or why, in the moment that he took her wrist, what he really wanted to do, what he *almost* did, was move her hand lower, to a place that was already eager to welcome her touch.

But he didn't do it. He pushed her hand away, more roughly than he originally meant to, because it was so hard to do it at all. "I'm not married," he said. "That's the point." And then he walked away. Which wasn't all that easy. He needed to reach a hand inside his crotch to readjust himself, and couldn't really do that in a crowded corridor.

Instead he ducked into an empty classroom and, not caring

whether she followed him and found an empty room, gated himself to the spot on the hill where he and his friends regularly met.

And there they were.

"Well, hello," said Laurette. "Where were *you* all day?"

"And what's her name?" asked Sin.

"Whose name?" asked Xena.

Sin just rolled her eyes, looking at his bulging jeans, and laughed. Xena looked, too, and laughed.

Danny sat down at once. "You guys are twisted," he said.

"Name," said Sin. "Say who, or we'll cut it off."

"I was walking through the halls at school," said Danny.

"Always a dangerous place," said Hal, who clearly had no idea what they were talking about.

"When I ran into Nicki Lieder," said Danny.

"Apparently very *slowly*," said Sin.

"The coach's daughter?" said Wheeler. "What about her?"

"She's kind of a nothing person," said Hal. "She never seems connected to anything."

"She *was* at the point of death when she suddenly got better," said Laurette. "Maybe it takes a while to rejoin the world."

"She's all for joining Danny, apparently," said Sin.

He closed his eyes. "I didn't sleep at all last night." And, to forestall Sin's inevitable lurid assumptions, he told them what had happened. And what it meant. War.

Everyone in the Families understood that Danny had made all the gates that anyone had used; everyone knew that if they offended him, Danny could gate anyone to anywhere.

That had always been true of any war that involved gatemages. "We're like kickers in football," Danny said to his friends. "We wear the uniform, but we're not really part of the team. We play a completely different game."

"Just beware of roughing the kicker," said Hal.

"Do you even know what 'roughing the kicker' *means*?" asked Laurette.

"Just because I look like a goal post doesn't mean I don't understand the game," said Hal.

Pat was the one who moved the discussion to a practical level. "How can you even *think* about high school when you know that the whole world is about to change?"

"I can't," said Danny. "But it's the only thing I can think of to do. If I go to the Family, they'll be all about how I can move the enemy mages all over the place, which I'm not going to do."

"Why not?" asked Sin. "I mean, they're your *family*."

"I kind of thought you guys were my family," said Danny. "You didn't spend my whole childhood despising me and threatening to kill me if I couldn't raise a clant."

"The question isn't whether you *want* to fight in a war," said Wheeler. "It's going to happen, and it's going to involve you."

"Why?" asked Xena. "Why does he have to get involved? Why can't he just study for the SAT like everybody else?"

"First," said Hal, "Danny doesn't study for anything, ever."

They all nodded their agreement.

"I study," said Danny.

"Like, never," said Laurette.

"I stud*ied*. When I was home schooled," said Danny. "High school just hasn't caught up to what I already learned."

"Second," said Hal.

"Thus proving that Hal can count all the way to two without losing his place," said Sin.

"Second, and this is the actual point: When people start getting hurt, Danny's going to get involved. Because he's the only combat medical officer in the whole war."

Danny remembered how carefully the family always avoided discussing why casualties had been so much higher in the wars since 632 A.D. Everyone's powers were reduced, but there were no gatemages to heal people. Now there was Danny. And the North

Family undoubtedly expected that Danny would use his healing gates only for the good-guy team.

"That's why I don't want to talk to my family about anything," said Danny. "Because sooner or later they're going to catch on that I intend to use gates to heal *everybody*."

"On both sides," said Pat, as if to make sure he really meant it.

"On all three sides," said Danny. "Because whenever there's a war among the gods, they end up using drowthers as surrogates. Mage-to-mage combat is rare and potentially destructive. So they're going to get the Danae to come attack the Trojans."

"'Danae' is what the Greeks in the Iliad called each other," Wheeler explained to Xena.

"And where did you learn that?" asked Xena.

"From a role-playing game in fourth grade," said Wheeler.

"I'm so tired I could die," said Danny. "That's one thing that passing through a gate doesn't fix. I'm fit, I could run for miles right now and hardly feel it, but my brain needs to sleep. I think if I did run I'd fall asleep doing it."

"What do you think these guys will do now that they're, like, really powerful?" asked Wheeler.

"Is this going to be like NASCAR, Wheels?" asked Hal. "Are you going to pick your favorite Family and root for them in the wizard war finals?"

"My whole life, when I wanted a taste of something magical, I had to play a videogame or roll a bunch of dice in an RPG," said Wheeler. "But Danny's given us rides around the world. Or at least to places around here, but *instantly*. And that was cool, don't get me wrong. But that's, like, a transportation spell. Very convenient, but I want to see some really major combat spells."

"There *are* no 'spells,'" said Danny. "Just persuasion."

"Yeah, well, I want to see a windmage persuade him a tornado," said Wheeler. "And clants. I want to see a stonemage turn stone into a walking monster, like the Incredible Hulk."

"A tornado's a terrible thing no matter how it comes into

existence," said Danny. "And your stone clant isn't going to care who it tramples."

"I know that," said Wheeler. "And I deplore it, abhor it, I *roar* it—"

"As you bore us," said Hal.

"And we ignore you," added Laurette.

"I didn't make the magic come back into the world," said Wheeler. "Can I help it if it's exciting? All those extras in the movies who run screaming from Godzilla or wave like idiots when the aliens come to blow them up in *Independence Day*—sure, they get squished, they get barbecued, but they were *there*."

"You'd buy tickets to *anything*," said Sin.

"I would," said Wheeler. "Once."

Danny sighed. "I just wanted to go to high school."

"Why?" said Laurette. "I mean, we're glad you're here, but why would anybody in his right mind *choose* to spend your days like this?"

"Sitting in the woods?" asked Pat.

"Down there in Parry McCluer," said Laurette.

"Come on, Rette, you've got the system sussed," said Xena. "You've got the teachers and the principal eating out of your hand, the office staff loves you, your grades are good, and you've got a great body. There is just no reason why *you* should be allowed to hate high school."

"Because it's not how I'd spend my days," said Laurette. "If I had a choice."

"But Danny does have a choice," said Pat.

Danny was thinking that if Laurette came from one of the Families, her ability to make people from every group like her might be considered a sign of manmagery. Then Pat turned the conversation back to him, and he could barely remember what they'd been talking about. He was that sleepy.

"High school is boring," said Danny, "and if anybody cared,

you could finish the whole curriculum in a year. It's mostly just a tool for keeping kids out of the work force and out of criminal activities for at least half the day. But I swear it looked like the coolest thing in the world when I was reading about it in young adult novels."

"Young adult novels," said Pat, "are no closer to reality than Wheeler's videogames."

Wheeler laughed. "Reality is so overrated. In between catastrophes it settles down to the most-boring-possible-explanation-for-everything. 'That can't happen,' until it does. 'Things don't work that way,' until they do."

"Girls can never find a god to fall in love with," said Xena, "until they do."

"Girls find gods to fall in love with all the time," said Pat. "Then they wake up pregnant and the god is gone. All that's left is an asshole."

Everybody laughed at that, even Danny, tired as he was.

" 'Who's the father of your baby?' 'Oh, Daddy, it was a *god,*' " said Pat. " 'What does he look like?' 'Oh, Mother, he forbade me to turn on the light and see his face.' Nobody ever wants to admit they fell for a lying moron. Every bastard ever conceived is the love child of a god."

"Yeah, but there's also been a *lot* of genuine drowther-boinking," said Danny. "The Mithermages have a lot of descendants scattered through the human race. In fact, by now I'd say that every living human has a Westilian ancestor."

"So why didn't the Great Gate waken the mage in me?" asked Hal.

"Maybe it did," said Danny. "It takes time to learn how to find your affinity and make things happen."

Right then, a little dust devil formed in the middle of the group, stirring up a bit of dust. And then it was gone almost as soon as they noticed it.

"OK, who did that?" asked Danny.

Nobody said anything.

"We're talking about finding your affinity," said Danny, "and one of you shows the power of a windmage."

The dust devil reappeared and then skittered over to spatter dust and leaves on Wheeler. He jumped up and brushed himself off. "Sneak attacks are against the rules," he said, brushing himself off.

"You wanted to have a monster chase you," said Hal.

"Seriously, who did that?" asked Danny.

Everybody acted innocent. They were all curious about it, looking at each other, but nobody fessed up.

"What's the point of hiding who can do this?" said Danny. "That's really good, that's like what a second-year windmage learns to do. And dumping the stuff on Wheeler, if that's who you were aiming at, that's why I call it a second-year thing. Nobody can do that in their first year."

Danny watched to see who showed pride when he said that. But nobody showed anything on their faces. Which is why Danny was reasonably sure that it was Pat. She was the only one who could keep her face a complete blank, when she wanted to.

But if she had some reason for not coming forward in front of the others, Danny would respect that.

"I know why you're in high school, Danny," said Sin. "It's your secret identity."

"Clark Kent at the *Daily Planet*," said Laurette.

"Without the glasses," said Sin.

"And you don't even need a phone booth," said Hal.

"He doesn't wear a costume so he doesn't need to change clothes," said Laurette. "Or a bat cave to keep his car in. Or anything."

"But it's still his secret identity," said Sin.

" 'By day, a mild-mannered high school track star,' " Laurette fake-quoted. " 'By night, Loki! Mercury! Thoth! Faster than a speeding bullet!' "

"Mightier than a thrown spitwad," said Hal.

"Able to leap onto curbs in a single bound," said Pat.

"And look inside the girls' bathroom whenever he wants," said Wheeler.

"Eeew, you *could,*" said Xena. "But why would you want to? It's poo and pee, just like boys."

"*Not* just like boys," said Wheeler. "Most definitely *not.*"

"How did we get onto poop and peeping toms?" asked Pat.

"I don't spy on people without a reason," said Danny.

"Yeah, like you want to see whether they drop their dirty undies on the floor or put them in the hamper," said Laurette.

Danny lay back and closed his eyes. "Wake me when it's over."

"It's over," said Pat. "Because we're all growing up. Right now. I declare puberty to be finished."

"I hope not," said Wheeler. "I was really hoping for more body hair."

All the girls but Pat said "eeeewwww" at once. Wheeler was delighted.

"I'm supposed to be at track practice but I've got to get home and sleep," said Danny. "It's getting cold and the sun is still up."

"Supposed to be a storm coming through tonight," said Xena.

"Not snow," said Laurette.

"No, just rain," said Xena. "To make little things grow."

"Xena likes to make little things grow," said Hal.

"As long as they're attached to Danny North," said Laurette.

Xena turned on Hal in fury. "Hal!" she growled.

Before she could say anything or throw something at him, Hal moved away. "Why are you going after me? It was Laurette who—"

"Girls can say things like that *to each other,*" explained Pat.

"I've got to go talk to my parents," said Danny. "And I have to get Veevee to write out an excuse for my absence today."

"You need to get a nap first," said Pat.

"Do you think they're going to do like Zog in *Superman II* and make the President kneel to them in the Oval Office?" asked Wheeler.

"If they feel like it," said Danny. "If they even care." And then Danny said, "They won't make anybody kneel, but they'll definitely want to get control of the army and navy and air force and all. Because we're not immortal, and so we have to know where the weapons are so we don't get blown up or beheaded while we're trying to control a clant a hundred miles away. Especially because weapons got really powerful since the Gate Thief closed things down in 632. So you don't necessarily get advance warning."

"It really is going to be war," said Hal.

"Yeah," said Wheeler, grinning.

"Danny, take me home with you, just for a minute," said Pat.

Several woos and wo-hos from the others.

"I need to *talk* with you," said Pat, rolling her eyes.

"'Please put your baby in me,'" said Hal in a falsetto.

"Let's get out of here so they can gossip about us," said Danny. He reached out a hand for Pat. She took it.

He gated to his living room and the moment she saw where they were she clung to him, her whole body pressed against his. Hungry. Frightened. "It really *is* war," she said. "What you did with the Great Gate last night and this morning, taking all the mages in the world through it, because that disloyal *bitch*—"

She stopped herself. "No. If you're not angry, I'm not going to get angry."

"I'm angry," said Danny. "I just can't do anything about it, so why develop an ulcer?"

"People will die," she said. "*You* could die. If somebody blows you up, who'll put you through a gate to heal you?"

"It's not likely, but it could happen," said Danny. "I'm more worried about a completely different enemy, though. One who can take over people's bodies and control them."

Pat looked up at him, without letting go. "You're talking about being possessed by the devil."

"Who knew it was true?" asked Danny. "But it is. And I don't even know if anyone would be able to tell if I was taken over."

"I'd know," said Pat.

"Would you?" asked Danny. "I'm worried that maybe *I* wouldn't even know."

"If somebody was inside you? Making you do stuff against your will?" Pat shook her head. "You'd know. And I'd know, because I'd test you. I'd ask you a question and if you didn't know the answer, I'd know it wasn't you." She pulled on his head and neck to draw him down and kiss him. Then she licked the tip of his nose. "I'd ask what I did right after I kissed you."

"What if he had access to all my memories?" said Danny. "What if he could answer all the questions?"

"I'd still know," said Pat. She kissed him again, this time long and hungrily. Her hands moved across his back, gripped his buttocks.

He pulled away from her. "No," he said.

"This isn't a game for me," said Pat. "Like for the others. I'm not playing 'sleep with a god and tell your friends.' I love you, Danny North. I'm not too young to know that. Girls married a lot younger than me. Juliet was thirteen."

"That was fiction, and it didn't end all that well," said Danny.

"You're going off to war. When you told us what you spent all night doing, I thought, what if something had gone wrong, what if Hermia had trapped him or tricked him and he simply never came back? And instead of crying when I thought that, my hands just instinctively went to my belly. My empty uterus. It's an *instinct,* Danny. We want to be pregnant when our man goes off to war."

"I'm not going to make any bastards," said Danny. "Period, ever. You think your parents are ready to let you marry a high school kid with no job, who lives in a shanty like this?"

"I don't care about marriage," said Pat. "People don't, they just don't care about that."

"The smart people do," said Danny. "The people who want to raise a family, and not just get pregnant."

She had her hands inside his waistband and was pushing downward on his pants. He thought of Lana the first time he met her in Stone's house in DC. His body was responding the same way, only this time he wasn't surprised and frightened. If anything, he wanted Pat more than she wanted him.

"I love you, too," said Danny, "but I'm not one of those gods." And, just as she got his pants down to his thighs, he gated her away, back to her own bedroom.

He wanted so badly to go through that gate after her.

Instead, he ate the gate so Hermia couldn't use it to get into her house, just in case she decided to start going after his friends. And then, too tired to make a decision about pulling his pants back up or taking them off the rest of the way, he gated himself to his own bed and fell asleep exactly as he was.

He dreamed of her, though. He vaguely remembered dreaming of other things, forgotten things, strange things, he dreamed that she was on the bed beside him, pressing herself against him, naked, whispering to him. "I love you, Danny," she whispered.

In the dream he held her, explored her body. He tried to kiss her but for some reason she evaded his kiss. He laughed and moved his hand up to her face and still she tried to turn her face away when he went to kiss her. He was ready to explode with desire for her. She didn't want his kisses, she wanted his baby, and that's all he wanted, was to give her that.

In the dream his body was poised over her. She was pulling his hips down. Then he kissed her before she could dodge.

It wasn't Pat.

He opened his eyes.

It was Nicki Lieder, the coach's daughter.

"I came to see you, the door was unlocked," she whispered, "and here you were, so ready for me."

It still felt like a dream. But it also felt completely real. Real, but with the cloudiness of a dream in his mind. Nicki Lieder. Not Pat at all. He didn't love Nicki. But she was naked under him, and he knew how much she wanted him, and at this moment all he could think of was that he wanted her, too. Not *her*, but a woman, the woman here under him, the woman who had come to his bed. The woman in this extraordinary dream.

No, it's not a dream, said something inside him. It's not a dream, it's someone who has the power to cloud your mind.

"You want me inside you," said Nicki.

"Yes," said Danny, even as something in his mind screamed at him, Listen to what she said, listen to what you just agreed to, it's not *you* inside *her*, it's someone asking to come into *your* body, and you said yes, you said yes, you fool.

And in the moment of ecstasy and release, he could feel it, this thing entering him at the groin and filling his whole body, taking control of his body. He tried to fight it, tried to move, but already he couldn't, already it had him.

He could feel his body roll off the girl. He could see her lying there, gasping, looking confused. Looking relieved. And then weeping.

"That's right, Nicki," his own lips said, though he was not speaking, and only found out what they were going to say when they said it. "I'm gone now. You can have your body back, nicely healed by Danny North here. Maybe pregnant. Wouldn't that be nice? Now be a good girl, get dressed, and go home."

Danny's body sat up and watched her as she gathered her clothing and put it on, still weeping softly.

"I enjoyed being inside you," said Danny's mouth. "You're a sweet thing and you'll find that this all becomes like a bad dream, and then like a good dream, and then you'll miss me, you really will. They all do. The ones that live."

And Danny was thinking: He was here for weeks. He found me weeks ago, when I came to Lieder's house and healed his daughter. Was he already inside her then, or did he find her afterward, take control of her when she was clean of her cancer? Maybe Danny could have fought him off any other time, but now, asleep, exhausted, half in a dream, and then the Dragon asked him through Nicki's mouth, asked him to let him come into Danny, and Danny said yes. But I didn't realize what I was saying, I thought I was consenting to the sex, and it was sex in a dream, not real, nothing was real, it's not . . .

Not fair.

Except this was war. Shaped like love, a moment ago, but it was the crucial battle in a war. The enemy had stolen a march on him, was suddenly in a place where he wasn't supposed to be.

Now he has control of a gatemage.

But he doesn't, thought Danny. Because I can still think these thoughts. I can still . . .

Danny tried to make a gate and pass himself through it, to see if he could shed this creature like a disease.

"Uh-uh-uh," his own throat said, the glottal stops that said, No no no. "Let's make a gate for *her,* to send your little girlfriend home."

In that moment Danny learned several important things. The Dragon had no idea that Danny really had just gated his girlfriend home—the real one, the one that he *hadn't* had sex with. The Dragon also had to use Danny's mouth to talk to him—it couldn't just put thoughts into his head. So it wasn't completely in control, and didn't even have complete access. He controlled movement and he controlled speech. But that was all a matter of muscles.

Except he could block Danny from creating the gate he wanted to create. Could he *make* Danny create one?

No, no, that's not the question, not the question at all.

Inside Danny's hearthoard, he now realized who had been warning him, screaming at him. Loki's gates.

Loki knew. Loki had never been possessed, so his outself could not *remember* having been possessed by Set. That meant

Loki was observing him from the outside. From another planet, however many lightyears away it was, Loki had realized what was happening, had seen past the fog in Danny's mind, past the belief that it was an erotic dream, into the truth.

But what Loki's gates *did* remember was being *given*. They knew how one Gatefather could *give* the obedience of his gates to another.

And so Danny tapped into their kinetic memory, and with their consent, Loki's gates obeyed him and showed him how to give them back to Loki.

The act of giving back the gates didn't move them or make them. Those would have been physical acts, apparently, and the Dragon who possessed him could have felt such an action, could have blocked it. But in all likelihood, the Dragon had never possessed a gatemage who gave a gate to another. It had no idea what was happening.

He felt his control over Loki's gates slip away.

But now he knew how to do it.

So, again without moving or making his gates, leaving them wherever they already were, Danny gave all of his own gates, every one of them, to Loki.

And just like that, they were not under his control. He was still aware of them. They were still where they were supposed to be. But they weren't his. They didn't belong to Danny North.

Nicki was dressed now. Danny could feel it when the Dragon gave the command to make a gate to take her back to her home. He could sense that the Dragon knew how to do it, knew where both the mouth and the tail of the gate should be.

But no gate came rising out of the hearthoard at his command. No gate formed.

Danny felt a kind of blindness come over him. No, it was rage. Fear? It wasn't an emotion of the body, it was a transformation of some kind within the Dragon itself, and then Danny's own body responded to it. Blood flowed hard and hot, his face flushed.

"What's wrong?" asked Nicki, sounding frightened.

Danny's body rose from the bed and stood on the floor, pants dropping around the ankles, but definitely not aroused, not as it had been. No, it was filled with rage and terror and it screamed.

Nicki screamed back and then ran from the room, ran out of the house. Danny heard the screen door slam behind her.

"What have you done?" demanded the Dragon in Danny's own voice, with Danny's mouth and throat and lungs, his tongue and teeth.

I've done nothing, Danny said silently. I gave a gift to a friend.

"The gates are still there, I can *feel* them," said the Dragon. It used Danny's body to dance around the room, jump up and down, as if somehow this would jar something loose. "You're a Gatefather, I took a Gatefather, why can't I touch your gates!"

He ran to the kitchen, and Danny understood that his body was in search of a knife. It was the animal mind that sought for one—for the first time Danny could feel the distinction between animal intention and his own will, his own ka. The animal's desire did not reach inside him and kindle any answering wish. The body wasn't his to control now. But he was still inside it, still absolutely tied to it, feeling all its sensations.

The knife was in the hand.

It stabbed down, into Danny's thigh. Again. Again.

The pain was excruciating. The Dragon felt it too; he groaned in agony.

"Make it better," said his own voice. "Make a gate."

But there was no gate that belonged to him.

Another stab. "You'll bleed to death unless you heal this. Do you understand that?"

I do understand it, thought Danny. I understand that I'll die. But what happens if I die with you inside me?

Nothing happens, thought Danny, despairing. Because Set

isn't tied to my body the way my ka is. When my body dies, I'm done, my ka moves away from here. But *he* will remain.

"I can keep it going after you bleed to death," said Danny's mouth. "Not terribly long, but long enough to get to somebody else. Someone you know."

He was trying to call up a clear memory. Danny immediately thought of Hermia.

Hermia was the one. Let him find Hermia and take possession of her.

"I don't want your enemies, I want your damn friends! I want to make you watch me kill them, slowly! Rape them and kill them! I'll do it to everyone you love if you don't let me use your gates! And then they'll come for you and take you and execute you, and *you'll* be dead, not me!"

It wasn't even making sense. Was it crazy? I'll let you bleed to death, I'll keep your body going, and then they'll kill you *again*? No, Set was confused. His rage was clouding his mind.

Because it was a human mind he was controlling.

The human brain, rather. Because Danny's *mind* was still there, thinking his own thoughts. Hermia, he was thinking. Imagining her body in a way he never had before—with desire, with lust. Never mind that it was someone else's body that he had felt all those desires for. The face he put into his memory, the name he thought of, they were Hermia's.

One more time he stabbed. One more thrill of agony. But it didn't hurt as much. No, it *did* hurt, every bit as much, perhaps even more. But Danny didn't care as much.

I'm detaching. My ka is fleeing from the pain. From the threat of death. I can't let that happen. I can't let him drive me from my own body. I gave away my ba, my outself, all my unmade gates, but I can't let him take away my body or I'm dead. Literally dead.

For a moment he had the idle thought: Then I'll know. What happens to the ka after the body dies. Do I return to Duat, as the desert hermit said? Or do I go somewhere else, or just haunt the place I died? Or do I dissolve like smoke?

But he stifled his curiosity and forced himself to connect with the pain, to feel it with the greatest possible intensity. You won't drive me out of my own body this way.

As if the Dragon could feel him dig his ka more deeply into his own body, the Dragon again gave a cry of frustration and rage. "Bastard!" he cried. "You're no match for me! Give it up! No one ever withholds from me the thing I want!"

Obviously the statement was false, or it wouldn't have needed saying.

But the pain in his thigh was a high price to pay for that small satisfaction. And Danny could feel the blood pumping out. This last time, Set had used Danny's own hand to drive the knife deep enough to find the femoral artery.

I really am going to die.

They'll rule it a suicide. Died by his own hand. Literally true, and yet utterly false.

In that moment he remembered that there were other gates. The captive gates. Not Loki's and not Danny's own.

Danny reached to make a gate and this time the Dragon let him, for now he felt for the first time the existence of the captive gates. Using Danny's mouth, Set cried out with triumph as Danny formed a captive into a living gate, passed it over himself so it could heal him, and then . . . gave the gate to itself.

Just like that, the gate was gone.

But not before Danny himself was healed. No pain. No injury. No bleeding.

The other captive gates sensed what had happened, and the clamor began afresh, now with a new goal, a different goal. Give me to myself and set me free! cried every captive in his heartho-ard.

"You bastard," muttered the Dragon with Danny's mouth.

It swung Danny's body around and smashed his head into the

corner of the kitchen counter with such force that Danny instantly lost consciousness.

He woke up hours later on the kitchen floor. Alone in the dark. His head throbbed.

He reached for another captive gate.

"No," whispered his mouth.

What was he doing while I was unconscious? Was he unconscious, too? No, he isn't as deeply tied into my body as I am. He was conscious and had nothing he could do but lie there feeling the agony. Or was it eased while I was asleep?

You won't drive me out of my own head with pain, thought Danny. So if you refuse to let me use a gate to heal the body whose agony we both feel, then so be it. I can bear it. Or I can die. Whatever you choose. What you will *not* do is make a gate that lasts.

Finally Set relented and made a gate. Danny let him draw on one of the captives and then, the moment the gate had passed over Danny and he felt no more pain in his head, Danny gave the gate to itself and it was gone.

"What are you doing!" his own voice demanded. "I don't know what you're doing. How can the gate be *gone*?"

But my head feels so much better.

"Until you learn who is master in this house, I will make your life pure hell," said Danny's mouth.

I'm sure you can do that, thought Danny. What you can't do is make gates that I don't approve of. And when we run out of captive gates, then you're done, because none of *my* gates belong to me anymore, and so you can't use them.

22

The Queen

When Anonoei arrived in Keel's office, he wasn't there. Nobody was.

Yet she could sense that Keel was near, now his dread was so strong it nauseated her a little. He was terrified for his life. Where was he?

She looked up.

He was hanging upside down from the rafters in the high-ceilinged room. His arms were trussed like the wings of a roasting fowl.

"When it all burns, won't he make a delicious smell?" asked a woman's voice.

Anonoei turned to see a woman standing in the doorway. She was simply dressed, like a peasant woman, and she was well along in pregnancy. Depending on how she carried, she might be two months from delivery, or the baby might be due right now. She smiled, and she was beautiful.

Anonoei recognized her then, though the pregnancy, the clothing, and the great length of time since Anonoei last saw her from a distance had delayed her.

"My Queen," said Anonoei. She sent a calming influence to the Queen, only to realize that Bexoi was already calm. No agitation at all.

Or none that Anonoei could feel.

"I know what you are," said Bexoi. "It's not as if you tried to conceal it. Who but a manmage could interfere with so many of my most trusted friends? That is, without sleeping with them. And now I see who you are. You were pointed out to me, years ago, back when you still shared my husband's bed and I did not. Anonoei, is it not?"

"It is," said Anonoei. Now she tried turning Bexoi's emotion to amusement, but again there was no change in Bexoi's feelings. Until it dawned on Anonoei that Bexoi might *have* no feelings, not about little things like murder and torture to advance her cause. She wasn't even angry, apparently.

"I've made a great study of manmages, because once I discovered what *I* was, I realized that only two kinds of mages could thwart me. Gatemages—but I knew the Gate Thief would take care of them. And manmages, because I feared that they would be able to overmaster me. So I learned all the lore about manmagery, especially what happened during the great war of Dapnu Dap, when the sandmages turned the steppe into a sandy desert in the effort to destroy the manmages of the far south. History is very important, when you prepare to defeat enemies you haven't met yet."

"I admire your scholarship," said Anonoei. Through the shred of outself she had left in Wad, she called him urgently. Take me out. Get me away from here. Take me *now*. But Wad must have been caught up intensely in whatever he was doing, because there was no response. Not even a flicker of annoyance at the nagging doubt she knew she was causing him. Come to me, if you won't bring me! But still he ignored her.

"Your pet gatemage hasn't come for you yet," said Queen Bexoi. "Whatever could be wrong?"

Bexoi couldn't have had anything to do with the business with the Great Gate that had kept Wad from paying attention to her. But she clearly meant Anonoei to think that she had.

"We're both on our own," said Anonoei. "To match up head to head, so to speak."

"Nose to pretty little nose," said Bexoi, smiling slightly but without a trace of amusement. "Neither of us is particularly beautiful, though we've both learned how to appear more beautiful than we are. No doubt it came naturally to a manmage like you. But to me, it was painstaking effort to become a beauty. To know just what angle, just what degree of smile. Ambition is the great driver, but it lives on hope. I could persist in my study, in my solitary practice, in my hours before the mirror, because I had hope."

"I've heard you're a great firemage," said Anonoei.

"I do well enough, in this decadent age of the world," said Bexoi.

"A self-seeming clant that bleeds," said Anonoei.

"Wad was so impressed by that simple illusion."

Anonoei could not find any road into her. The woman had no emotions.

"I have no emotions," said Bexoi. "I can see that you're frustrated. What do you think my studies taught me? That when manmages send their outselves into a victim, they use the low road by preference—the deep emotions. So you block them by having no emotions. Feeling nothing. It came quite naturally to me, and helped me during the long years when my husband only desired *you* and ignored me almost completely."

Anonoei knew of no road but the low road—no way into a person except by way of their emotions. But Bexoi must have learned of others. I should have studied more, thought Anonoei. But members of royal houses have better libraries than my father and his friends. There may also have been books in Gray that were lacking in Iceway.

She thought of the things that Wad had just remembered about Set, the Dragon, and how he possessed people completely, sending his very ka into their bodies, instead of using the insidious ba, the gentle outself.

"And still no rescuer comes for you," said Bexoi. "I assumed I'd only have time to say a few words before you were gone. Or before dear Wad, my former lover—he did tell you that, didn't he?—moved *me* to someplace else. Yet he does nothing. He must have sent you here. But he's busy, isn't he?"

"There's a Great Gate open between the worlds," said Anononei. "Soon the lands will be flooded with mages more powerful than you."

Bexoi's face flared momentarily with excitement, but before Anonoei could exploit the emotion it was gone. "The Great Gate turns a needle into a bludgeon, even though a needle is so much more subtle and piercing. I will face whomever he brings here. No longer the Gate Thief, is he? Now he makes Great Gates."

Anonoei did not correct her. Let her think Wad was still capable of making a Great Gate. Let Bexoi keep her fear of Wad, even if she had no fear of Anonoei.

"And yet the Gate Thief does not come to retrieve you. Do you think he sent you to me as a love offering? 'Here is your enemy, Bexoi. I give her to you, so that your child can be born into a world at peace.' Or did you think he really loved you? He loves no one."

If Bexoi was gloating, she gave no sign.

"But the longer I delay, the more chances Wad will have to change his mind and come to your rescue. So I'll kill you now, I think, and use the heat of your body to ignite the wood of this building. Keel can see how powerless you are before the flames roast him. I'm betting he's still alive when the rope breaks and drops him down onto the burning floor. I really wouldn't want him to miss any of this. When servants choose the wrong master, it's very important that they understand their mistake. But then, did Keel ever have a choice? Manmages like you don't let them. And here I go, talking more. But it's important to me that you understand just how thoroughly you have been lured, trapped, defeated."

The gloating showed that there was *some* emotion in play here. Anonoei probed for it. Not an emotion of the body. Pride and ambition were emotions of the ka, so they followed different rules. But it still offered a road in, and now Anonoei had it.

She made a move, sending her outself to turn Bexoi's vanity into complacency, and her complacency into unwariness.

Instead, Bexoi's eyes widened. "Is nothing sacred?" she demanded. "Are there no bonds between women?"

Anonoei thrust with all her might. And now Bexoi grew afraid, alarmed. The emotion touched her body. I have her now. I will win.

At once she felt her body grow hot. A fever beyond any she had ever felt.

"The trick," said Bexoi, gasping, "is to heat all the body except the head, so that you can remain conscious through the entire process of burning alive." Bexoi was hurrying, heating her body quickly, trying to distract Anonoei from her probe. And it was working, Anonoei knew, because it grew harder to concentrate on her outself. Her inself was screaming: I'm going to die!

In that moment of desperation she thought of Set, the manmage who never dies, because his ka is free of any flesh. But that's because he has never fully bonded with a body. I have. This body, this burning body.

Flames erupted from her skin. But she could still see. Her muscles still, for this moment, responded to her will. So she leapt forward, threw her arms around Bexoi, embraced her.

"Don't you know that I can keep the fire from touching me?" said Bexoi scornfully. "Now die, whore."

The sudden surge of heat destroyed Anonoei's whole body in an instant.

But in that instant, Anonoei followed the road she had found into Bexoi's mind, and then on into her body. I am not dead yet, she thought—but, lacking a mouth, could not say. I am here in *you*, Queen Bexoi. Not as a visitor, not as a beastmage partnering with his heartbeast. I am here as a ka that knows how to fully possess a body of flesh and bone.

Anonoei felt the cool skin of the new body, the Queen's body. Suddenly she could see again—through Bexoi's eyes, because they were now Anonoei's eyes. She willed herself to move, and she moved.

Moved, and in the movement became the master of this body. She could still feel Bexoi inside her, struggling to control the body, failing, failing.

Anonoei's dead body was still brilliantly hot, and the bones, not yet crumbled, still held it up. The arms were still wrapped around Bexoi. But Anonoei had no skill as a firemage and did not know how to control it. Nor did Bexoi have access to the body's ability to command the fire.

So the heat of the fire suddenly passed the boundary between the charred corpse of Anonoei and became an agony of burning flesh in Bexoi's body, whose pain *both* women felt.

Anonoei screamed and thrust the burning mass away, but too late. Her own—Bexoi's own—clothing had been charred in the instant, and the skin of this unfamiliar new body was burning. Anonoei had no knowledge of how to put the fire out. Bexoi knew, but if Anonoei let her have enough control to block the flame, Bexoi's strong ka would take her body back.

Either die now by being thrust out of this body by its evil owner, or die later from these agonizing burns. Nobody could burn like this and live. I will have died twice by fire, Bexoi only the once.

But then she thought: fall to the floor, smother the fire.

It worked to put the fire out. But it restored nothing. Her flesh was charred. Her bodily fluids were flowing out of the entire front of her ruined body. The pain was so agonizing that Anonoei knew she would faint.

But she could not faint. If she did, Bexoi could take her body back.

Then, to Anonoei's surprise, she felt something else: Bexoi's inself was retreating, fading, ceasing to reach into every corner of this half-burnt body. It had never occurred to Anonoei that Bexoi might surrender. It had to be a trick.

No. Not a trick. It was death. Bexoi's body, the ape her ka had once controlled, was dying, and Bexoi knew it, not intellectually, but deep in the core of her being. It was time to shed the body and move on. Bexoi was no manmage. She did not know how to attach herself to a body and hold on. But Anonoei did.

I will be alone in here.

For a moment that felt like triumph. In the next moment she realized it was failure.

Only if Bexoi's ka remained in this body was there any hope of having access to her firemagery—not to mention her role as Queen, the love of Prayard, and . . .

The baby.

The baby, thought Anonoei. The baby! she screamed inside her mind.

If Bexoi heard the thought, she did not respond. She continued receding, dying.

Stay! It was Anonoei's will, her demand that Bexoi refuse to die.

Here, thought Anonoei, I give you a place to remain. Here are the hands and feet, here is the mouth, the eyes, the groin, the belly with a baby in it. See? I invite you back. No, I will not leave to make room for you. There is room for both. We can both control this flesh, this tortured and dying flesh.

Only half understanding what she was doing, Anonoei drew Bexoi's ka more firmly and fully into the dying flesh. You will stay through all of it, thought Anonoei. Just as you were going to make me stay conscious until I burned to death—you will stay here in this body until it dies.

But Anonoei knew that was not what she meant at all. For she had not despaired. To her, this body was not dead, was not going to die. For the flake of ba that she had put in Wad was still there, still calling, still demanding that he come. And if he came soon enough, if he came now, he could still pass her through a gate and save this flesh, save even the baby.

That was when she felt the vibration in the floor. Someone standing there. No door had opened. No one had heard the talking or the shouting, or if they heard, they didn't want to intrude. So only one man in all the world could be standing here, though Anononei had no power to raise her head, no voice with which to speak, no strength to move.

"You killed her and then you burned for it. Justice." Wad's voice was quiet. She could feel the grief and rage. "Everything I love you take from me." So he did love her. It was not just any-bed-when-the-need-comes-on.

And then she realized: He is talking to this dying body on the floor as if it were Bexoi and *only* Bexoi. He has no intention of healing her. He is going to watch her die.

Save her! Anonoei shouted through the bit of her ba that dwelt in Wad's mind. She did not try to control him; she did not dare use more than this small bit of her attention, lest the distraction give Bexoi a chance to either slip away entirely, and die, or to wrest control of her body back again.

She could feel Wad's torment as he wrestled against the impulse she was sending him.

I am Anonoei! Yet how could her wordless ba make such a strange thought clear in Wad's mind? The ba dealt only in emotions and kinetic memories.

It was emotion, not identity that she needed to send into him. All her love for him.

The trouble was that she did not love him. Not so very much. Enough, yes, to share his bed. But he was also the torturer who had damaged her children. She had managed to thrust her rage into another compartment in her mind, to save it for another time, when it might more usefully be expressed. But it meant that she could not thrust into *Wad* her love for him because there wasn't enough of it. Nor could she control him enough to remind him of his love for *her*, because she knew that he did not love her so very much, either.

But she loved her children. And she knew that he had loved his own child. And there was a living child—still, for one moment more—in the belly of this woman. A child who did not deserve to die, whatever the mother might have done.

Love of a child. Anonoei's love for Eluik and Enopp. She also reached for his own memories of holding his son, Trick, of playing with him, talking to him. Anonoei had no idea what Wad had said to his son, but she knew that he had talked to him, and she could touch those memories and rekindle them. And she could make him think of the belly of the dying woman lying on the floor of Keel's office.

She felt his decision at the very moment he passed a gate over her body—for it was hers now, as surely as it was Bexoi's. The gate did not drive her out of the body; nor was Bexoi any longer trying to die.

"It's the baby that I'm saving, not you," said Wad. To her? Of course not. To Bexoi.

"I'm Anonoei," she said.

But no sound came out.

Nothing.

For Bexoi's ka was fully in this body, and so was Anonoei's, and Bexoi would not let the body act on Anonoei's intention to identify herself as present in this flesh.

Bexoi wanted her gone. Sole control of this body, that's all that she would settle for.

I should have let her die.

But if I had, would I have been able to keep the flesh alive? Do I still need Bexoi to maintain my life? It doesn't matter whether I do or not. She's here, and the opportunity to let her die is gone, now that the body is healed. Does she choose to block me from speech? Then I choose to block *her.*

"A simple thank-you would do," said Wad. "Or even a curse—I have no fear of your curses. Or are you trying to work up the strength to burn me to death the way you burned Anonoei? She was worth ten of you, you know. A better mother than you—and not just because she never arranged for the murder of her first-born. Burn me if you can. See what happens."

And then he wept.

Maybe Anonoei loved this man more than she had supposed.

Anonoei wanted to look at him. To use these eyes to see him, these hands to reach for him. But Bexoi blocked her.

The weeping stopped. Wad spoke again, whispered. "You knew that I couldn't kill your baby, even though you killed mine. You knew there was a line I wouldn't cross. But once the baby is born, anyone can nurse it. Do you understand?"

Anonoei understood, and so did Bexoi. If they did not manage to end their struggle and find a way to make this body speak aloud, then after the birth of the baby, she would die. *They* would die.

But there was still a little while before the baby was due.

Wad rolled the body over so it was lying on its back. He pried open an eyelid. The reflex for the eye to focus was under the control of the ape-brain, not the two kas that warred within it. So Anonoei saw and therefore remembered that Keel still hung, alive, from the rafter overhead.

Look up, she said to Wad. And then she filled him with the kinetic memory of looking up.

And so he looked.

"Keel," he said.

In a moment he had gated himself to the rafter and the open eye watched as Danny untied the man, as he caught Keel in a gate so he landed on the floor after the fall of half an inch rather than ten feet.

I am not utterly helpless in this flesh, thought Anonoei. I am still a manmage, I can keep communicating with the portion of my ba that already dwells in him.

There were other splinters of her outself that connected her to Eluik and Enopp, and to the couple in Mittlegard who were looking after them. Her connection with the Gatefather Danny North, with Bexoi's nephew Frostinch, with King Prayard—all these persisted, along with her links with the enemies of Bexoi. Bexoi would probably be able to block her from making new connections, but she could not interfere with the ones that still existed from before. They were part of Anononei's self, her ka-and-ba, and Bexoi had no part in them.

So while Bexoi was fully trapped inside this stalemated, unmoving body, Anonoei could still influence the actions of dozens of people, could still reshape events, at least a little.

That's a tiny bit of justice on my side.

23

Resolution

Wad listened as Keel told him how Queen Bexoi and two soldiers arrested him and brought him to his office and hung him from the rafter. There was no explanation, no threat. Keel had kept quiet, expecting her to ask him questions, to accuse him of something, but not a word was said until Anonoei arrived.

"It was hard for me to concentrate on what they were saying," said Keel. "The Queen called Anonoei a manmage, which is true enough. I don't think the Queen knew that the manmage who was interfering with people like me was Anonoei until she appeared here. Bexoi said she had studied manmagery because manmages and gatemages were the only ones who posed a threat to her. Bexoi kept waiting for you to come. I think she was using Anonoei as bait."

"I was busy," said Wad. "I didn't realize that Anonoei was calling me until too late."

"Bexoi is a firemage."

"I know," said Wad.

"The way she burned up Anonoei, it was . . ."

Apparently there was no word in his mind for what it was.

Keel broke into convulsive sobs. "I thought I was going to die."

"Why was Bexoi burned as well? Her fires never harmed her before."

"Anonoei threw herself on her at the last moment and held her close," said Keel. "That's how it looked to me, at least."

"That shouldn't have made any difference," said Wad. "Bexoi could stand in a furnace that would melt granite and the heat would never reach her."

"Then Bexoi must not have burned," said Keel.

"Getting some sarcasm back, I see," said Wad.

"You're the kitchen boy. Hull's errand runner."

"I am," said Wad.

"And you've been a gatemage the whole time."

"It made me a better errand runner," said Wad.

"Why hasn't the Gate Thief eaten your gates?" asked Keel.

"Do you really want even more of the kind of information that will make me need to kill you?" asked Wad.

"If you didn't kill Queen Bexoi when you had her in your power, you won't kill me," said Keel.

"You don't know what I'll do," said Wad.

"I know that if you're Queen Bexoi's friend after all, I'll kill you if I ever get the chance."

"I'm not her friend," said Wad.

"She told Anonoei that the gatemage was once her lover. Was that you?"

"I put a baby in that belly once," said Wad. "The boy that she named 'Oath' was mine."

Keel's body shook again, but now with laughter. "Poor Prayard. Cuckolded by a kitchen boy."

"By a spy that he often resorted to himself."

"So he knows you," said Keel.

"And trusted me, once upon a time. The question now is, what should I do with you?"

"I'm now the open enemy of the Queen, known to her. If she lives, my life is as good as gone. I don't know why she isn't killing us both right now, but even if she chooses to bide her time, I'm a dead man. I doubt there's anywhere that I can flee where she won't follow, or send an assassin after me. So I will do whatever I can to kill her. Does that make us allies or enemies?"

"Not until her baby is born," said Wad.

Keel nodded. "Yes, you told her that. You spared her for the baby's sake."

"And so will you."

Keel nodded. "Unless she comes after me. I *will* defend myself."

"Whatever is keeping her silent," said Wad, "does not make her deaf. I think she hears us and she understands, even if she can't give us a sign of it. Maybe pride alone holds her tongue. But I tell her now, in front of you, that if she harms you in any way, or Anonoei's children, I'll overcome my scruples about not killing her unborn child."

"Thank you," said Keel. "I can't understand why I don't feel any pain. I hung there for hours."

"Passing through a gate restores your body to perfect health, maintaining the age and shape that you've achieved."

"I didn't know that," said Keel. "So gatemages are all healers. Yes, I think I had some vague knowledge of that. Old stories."

"Keel, I need your help."

"I doubt you want a ship, you who can travel anywhere in the blink of an eye."

"I have the body of the Queen, apparently in some kind of trance. But she's in your private office. Surely this is not where she should be discovered."

Keel thought for a moment. "Can you take her back to her own rooms in Nassassa?"

"And let her simply be discovered? The problem is that her clothes are half burnt away."

"No woman in my house has clothing fit for a queen."

"Then I think our purpose will be best served if she is found in some strange place, without clothing. She needs to be discovered quickly, because in this weather she would soon die of exposure."

"You want me to discover her."

"Tell me a place where you or a workman would find her, but where you would not be suspected of having put her."

"In the water," said Keel. "If she bobs to the surface where fishermen are passing on their way home, then she'll be found. Found naked in the river, no one will know where she might have been thrown in."

"Should we bind her hands and feet?" asked Wad.

"No," said Keel. "No one would believe that she hadn't drowned. Better to have it thought that she was struggling to swim and then fell victim to the cold."

"And the cold would explain this coma. *If* it persists. There's always the risk that the moment she's not in my direct control, she'll start to speak. I'll keep a watch on her. If she starts to talk to anyone, I'll warn you. I'll gate you wherever you want, you and anyone you want to take with you."

"So much simpler just to kill her," said Keel.

"For a man who was almost the victim of assassination yourself, you're awfully bloodthirsty."

"You don't understand," said Keel. "She murdered Anonoei, a woman I honored and admired and obeyed. Even if Anonoei, as a manmage, put these feelings in my heart, that doesn't make them any less real. The murder was terrible. I will not let this monster live. If I'm in exile, I won't be in a place where I can kill her."

"If she starts to talk," said Wad, "I'll bring you to her with a knife in your hand."

"I wish I had realized, years ago, that you were something more than the palace monkey," said Keel.

"But if you had realized it," said Wad, "would I have let you live to reach this happy day?

"This happy day," said Keel bitterly. He moved to the burned clothing, the ashy corpse of Anonoei, and knelt. "She used me, but in a way that I was happy to be used. If she was compelling me, it was to do what I would have done by choice, though with less boldness—work against the Queen. May I take these ashes and these clothes, and give them a proper deeping in the river?"

"As long as no one knows whom you're deeping, then I would also like her to have such honor. I did her great harm once upon a time. Now I can never redress that wrong. But her sons are still in my keeping, and my own way to honor her will be to keep them safe and whole, and help them reach a happy life, if they choose it."

"Are we friends, then?" asked Keel. "I don't know what I can offer such a mage as you. My powers are not worth mentioning, compared to yours."

"It's not the magery that makes the man, but what he does with it, and with any other opportunity that he is given," said Wad.

"You say that as if it were an old saying, but I've never heard it."

"I learned it in my childhood, more than fourteen centuries ago, and in another language."

Keel took in this information calmly. "There are tales in this that someday I'd like to hear. How a man can live so long. How you kept your gates when the Gate Thief took everybody else's. What harm you did Anonoei, and how you came to be the lover of the Queen."

"What parts I could tell you, you would not believe, and what you would believe, I dare not tell you," said Wad. "But I know the service you have done for Iceway, and if it comes to war with Gray, I know that Iceway will have a mighty fleet, only because of your brilliant and devious mind. That's what you bring to our alliance—your loyalty, your love of country, your intelligence, your resourcefulness, and a deep goodness that Anonoei admired."

Again a sob caught at Keel's throat, but then he mastered it. "Few will know, except for you and me, the greatness of Anonoei's heart, and how faithfully she served King Prayard and the people of Iceway."

"Everyone will know, if one of her sons someday inherits this kingdom," said Wad. "But now it's time for you to place yourself where the fishermen who find Queen Bexoi in the river will come directly to you. Tell me where you want to be, and I can put you there. Or you can go yourself, so that the ordinary witnesses will believe that you were there on business and it was only chance that made you the official into whose hands the fishermen delivered the half-drowned body of the Queen."

Keel told him a place on the docks where he had a team of workmen refitting a ship for a long voyage. "I'll be there in ten minutes," he said. "And I have work enough to keep me there for another ten."

"Make sure there's a likely fishing vessel coming in or going out," said Wad. "The Queen will bump against the side of it."

"There's always at least one fishing boat, and usually a dozen, within hail of the docks."

"Then gather up Anonoei's remains," said Wad, "while I undress the Queen."

It took Keel very little time to gather the sad ashes of Anonoei, along with her half-charred clothing, and put them in a pot that previously held nuts, which now were strewn on his writing table. Wad did not remove the last of Bexoi's undergarments until the man was gone. She *was* the Queen, after all, and once he had loved her. With his hands on her unresponsive body, with the warmth of her flesh under his fingers, old feelings came flooding back. He had loved her with the intensity of a boy's first love, for she *was* his first love after the long amnesia of the tree, and when it began he *was* a boy again, though old memories came back quickly enough, along with his knowledge of how a woman might be pleased. By habit he found his fingers stroking her as if in lovemaking, but he caught himself and stopped. She was no longer the woman he had been besotted with. Now she was the murderer of their son, the boy whom she called Oath and he called Trick, and he did not love her. Yet those feelings were so strong within him that he could hardly drive them away. He had to stand up and pace the room until he judged that Keel had been gone for long enough that it was worth checking on his progress.

Yes, he was at the dock, and already heavily engaged in conversation with the foreman and a couple of workmen. Wad looked out across the water and chose the ship, an inbound vessel with a crew that seemed alert enough as with long sweeps of two oars on a side they rowed upstream.

"Don't inhale," he told Queen Bexoi, "and you'll be fine. Or if you can't control your body well enough to manage that, I'm sure the fishermen will be able to revive you. Trust me: After saving you from the ravages of fire, I will not let you drown or freeze to death. Whatever the sailors do to revive and warm you, I can promise it will work."

Then he gated her into the water, just below the surface, so she would bob up between the portside oars. He watched them notice her, drag her into the boat. He was glad to see that she was capable of choking and sputtering and struggling to breathe—it meant she wasn't paralyzed. But when the sailors peppered her with questions, she said nothing. And so they took her in to shore, where Keel performed his show of recognizing her, modestly covering her, and taking her to Nassassa, where King Prayard rewarded the sailors, and Keel as well, for bringing his wife and unborn baby home to him.

THEN WAD WATCHED as Danny North sent all the other mages of Mittlegard to Westil, making sure they immediately went back again. The boy learned well. He was careful. If Wad was fated to lose his gates to a greater Gatefather, then fate was kind to let it be a responsible, intelligent, persuasible lad like Danny North.

Throughout the day, Wad checked on Bexoi many times, but she never spoke or did anything that seemed volitional, though she breathed and took in food when it was given to her. If she was putting on an act, she was astonishingly consistent; someone less clever would have feigned a coma, and then it would have been easy to discover that she was really awake. By pretending *this* sort of catatonia, her eyes could be left open by someone else so she might see; her breathing could show responses to what went on around her without provoking suspicion that she was faking all of it.

There was also the possibility that it was real. Though with Bexoi, to have something really be exactly what it seemed was so unlikely.

At last, late in the day, Wad allowed himself the luxury of sleep.

He was wakened by an urgent stirring of his outself. It was the gates that he had given to Danny North. They no longer obeyed him, but they were still part of him, and their agitation, their panic, filled him with fear as well. Immediately he tried to make sense of what they were perceiving from Danny's mind.

The boy thought he was dreaming, but he was not dreaming. There was a woman in his bed, a woman that he did not love and did not want. He knew that he did not want her, and yet his body wanted her, and so he continued to believe it was a dream, or to pretend to himself that he believed it.

But it was this very dreamstate that had alerted Wad's outself to the danger. For Wad had seen possession many times and his ba remembered it. A dozen of the Sutahites were in and out of Danny North, possessing him only lightly, only enough to whisper reassurance to him. This is safe, they were saying wordlessly. What harm can it do. It's a dream. Nothing is real.

Wad joined with his given-away gates in shouting their panic to the boy. Someone as strong-willed as Danny North, the Sutahites would never bother with. They could never own him; he would drive them out. What could they possibly gain by encouraging him to be intimate with this girl? And why was she there, uninvited?

Wad came quickly to the conclusion that there was something in the girl, something that wanted very, very much to have her body intimate with Danny North's. Something that hungered for a clear pathway from one body to the other.

It was Set, the Dragon, making his first assault upon the greatest Gatefather in the history of the world. And it was working, because the boy was an adolescent who was easy to arouse to passion, and he was deeply weary, and he was coming out of a sound sleep, and he knew the girl and did not fear her. All of it worked together so that even though Wad knew the boy felt the deep dread, the warning of Wad's gates inside him, he went ahead.

He not only coupled with the girl, he consented when her voice asked him for permission to enter him.

Fool. Fool.

Not Danny—in his confusion, he was only as foolish as any boy would be.

The fool was Wad. When Danny 's exploration of Wad's memories had brought everything back to Wad with such clarity, it had not been half so clear to Danny North. Wad should have dropped everything then, should have used the Great Gate again to go to Danny North and explain everything, not in the vague way Danny would have learned it, but with the clarity of Wad's bright memory, and of all that he knew beyond the information that came from Kawab during that desert conversation.

I should have prepared him for exactly this danger. But in my arrogance and solitude, I thought it was enough that *I* knew. Why would I think that? I'm in Westil. Danny's the one who was in danger, the one who needed to be alert to the way this sort of thing is done, and I betrayed him by my silence, my delay.

Now all is lost. Set has him, and can make as many Great Gates as he wants, a thousand of them. He can flood Westil, the world of Mitherholm, with his Sutahites, and find a people totally unready to resist them. All the powers of the Mithermages will be in their hands, compounded by as many passages between the worlds as they might need or want.

Everything I tried to prevent has now taken place. So what if I delayed this day by fourteen centuries? All that happened in the meantime was that drowthers had created terrible weapons that now would be completely in the hands of the mages who had the power to take them and wield them, or induce the drowther armies to use them. How long before those terrible machines made their way to Mitherholm as well? How long before they were used, and Mitherholm destroyed, along with Mittlegard? Then Set would have his great triumph over Duat, having ruined both the other worlds.

In that moment of despair, Wad was shocked to feel himself awash with a sense of power and connection.

He had never felt this thing before, because he had never given his gates away before. It took a moment to realize that this was how it felt to have them given back.

He didn't *have* them; they were still in Danny's hearthoard. But he *owned* them. They would obey him now, if they obeyed anybody. If Set, through Danny, tried to make them into gates, they would not become gates at all, they would simply return to Wad. Wad wasn't sure if Danny understood that. It was likely that Danny knew only that they were no longer Danny's to command, and therefore they were out of the reach of Set.

The boy was braver than Wad had imagined. Danny must realize now that he had lost his battle with the enemy, but he was not giving up. Inside his own body, which Set must now control like a beastmage riding his heartbound, Danny North was still himself, and was still capable of doing things that Set had no idea how to prevent.

But since Danny did *not* have the power to free the gates he held captive in his hearthoard, this gift would only be a small limitation on Set. A futile gesture, really.

Then Wad realized that it was not as futile as it seemed. There were things that Wad knew how to do that required him to have a huge aggregate of gates—and his own store of them had seemed huge indeed, until he met Danny North, whose natural hearthoard made Wad's seem small and shallow. Wad might not have his gates *with* him; he might not be able to *make* them into gates; but they were his gates all the same, and if he reached out to swallow up another mage's gates, these captive gates of his would be part of his strength. If Wad was careful and clever, he might be able to find some way to resist Set after all. At least to slow him down.

For one thing, Wad would have the power to swallow up the rebellious gates that were woven into the Wild Gate the Greek girl had moved out of Danny's control. Unfortunately, half of the outbound Great Gate and all of the inbound one was made up of Danny's own gates, and those would remain in place.

Wad was still trying to think of possible uses for his newly restored power when he was overwhelmed by a force so strong his body could hardly cope with it. He fell to the ground, gasping for breath, whimpering with a feeling so strong that he could not tell if it was ecstasy or pain.

In moments, though, he understood what had happened to him.

Danny North had given Wad his gates. The seemingly infinite store of Danny North's own natural endowment was now utterly placed in perfect obedience to Wad, and Wad alone.

Danny was still connected to them; they were still part of his ba. But they were almost as deeply connected to Wad. They were part of his power.

Having his own gates returned to him had given Wad the scope to swallow the gates of any mage but Danny North, for Danny's strength was like the sun compared to Wad's otherwise-impressive moon.

But with Danny's gates as part of his own strength, Wad had power to swallow anything.

He still could only *make* the eight gates that Danny North had left to him in their original struggle. But anytime he wanted to, he could change that. Though he had no way to make the gates that Danny held within his hearthoard—Set could force Danny to hold on to those, to prevent their being made.

But the gates that were outside of Danny's body, the gates that *he* had made before Set took him, those were there for the taking. For with all of Danny's strength under his control, Wad had the power to swallow all of Danny's made gates.

And so he did it.

He swallowed first the Wild Gate that Hermia had moved, including all his former captives. They were in Wad's hearthoard once again, under his discipline again. Their freedom had been shortlived, and they despaired and fell silent almost at once.

Then Wad reached out, gate by gate, and swallowed the rest. But now, knowing that Danny North had made them all for a purpose, and Danny's friends relied on them, Wad remade them immediately, only now as gates of his own making, though the gates were Danny's.

It was a subtle thing indeed, but with enormous consequences. If Set had understood his danger, he could have quickly gathered in all of Danny's made gates. But Set had only a little practice at possessing a gatemage; he would know only what was known to previous gatemages he had possessed, and there could not be many of those. He could not possibly know what was possible to a Gatefather of such magnificence as Danny North.

Now, though, the gates were not of Danny's making, though they were his gates. Danny, under Set's control, could not gather in these gates. They would not obey him. And because his hearthoard was reduced to zero, Danny North couldn't even do what Hermia had done—move another mage's gate.

Wad was astonished at the things that Danny North had done. Gates attached to amulets, which his friends could use for quick escapes. Gates that chained from place to place, which could be found only if you knew where the mouth was hidden. Wad understood now that Danny had provided highways for his drowther friends, to keep them safe if the Families went after them. The boy had more love for ordinary people than Wad had ever heard of in a mage—more than Wad had ever shown, though he considered himself a drowther-friend, compared to most.

The Great Gates were harder. He could not unmake them and then remake them as a whole. Instead he spent hours carefully gathering each single strand, then remaking it by weaving it into the existing Great Gate, exactly where it had been before. It taxed all of Wad's power of concentration to hold the shape of it in place, but finally it was done. Even the Great Gates were now outside of Danny North's control, and therefore beyond the reach of Set to gather them back in.

What irony, thought Wad. The outcome is almost identical to what it would have been if I had won our little battle when I first tried to eat the gates of Danny North. His hearthoard is full of gates, that's true—most of his and most of mine. But he has no gate in either world that will respond to his commands. No gate that adds to his strength. He is as bereft of power as if I had stripped his gates away.

Only the captive gates remain within him. He can't give them to me. But if Set tries to spin a Great Gate, it will be completely wild.

And then, as Wad observed Danny from inside, he saw something that he wasn't sure he would have thought of, or, having thought, had the courage to act upon. The Dragon was torturing Danny to try to get him to do what Danny no longer had the power to do—allow the Dragon to control the making of Danny's gates. The game was simple enough: The Dragon was threatening to kill Danny and move on if Danny didn't give him what was no longer Danny's to give.

By the time the Dragon understood how Danny had deceived him, he had done so much damage to Danny's body that Danny

North would surely die unless he made a gate to pass himself through. At first, Set might have been content to let him die, as punishment for Danny's clever, stubborn disobedience. But then it must have occurred to Set that he was nowhere near any other person. Cut off from a human body, Set was weak again, unable to jump right in and control a person who had any willpower at all.

If Danny's body died, it might take Set weeks or months to get control of a body that was worth controlling.

Meanwhile, there was Danny's hearthoard. So many gates—and so many captives, too, including Wad's own gates. Even though Set hadn't the power to use them, if Danny died then he would never have the power.

As long as he remained in control of Danny's body, and Danny's body remained alive, then Set had a hope of persuading Danny to cooperate; and if that never happened, he could use Danny's body to bring him close enough to another person to make the jump smoothly and easily.

He could always kill Danny later, he doubtless thought.

And so he made one of the only gates remaining under Danny North's control—the captive gates. He made it and then moved it so that it passed over Danny's body, healing him. Danny North would not die.

And then Danny did something Wad had not known was possible. He gave the captive gate *to itself.* The ka that the gate had once been attached to was long dead, gone wherever the kas of dead gatemages went. But the ba was still part of that self, wherever it was, and even though Danny could not find that ka, he figured out that the ba could find it, could always find its ka, and so he gave the ba to itself, and through itself, to its original maker, even though he was dead.

The result was that the ba was gone. Simply gone. Danny hadn't unmade the gate—Set would have known what that felt like, would have prevented Danny from doing it. But Set did not know what Danny was even doing, when Danny performed the act of *giving* a gate. Because as far as Wad knew, he was the first mage ever to give a gate to another mage—if someone else had done it, Wad had never heard of it. And Danny had taken that new technique, had *learned* it, and then extended it to a use Wad would never have imagined.

Danny's body was healed, and Set was in check. His total supply of gates was limited to Wad's old captives, and now he knew that each time he made such a gate, he could use it once, but then it would be gone. Danny North would set it free, would let it die and disappear. And though there were many hundreds of gates, that number would be exhausted very soon if Set made heavy use of them.

If spacetime really had brought Danny North into the world as a giant prank, it was a good one. Because even though Danny North tried hard to be a decent man, he still had a prankster's heart, and he had chosen his victim well. Set had thought he would be master, and he was; but Danny had taken the mastery out from under him, even though it meant that Danny would be left utterly empty when Set abandoned his body. If Set let him live, Danny would be an empty gatemage, just like all the mages Wad had emptied through the years.

Wad knew well how rare it was for a mage to make such sacrifice. The usual thing, when a mage had been possessed, was for the mage to yield, to surrender quickly to the Sutahite's will, and then become its partner, obeying it but receiving the rewards of power ruthlessly applied.

Danny North could have taken that road. Set would have used Danny's gates to become the most powerful mage in history, forcing all the other mages to bend to his will. Truly he would have been the Great Dragon then, master of two worlds, manipulator of humankind, mage and drowther alike. Mage of mages. God of gods, at least in the eyes of drowthers.

Women, money, mastery of everyone. Anyone that Danny hated, he could have punished; Set would have had no scruples about the taking of a life, of many lives.

But Danny had thrust all of that away, removed it from himself with no hope of getting any power back, so that Set would not have the use of that power. So that Westil was still safe. So that Wad's work was not undone.

Danny North, I admire you for your courage. I honor you for your cleverness. I pity you for your loss.

Because even if Set moves on to someone else, even if he doesn't kill you in revenge for having tricked him, do not think for a moment that I will ever give these gates back to you. I do not even *want* to be as noble as you. For a while you were a greater mage than me. I am now, again, the greatest Gatefather in the world, and you are nothing. I will never give that up. I am the Gate Thief, and because of your nobility, the victory is mine.

AFTERWORD

For those who wish for an afterword that is a continuation of the themes of the book, I must disappoint you. Instead, I want to talk a little about the practical difficulties that only the writers of fictional stories have any reason to care about.

This book was six months late, but for good reason. If I were still the young writer of *Songmaster* and *Treason,* or even the not-so-young writer of *Saints* and *Ender's Game,* I would have delivered the book on time. It would also have been a very different kind of fiction.

In the years since then I've learned something about the structure of storytelling. I realized, just as I began writing the book in time to meet the original deadline, that I had the structure all wrong. I was going to use this book to tell the story of the wars of the Mithermages who had received the enhancement of their powers—thus melding the world of meddling gods shown in the *Iliad* and *Odyssey* with our modern kind of warfare.

Then I realized that I couldn't tell that story and only bring in the conflict with Set at the end. That had to be at the heart of the story all the way through, or it would feel tacked on, an extra element when the real story was over. As I tell my writing students, you have to promise the story you are going to end. The ending of this series is the climax of the struggle with Set. Just as the Mithermages will supercede the wars and geopolitics of the drowther world, so also the war with Set must supercede all other concerns in the minds of those few who know that it's going on.

Once I faced that structural necessity, I realized that I was not ready to tell that story. All my thought and development had been in the world of the Mithermages, while the magery of gatemages and manmages remained nebulous and ill-formed in my mind. In order to tell this story, I needed to develop a complicated rule set. What is it, exactly, that a manmage does? Or, for that matter, a gatemage?

So instead of delivering a book, I essentially started it over—always a depressing bit of news for an editor who trusted you to deliver when you said you would. But Beth Meacham, my editor for most of my career, also understands that it's better to deliver the best book I'm capable of than whatever book happens to be ready on the due date. Her patience is extraordinary, because the patience of editors is not passive. She has to fend off and placate marketing staff who are wondering just when (or whether) the promised book will appear; she has to make decisions about whether to go through the expensive and disappointing process of changing the publishing schedule. Fortunately, her employer and my publisher, Tom Doherty, shares the same literary values—that getting it right is more important than getting it now. My responsibility, then, is to be sure that any delay is worth it.

I happened to be listening, during this time, to a course on ancient Egypt from the Great Courses series. When I heard the description of Thoth as being very much like Hermes and Mercury, including healing, I realized that I could benefit greatly by adapting a version of Egyptian lore to my literalizing of Indo-european gods. *Ka* and *ba* corresponded—or could be made to correspond—with the way I was already using "inself" and "outself" in the Mithermages series. That allowed me to *name* the Belgod I had taken from Semitic and biblical tradition. Set made a lovely, dangerous enemy. And as I invented more and more of the lore surrounding him, tying him to the dragon in the book of Revelation, the workings of manmagic became something rich and fascinating, and very close to what I had already developed for gatemagic. In other words, they made a consistent whole, and one that I believe corresponds with the real world in significant metaphorical ways.

Having invented the world I needed, I then had to find a way to make it clear to readers. What made it especially difficult was my determination that all the communication between ka and ba had to be on a pre- or sub-verbal level. We don't talk to our own minds and bodies in language, and so when I had Wad-Loki's ba trying to share his memories with Danny North's ka, I had to put it on a nonverbal level. Yet books are written in words. Finding a means of representing non-speech in speech was daunting. I hope that for most readers, I succeeded.

As I learned more about manmages, the character of Anonoei began to grow. I began this novel with no idea that Anonoei would be important in it; she insisted on growing into something important, she and her sons, and so they will be major figures in the third and final volume.

Another problem was to keep from getting so caught up in the lore of magery that I lost track of the real world—*our* world, and Danny's place in it. It was very important to me that his friends become memorable individuals, and that Danny fall in love in a serious way. These high school students should not be merely Danny's foils, people he can talk to in order for us to learn what he is thinking. In this novel, they represent us, the drowthers, ordinary people who are in awe of the gods, if we believe in them; and I have met few people who didn't have some conception of a god, whether they would apply that title to it or not. How would these teenagers respond to having the new kid turn out to be the equivalent of Hermes and Mercury and Loki and Thoth?

One theme that runs through mythology is the amazing fecundity of the gods—the world seems half-populated by their bastards. While a few of these are rapes (in the old sense of "carrying off" the human female, whether the sex turned out to be consensual or not), it's also a fact of human life that there are certain women who are irresistibly drawn to powerful males. As Henry Kissinger pointed out, power is the ultimate aphrodisiac. This is not true for all women, or for all powerful people. But Danny North would not have to look like a young George Clooney or Robert Redford in order to attract the notice—let alone the eager desire—of a certain contingent of young women. His power, his intelligence, and, I must add, his innate goodness would make him desirable to many girls, for reasons as various as the girls themselves.

The result was that my original outline for this book is now an amusing cast-off; that which survives from it will be in the third volume, while most of what's valuable in this book was not in the outline. Stories are invented as you go along, if you're writing them properly, and that means that characters and situations that come out of nowhere can blossom into productive mines that bring out tramloads of metal-rich ore. My skill as a refiner is a different issue. But I think the ore I smelted to make this book is of a much finer metal than what I originally planned.

How can we tell, though? The earlier version was never written, not a word of it. It existed in my head, so I think of it as real; but no graduate student will ever pore over the differences between drafts, because the book you just read is the only draft that actually hit the paper.

How do you unfold the tale in an order which will be clear and interesting to readers who obviously begin the book knowing almost nothing about the story, and must end it understanding all? I regard it as the essence of good structure that all the key information will have been presented earlier in the book, so when you move through the climactic scenes at the end, everything is *already* clear to the reader, because it was so well explained earlier on. This means that the exposition is front-loaded. But readers won't tolerate (nor should they) a story that begins with nothing but exposition.

The device that works best is for the point-of-view character to know little more than the reader does. Thus when the viewpoint character learns it, so does the reader.

But what if the viewpoint character's learning is also vague and highly subjective? And how much information is too much for a given scene? Boredom and inclarity are the ways to drive readers out of a book, to make them close it and never open it again. The goal, then, is to provide the light with enough sweetness at every stage that the reader will stay with you, learning constantly but also getting the rewards of a good story along the way. This is not a trick—here are the good bits, so you'll keep reading the boring bits. On the contrary, the good bits *require* the explanations, but the explanations themselves need to be part of the action, so that it never feels as if the story has stopped cold while the reader is brought up to speed. This is such a delicate dance that most writers fail at it most of the time. And most of us realize that we will never find the perfect way to tell a story; it's likely that there is no such thing. We just keep dancing as fast as we can, hoping to take you far enough into the workings of the world that, when you move from one event to the next in the story, you always know where you are and what's happening, and you always understand just what is at stake.

This is hard enough with fiction that takes place in the "real" world; when the world itself must also be explained, the expository burden becomes dreadfully heavy. The result is that some writers skimp on world development, coasting along by borrowing the stereotypes of earlier writers in the field. Others include every detail of their world creation, whether it's relevant to the plot or not, as if they wanted to make all their readers memorize *The Silmarillion* before they were worthy to read *The Lord of the Rings*.

This is a long way of saying that the better your world creation, the heavier the expository burden. And sometimes your world creation is so deep and rich that the actual story never measures up to it.

In the effort to create a story that *does* measure up, sometimes you're late; but that does not imply that being late will make your story better. My most popular book was written in a single swath, more quickly than I could have imagined possible. This does not imply that moving quickly through a tale will make it better, either. Each story poses its own unique set of problems. It merely happens that the problems I had to solve in order to tell this story were some of the hardest, creatively and technically, that I've ever faced in my writing career.

That's the problem with growing older and more experienced. Decisions that would have been "good enough" when I was thirty now seem like cheap shortcuts to me at sixty-one. I know how to write better than I did before; but knowing better usually means that I have to work harder, invent more, and find solutions to ever-more-difficult expository problems. This is why writers never retire. If we're doing our job right, we're always just figuring out how this thing is done; we're always novice writers flailing about to find some kind of solid ground for moving forward.

TOR